D0837144

———— ★ ————

We exited the Garden the way we had come in, three employed people merely using the employees' entrance. We stepped out into the sunlight onto the sidewalk.

Across 33rd Street, I caught a flash of bright metal reflecting the morning sun. Without thinking, I flattened Ike to the wet, filthy pavement while I hauled Church down by his vest.

And the shotgun blast sprayed about ten cars and the Garden door.

———— ★ ————

"As high-spirited as Abby and Ike's first two cases..."

—*Kirkus Reviews*

Polly Whitney

UNTIL
IT HURTS

WORLDWIDE.

TORONTO • NEW YORK • LONDON
AMSTERDAM • PARIS • SYDNEY • HAMBURG
STOCKHOLM • ATHENS • TOKYO • MILAN
MADRID • WARSAW • BUDAPEST • AUCKLAND

*I am fortunate to have the two best editors in the world,
and I would like to dedicate this book to them:
My husband, Michael R. Whitney, who is always my first
reader, and Ruth Cavin, the final authority.*

UNTIL IT HURTS

A Worldwide Mystery/May 1998

First published by St. Martin's Press, Incorporated.

ISBN 0-373-26272-8

Things are seldom what they seem,
Skim milk masquerades as cream.
—Gilbert and Sullivan
H.M.S. Pinafore

ACKNOWLEDGMENTS

I'd like to thank a whole passel of on-line buddies for their gracious help while I was writing this novel: Dr. Leonard Greenberg—for medical information; Jean Geiger and Elena Santangelo for helping me find the waltz; and my favorite gangster friend, Terry "Spats" Burkhardt, who keeps the E-mail I.V. going. Not on-line pals, but equally important to this book, are Dan Rather, who gave me a sound idea; Tim Fuchs, who drew the "Rocky Mountain Torture"; Chuck Wilson, who educated me about weapons; Claudio Pimenta, for giving Abby some admirable colloquial Portuguese; and Mike Kilfoil, who explained the game and taught me to talk the talk, if not walk the walk— and helped me fire a gun for the first time in my life. And thanks to all of DorothyL (you know who you are) and to the Prodigy gang for allowing me a leave of absence.

AUTHOR'S NOTE

I wouldn't deny that the New York Knicks, the Chicago Bulls and Madison Square Garden exist in reality, but the versions of them in this novel are fictional in every respect. All other people, places and events in *Until It Hurts* are either fictional or are used fictionally. Any perceived relationship between aspects of this novel and aspects of reality is an aspect of coincidence.

ONE

KEEP ROLLING, and get down!"

What I yelled was reflex, not a plan.

There wasn't time for thinking.

When the explosion came, somewhere behind us in the stands, we hit the deck almost instantly. It took us one second, tops.

As a television director, I'm on intimate terms with seconds. I make my living by filling and counting seconds. I much prefer the luxury of enough minutes to plan and think about my seconds before acting. Without that luxury, though, my field experience got connected to my vocal cords, and I hollered about keeping the camera operating.

That was all I could do—yell something on instinct, take a dive, and hope my cameraman had his finger glued on the "record" button. On my way down to the classic flat-on-belly, hands-over-head position, I grabbed a glimpse of what was happening on the arena floor.

The scene that had been a routine warm-up on the basketball court in otherwise empty Madison Square Garden—the Knicks and the Bulls shooting baskets and talking Trash while a few of their coaches baby-sat them—suddenly froze. And I mean froze.

Froze solid.

One second, it was a show, choreographed by a master who was lucky enough to have superhuman bodies to work with. A second later, after the explosion, it was a still portrait. The action just stopped dead. On that celebrated court, famous for unforgettable moves, twenty big men turned into statues.

Another second later, I was pretty sure none of my crew—a producer, a cameraman, and a sound technician—had been hit. The only pain I felt was in my ears. All I could hear was the thundering, rolling echoes of that single shotgun blast. I didn't know then that it was a shotgun, but I sure as hell knew it was a gun.

It was in the fourth or fifth second that I raised my head, swallowed hard to pop the deep hum in my ears, and was able to sort out sounds other than the reverberating boom of the gunshot—sounds coming from the court. The Knicks and Bulls were moving again, breaking out of that stunned and silent shock.

I glanced at my sound technician's recording mixer and saw the needle moving. He was getting it all, or most of it: The players and coaches swearing, and screaming, and yelping. And the squeak of basketball shoes on polished wood. And the softer, less distinct impression of a man falling. A man dropping on a basketball court makes about as much noise in a major sports arena as a Styrofoam cup tossed onto the wood. I remember thinking it was weird that a shoe made a bigger audio statement than a man going down.

My crew was absolutely quiet. An experienced television field unit, when it decides to eat concrete, dines in silence. You've already got metal scraps of death whizzing over your head, you don't open your mouth and ask, "Got a little something for me in a nice shade of lead?"

We just lay there in a noiseless heap, wadded up against the short Plexiglas wall separating the twenty thousand seats and the basketball court. I'm not sure any of us was even breathing. I wasn't.

Our long extension microphone (ironically, it's called a "shotgun mike," the kind of thing we use over the heads of a crowd to ambush a sound bite) was hanging on the barrier and the video camera was running, rolling tape and presumably getting nice dark shots of high-grade concrete. I found myself staring at the needle on the sound recorder. The needle wobbled with the echoes, trying to hit the other noises but still riding the waves of that blast.

When the echoes of the gunshot stopped, our news reflexes kicked in. We scrambled for our gear and cautiously got ready to cover a sudden violent crime instead of the predictable sports feature we'd come for.

Journalists who've worked in Bosnia, and done time in the Gulf War, and taken broken bottles during inner-city riots— they don't turn into heroes. They get smart. If they're really smart, when they get up and dust off their clothes and gear, their reward is they get to go to some new Armageddon and do it all over again.

But we hadn't expected to use our battle smarts or chew concrete in Madison Square Garden. This was just supposed to be a tame remote shoot we could put in the can and take back to the NTB studios for editing.

Now, however, we could see there was one very famous body on the court, and it looked to me like he wasn't ever going to get up again. From my vantage point, say twenty feet from him, that small stain on the front of his pure white silk warm-up jacket was in just the right place for the wrong turn into the Beyond. It looked like the New York Knicks' center was down for good.

If we had to duck incoming in the presence of a murder, it was a shame we were such useless witnesses and journalists. Somebody had come to the Garden to blow away the most famous basketball player in the world, and we had missed it— with a *fully equipped* television crew at courtside, we missed the killing. In the last place we would have expected, death walked into the arena, put on a show, and then departed without us catching his act.

I was scared and mad.

But I'd been mad all the way to this assignment, which maybe explains something I did after the shooting.

The crummy way the trip to Madison Square Garden started, I probably looked angrier than your average surly New Yorkers out in the cold on their way to work at night—I was mad enough to core a pineapple with my bare hands. I had my reasons. For one thing, I'd just had a fight with my ex-wife. Plus, earlier, the ATM machine at 58th and Broadway had lied to me about my checking balance and refused to fork over any cash. And, probably worst for a guy like me who makes a point of navigating the city on his own private wheels, I couldn't find a cab. I was standing on the sidewalk in Columbus Circle, squeezing my icy hands into the pockets of my jeans, stamping my feet, at the mercy of fate. The snow had started to fall, and I was beginning to think I'd kill for a cab, or at least hire a hit man to do it for me. Except I didn't have any money and there weren't any unemployed hit men standing around in the cold, wearing signs that said RUBOUTS FOR SALE—BUY NOW, PAY LATER.

And, just to make things as nasty as the weather and my mood, I had Church Finnegan tagging along with me, the very man who was winking his eye around the network that he was maybe dating my ex-wife. Sharing a cab to the Garden with Church was not at the top of my list of new hobbies to take up after crocheting, which was at the bottom of my list of hobbies to take up. I probably didn't hate Church enough to slaughter him, or hire someone in the slaughtering business to take him out. But I did hope he was as cold as I was. Or, even better, cold and occupying some other street corner—across town.

With eight million of us living on top of each other, New Yorkers generally get used to sharing space with people they'd prefer to avoid. Still, there are ways to squeeze out from under the teeming throng. That's one of the reasons I usually make my way around town on Rollerblades—they give me breathing room.

However, at six o'clock on that pitch black late November Tuesday evening, with the temperature hovering just around twenty-five degrees, and the fat snowflakes coming down like they had little weights on them, and a fickle wind alternately howling and bleating in across the Hudson, and a professional need to keep my hair combed and my tie around my neck because of an appointment with the most famous athlete in America—as well as any other part of the earth that was populated—I'd left my skates in my office.

So it was either share with Church or walk twenty-five blocks, because he had the cab fare. I didn't have as much as a subway token on me. I almost never have much cash on me, even when the ATMs are telling the truth, and cabbies look at you funny when you wave your American Express card. I could just imagine a New York cab driver presented with plastic: "Hey, I look like a department store to you, buddy?"

After Church and I spent about five minutes of misery not loving company, a little yellow army of six cabs came sloshing through the Circle at once. We snagged the first one, a cab that had just dropped off a couple of kids carrying their leather backpacks and some shopping bags from Bloomingdale's. They were shouting at the cabbie about something, but I didn't catch it over the wind.

I grudgingly climbed in the backseat beside Church and told the driver, "Seventh and Thirty-third." A burst of wind came out of nowhere and slammed the door against my shin before I could get myself folded into the cab.

"Shit!" I yelped. Now I was really mad. Stuff like that hurts worse when it's cold, when your bones already feel like dried bamboo and your skin feels so tight, it could've been glazed with shellac.

Church didn't waste any sympathy on me.

"Abagnarro, I already leaked it to the driver that we're going to the Garden," he said, irritation showing in the frown that creased the skin between his deep blue eyes. He wasn't wasting any of his charm on the former husband.

"Oh, yeah?" I said, clutching the fiery spot on my leg. "How much you want to bet this cabbie doesn't have a clue where the Garden is?"

Church pulled a single out of the inside pocket of his down vest and held it up in the air between us. "Everybody knows where the Garden is. Even a newcomer like me. You native

New Yorkers think you're the belly button of the universe."
He said it with a slight Irish brogue, so totally cool and musical it made his philosophical insights even more annoying.

My wallet was empty, but I considered the odds, thoughtfully rubbing my sore leg and giving the cabbie and the taxi a quick once-over. I could use the money, even mere crap like a dollar, and this looked like a good bet, with the low vowel content of the driver's Taxi and Limousine certificate, the last name something like Schmedzckt (although there may have been a *J* in it somewhere), with his pale pink fez, with the aromatic musk coming from the Infant of Prague air freshener on his dashboard, and with the magnifying glass chained to the rearview mirror. Plus—a big tip-off—Schmedzckt didn't have nearly enough B.O. to indicate he'd been driving a cab in the city the required amount of time to have mastered even the rotten-customer-relations part of the trade yet.

"You're on," I told Church. "Double or nothing?"

"Sure, and I'll throw in a pint of the best."

"I ain't drinking with you. Listen and learn, farm boy." I turned to the driver and leaned my arm on the open plastic partition. "We want to go to the Garden," I said. And to make it fair, I gave the driver an extra hint. "Madison Square Garden."

A happy grin split the driver's face and gave me an intimate view of broken and yellowed teeth and a nice close-up of the brown wad of something chewable in his mouth. It wasn't Juicy Fruit.

"Ah, botanists." With the handicap of the tobacco cud, his accent only placed his roots as somewhere between Siberia and Algeria. Usually I can guess within a country or two, but not with this guy.

"Garden, yes," he said, nodding his head happily, "not so full of delights this time of year." Slurp. Smack. "Very cold now for flowers in the Large Apple. You fellas from out of town?"

I glanced at Church, who was rolling his eyes at the back of the driver's head.

"Yeah, we're from North Korea," I told Zchmedzckt or whatever his name was. "And you're absolutely right. It's too cold for a flower garden. How about the Bronx Zoo instead?"

The cabbie looked puzzled, but only for a moment. "Ah, this for you is the universal nature love, yes?" He transferred the tobacco from his right cheek to his left. In an odd way, doing that made him look like he was a little more plugged in than I had thought. He did it so smoothly.

"Yeah," I said. "We're practically the Mother Teresas of flora and fauna. Can you take us to the zoo?"

"No sweat, you fuckin' pal." He smiled and slipped the magnifying glass off the mirror. He bent over his lap and fished around under the driver's seat, coming up with a shiny and obviously brand-new map of the subway system. "Me, I can get you anywhere." The map crackled as Zchmedzckt opened its folds. "I know this city like the back of your hand."

I looked at Church, not amiably and not bothering to lower my voice on account of the driver. "Listen good: You've probably never heard a belly button talk this much sense before. We don't have time to monkey with this guy. He's totally lost. Even with us pointing the way, he'd never make the crossover at Times Square."

Church grabbed another single from his vest pocket, slapped my hand with two bucks, gathered up his audio equipment, and opened his door. I opened mine, two dollars richer. More bets like this, and down-on-their-luck hit artists would be lining up at my door for work.

We got out and hijacked the next cab, which was easy because the only other competition for it was a couple of women in big black coats, and we had bad manners and worse—attitude—on our side.

I happened to look back and noticed that Zchmedzckt was

still poring over his map, hardly aware he'd lost us but had been resupplied by the women in big coats. They'd be sorry.

But I didn't think their happy driver would be very sorry for anything, at least not until he'd spent a few months in the city. So far, he had a nice outlook, for a cab driver. Maybe Schmedzckt was woozy from the fumes his air freshener was dosing into his nose, maybe hypnotized from studying the subway map, the Big Apple's version of his name: the BMT, IRT, and IND. I swear, letters of the alphabet will soon replace words in this country—ASAP, FYI.

Our new cabbie was a woman. Her certificate said she was driving around the city under the name of Angel Rosenbloom, and her shiny black hair and sparkling brown eyes and deep dimples said she probably deserved at least the first name.

I was tired of playing "Stump the Foreign Transit Department," so I simply told her "Seventh and Thirty-third," and crossed my cold fingers.

"You catching a train at Penn Station, or buying tickets at the Garden?" she said, in friendly Brooklynese, which is almost English. "You're too late if you want tickets for tonight's game. It was sold out two weeks ago. The Knicks and the Bulls always sell out. PDQ, if you know what I mean."

I sighed contentedly. PDQ. She definitely spoke American.

"Press credentials," I said, relaxing against the seat. "Complete with a laminated color photo of yours truly, the navel of the universe. Aka—VIP I.D.''

TWO

CHURCH CLOSED HIS EYES and pretended he hadn't just lost two bucks on a dumb bet.

Not that it made me feel so smart myself to win a measly two from the man who was doing a good job of convincing all the network gossips (roughly one hundred percent of the staff) that he was dating my ex-wife. After all, I was the dope who had ruined a perfectly good marriage and opened the door for this dark-haired, blue-eyed Irish Romeo. And a couple of other guys. On my way out, I might as well have hung a sign on the doorknob of my former conjugal apartment that read BLONDE AVAILABLE. MAKES A LOT OF MONEY. INQUIRE WITHIN.

I didn't want to think about the lucky sound tech who was seated to my left and who was probably my ex-wife's latest pastime, but it's almost impossible not to think about your companion in a New York cab. Cabs are not as predictably insistent as elevators—those other voluntary urban jails—for spontaneous and nonconsensual intimacy; in fact, with the right companion, the unpredictability of cabs can be fun. I just didn't have the right companion.

The way it worked out, after we shot over one particularly deep and jagged pothole on Seventh Avenue, I knew things about Church's right thigh that his doctor probably didn't know and that I didn't especially want to know and that maybe he'd been showing off to the blonde.

Not that Church looked like he needed to see his doctor much. Or his dentist. When he wasn't losing bets in taxis, Church had a smile that revealed these great teeth, like they'd been polished, and everything else about him matched the smile. As far as I could tell, the only professional that Church needed to see regularly was a barber, what with his five-o'clock shadow starting probably after he put the razor down and leered at his face in the mirror. And that pothole had foisted on me the solid data that Church either didn't need a personal trainer or already had the best one in town.

Church Finnegan, fresh from Steven Spielberg's "Sound Circus Stage" in Shannon, Ireland, was—my female colleagues were happy to inform me—the new darling of the staff of *Morning Watch,* which in turn was the new darling of media watchers because our program had climbed out of its thirty-year hole in the broadcasting basement to overtake *CBS This Morning.* We were now number three in the daybreak ratings.

That may not seem like much to crow about, but roaring out of a decades-old ratings niche Just North of Hell had shocked everyone so much that we were being treated in print like we'd revolutionized morning TV. The word in the industry was that Tom Shales, one-man TV think tank for the *Washington Post,* had keeled over into the reflecting pool in a dead faint when the ratings first showed our sprint out of nowhere.

Don't get the idea that my cab companion had anything to do with Tom Shales's impromptu half gainer. Church Anthony Finnegan wasn't the darling of *Morning Watch* because of any spectacular talents, other than that brogue. In fact, as the show's director, I was in a good position to know that he was certainly competent but unusually lazy. Show business—even news—is a funny game, where charm and good looks in guys like Church can compensate for any number of failings, and there have always been significant pockets of charming, good-looking, I'd-rather-not prima donnas in the broadcasting wing of show business. In TV News that's from anchors on down to the lowliest production assistant. Plenty of people who break into television hope to move up to the next level so they can do even less than what they're currently not doing.

It's the exceptions that keep us on the air, exceptions like my former wife, Ike Tygart, broadcast producer of *Morning Watch* and super babe. She had supplied the energy and the

ideas that accounted for our show's rise from invisibility to
something like real competition.

And I was sharing a cab with Ike's reported new romantic
project because of her latest hot ratings idea. Having helped
Morning Watch crawl out of the cellar of morning TV by
capturing the eighteen-to-forty-year-old female audience with
thoughtful weeklong story packages on medical, social, and
cultural issues, Ike was aiming now to add another demo-
graphic idol worshiped by advertisers—what Ike calls the
"S.G.Q.," or Stupid Guy Quotient. Mind you, she wasn't using terms like that with Tom Shales, but she'd been candid
with me about supplementing our issues focus with more
sports reporting on *Morning Watch*.

Ike's a football fan herself, so automatically it's not stupid
for a guy to watch that sport. But she thinks *basketball* is for
people who like to go blind in front of their TVs, and those
blindness freaks are all guys. And she was going to corral
those guys by programming more sports on *Morning Watch*,
especially sports she considers stupid, like golf and basketball.

I've tried to change Ike's mind about some of those sports
she despises. Her idea of world-class sport is racing on her
Rollerblades through a traffic jam or ballroom dancing in a
dress with razor-sharp sequins. Once I pointed out to her that
Fred Astaire had been an avid golf player.

"Doesn't count," she said, laying down the law. "He was
charming and intelligent at anything that required *motion*. Besides, he probably wasn't really playing golf."

"Oh yeah? Then what was Astaire doing out on the links?"

"I imagine he was choreographing an original dance step,
using the club gizmo as a prop."

Sometimes you just can't tell Ike things.

Still, as someone with a high S.G.Q., I was all for her latest
idea, but Church and I had missed the NTB News truck. It
was carrying the rest of our crew to the Garden to start the
big wave of *Morning Watch's* exclusive sports interviews tar-
geting the early S.G.Q. audience. Assuming, of course, that

audience wasn't too mentally uncoordinated to handle the really complicated exercise of watching television while they were tying their shoes and waiting for the coffee to finish percolating.

We had missed the NTB truck because Church and I had both overslept. I don't know where he had done his oversleeping, but I had done mine in my own apartment, alone.

I had a pretty good idea that Church had been unaccompanied in his sleep, because Ike had hissed at him, too, when we showed up late. She didn't show her usual preference for giving me the exclusive screw-eye when we made our tardy appearances at her office in the O. Armitage Broadcast Center on Columbus Circle. She was wearing a pretty green wool dress, which went very well with the hissing.

The building is that ugly green skyscraper everybody calls the "Emerald City," not because it looks like something from *The Wizard of Oz* or Tiffany's window. It's just a tall green granite building. Clever name.

Of course, there's nothing clever about the name "Macy's" for a building either, but that's a New York landmark. NTB News doesn't even host a Thanksgiving Day Parade, but our place of business counts as a landmark in every guidebook to the city. The photos are doctored to look more like emerald green than like the actual pigeon-shit color of the place, but those of us who work there try not to disappoint with more than our architecture, and sometimes we manage to entertain and inform, in our own little unspectacular way. The Emerald City houses the News and Entertainment divisions of the NTB Television Network, which, until recently, had kept Tom Shales nice and dry.

Under Ike's leadership, *Morning Watch* was finally pulling its weight. She's an excellent leader, and everyone likes to work with a winner, but she's apt to be a little intolerant of me. That makes my working with her touchy, partly because of the fact that, while she technically runs the show, she doesn't run me. Directors are princes of the television kingdom, mostly because nobody can figure out what we do, and that means they can't do it themselves.

I could have lied to Ike, come up with some potent excuse for being late that night, or at least said I was sorry, but I rarely lie or apologize about oversleeping. Since we all work the overnight shift, and since I usually get by on only five hours of shut-eye per day, I'm proud when I outmaneuver my alarm clock. And this particular gig at Madison Square Garden had been scheduled into my R.E.M. cycle.

Church, by way of contrast to my honest sleep deprivation, had taken Ike's hand and apologized like a gentleman.

The apology, I mean, was like a gentleman. Taking her hand was merely showing off.

Ike hadn't snatched her hand back, but I could tell from her mood that Church's gesture was about as productive as if he'd gone down into the subway and stuck his hand into one of the high-voltage transformers. Which—it occurred to me in that moment—are sort of like self-service hit men. And very cheap if you could get your victim to volunteer.

"You missed the truck," Ike said, in that tone we used to tease each other about as being "very Szechuan"—meaning hot and sour. And she was drilling holes in us with her eyes.

Ike's eyes, by the way, don't match, which is only one of the things that makes guys like Church take advantage of any excuse to hold her hand. One of Ike's eyes is blue, a golden-flecked Caribbean, that color you can catch if you get up early and walk on the beach in Cozumel; her other eye is green, plain and simple, just pure unadulterated dark green, like the deepest part of a forest. I've never been in a real forest, just some lousy jungles, but a really good forest would be that color.

"We'll take a cab," I said, covering a yawn that I'd invented on the spot. "Keep your hair on, Ike."

"Oh, right. And *do* try to arrive before Hannah if it's not too much trouble. Her limo will be on time. And you guys are supposed to be set up, with the preliminary taping done by the time Her Highness gets there to do the interview."

Our thousand-year-old anchorwoman never missed a deadline. Must be all those centuries of practice.

"Ike," I said, "Hannah Van Stone will have me all over her, kissing her four-million-dollar behind."

"Goody. You do that. Hannah happens to be worth four million. Let's not get started on your street value. Be sure to put the cab fare on your expense account. Go ahead and spend my paltry budget until you can't see straight. Have a spree. Go ape. Paint the town while you're at it, Abby. Why don't you stop at Sardi's for a beer on the way? Maybe you can tell the bartender that parrot joke you can't shut up about lately."

"It's a great story, Ike," I said, interrupting her flow. "If we had more time, I'd tell you now."

"I don't want to hear it, Abby." She glared at me. "I wasn't finished ragging you out. Where was I? Oh. Just tell the driver to keep the meter running. Take your time. Have two beers. After all, you're only going to Madison Square Garden to get pictures and sound of the Big Chill on his home court. I had to have the Devil's assistance scheduling this interview—never mind what *The Guy with the Pitchfork* got out of the deal. The point is, as you very well know, the Big Chill never grants interviews anymore. So I work my tail off getting *Morning Watch* the one thing nobody else in the world can get—permission to ask Mister No Comment some easy questions. You wanna know how big this is? The biggest. The biggest athlete on the planet. Newborn penguins in Tierra del Fuego would recognize the Big Chill's face. So what do you do? You stroll in here yawning as though you've been assigned to cover the Hoboken Poodle Grooming Club. You bring up that story about the three parrots."

"Hold on, Ike. *You* brought the parrots up."

"I did not. And you know what else? You—"

"Oh, cut out the yapping, Ike. We'll make it to the Garden on time."

"Stop that. You're always accusing me of yapping. I'm sick of it. Can't you find something fresh to torture me with?"

"Probably."

"Well, I don't yap."

"You do, too. You're doing it now."

"I am not."

"Okay then. You leave baby powder all over the bathroom."

"Oh, right." She sneered at me. "I've practically cemented the faucets shut."

Church cleared his throat. He got drilled by looks from both of us.

After she'd finished with his face, Ike finally looked at her hand and took it away from his clutches.

"What I'm getting at," she said, straightening up her dignity, "is—don't you think you two ought to get going?"

"Ah, that's different," I said. "That sounds like a question, one colleague to another. No whining, no barking, no yapping." I paused. "No baby powder."

I thought she was going to do some more drilling. She pulled a fast one on me, however. She turned away, sat down in her chair, ran a hand through her blond hair, booted her computer, and pretended we didn't exist.

Which is very good technique because it makes you feel like dog meat.

It wasn't so easy then to ask her for money. When you feel like dog meat, you don't like to call attention to your condition.

"Ike," I said.

She ignored me.

"Ike, I need a loan from petty cash. I don't have any money on me for a cab."

"Church can pay for it," she grumbled, and I could hear her teeth working against each other. "I have to sign his expense account, too, you know."

Church cleared his throat, apologetically.

Ike stayed glued to her computer, but she kicked her desk hard. She yanked open her bottom drawer without turning around, grabbed her purse, dumped it out on the floor, and said, "Take more than ten bucks and you're a dead man, Abby. In fact, Church, you take the money. Don't touch my stuff, Abby."

Church stooped and wrestled ten singles from her junk and we bolted.

Now, riding with him, with a throbbing red bump forming on my shin from the first cab door's attack on me, I pulled up my pants leg to inspect the damage, and sure enough, it looked like dog meat. I was wondering how to sue a cab driver who had not wind-proofed his doors when we swerved to a halt in front of the Garden.

The meter said NTB News owed Angel Rosenbloom $4.25. I looked at Church. He looked at me.

"What the heck," I said, pulling the two singles out of my back pocket. I handed Angel the cash I'd won off Church. "That's the tip."

Church shook his head, like he was having an irony attack. But he had to fumble around with his audio gear—which, even with the retractable microphone, is cumbersome—and reach into his vest pocket to come up with the fare. Watching him work to get the money, I found my shin didn't hurt quite so much. The healing power of spite.

"Church," I said, not smugly, just stating the facts, "this is your night for shelling out my wife's money."

"Your *ex*-wife. Anyway, now we both have to file expense reports to reimburse Ike."

"Tut-tut. Maybe I won't bother over a mere two bucks. If you think about it, that two bucks was pure profit for me. It may have come out of Ike's purse originally, but speaking only as a belly button, I'd say now it's coming out of your hide."

"You're being really petty, Abby."

"Not by accident. Another New Yorker trait."

Church gave me a look. "Abagnarro, you never run out of words, do you?"

"Not in this country. I might have some problems in, say, Cambodia."

Our cabbie cleared her throat, which I could see was an excellent throat, smooth and long. "You guys plan to step out of the cab? I'm just wondering if I should reset the meter."

Again Church grappled with his boxed retractable microphone and recorder. "Yeah," he said, "we've got a star to shoot. Sure hope he speaks Cambodian."

Angel slewed around in her seat to look at him. "A star? What star?"

"What other star is there? The Big Chill. The New York Knicks' very own center of the world. Archibald Tyrone Thorpe."

"You're kidding. That Q-tip brain never lets you media wolves get near him."

"Well, he is this time."

"What station do you guys work for?"

I thought it was time to intervene. Why should Church get to talk to a good-looking woman in a cab when I'd paid the tip?

"Not a station," I said, with a smile, a Sicilian version of Church's supposed Irish charm. "NTB Television Network. We're the big boys."

"Well, big boys, when you see the Big Chill, you can tell him from me that I sold my season ticket because of him. I didn't scalp it either; I sold it for what it cost me."

I raised my eyebrows. A season ticket to the Knicks goes for about four thousand bucks. I didn't know cabbies had that kind of money.

Why she'd sell something at cost that she could scalp some sucker for puzzled me. Hating the Big Chill did not seem a good reason to scoff at profit.

Archie Thorpe, known as the "Big Chill" for the freeze he put under the basket when opponents were trying to get hot and for his absolutely cold and concentrated demeanor on the court, was the most sizzling draw in New York. A lot of people didn't like his eco-politics or his membership in the NRA, but he undoubtedly dominated the NBA. The Big Chill was putting New Yorkers in the mood for a championship. And in New York, we are not kind to losers. We're not nice to them. And we're excellent at not being nice. In this city, not being nice is like having skin: it's a prerequisite for getting around the city without losing your organs.

The controversial but magnificent Big Chill was like a magnet for New Yorkers looking for a sports franchise they could be nice to. It was hard to believe Angel had not made any money on that Knicks season ticket. She didn't look like a chump to me.

Church and I got out of the cab without hurting ourselves. I shut my door and patted the roof of the car.

Angel stuck her pretty head out the window.

"You want me to wait?"

"No, thanks," I said, "we'll probably stay for the game. It'll be a long wait—on the other hand, I don't suppose you take American Express, do you? We could get coffee after the game."

She shook her head and gave me a serious look. "But I'll wait for free if you promise to tell the Big Chiller he's a disgrace to the pro game. They ought to bury him under the Holland Tunnel instead of putting his star on the Walk of Fame. Like the Chiller deserves a piece of that floor! Thirty stars on that marble and one of them belongs to a seven-foot doorknob. Hell. Michael Jordan's star is in there. So is Larry Bird's."

"Angel, I hate to disappoint you and lose this promising friendship," I said, and I heard Church make some kind of noise where he stood beside me on the street. "And you've got beautiful hair. But when I talk to the Big Chill I'm going to fraternize and ask him how I can improve my drop step to the basket. So you'd better not wait."

"Traitor," Angel said, not in an angelic voice. She threw me a nasty glance before she turned to her side mirror to catch a place in the stream of traffic headed downtown.

Church and I walked up the steps and headed for the big Bulova Clock just inside the entrance across from the twenty-four ticket windows, where our producer and cameraman were waiting for us with a Madison Square Garden security escort, a little guy in a blue uniform.

We'd have to stroll right over the Walk of Fame. Maybe step on Michael Jordan. I toyed with the idea of trying out a limp, because of my injured shin, but decided against it on the grounds that I didn't want to entertain Church Finnegan.

In fact, I'm sure he couldn't have cared less about my injuries—phony, exaggerated, or otherwise. He was more interested in my height, a mere six feet one inch, which makes me practically Tom Thumb in Madison Square Garden.

"Abagnarro," he said, "a drop step is a big man's move."

"Yeah? Well, I'm going to tell you something, Mr. Hand-snatching Finnegan. It takes a big man to hold my wife's hand. *And* hang on."

THREE

MADISON SQUARE GARDEN has been like a rock-solid cathedral for me all my life, one of Manhattan's reliably sacred places, even though the actual arena has floated around New York's architectural landscape four times and is probably going to move again soon. It isn't anywhere near Madison Square these days, not that anyone knows where Madison Square is.

But wherever the arena is physically located, it will always be Madison Square Garden, and there's only one *Garden* in the world. How many major sports arenas can *you* name? If you haven't heard of the Garden, you just haven't been paying attention. Heroes have been anointed in Madison Square Garden, But as far as I ever heard, nobody had the last rites administered in the Garden until that November evening when Theo Hornachek, Knicks co-captain and all-star power forward, knelt on his own bloody knee and put his thumb on the Big Chill's forehead to make a little cross on the dark skin and mumbled something that nobody but Hornachek will ever know. He never told the media, so his words never entered sports lore.

Hornachek was not a talker. But evidently he could pray.

There hadn't been much praying in the Knicks' organization during the explosive four-year professional career of the Big Chill, under Head Coach Max Edward Hall, but there'd been enough talk to make New York basketball the Trash capital of the NBA. Unlike Hornachek, Hall either liked to flap his mouth or was congenitally incapable of keeping his flapper buttoned.

And Hall's flapper had most affected his megastar, the Big Chill, with words that not only entered sports lore but should have cost the coach his job. Among other times that Hall ought to have taken lessons from the quiet, prayerful Hornachek was the five-month period when the Big Chill had dated Didi Hall, the coach's only daughter. There had been rumors that a marriage was in the works. Hall had opened his fabled big mouth and told the New York *Daily News*, "I'd be disappointed. I'd rather see Didi marry Bobby Knight and have him kick her ass across the court every time Indiana loses. Knight's mean as hell, but he's Caucasian."

Hall had later apologized for the racism of the comment, trying to pass it off as a joke that went bad. After Didi disappeared from the picture and the Big Chill married a woman from South America who happened to be darker than Didi Hall, the coach's comment lived on in Trash Talk legend, but the exact words of his apology didn't.

And, it was said, the apology didn't go very far in sweetening the relationship between the star center and his coach. Everyone knew that both the Big Chill and the usually reticent Hornachek had asked to be traded after the coach's remarks, that Hall had begged to get himself a new center to replace the Big Chill but wanted to keep Hornachek, that many players around the league had demanded Hall's resignation, and that the Knicks' president had told the three men involved (in private, but it leaked out because it was too good a piece of Trash to keep behind closed doors) that the Big Chill and Hornachek would be traded when a pregnant woman was elected pope.

The bottom line in the dispute was, well, the bottom line: Hall had the best winning record in the NBA for five years running, so all he was forced to do was make a credible apology, explaining that he'd only been kidding about Caucasians and was actually making fun of Bobby Knight—not Archie Thorpe, the Big Chill. Three really nice people in Little Rock, Arkansas, believed the coach.

I wasn't surprised by the tenderness of Hornachek's touch on the Big Chill's forehead. Or by the bewildered look in the kneeling man's eyes. In a league where the Big Chill didn't have many friends, Hornachek had always quietly stood by his teammate, never once uttering the kind of bitter invective the Big Chill usually got off the court, even while he was respected and feared on the court for his play.

The NTB crew all witnessed those last rites from Hornachek. We were up on our knees, shifting our equipment into place to get pictures and sound of the mess on the court. Of course, we were watching our backs, too, stretching peripheral vision to its limits. But it was the basketball court that drew our primary focus, even with a shooter in the arena, maybe still in the stands.

The sight of the Big Chill on the floor and the blood on Hornachek and the other players gave our crew one big piece of information: the shooter had been aiming at the court, not at us—unless the shooter was really inept. He'd aimed at the broad side of a barn and had hit all of it. There wasn't a man on the court who wasn't carrying a piece of buckshot in his anatomy.

The explosion had come, as we would soon learn, from a sawed-off twenty-gauge shotgun, the design whose whole idea is to spray as much buckshot as possible in as wide a circle as possible. Evidently anybody can hit the broad side of a barn with a sawed-off like that. All you have to do is hold the gun in the right direction and pull the trigger. Result: an extremely holey barn.

Because the barrels were cut down to only eight inches, the dispersal pattern of that one blast from the gun had been so great that not a single man on the arena floor had escaped without at least a pellet in the leg, but the wide pattern of shot, spread out like a cloud of BBs, had also meant that nobody was hurt so bad they couldn't bitch and whine and carry on like they'd been hit by cannonballs. It was like a fine spray of vicious, oversize mosquitoes had invaded Madison Square Garden and had brushed through the players on their way out.

Except for Hornachek, the players and assistant coaches were up and hopping around, and everyone was hopping mad, until they noticed that the Big Chill was still on the floor, on his back, not moving.

When we realized what the Big Chill's condition was, the crew and I were up on our feet, too. None of us was hurt. Even if we had been, the cameraman didn't need to be told which way to point his lens. Ronnie Kovacs was a veteran of Sarajevo and Somalia, and he was more than familiar with shooting tape in the presence of that other kind of shooting. He had the camera pointed at the court, at the dazed and angry but only slightly wounded players and coaches. There were small sting-sized splashes of blood, and a lot of cussing, but it looked like nobody was seriously hurt. Except the Big Chill.

The cussing and bitching stopped when it was clear that the Big Chill wasn't doing any.

While Ronnie kept his eye and the camera on the court and Church Finnegan handled the microphone as if he were a sound tech veteran of more than Irish sheepdog trials and pub singing contests, I turned to where I thought the blast had come from, behind us in the tiers of seats on the south side of the arena. I saw a shape vanish into one of the tunnel gates. That's all I saw: a shape, a blur.

I jumped and stumbled up over maybe ten rows of seats, skidded onto the aisle stairs, and almost tripped over the shotgun, lying there between the rows of seats like an arrow pointing the way out of the arena. I knew better than to touch the gun in any way, so it took some fancy footwork to avoid the weapon while attempting to stay upright. After I got myself steady, I had the strangest impulse to reach down and touch the gun, just to feel if it was hot.

I did bend down and get a sniff. It smelled like it had been fired. You can bet I didn't smell it so thoroughly that I put my nose on it. But I did look close enough to see that the gun appeared to be shiny and brand-new; and I read the text on the first six inches of the left barrel:

FOX   model BSE series H   20 GAUGE
               2 3/4 & 3 inch shells
               Savage Arms, Westfield, Mass. USA

I was the first one to see the gun after the shooting, and
I'm no ballistics expert, but I was pretty sure this thing was
so nasty, you'd have trouble buying it even illegally in New
York, or importing it from Virginia. The butt and both barrels
had been sawed off, leaving a shotgun that was, to my eye,
less than fifteen inches long. A city where you can own a nine-
millimeter semiautomatic—and even take it to bed with you
and kiss it good night with the mayor's blessing—won't tolerate a sawed-off shotgun.

I quickly considered my options.

There was the weapon, a used and solitary block of pure
ugliness all by itself on the stairs.

There was my crew, down by the barrier. Hannah wouldn't
arrive for maybe another ten minutes. Even without her, the
crew wouldn't stay put long, not with Sally Goldberg-Petit,
the producer, on top of the fastest-breaking story in New York,
and she had it exclusively. Sally would have the crew on the
basketball court pronto unless I yanked her chain, and yanked
it hard. The Garden's own cameras weren't turned on yet, so
even the MSG Network would have to beg for our video if
they wanted to cover the story with more than well-written
copy for their five million cable subscribers. I wasn't going to
yank Sally's chain.

There was the cell phone in my jacket pocket, and considering that *Evening Watch* was on the air, I needed to flip that
phone open fast and give NTB's flagship news program a hot
item for their twelve million viewers.

But somewhere out in the massive structure whose fifth
floor was the basketball court was the owner of the sawed-off
shotgun, that human blur I had seen exiting the arena. I was
assuming the "human" part because of the weapon, not because anything about that blur identified it as part of the shot-
gun-toting species. It was just a blur.

My instincts told me that nobody in the Garden, except maybe the basketball players, was any dumber than I am, so the gun would be okay if I left it unattended. Hornachek was yelling now for the team doctor, and I *knew* I was dumber than the doctor when it came to the medical mess on the court. I couldn't do anything for the Big Chill.

That left the shooter, out in the vastness of Madison Square Garden's cavernous halls and tunnels. At least five stories of halls and tunnels, assuming the shooter was heading down and out to the street. Five more if he was heading up. The presence of the gun on the concrete made my decision easy—find the shooter, who was now unarmed. I hoped.

I sprinted up the remaining stairs to the tunnel, passing twenty-five rows of seats and flipping open the cell phone as I went out into the dimly lit corridor.

I listened carefully to that corridor. Nothing. Nothing real, anyway. Just the memories of the sounds of screaming fans, echoing along the corridors of my mind. But in the here and now, nothing.

There was no way to tell which way the shooter had gone. One man wasn't going to find one shooter in that titanic sports warehouse unless the one man was blessed with X-ray vision. I've got good eyes, but not that good.

Feeling about as useful as a poodle on ice skates, I dialed the cell phone directly into the control room for *Evening Watch.* As quickly and coherently as I could, I told Tom Hitt, the show's executive producer, what I knew. And hung up.

I considered calling 911, although surely someone on the Garden staff had already done that. I thought about it: 911. I didn't believe for one minute that I'd get a dispatcher who hadn't already heard at least fifty prank calls that evening about alligators in the Empire State Building, marauding transvestite neo-Nazis in Central Park, or just plain lonely people looking for a date. Who'd believe the arena at Madison Square Garden had just been peppered with buckshot and that the Big

Chill was down? I mean, believe me without first giving me a hard time.

Ike.

She'd believe me. And she could call police officers by their first names. She wouldn't need 911.

I dialed Ike's office.

She didn't waste time yapping at me. She listened to my fast narration. And then three sentences is what I got from her: "*Evening Watch* already has this on the air, quoting you. I can call the cops, assuming they don't already know. Is the crew okay?"

I gave her the two sentences she'd want right away.

"We're fine," I said. "Sally's got her Gestapo cap on and she's getting the story."

Then came the most important news question from Ike.

"Is the Big Chill alive?"

"I don't know." I hung up.

I stepped across to the big plate-glass windows and heard the sirens coming down Seventh Avenue. Either Ike had been dialing her other phone with her left hand while talking to me out of the right side of her mouth, or somebody else had called the cops. Or, I couldn't help thinking, there was some other big crime in progress in this neighborhood.

I looked at my watch: 6:34. The game was scheduled for 8:00. If the NYPD was going to seal off this crime scene, they were going to have to send heavy troops immediately, maybe in riot gear. A piece of yellow tape wasn't going to hold back thousands of ticket holders and maybe hundreds of jerks who like to hang out when they get a whiff of a free show in town.

And the media. NTB was already inside. Already shooting tape and collecting sound bites. Luck. Even if our anchorwoman couldn't wrestle her way past the crowd, the police, and the confusion, Sally could do interviews. We just couldn't put her face on the air. Union rules. But I wasn't too worried about our anchorwoman.

If Hannah did get through Madison Square Garden's front

door, it would be on pure bitchiness. Since she's the Queen of Bitches, I had no doubt I'd see her any minute.

That other news organizations were on the way was an even easier bet than the one I'd made in the cab with Church Finnegan. How they'd get in to the crime scene was their problem. They'd all be here soon, trying to get in somehow, but without Hannah's overwhelming gifts.

My media brothers and sisters didn't need a phone call from me to find the trail to a good murder. I've never seen any statistics on this, but I'll make another easy bet: there are more police scanners in civilian hands in this media-owned city than the cops will ever have.

Despite what I'd seen Theo Hornachek doing to the Big Chill's forehead, I didn't know for sure the big Knicks center was dead. So I didn't know if a killer was on the loose or if that shattering blast had been engineered by someone who was technically guilty only of assault with a deadly weapon. Either way, the gun was in the arena, and I thought it wouldn't hurt to check the most obvious exit—the front door—just to see if there were any blurry shapes I could have a word with.

I took off running toward the box office, practically leaping down the escalator that was flowing like a lazy steel river on its way to the lower floors. At street level I slowed a little. Down here it was noisy. If that human blur had come this way, he or she was already either gone or milling around anonymously with the crowds lining up for tickets to future games or looking to get ripped off by scalpers so they could see the New York Knicks play the Chicago Bulls on the home court that night. Which was exactly what nobody was going to see.

I slowed down even more. I didn't want to walk into the crowd and lose my place in the inner sanctum. The only thing NTB had going for it was that it was already inside the Garden. There was no percentage in me wasting any time fighting my way back to an already perfect position.

And the cops were starting to block off the Garden's main

entrance. My personal favorite cop, Homicide Captain Dennis
Fillingeri, had come striding under the Bulova clock with
about ten detectives and twenty uniforms fanning out behind
him like a really good marching band, all in step, shoes tapping on the marble floor in impressive rhythm, and apparently
to the same tune.

Other uniforms were making their way around the lines at
the ticket windows, and the flow of fans was being bottled up
at the Seventh Avenue entrance. There was some pushing, but
it didn't look like serious pushing. And, of course, some
"What for?" and "What the hell?" and "Get out of my
face," but that was just urban background noise. What the
customers really wanted was *in*.

I backstepped, hoping Fillingeri hadn't seen me. We don't
run into each other all that often, but when we do he usually
wants to arrest me a few times for opening my mouth, which
is unconstitutional and pretty irrational for a lawman. I never
did anything to him, unless you count a few remarks, but Fillingeri had briefly dated Ike, giving *me* the decided edge in
the resentment department, which was always open for business between me and the Murder Captain of Midtown Manhattan.

So I turned and headed back, fast, the way I had come, to
take advantage of NTB's position while we still had position.
The inevitable argument with Fillingeri could wait.

On my way up to the court, running all the way, I had a
superbly selfish thought: I may have been an eyewitness to a
crime, but there were plenty of eyewitnesses to the fact that I
was only an eyewitness. Fillingeri couldn't possibly have any
complaints with me except for whatever bad attitude he could
find time to cultivate at the scene of the crime, and I was
guessing he'd be too busy for much attitude.

The shotgun was still there on the stairs. I vaulted over it
and on down to the court. The crew wasn't interfering with
any medical attention from several team trainers, but Sally and
the technicians weren't being shy about their jobs, and they

were well established on the court, like they belonged there with the injured men. Even Church Finnegan seemed to be using some energy with the mike and with the audio gear strapped to his waist.

We'd be hated by every other news outfit in the city, maybe on the planet. We only had one camera and one microphone, but we had one hell of an experienced producer, and I could tell she already had a lot of talk, speculation, and crying on the record. When I arrived by her side, Sally was speaking quietly with Head Coach Max Hall, who had apparently just arrived on the court. His designer suit didn't even have a wrinkle, much less any bloody buckshot wounds. Sally and Hall were not looking at the seven-foot man lying on his back at their feet, with the team doctor down on his knees beside the player, along with Hornachek.

"He can't be dead," Hall was saying. "Everybody else is okay—except for this little BB shit."

The team doctor glanced up at Hall and looked like he felt almost as bad as the injured men. He wasn't brandishing his medical diploma, but I could tell from the look on his troubled face that he was basically an orthopod in running shoes, not a cardiologist or pathologist. He had unzipped the Big Chill's jacket and was doing his best to stuff a wad of gauze over the heart. He held it there like he was trying to glue it to the Big Chill.

I saw that the doctor's left ear and cheek were streaked with blood, and without having seen the action with my own eyes, I knew he must have been listening for a heartbeat in that big slab of humanity on the floor. The doctor, whom Sally identified as Sam Rice, obviously thought he had heard something in the chest, because he was holding that gauze with shaking hands while he kept twitching a look over his shoulder for medics to arrive.

"Coach Hall," Sally said, "did you see any of what happened on the court?"

"I heard the gunshot when I was downstairs. I ran all the

way up here.'' He glanced sadly around at his bleeding players
and down at the Big Chill. ''And this is what I saw.''

''Coach Hall,'' Sally said, ''does the Big Chill have some
medical problem that hasn't been reported? Like Hank Gathers
or Reggie Lewis?''

''Of course not,'' Hall said, working up to some serious
anger. ''The Chill plays as healthy as anybody in the game.
Healthier. He's never even had a serious injury. What do you
think, this organization is putting sick men out here on the
court? You think *I'm* starting a sick man? Is this some of that
old crap about me and the Big Chill?''

Hall didn't get to work up enough steam to haul off and
punch Sally, because a stretcher was wheeled in just as the
head coach was revving up. We all stepped back, including
the team doctor with the bloody wad of gauze stuck to his
hand, while the Big Chill was loaded and the paramedics
started frantically doing things to that long, long basketball
star's unmoving body. They got an I.V. started and covered
him with a blanket, a blanket that looked about the size of a
bath towel on that seven feet of impossible talent. The
stretcher was on its way out the north entrance to the arena
floor when one of the paramedics climbed on it, peeled back
the blanket, and kneeled over the Big Chill's chest. I knew the
Garden kept an ambulance on standby, and I expected that the
emergency room at St. Vincent's Hospital was on full red
alert, with the Big Chill's private doctor tearing down there to
meet the ambulance.

I almost got Hall's elbow in my eye when he suddenly
jerked his arms and swore. I blinked and stepped back from
him. He was feeling around on his face, and at first I thought
he was mopping up phony tears. But he peeled a deep blue
contact lens off his cheek, licked the lens, pulled his eyelids
apart, and stuck the thing back in his eye. He'd come a long
way from the ugly prescription goggles that had made him so
recognizable when he played for Louisiana State. He was as

big as most of the players on the court, but not as hard any-more.

Ronnie Kovacs had good eyes without any help from Pearle's and was shooting tape of the Big Chill's exit from Madison Square Garden. Church Finnegan was getting the sound. And I was getting nervous. Fillingeri was on his way. I'm all for cooperating with law enforcement, and I planned to cooperate fully—just not immediately.

That's when I realized it wasn't exactly nerves that were bothering me. I'd never had a chance to get over being mad. My mood on the way to the Garden had crystallized into a purpose, one single obsession. I'd come down here for a story, in many ways against my will, after another stupid fight with my ex-wife. And here was a better story than anything we had imagined. Ike Tygart was going to get that story with all the trimmings.

I wanted that tape from Kovacs.

I grabbed my cameraman's elbow.

"I need that tape," I whispered to him. "Now."

Ronnie popped open the camera and handed over the tape without a word or a second of hesitation. I stuck it in my jacket pocket. While Ronnie was loading a fresh tape in the camera, Sally shook her head at me.

"What?" I said.

"You might as well wear a sign saying 'I've got a really fascinating videotape in my pocket.' Jesus, Abby, use your brain. If the cops happen to bring the Special Forces Mindless Homicide Unit, even they'll know immediately what you've got sticking out of your jacket."

I thought of Church's down vest. I crossed to him where he was holding the shotgun mike and snatched his collar. I jammed the tape into the inside pocket of his vest.

"Don't say anything," I told him.

"About what?"

"Good boy."

With a new tape inserted in the camera, Ronnie and Church

were ready to go again. Since I was the director, I did some directing, telling Ronnie to get a good clean shot of Fillingeri's face when he saw us on the court getting an exclusive video grope on the actuality at a crime scene after the principal victim had been removed and before the cops had done a single bit of detective work.

If Fillingeri was going to confiscate a videotape from NTB Television News, I wanted to be sure he got an educational one.

FOUR

I HAD NO IDEA how sprightly Church Finnegan's mind was, but I had every reason to think Fillingeri's was dark, suspicious, and quick. I didn't cross my fingers, because Fillingeri would have noticed that, and I didn't say a mental prayer, because God would have fallen off his throne in shock to hear from me, but I did go so far as to give Church a glance, just to see if he was fiddling self-consciously with his down vest.

He was all business, holding his sound mixer against his thigh and doing his best to gag Fillingeri with the shotgun mike.

"Get that thing out of my throat," Fillingeri said, but not in a nasty way. More like he was a weary Macy's Santa Claus who'd been on duty too long without a break and some ugly kid had stuck a lollipop on his beard. Annoyed, but not violent.

Fillingeri ran a hand through his thick brown hair. He must have it cut by a gravity expert, because it always falls back into place perfectly.

Church didn't move the mike.

"Abagnarro," Fillingeri said, without taking his eyes off Church, "tell your punk to get that extension of his manhood out of my tonsils. And you guys can turn off the camera. Show's over."

I thought about it. I wanted that videotape to stay put in Church's pocket. The cops were welcome to the tape in the camera. It would be in character for me to give Fillingeri some lip, and I didn't want him suddenly using the suspicious part of his mind because I'd turned into someone who obeyed orders promptly.

On the other hand, I didn't want to make him too mad, mad

enough to use the dark part of his mind to turn on us as the focus of his curiosity.

I compromised with myself.

"Church," I said, "back off far enough so the captain doesn't hurt himself on your manhood."

Church smiled—meagerly for him—and backed up a step, drawing the long mike away from close contact with Fillingeri's mouth.

Fillingeri raised a hand. Two uniforms immediately were at his side.

"Abagnarro, I want the tape in that camera. Tell your man to hand it over to these nice officers."

Ronnie looked at me.

"I want to say something about our First Amendment rights," I started, as though I were about to launch into the first class in Journalism 101.

Fillingeri wasn't about to let me lecture him on fundamentals.

Without raising his voice, he said, "Give us that tape or I'll pull out my gun and put a hole through your First Amendment."

"Too bad you can't confiscate our memories, Captain. We all heard that threat."

"Take it to court, Abagnarro."

I nodded at Ronnie. He popped open the camera and extracted the new tape. He gave it to one of the uniforms, the guy who had stepped over to receive it. The cop was about to put the tape in a big plastic evidence bag when Fillingeri reached over and grabbed the treasure out of his lackey's hand.

"I'd like to see what you've got on here," Fillingeri said. "Play it back for me on your camera. You can, right?"

"Not this kind of camera," I lied. "But you know I'd oblige you if I could."

Fillingeri gazed at my open and honest face for a few seconds before he handed the tape back to the uniformed lackey, who plopped it into the evidence bag and sealed it up tight.

"Abagnarro," Fillingeri said, shrugging himself out of his tan camel's-hair overcoat, "that tape. How long's it been running? How long have you been here?"

Now what was worrying me was the quick part of Fillingeri's mind. I was trying to figure out what was the typical *Me.* I decided to answer his question like a trick question.

"On this spot?"

"In the Garden, you clown. Since what time?"

"We've been here since six-seventeen. That's p.m." Fillingeri's fingers curled up into a fist. "Anyway, Captain, we started rolling tape almost immediately. It doesn't take us long to get set up on this kind of remote. We were shooting the warm-up, waiting for Hannah, who was probably having her roots touched up in the limo."

"So you saw everything?"

"No."

"No? Why not?"

"I was down on the floor part of the time, hiding from buckshot pellets."

"How do you know what kind of ammunition you were hiding from?"

"I saw the gun. The gun on the stairs that those five cops from the crime scene unit are now guarding." I gestured toward the stairs where I'd danced around the gun. "Did you see that weapon? Nasty-looking thing. I didn't care for it. I wouldn't own one of those. It looks just like one I saw in a movie, I think with Al Pacino. If I was going to buy a gun—"

Fillingeri turned away from me and went into conference with his platoon of investigators. They dispersed over the court, in what seemed to be an orderly fashion, headed for the wounded and the trainers. The head coach was already in conference with a woman lieutenant I'd seen before and not lusted after. I didn't see the team doctor on the court and figured he'd gone with the ambulance carrying the Big Chill to the hospital, with the paramedics trying desperately to keep whatever flicker of life they'd found in the player from going out for keeps.

"Abagnarro," Fillingeri said, "if I believe all the things people say about you, the only difference between you and a videocamera is that you don't need a battery pack. Why don't we test this out and have you tell me what happened here. Start at six-seventeen. That's p.m."

The two of us stood there, at the center of the sports and entertainment universe. I looked up at the fifty-thousand-pound center display unit directly over our heads. When it's working during a game, it's called "Garden Vision" and shows the score and bombastic cheers. Now it was alive with advertising and changing electronic pictures of coming attractions. It wasn't going to show any scores or fireworks tonight.

I decided to tell the unvarnished truth, omitting only the switch we had pulled with the videotapes and my fib about the fact that our video camera can play a tape backward, forwards, and sideways. I admit I had a qualm or two. I mean, I like law and order. But I was obsessed about that videotape, beyond the fact that it represented a huge scoop for NTB, a scoop we had only if Fillingeri didn't get the tape. Without pictures, we weren't any further ahead than the rest of the media. In fact, without pictures, we were *behind,* because everyone would wonder what, if NTB was on the scene, we'd been doing with our time.

I could just see the headline in the New York *Post* if the worst happened:

BIG CHILL ICED IN GARDEN
NTB News Snoozes Through Murder

And I could just picture Ike's face when we got back to the studios with nothing more to show her than our sheepish grins. I had to cooperate fully now without volunteering to hand Fillingeri something that he'd consider evidence but that I knew wasn't. We hadn't taped the shooter or the Big Chill going down.

"Well," I said, "I can also dance better than a video camera."

"Yeah, yeah. Mr. Ballroom Dancing. The reincarnation of Arthur Murray."

"Arthur Murray was a kangaroo compared to me. Think of me more as Fred Astaire."

"Arthur, Fred, I don't care," Fillingeri said. "Just open your mouth and see if you can make more sense than Bugs Bunny."

So I told Fillingeri. About the explosion, and the sound of basketball shoes, and the players yipping and cussing, and, later, our producer, Sally Goldberg-Petit, asking Coach Hall about the Big Chill's medical history and Hall getting mad. I told Fillingeri about those last rites from Theo Hornachek. I told about the paramedics taking the Big Chill off the court. I told about finding the gun and looking but not touching. And I told about the blurry shape. I told about my wild idea of chasing the shooter around Madison Square Garden's winding caverns.

"You left something out," Fillingeri said, giving me a look that said "Fred Astaire is ad-libbing this dance."

"What?"

"You know. The part where you phone Ike and tell her the part you're not telling me."

"Captain, you have a dark and suspicious mind."

"I also have nightmares about you, Abagnarro. So what about the phone call?"

"I'm even worse than you think. Before I called Ike, I called *Evening Watch* and gave them the sketch of what happened here. Only a couple minutes after the shooting. I had enough time to run up the stairs, almost kill myself not stumbling on the gun, dash out into the hall, realize that I couldn't find the shooter without a map or Sherlock Holmes, and then

I flipped open my cell phone. I called Ike after I called the show."

"What time did you call the show?"

"Six thirty-three. That's p.m. They'd already started the lead story."

"So the shooting happened when? Six thirty-two?"

"I could be off by a minute."

"That wouldn't be like you, Abagnarro. But your videotape will show the exact time, won't it?"

That's when I almost changed my mind about the tape. After what Fillingeri said, I knew for sure I was withholding evidence of a crime. The time code shows on unedited videotape. And in Church Finnegan's down vest was a spool of videotape that would establish the exact minute of the shotgun blast.

"Of course," I admitted, the master of candor. "But you said it yourself. It wouldn't be like me to be wrong about the time. Why don't you ask some of these other guys on the court?"

"What do you think we're asking them? How they like their play-off chances?"

"Probably not. I wonder what the chances are they'll play even the next game on their schedule."

Fillingeri made a noise that, in a man who looked less like Alec Baldwin, would have been close to obscene, and which, if you did it to a New York grocery clerk, would get you the finger no matter who you looked like.

"Let's talk about before the shooting," he said.

"There wasn't much *before* before the shooting."

"I'll make this easy for you, Abagnarro. Let's say it takes you and your crew three minutes to get up here from the box offices."

"Okay."

"That's at least ten minutes of *before* that I'm interested in. I'll give you an example. Was there any, you know, shoving between the Big Chill and Lasalle Parker?"

"'Fedex' Parker?''

Now Fillingeri made a different noise. If I weren't on thin ice about a certain videotape he didn't know about, *I* would have given him the finger.

"How many Lasalle Parkers do you think there are, Abagnarro, that play point guard for Chicago?" He stared into the thousands of seats with an odd look in his brown eyes and mumbled, I guess to himself. "Nicknames. Fedex. A guy gets a nickname like that because he can deliver the ball on time."

"I deliver on time, and women call me Abby," I offered, brightly.

Fillingeri shook himself out of his reverie and returned to me. "Everybody calls you Abby. I thought it was because you're as gullible as that woman who writes the advice column."

"Dear Abby is not gullible. People really have problems like that."

"Tell me about it. I'm thinking of writing to her now. Let's get back to Parker. How many Lasalle Parkers got fined five thousand dollars by the NBA when they played the Knicks two weeks ago? Five thousand dollars for the most flagrant foul I've ever seen—that guy grabbed the Big Chill by the ankle and flipped him on the floor like a fried egg. And *swore* he'd bring cash to every game so he could foul the Big Chill and pay his debt to the league all in one night? So I want to know if there was any trash between those two while you were spying on them with your lousy camera."

"Fedex Parker was out here on the court, and yeah, there was some talking between him and the Big Chill. But so what? Fedex didn't let off a shotgun down here on the court. The shot was fired from up there in the seats. I know because I heard it."

"Parker was on the court that whole time?"

I closed my eyes and pictured the pregame warm-up. Lasalle "Fedex" Parker had left the court about five minutes after we arrived at the Garden.

"No," I said, opening my eyes. "He left." I pointed to one of the six gates athletes could use to enter or exit the performing surface. "He went out there. I figured he was answering a call from the porcelain telephone."

"I don't suppose you saw him carrying a shotgun, did you?"

I raised an eyebrow. This was a dark, suspicious, and quick mind at work. Within five minutes with me, Fillingeri had a suspect. I didn't know whether to feel guilty, glad, or just stupid. I hadn't thought of Parker.

"Jesus. I'd have *told* you if I'd seen him with a gun."

Fillingeri turned and signaled to a uniform, who trotted over like he, too, had received an urgent call from the porcelain.

Fillingeri gave the cop my name, even spelling it correctly, and said, "Start taking this down." The cop already had his stenographer's pad open. Fillingeri once again tried to challenge gravity by running his hands through his thick hair.

"Repeat what you said, Abagnarro. About Parker leaving the court."

I did, while the stenographer wrote down what I said. I was thinking of all the ink that had been used to analyze and comment on the feud between Parker and the Big Chill. *Sports Illustrated* had quoted Parker, after he paid the fine, as saying, "The Chill's head's so thick, he should play hockey. He could step right in as goalie for the Rangers and the equipment manager wouldn't even have to give him a face mask. All the Chill would need is some fancy eyeholes."

Parker was further on the record, with a threat that every publication, with the exception of the Victoria's Secret catalog, had carried: "I don't care how many fines I get. I'm gonna keep the Big Chill on the floor until his wooden head splits open, even if it takes ten years—unless his cranial termites get him first."

Fillingeri apparently had done his reading, leading me to suspect he had a higher S.G.Q. than I'd have given him credit for. Fedex Parker was not just eco-chic like a lot of celebrities.

He was an eco-freak, and among his many charities, saving the rain forests came first. With the Big Chill, cutting them down came first. And Parker had recently taken his politics out onto the basketball court and started using his hands on the Big Chill to make his agenda clear.

When I was finished spilling the beans about Fedex Parker, and the stenographer's pen was still, Fillingeri said, "What I'd like to know is what *Morning Watch* is doing here. You're not a sports show."

"Well, we are now, sort of."

"Since when?"

"Since Ike decided."

"Ike."

"Yeah. Ike. The blonde who spurned you."

Fillingeri cracked a mean smile. "She spurned you first, Abagnarro."

Okay, he started it. "She did *everything* with me first, Captain."

No more smiling.

"If NTB is here on Ike Tygart's say-so, you're here for a good reason." Fillingeri frowned at me. "Like maybe she got you an interview with the Big Chill. You're not here to practice your dribbling."

"Good guess." Sometimes Fillingeri impresses me against my will.

"So how did Ike work this miracle? The Big Chill doesn't talk to you guys. *Any* of you guys."

"We're doing a week of shows on the rain forests. Next week."

"Oh."

"Yeah."

"The Big Chill wanted equal time?"

"I think so. Something like that. Listen, Fillingeri. The Big Chill's had so much bad press from burning down half of Brazil for his cattle ranches that nobody's offering him endorsements or asking for his autograph or voting him onto all-star teams. His life has been really, really tough. Maybe he'll get some endorsements wherever he's headed now.''

"The hospital?''

"I think he's going farther than Saint Vincent's, Captain.'' Fillingeri shook his head, slowly.

I thought he was going to make a remark about whether I thought I was a doctor, but I watched his eyes and he'd lost interest in me. He was looking at the crime scene unit studying the shotgun. And at Hannah Van Stone, our show's anchorwoman, who stood there over the gun, her fist on her ample hip, her feet spread apart like Cleopatra acknowledging the crowds from her barge before she threw a few crew members to the crocodiles. Only, I don't think Cleopatra had dyed blond hair.

"I'll be damned,'' Fillingeri said. "I'll just be damned. She wasn't here when we got here, was she? This arena is sealed off.''

I was, frankly, a little proud of Hannah. "She probably dropped her limo and hired a tank, Fillingeri. You don't have the kind of seal that will keep Hannah Van Stone from a story.''

"That woman ought to have an electric shock collar around her neck.'' Fillingeri took off for the stairs at a trot.

I watched him go, thinking about collars and other instruments of torture, wondering what the NYPD would use on me when they found out I was personally responsible for misleading them about a videotape they'd really like to have, probably as much as they'd like to have a bigger pension fund.

Especially if the Big Chill's journey on that cold, cold night was taking him farther than St. Vincent's.

FIVE

THE BIG CHILL was pronounced dead at 7:04 p.m. by Dr. Martha Rodriguez, chief of staff in St. Vincent's emergency room. She held a press conference to make the announcement. The personal physician for the Knicks' center was not on the scene, having failed to beat death to the hospital. Probably the traffic, and I don't mean anything theological by that.

Other reporters at the hospital who saw the Big Chill's body told me that there had been a lot of blood by the time the ambulance got to St. Vincent's, but that was because the paramedics had been working furiously on the Big Chill to restart his heart, which had failed en route. I don't know CPR, and I'd hate to pound somebody's chest hard enough to make the heart acknowledge my presence, but I didn't think the paramedics had made much difference. I guess I knew in *my* heart that the Big Chill had bought it when he hit the floor in Madison Square Garden, even if delivery was delayed for a while.

But paramedics in this city are tenacious, with a reputation for toughness and brutal fierceness in the face of all the tragic challenges New York deals out on a daily basis. On the battlefield known as Gotham, our medics almost always assume the presence of life in a body until somebody in higher authority peels them off the corpse.

And it might have entered their minds that this was a particularly expensive potential corpse. The Big Chill's contract was no secret, and I guess you work pretty hard to save a heart that pumps at a rate of eight million dollars a year.

During the press conference, a tape of which I saw a few hours after the fact, Sam Rice, the Knicks' team doctor, was in tears. Dr. Rodriguez did what little talking there was, but the best pictures were of Rice, who made his living by man-

aging ice packs and taping up knees and hanging out with
basketball giants.

He was bawling.

Rodriguez did not announce the cause of death at the press
conference. The videotape showed a police officer by her side,
and I thought he was her partner in omission. She made a
brief statement about an autopsy to be conducted on the Big
Chill, and that was it. She didn't take any questions from the
media, all of whom wanted to have everybody's favorite guess
about the cause of death confirmed for the record. When something is obvious, it's obvious. The Big Chill had taken buckshot in the heart.

There was a lot of shouting from the press corps about
buckshot and some obligatory whining about preexisting con-
ditions in the Big Chill's medical history. Rodriguez ignored
the noise.

But noise in New York travels fast, and the word filtered
back quickly to the Garden and us that the Big Chill was dead.

I didn't see the press conference live because Fillingeri kept
us at the Garden until he ran out of questions for his minions
to ask the crew, and out of reasons to think he might come
up eventually with more questions for us, which was at about
8:30. At that hour the crime scene unit was still crawling all
over the court, and they even removed a few of the two hundred wooden sections of the floor, the sections that were most
heavily pocked by buckshot. They examined the ice under the
court, and by golly, they found one shotgun pellet. Imagine if
the New York Rangers had skated into that thing.

The time wasn't completely wasted for me. I learned,
among other things, during the course of Fillingeri's investigation of what was now a murder scene, that the Garden staff
can put the basketball court over the ice in only two hours.
I'd have guessed it took them much longer. You look at the
court during a game, and you'd swear it was a seamless sheet
of highly polished wood that had been there permanently,

maybe since the Bronze Age, instead of a jigsaw puzzle put together since the last hockey game.

I also learned that the Garden has a whopping one thousand employees, and I wondered how many of them owned shotguns. And saws. And how many of them knew how to put the basketball court together. And how, when the circus is in town, they can take up the basketball court, lay down some plywood, and never have elephant damage to the Rangers' ice. I was wondering about elephants and floors because I didn't want to wonder how long it was going to take the cops to search the crew. And find that videotape. By eight o'clock I was almost wishing they'd search us and get it over with so I could go Windex my conscience.

But the NTB crew was apparently out of the running as suspects. We could all alibi each other. In fact, everyone could alibi everyone who'd been present during the shooting, except for Fedex Parker, and nobody had seen him with a shotgun.

Fillingeri himself had found something a lot more interesting than that lonely pellet under the court. In the visitors' locker room downstairs, he discovered the most well-stocked piggy bank I'd ever seen. In Fedex Parker's locker, there was a neat stack of hundred-dollar bills in a white envelope, totaling ten thousand bucks, tidily wrapped in a thick rubber band.

I wasn't allowed to hang around while Fillingeri questioned the Chicago Bulls' floor general. But I did get to see a technician spray some fine chemical mist from an aerosol can onto Fedex Parker's hands, front and back. Parker was told to hold out his hands while the tech aimed a beam of ultraviolet light on them. Probably the biggest hands the tech had ever sprayed.

"What are you studying my hands for, man?" Parker asked, not unreasonably, I thought.

"Trace metals. We can tell if you've held a firearm in the last twenty-four hours."

Parker laughed at the tech. "You find any trace metal, it's because I've been hangin' from the basketball rim."

"I can see the shape of the rim on your palms."

I looked at Parker's palms and saw the small arcs under the black light. I didn't see anything that looked like the shape of a gun.

"Will you look at that?" Parker said, a huge grin revealing an expanse of pink gums. "I got a piece of the Knicks' rim on my own hands."

The tech took a cotton swab, that big kind like they use for throat cultures, and spread a different chemical over Parker's hands, again front and back.

"What's that stuff for?" Parker asked.

"Gunpowder residue."

"You find any, they been putting it on the rim in the Garden. Always said the Knicks play dirty."

The tech shook his head while he did things with the swab. I took that to mean he had found no residue even remotely related to gunpowder. He certainly didn't say "Tsk, tsk, you're a killer."

A fresh cotton swab was produced, along with a different chemical, which I could see from the label on the bottle was nitric acid, and the tech did Parker's hands again.

"Now what?" Parker asked.

"Neutron analysis."

"Well, I ain't been hangin' from no neutrons."

The tech didn't see anything funny about that. Or maybe in his line of work he wasn't used to holding hands with a man who'd made five NBA all-star teams, one Olympic squad, dozens of shoe commercials, the cover of *Sports Illustrated* six times, a reputation as the least selfish of America's premier basketball hogs, and more friends in inner cities than crack cocaine because of his tireless work with kids in his basketball camps. And he had bought up thousands of acres of rain forest in Costa Rica and Belize, donating that land, acre by acre, to elementary schools so the kids could learn to take care of the planet. Fedex Parker didn't put as many basketballs through the hoop as the Big Chill did, but everyone liked him, probably including this NYPD technician. The only blot on Parker's role-model chart was the way he roughed up the Big Chill—both on the court and in the media. A lot of people, even some of Parker's groupies, thought the five-thousand-dollar penalty for fouling the Knicks' center had been overdue and underassessed.

Whatever the tech thought about Parker, what he thought about these on-the-spot forensic tests was clear:

"Captain Fillingeri," he said, "both field tests are negative. We'll have to send out the neutron analysis."

That's when Fillingeri signaled for me to get my nose out of the locker room so he could chat with Parker about the cash in his locker and about other things that occurred in the dark, feverish mind of a police captain.

The word got passed quickly, from the players outside the locker room, that Parker had brought the stash openly and brazenly and even proudly in anticipation of paying a fine for the next flagrant foul he was planning to inflict on the Big Chill. As far as I was concerned, that made Fedex a nut, or maybe a man with a cause, but not a murderer. That cash told me his plan to get at least the Big Chill, if not all of the Knicks, didn't involve a shotgun. Parker was going to hurt the Knicks' center during the game and give "contact sport" new meaning. Fillingeri, however, thought the money proved no such thing, that maybe it was what he called "alibi money."

He returned to the court after his first session with Parker.

I asked Fillingeri about the money, maybe not tactfully.

"Abagnarro," he said, "this is a no-brainer. If I was Fedex Parker and I was going to play with a shotgun, I wouldn't mind having a little cash in my locker that said I had different plans. Am I going too fast for you?"

"No, you're not going too fast. You're going too *far*. You don't even know the shooter was trying to kill the Big Chill. He shot the whole team, the way I saw it."

"Well, you ought to know all about that, Mr. Eyewitness. If ever there was a world-class expert on going too far, he's you. I told you to shut off that camera."

"I forgot."

"Get out of here and take your crew with you. Especially Hannah."

"What's your beef with Hannah?"

Fillingeri closed his eyes for a second and sighed. "She's vamoose-challenged. Go. Get her to go."

Music to my ears. Hannah had done her job, being a world-class expert on going too far by getting in the cops' way and asking questions in front of the camera that Ronnie had slipped his third videotape of the night into (making me nervous because that action might have given Fillingeri ideas), and she was probably the main reason we were allowed to go so soon. Every time Fillingeri and his crime scene specialists turned around, there she was, like a shadow, only a shadow that doesn't keep its mouth shut like your nice, ordinary shadow, the kind without vocal cords. Hannah's difficult to ignore, mainly because she sees no reason why anyone *should* ignore her, the most important anchorwoman in the world.

Hannah's also difficult to ignore because she smokes so much that she smells like a cross between a brush fire and an R.J. Reynolds convention. Despite the no-smoking signs posted everywhere, and despite New York City's stringent law about smoking in a public building, Hannah was stinking up the Garden with Virginia Slims. That's impressive smoking: it's 192 feet from the arena floor to the ceiling of the Garden, yet one woman with a pack of Slims and lungs like a humpback whale managed to pollute enough of the air to make us all a little sick. It's a good thing you can see and hear her on television but not smell her. At least, I don't *think* you can smell her.

The NYPD escorted us to the employees' entrance of the Garden, because the main box-office entrance was still sealed by tape and cops with guns. As he passed in front of me to get out the door, Church Finnegan gave me a broad wink, and I wanted to reciprocate with a kick. Fortunately, Fillingeri was not our escort, so Church got away with almost giving it away.

Fillingeri, I heard, was then back in the visitors' locker room, having another extended chat with Fedex Parker, who looked like the man of the hour. If he wasn't read his rights before the night was out, it would only be because Fillingeri's too smart to walk into unnecessary bad publicity without solid armor.

Clearly Fillingeri wanted to make a quick arrest. I know he can read. Editorial writers would be howling for the cops to get the killer who had so boldly opened fire in the sports shrine of the world to kill the Knicks' "Man" in cold blood. Plus, there was the matter of all the other men who had been injured in the blast from the shotgun—surely they and their agents wanted to know as soon as possible who they could sue. But Fillingeri would not let that pressure force him into a premature move. And, like I'd told Fillingeri, it was hard to say that the shooter had intended to kill the Big Chill. What if he'd been after *all* the players?

But you couldn't argue with the fact that it was the Big Chill's dead body down at St. Vincent's.

Fedex Parker had history to show he was after the Big Chill. And he apparently had the opportunity (unlike the rest of us) to get into the stands with a shotgun, because he had left the court before the shooting. But if he had used that opportunity and that shotgun, the cops couldn't prove it—yet.

At the same time we left the Garden, the forensic chemist left, holding two sealed, labeled glass bottles containing the cotton swabs he had used on Fedex Parker's hands. I caught up with the chemist and asked him about the swabs.

"The second one's going on an airplane out to Missouri to a nuclear research facility where they'll analyze it for the ratio between antimony and barium."

"Oh," I said, nodding wisely. "*That* ratio. Why won't they be looking for gunpowder instead of barium and whatever you said?"

He pushed his glasses up on his nose and said, "Who are you?"

"Lieutenant Abagnarro."

I was afraid he was going to salute me.

Instead he answered my question respectfully. "Gunpowder residue leaves a telltale signature—that ratio I told you about. They can find it even if the killer washed his hands or did the shooting three days ago."

"What if the shooter wore decent gloves?"

"Then we're shit out of luck, sir."

"How long before you get the results?"

"Maybe four, maybe three days."

"Why don't you send it closer, somewhere in this state?"

"Because it's in Missouri where they do this test."

I dismissed him politely and he took off toward a squad car.

I knew then that the cops had to be searching the ten-story structure known as Madison Square Garden for gloves, Fedex-size gloves. Good luck.

Not only does the Garden have extensive plumbing (twenty thousand beer-drinking fans have rights) where you could conceivably shred and flush a pair of gloves, but the arena sits on top of Penn Station, that underground nest of trains and vagrants and drug dealers that can get you to almost any place you're longing to go or would like to send your gloves.

The snow was piling up when we left by the employees' entrance, making the street a trial of balance and good fortune. We headed for the NTB truck, even Hannah, who had misplaced her limo driver. Across 33rd Street, waiting a couple of spaces behind our truck, which was illegally but untouchably parked courtesy of New York press plates, was a cab I'd recently ridden in. When she saw us, Angel Rosenbloom turned her head away to gaze thoughtfully at the ugly vertical morgue slab known as One Penn Plaza, like she was doing research for an article she was writing for *Really Dumb Architecture Magazine*.

Now, here's an interesting coincidence, I thought. I slopped through the snow and tapped on her window. She rolled it down.

"Change your mind about coffee?" I asked.

"I never made up my mind about coffee."

I thought about that. "You're right. So what are you doing here?"

"Same thing you are."

"What? Leaving?"

"Yeah. I was just about to. There's nothing to see."

"That's why you're here? To see something? What makes you think there's something to see?"

She gave me a look almost worthy of Ike's best efforts.

She pointed to her dashboard. "I heard on the radio—NTB Hourly News—about the Big Chill. You gotta get with the program. Don't you know what goes out on your own shows?"

"Not on radio. On TV, I usually know at least ten seconds before our audience does. But I've been busy. What have you heard?" I said, putting my hand companionably on her door handle. I almost shrieked from the icy touch and withdrew my paw. I wanted to stick my fingers in my mouth, but didn't think that would help the impression I was making.

"The Chiller's dead," she said. "Shot through the heart right there across the street in the Garden."

"So you're here looking for the trail of blood? I was hoping you simply found me irresistible, Angel. Let's say you do. Did you circle the block after you dropped us off and just station yourself as a lookout until I came back out?"

"No, I drove back up here when I heard the news. What are you, my mother? Or a cop?"

"I'm not sure. I've certainly been impersonating a cop. Maybe something rubbed off."

"Well, don't rub any on me. I don't like cops."

"You didn't like the Big Chill, either."

"So?"

"So nothing. I'm just making conversation."

"Can't you find a different topic?"

"Well, I could, if I were still impersonating a cop, ask if you know anything about shotguns."

"What's it to you?"

"The Big Chill was shot with one."

"I heard. And it's got nothing to do with me."

I wasn't doing very well. I put my hand on the roof of the cab like Fred Astaire would, gracefully. I immediately snatched it back and stuck it in my pocket. That roof was cold and snowy. "I wish it was spring and you were parked on Central Park West."

"What's your problem? I've got a right to be here."

I didn't have to study the signs sprinkled around by the Traffic Department. "Well, actually, you don't. You're parked illegally."

She laughed. "Oh. Are you a tow truck?"

"No. I'm—"

I was interrupted by a famous voice, a deep, regal voice that sounded like it wasn't used to having its vocal cords exposed to nasty weather. Hannah Van Stone, who had covered the Gulf War in a jeep, apparently didn't like the accommodations of the NTB truck.

"Abby, if I have to ride in this piece of shit, the least you can do is get a move on. I don't want to spend the night in a refrigerator truck that feels like an RV for Frosty the Snowman. Is that cab driver off duty?"

Being Hannah, I thought, must take a lot of practice.

"Your name's Abby?" Angel said. "That's a girl's name."

"Michael Abagnarro. Everyone calls me Abby. Why?"

"I just wanted to know who to tell to get out of my way. I'm off duty for sure."

I stepped back so she could pull the taxi away from the curb.

She didn't even wave good-bye. I've got a good memory, but I took the lying ATM receipt out of my pocket and wrote down Angel's certificate number next to my negative balance—which there was no way I had unless ATMs eat money.

I didn't think the cops were really rubbing off on me. Maybe someday I'd want to buy Angel a cup of coffee, and what if she wasn't in the phone book?

The snow slowed the NTB truck down some, but not as much as the plows and the sand trucks. Hannah was restless, griping about how cold it was in the truck and how I'd let the cab get away. She's got a fairly colorful way of concentrating out loud on her own needs, and after ten minutes of crawling up Eighth Avenue, she said, "I feel like a P.O.W."

I stared at her.

"You have an eye problem, Abby?" she said, lighting another cigarette and blowing the smoke at my face.

I rubbed my eyes. "I do now."

"Stare at somebody else."

I kept my mouth shut and looked at my shoes. P.O.W. Only Hannah, after living and working in New York for more than thirty years, could get that exercised about slow-moving vehicles on the city's streets. Good thing she didn't make her living as an ambulance driver.

SIX

WHEN WE FINALLY got to the Emerald City, Ike was in her office waiting for us, with all five of her television monitors on, watching NTB, the other broadcast networks, and CNN. We arrived right during the 9:00 p.m. adjacency between broadcast programs and at the top of CNN's hourly, and everyone was trying to report the death of the Big Chill without pictures and with very little information, including us. All their scripts must have looked something like this:

PICTURES:	SOUND (ANCHOR'S VOICE):
Close-up on anchor	Good evening.
	He's dead. A doctor said so.
picture of hospital E.R., Dr. Rodriguez's mouth moving	The cause of death has not been released by officials, but eye-witnesses in Madison
sorry, zilch	Square Garden say they think someone with a shotgun got him.
slide of Sistine Chapel's ceiling	We hope to God we've got better coverage at eleven.

"We have a little something for you, Ike," I said, eyeing all the talking heads on her screens. "Church, give her the tape."

He pulled videotape *numero uno* out of his down vest and handed it to Ike. He did not clutch her hand. He did not seduce her with his brogue. He didn't give her the change from the ten dollars she'd given us for taxi money.

"This is what you were shooting when the Big Chill got it?" Ike asked eagerly.

"Yep."

"Fillingeri was at the Garden?"

"Yep."

"How'd you get this out?" she said, tapping the tape with a fingernail. "Was the captain asleep? Drugged? Also dead?"

I waved my hand nonchalantly. "I used magic, brilliance, and complete disregard for the law. I think I'm now a fugitive."

"Did Fillingeri ask you for this tape?"

"Not exactly."

"Did you lie to him?"

I had to think about that. Maybe two seconds. "Not about the tape."

She handed the tape back to Church, with orders.

"Get this dubbed immediately—and I mean immediately. Faster than immediately. Then messenger it to the 54th Street Precinct, addressed to Fillingeri. I'll meet you in Editing Room Three in two minutes. We have to get this on the air. Hannah, you'll do the narration."

Church obediently left the office and raced down the hall.

"I wasn't there," Hannah said. "I'll need help doing the voice-over for the pictures. And I need makeup."

"I'll send a makeup artist to the studio. Abby will narrate into your telex from the control room. You just say what he says."

"Since when is Abby a writer?"

"He's not. But he's the best eyewitness on earth. Just clean up what comes through the telex from him and make sense out of it."

I was offended. "I can make sense."

Ike didn't even bother to answer me. She turned to her

computer and started pounding the keyboard, sending notes to staff all over the twenty-seventh floor of the Emerald City.

The rest of the crew took off for their appointed stations. I dropped onto Ike's couch, intending only a twenty-second pause in the evening's horrors, time I could sneak in while they were dubbing the tape for delivery to the cops.

I used Ike's other extension to call the Graphics Department and instruct our resident computer geek, Fred Loring, to get the Special Report slide ready, on the double.

Ike's office is full of newsjunk. While I was talking to Fred, I plucked a blue UN beret off the cushions and put it on my head. I picked up a heavy bunch of metal lying on her coffee table. It was two horseshoes joined by some metal links and a large central circle of metal.

I hung up the phone.

"Where'd you get this?" I asked, shaking the metal and making a loud clanking noise.

"Get out of my office and get your butt into the control room, Abby." She didn't look up from her monitor screen. "Cal Brookins sent it to me from Colorado. I can't figure out how to get the middle ring off. It's supposed to be possible, but I've tried and tried for days. I think it's a hoax. Cal says it's called Rocky Mountain Torture. I call it baloney."

I held the iron puzzle in my hands and gave it a good look. I twisted the links around, folded the shoes back against each other, and slipped off the central ring. I held the ring up.

"It's not a hoax," I said. "See?"

She shook her head impatiently and swiveled her chair

around to blast me out of her office. When she saw the ring in my hand, she made a noise, like yipping.

"You broke it," she yipped.

"I did not. I solved it."

"Put it back together."

I manipulated the metal parts, but I couldn't restore the puzzle to its original design. The ring kept falling off.

"I told you it was broken," Ike said menacingly. "You've ruined it just because you like to show off."

"I didn't ruin it. I merely haven't figured out how to put it back together. Give me time."

"We don't have time. Put that thing down and get to the control room now. And try to make sense for Hannah."

"I'll try," I said, standing and letting the puzzle pieces fall with clanking noises onto her table. "But it's pretty hard for a dope like me to put complicated things together in a hurry."

"And give me my hat back."

I tossed the beret like a Frisbee onto the back of her couch and took off running down the curving hall to the control room.

By ten o'clock every snoopy journalist in the Free World knew we had aired exclusive footage of both the prekilling and postkilling activity in Madison Square Garden, including shots of the Big Chill dying on the court. As for the killing itself, we had a swooping shot of the ceiling of the arena, as well as pictures of the concrete where we'd taken our dive. I didn't say anything completely senseless into Hannah's telex, and our pictures were pretty good, even the concrete floor.

Fillingeri also knew about our exclusive, which we ran again in the eleven-o'clock show. Ike took his call in Control Room #1, close to midnight. The desk phones in our master control room really seem out of place around the hyperadvanced technology that makes that room in the Broadcast Center look like we warped into the twenty-fourth century. With sixty-six monitor screens on the wall we all face, and the lights and control panels on the boards, we should be having Close Encounters instead of telephone calls.

Ike told Fillingeri to hold on a minute and signaled me to pick up the phone at my station about three feet below hers and listen in.

After I picked up, Ike said, "Okay, Dennis. What can I do for you?"

"Let's begin by putting Abagnarro's ungodly nerve in the Smithsonian. He removed evidence from the scene of a capital crime."

"Would you please be specific?"

"Christ, Ike. The videotape. The one you've been showing to about eight million viewers."

"Did you ask Abby for that tape?"

"Of course I did."

Ike raised her dark brows at me. I shook my head. No way.

"Abby says you didn't ask for that tape."

"Well, he damned well knew which tape I meant."

Ike started tapping her pencil on the sound engineer's board. "That's interesting, Dennis. The part where you know what Abby damned well knew. Are you a telepath?"

"Don't play dumb, Ike. He knew. And he lied to me."

"Abby says he didn't tell you any lies about the tape."

"Bull."

"Abby's pretty careful about his lies. I think he even has a weekly quota."

That hurt. It was my turn to raise my brows at Ike. She pretended she didn't see the pained look on my face and went on.

"Dennis, it sounds to me like you just didn't ask Abby the right question. You should know by now that you have to be quite precise when you want information from Abby."

"Him and his information. I'll remember that next time. In fact, let me write it down: *Be precise.* Before I send a couple of officers over to the Emerald City with a warrant for Abagnarro's arrest—"

"On what charge?"

"Obstruction of justice. As I was saying, before I send for Abagnarro, *you* answer a precise question for me."

"Pooh. You won't arrest Abby for doing his job—because he'll spill his guts about you not doing yours. It's your own fault, Dennis, that Abby spirited that videotape out of the garden. He may have been ahead of you by one step, but it's your business to catch up."

"Ike. My precise question."

"Shoot."

"That copy of the tape you guys messengered to Fifty-fourth Street. How close is it to the original? How much editing did you do?"

"Don't insult me, Dennis. The tape we sent you is an exact clone of the original. *Exact.* We sent it as soon as we dubbed it, without editing."

"I want the original."

"No problem. I've got it locked in my office. We've dubbed enough copies for our use."

I could hear Fillingeri put his hand over the mouthpiece of his phone so he could make some noises for his own enlightenment. When he took his hand away from the phone, he sounded a little hoarse.

"How will I know it's the original?" he said.

"You won't, unless you take my word for it. In fact, you'll be wasting your time worrying about it. The copy I sent you looks just like the original. You now have everything we have. You don't need the original. Have you even looked at the tape I sent you?"

"Some."

"Well, look harder. There is absolutely nothing on that tape to show who fired the shotgun."

"You don't sound very disappointed, Ike."

"I'm not. NTB broke exclusive pictures of a great story. It's not up to us to catch the killer for you. And it's certainly not Abby's job or responsibility as a citizen to figure out what you need so you can do what our taxes pay you to do.''

"You know, that's probably the only reason he's not in jail right now."

"What? Our taxes?"

"No. Abagnarro trying to figure something out. If he was the brains behind sneaking that videotape out of the Garden, then it was probably just a mistake.''

I decided my quota of lies for the week was filled. I also decided the phone in my hand was in working order.

"Fillingeri," I said.

"How long have you been on this line?''

"Long enough to hear all the bad news about my brains and my morals. Here's the deal. When I saw you coming, I deliberately had the tape switched and hid the one I knew you'd be interested in. It was no accident. I practically felt like Richard Nixon. And I'd do it again.''

"You admit it? You admit you concealed evidence with purpose and forethought?''

"I didn't say that. I never used the word 'evidence.'''

"Did you know that tape was evidence?''

Time to borrow from next week's quota. "No. I knew we didn't have pictures of the shooter." But I did know we had the exact time of the shooting and of the action that followed the shot. Surely Fillingeri's experts could do something with the aftermath of the shooting—which we had on videotape— to learn something about trajectories and other gun mysteries. Of course that tape was evidence. Of course I'd concealed it. Of course it was a scoop, and we'd never have had it if I'd handed the tape over to Fillingeri. They don't dub tapes down at 54th Street so they can share with the media.

Fillingeri cleared his throat. Right into the phone. "Did you keep anything else to yourself?''

"Like what?"

"Like that blur you said you saw leaving the arena after the shooting. Was it a friend of yours?''

"My friends are not blurry."

"Could you distinguish anything about this blur?"

"No. I wasn't even certain it was human. I told you all this at the Garden."

"Yeah. The things you tell me."

Ike waved her hand at me.

"Dennis," she said, "when will the medical examiner have the autopsy results?"

"He just got them. Five minutes ago."

Big pause on both ends of the line.

"Well?" Ike finally managed to say.

"Well what?"

"Are you going to tell me?"

"You can attend the press conference in the morning. Here at the precinct. Eight a.m. Sharp."

"Aren't you being petty?"

"No. I'm withholding evidence from Abagnarro."

"He didn't keep any evidence from you."

"The hell he didn't. The Big Chill wasn't killed by that gunshot. He was killed by someone near him on the court. The very thing we could learn to a nicety from that video-tape."

My jaw dropped.

"Excuse me," I said. "Would you repeat that?"

"Which syllable didn't you understand, Mr. Nixon?"

"Come on, Fillingeri. I was there. It was just a basketball warm-up and then that shotgun blast. And then the Big Chill, the one and only, on the floor."

"Why don't you go watch your own tape? I'll see you in the morning."

He hung up.

Ike and I cradled our phones. We stared at each other.

"Abby."

"I swear, Ike. It happened just like I said. That videotape will show nothing—nothing about any killer. The killer was in the stands, behind us, not on the court."

"You'd better be right. Or you've put our NTB asses in a really tight sling."

"Let's take a good look at the videotape, Ike. Fillingeri's just giving us the business. If the Big Chill was murdered by someone on the basketball court, I'll eat your monitor screen and take a vow never again to try to get you in bed."

Shock showed on her pretty face. "Wow. Turn on the machine, Maestro. Roll the tape again. That's the very vow I'd like most to receive. You must have ESP."

Together we watched the videotape Ronnie Kovacs had shot in the Garden. We watched five times. There was *nothing* on our tape to show a killer on the court. Of course, we were missing the crucial moment, the space on our tape filled with pictures of ceiling and concrete.

We watched again and again as the Knicks and the Bulls shot baskets. The Big Chill didn't even look like he was trying when he dunked the ball through the net. Fedex Parker didn't look like *he* was trying when he shot from three-point territory and every shot swished through the hoop. The only time either man seemed to be trying at all was when they happened to pass each other and their mouths moved.

"Can't you get the volume up on that?" Ike asked.

"We were pretty far away then, and a shotgun mike can only do so much."

"Maybe we should get Church in here."

"Yeah. Maybe he *heard* what they were saying to each other."

"Abby, Church is a sound expert. Maybe he knows some trick you don't."

"You'd know more about that than I would," I said, not nicely.

"Oh, have you been gluing your ears to all the gossip, Mr. Potato Head?"

"No, but everyone's been gluing the gossip to their big mouths."

"Well, well." Ike crossed her legs and swiveled her chair. "And are we having a jealous rage, Mr. Abagnarro?"

"No. I just don't like gossip."

"Or Church."

"Him either."

She picked up her phone and dialed. "Church, this is Ike. Can you meet me in Control Room One, right now? Thanks. Oh, and bring the equipment you used at the Garden. Not the mike, just the audio mixer. See you in a flash." She replaced the receiver in its cradle.

"How nice," I said, leaning back in my chair and putting my feet up on the console. "A party. Great guest list."

When Church arrived—with what I thought of as suspicious speed—we went over the tape again, this time with Church making subtle adjustments and keeping an eye on the needle's level.

We were able to make out a few crumbs of words between the Big Chill and Fedex. Nothing about killing. A lot about parentage. Trash Talk, and not even very interesting or spirited Trash Talk.

We gave up after about twenty minutes and Church left the control room. I didn't sob at his departure.

Ike detailed two producers to make some phone calls, trying to get one measly detail from the medical examiner's office to explain what Fillingeri had said about the killing having taken place on the court. Nothing doing.

After they struck out, Ike assigned a crew to cover the 8:00 a.m. announcement from the M.E. We'd have to carry the news conference live. *Morning Watch* is on from 7:00 to 9:00 on the East Coast. That first hour, we'd still have our exclusive pictures from the Garden, but we wouldn't know what they were supposed to be showing us about the murder. Fillingeri wouldn't pull our legs about an autopsy report. He doesn't lie like me.

"Tell you one thing, Abby," Ike said, a slow smile forming on her lips.

"A good thing or a bad thing?"

"Good for us, not so good for Fillingeri."

"What?"

"Until we get that autopsy information at eight o'clock, we're not exactly helpless."

"I know. At least we have the pictures."

"We've got more than that."

"Yeah?"

Now her smile was very bright and her mismatched eyes gleamed. "Oh, yeah. We'll just quote what Fillingeri said on the phone."

"Jesus, Ike, you think he was speaking on the record?"

"He didn't say he wasn't."

I smiled back at her. "I'll bet nobody else but us has Fillingeri's own words on the M.E.'s conclusions."

"And we didn't have to sneak those words out of anywhere. Fillingeri forked 'em over. That wouldn't have happened if you hadn't provoked him, Abby."

"By golly, I'm Superman tonight. May I show you my secret identity?"

SEVEN

IKE'S a better journalist than Lois Lane, having already gotten the number of my secret identity long ago, but I hadn't sworn off trying to get her to see I'd revised it.

Anyway, she was busy, having a little problem with staff morale. The overnight shift was too quiet and the staff was on the jumpy side, waiting, half-prepared and underinformed.

We could put a tight script in place only for the first hour of *Morning Watch*, because we didn't know what would break loose when the medical examiner held his press conference at 8:00 a.m. to announce the autopsy results on the Big Chill.

We already had the only pictures of the Madison Square Garden shooting, and the only pictures of the Big Chill after the shooting. The player had beat even the media to his death at St. Vincent's Hospital. His official death, that is. His unofficial death had caught up with the Big Chill in the ambulance. I didn't know how Saint Peter would sort that out.

Down here on earth, all the other media would have to narrate their morning shows with footage from the past. Games—pictures of the Big Chill grabbing rebounds off the backboards like balls were so many flies and he was flypaper, pictures of him soaring above the rim and dunking the rock through the hoop, pictures of him crashing to the floor after that flagrant and massive foul from Fedex Parker, pictures of Parker tossing rainbow three-pointers into the basket or engineering passes behind his back or through his legs that resulted in some Chicago teammate scoring two points, pictures and sound of Parker badmouthing the Big Chill, with maybe the best Trash Talk in the league. We also had some nice video of Parker's spectacular play with the United States Olympic team, but this wasn't *his* obit. The Big Chill had not made the

Olympic Dream Team, even though he was unquestionably the most talented center playing in the NBA.

My favorite video was a clip we had of Fedex Parker on the court of Chicago's United Center, dancing around the Big Chill near the Knicks' bench—waving a huge Olympic flag with a big hole cut in it and yelling, "Hey, Chill! Look what I found. Your Mama's diaphragm."

We wouldn't be using that clip, but it was fun to look at.

All the media would have that infamous quote from Knicks Head Coach Max Hall about his daughter and Caucasians. Ike was deciding if something Hall had said almost two years before the shooting should be left alone or if it rounded out the obituary we were preparing on the Big Chill. She told the head writer to include it provisionally, and she had detailed an intern to scurry over to the archives to get the videotape of Hall putting his loafer into his mouth.

Obits aren't hard to produce when everyone loved the dead celebrity, someone like Lucille Ball. But Archie Tyrone Thorpe, New York's "Big Chill," was going to be passed along to posterity with some tarnish on the bright image he'd earned as a basketball player. The coverage was thorough and mostly fair even in the tabloids. My favorite item was "The Big Kill," the New York *Post's* front-page screamer headline, their best of the year, over a photo of the Knicks' controversial star, his icy "game face" glazed with sweat as he snatched a ball off the rim.

Every news outlet had their share of unflattering pictures of the Big Chill, too; the tricky part for us was editing them in around the pretty stuff so as not to be overly disrespectful to the recently deceased whose murderer was still at large. We had shots of Archie Thorpe, known familiarly even in Brazil as the Big Chill—*o congelante*—on his cattle ranches near Altamira in Brazil's part of the Amazon forest, personally overseeing the earthmoving equipment that was clearing his land of the endangered habitat that stood in the way of his walking hamburgers.

Since our upcoming week of shows was already scheduled to feature the rain forests, we had our ducks in a row concerning the background to the feud between Fedex Parker and the Big Chill, as well as the feud the Knicks' center was stubbornly conducting with every ecology-protection fraternity on earth.

And we had some nasty statistics and questions ready to air about turning rain forests into cattle ranches, a practice that is just now getting really big in Brazil. Journalists and ecology experts had had their eyes on the story, and all it had taken was one vitriolic piece a few months back in the *New York Times* to get Berkeley's Bank to sell its shares in a gold mine of cattle ranches co-owned by a wealthy family from Rio. Bad eco-press and the bank was out of the beef industry. Just like that.

Nothing, however, had made the Big Chill get out of the business. The increasing global demand for cheap meat was making him one of the world's richest men. In an interview he gave *Newsweek* before he made the decision to stop talking to the press, the Big Chill had made this defense of his ranches: "Man, I'm not even making a dent. I got a lousy quarter million acres of monkey-jungle in Brazil. Twenty-five million acres of Brazilian forest is destroyed every year. You're pickin' on one ant in a big hill."

Maybe. But he'd been getting a lot of heat when he entered any basketball arena lately, and he had lost the stupendous popularity that was his when he'd brought Ohio State two national championships and when he'd been named Rookie of the Year after his debut season in the NBA.

Once he'd invested in raping the rain forests, though, hardly anybody wanted his autograph. He was no longer surrounded by mobs of fans. The Big Chill, who had grown into manhood being courted and wooed and adored, had become a wealthy pariah, the object of boos, catcalls, and Trash Talk. And, easily the greatest center in the league, he hadn't been getting any all-star votes, from the fans or from the coaches.

People had questions the Big Chill wouldn't answer. He just kept on with his cattle ranching and got richer and richer financially; and poorer and poorer in popularity.

But the Big Chill had finally agreed to break his long silence and answer some of the questions, via the interview Ike had set up for us that fatal evening in the Garden. That interview would have won Ike an Emmy, a Peabody, and a raise.

Hannah and her producer had been given instructions to be gentle, but they were supposed to pin the Big Chill, on record, concerning a few points: One in five of all species of birds live in the Amazon forests—where were they supposed to go for low-rent housing after the land was cleared for cattle? And when the Big Chill was cutting and burning and mowing down those trees from the quarter million acres he owned, was he going to build oxygen factories to replace the trees? And would anything make him change his mind about the ranching business, especially since his former fans were clearly speaking out against him?

We had specifically been told by Ike to avoid bringing up the feud between the Big Chill and Fedex during the interview. That was then. Now we were working on an obit.

As a member of the species whose habitat happens to span the globe, I didn't blame Fedex Parker for his frequently quoted question about the Big Chill: "Takes a lot of meals to keep a man as big as the Chill alive, but I wonder if he'd rather eat South American hamburgers or breathe?"

There was more of the quote from Parker, concerning what the Big Chill *should* eat, but we wouldn't be putting that on the air. Networks are squeamish about certain words.

Morning Watch would be leading the way that Wednesday morning with more than the pictures from the Garden. We had that quote from Fillingeri about someone on the basketball court killing the Big Chill, so we could put some liveliness and the appeal of perfectly legitimate insider gossip into our on-air buildup for the press conference. I still didn't believe what Fillingeri had said, but it was great material, and if Fillingeri had hung himself, who was I to complain?

If Fillingeri and the M.E. had concluded that the Big Chill had been killed by someone *on the court,* during those four or five seconds when I had my head down, ducking buckshot, I'd be very interested in knowing what their conclusion was based on. And if they were right, what the hell was the buckshot all about? And who was the blur I'd seen? And how did the shooter and the killer work it so the timing came together so perfectly? And how come the Big Chill, all seven feet of him, didn't put up some kind of fight? And where did you hide a weapon in warm-up clothes if you were getting ready to kill a superstar with about twenty witnesses hanging around? And did the shooter and the on-court killer care that a network television crew was there, with the potential to get the entire thing on tape?

I strolled into the control room about four o'clock. Ike was at her station, on the phone, with the receiver on her shoulder. Her hands were on the keyboard of her computer, and I walked behind her to see what she was doing. She was switching screens, and it looked like she had turned into a meteorologist because she was playing with weather maps while she talked on the phone. She crooked a finger at me and pointed at a spot on one of the maps.

I've covered enough hurricanes to recognize what they look like in satellite photos. This one had a well-defined eye and was twirling around just north of Puerto Rico. It was almost December, there was snow coming down in New York, yet a walloping hurricane had popped up in the Atlantic like it hadn't read any books on tropical weather. November is technically still hurricane season, but this storm was on the highly unusual and really off-pissing end of the statistical spectrum.

Ike drew a line with her finger on the monitor screen. Apparently she was telling me that the storm was predicted to make its way toward Miami.

When she hung up the phone, I asked her, "What's its name?"

"Ricardo."

"Intensity?"

"Category three, but they're saying air force reconnaissance is reporting the pressure at the eye is dropping. It's gonna get bigger, Abby."

"How sure are they it's headed for Miami?"

"They're never sure. You know that."

"You been talking to the Miami Bureau?"

"Yeah. Guess what. They don't care that the Big Chill is dead."

"I'm not surprised." I gave the satellite photo a good look. The swirling bands of clouds sure looked mean.

"Abby, they've already made up a news riddle."

"Okay." I sat down in the chair beside her.

"What's the difference between the New York Knicks and Hurricane Ricardo?"

"What?"

"Ricardo has a center."

I laughed. I couldn't help it. Then I generously offered to tell her the story about the parrots.

"No, thanks. Please don't." She put up her hands, as if to ward me off. "Abby, I think I'm going to pull our crew out of Costa Rica and get them on a plane to Miami."

"What about the live reporting from the rain-forest village you lined up for next week? And all the reports on endangered species? And everything else they've already gathered?"

She put her hand in her hair and tugged at it. Unlike Fillingeri, Ike does not have her hair cut by a Ph.D. in gravity. Her hair gets messed up when she plays with it. She didn't look happy, and I knew it wasn't her hair that was bothering her. She could wear a big slab of cheddar cheese on her head and still look beautiful.

"The Miami Bureau's so decimated with the budget cutbacks," she said. "I hate to leave them understaffed if they're going to get hit by Ricardo. And wherever Ricardo hits, Miami will have to have the people to cover it."

"Maybe Ricardo will blow out to sea."

"And maybe it'll blow out Fort Lauderdale."

"Are you going to run this past Othello? NTB's terrifying owner gonna sign off on this?"

"Othello Armitage has never interfered with the way I handle this show's budget or personnel." She took her hand out of her hair. "Well, maybe once or twice he turned *your* knees to Jell-O. But that's because you can't control your mouth around him."

I took her hand now that she was finished destroying her hairdo. "Ike, I'm sorry about the way I was earlier tonight. Me and my mouth. I'm referring to the baby-powder crack I made in front of Church. I was mad at you, and him."

"I could tell. But I jumped at you first. And I think your anger probably helped us get a whopping big exclusive videotape. You were a tiger in the Garden. Or maybe I mean snake. Sneaky." She twisted her hand to get a good grip on mine and gave me a professional shake. "Pals?"

"Pals? I don't want to be just your pal, Ike. I want to be your husband again."

She tugged her hand out of mine. "I'm sorry, Abby." She swiveled back to her computer. "We're okay through the first hour of the show. Have you talked to Fred about graphics for the M.E.'s press conference yet? I just sent the lineup to your queue. You'd better take a look at it and see if there's any part you want to order. And I'd like you to vet the Big Chill's obit when it's done." She glanced at the clock on the line monitor, the screen that shows what's going out over the air. A call-in talk show. Revolving host. They just couldn't get *Late Watch* comfortable. "We should have the obit done in about an hour."

I rose from the chair. "Sure, *pal.*"

I started to walk out of the control room. I thought Ike

didn't notice. She was fiddling with the weather maps again and had reached for the phone.

"Abby?"

I paused. "What?"

"I'm going to try to get the National Hurricane Center to give us a couple of live updates on Ricardo, one per hour of the show. It'll just be a straight remote feed from the campus of Florida International University. We'll need some supers. I can never remember the guy's name who heads that operation."

"Bob Coates."

"Yeah, him. Will you see about it?"

"No problem."

I left the control room that time without any interruptions in my stride. Pals.

By 7:00 a.m. we were as ready as we could be. We may have had fascinating video on Brazilian cattle ranching, but we also had our own internal meat ranch to contend with. Hannah had enjoyed a brief snit because we'd given the lead story to her coanchor, J. D. Waters, in the news block that leads the show. Her face and voice were all over our postkilling Garden coverage, so it would have looked funny if she introduced our package of videotape, but Hannah had put the oink in "air hog," and she wasn't buying the argument that she wasn't being denied face time on the air just because we liked being mean to her.

Ike got Hannah settled down without allowing her to hurt J.D., and the two anchors appeared to be in perfect harmony during that first hour. I don't know what they were doing to each other under the newsdesk, but I didn't hear any groaning or sharp cries, and I was connected to them via their mikes as well as the monitors.

We were waking America up with plenty of drama, but it was old drama to us. In the control room we were all waiting for the M.E.'s press conference.

The pictures from our crew on the scene where the press

conference would be held showed up on a bank of monitors at about 7:50, giving us a clear view of an empty room in the 54th Street Precinct House. The empty room, brought into the Emerald City via a microwave truck a few blocks away, had an eastern exposure and the lighting was good. Sally was down there to oversee the crew, and I was hoping that our correspondent, Arden Boyer, was too preoccupied with his necktie or something to ask any really stupid questions after the authorities read their statement. Arden tends to be a little basic in his reporting. But that was Sally's project for now.

We came out of a station break at 7:59:30, and Hannah ad-libbed almost five minutes up to the press conference, as we watched Fillingeri and Dr. Stacey Richmond, the medical examiner, file into the room and take up position behind a lectern. I saw Fillingeri look at his watch, so he was aware, as I was, that the conference was starting late. They always do.

Church was with our crew, and damned if he didn't screw up the opening words Fillingeri uttered.

The sound we got, and *aired,* began, "adies and gentlemen. Dr. Richmond will read a brief statement and then we'll take your questions." Fillingeri unleashed a faint, self-deprecating smile that revealed his dazzlingly white teeth. "Hope we know the answers."

Richmond cleared his throat.

He pushed his glasses up on his nose and looked down at the paper he'd put on the lectern.

"Archibald Tyrone Thorpe was pronounced dead at 7:04 last night at St. Vincent's Hospital in Manhattan of a deep stab wound to the heart."

I couldn't believe my ears. But Church was then doing all right with the sound, because apparently nobody in the room could believe their ears either and their chatter was loud and clear from our microwave truck.

"Just a moment," Richmond said. The room quickly got quiet again.

"Thorpe was stabbed with great force, once, through the

right ventricle of the heart. The weapon was a blade approximately five inches long, maybe a little less.'' Richmond fiddled with his glasses again and looked up from the lectern. ''Let me make that clearer. The chest was penetrated by five inches, which we assume was also the length of the blade. The police have not found the weapon. We have been unable to determine anything about damage done to the heart by the removal of the blade, because Thorpe's heart was subjected to great stress in the extraordinary efforts of the paramedics to keep him alive and, when his heart failed in the ambulance, to revive him. Two other wounds to Thorpe's body were caused by buckshot pellets. Both were small wounds in his legs, both insignificant and not related to his death. Those wounds were quite similar to those suffered by the other men on the court at the time of the shooting.''

There was a stunned silence now in the room.

''Captain Fillingeri and I will now take your questions.''

EIGHT

THE FIRST question of the news conference, which came from Arden Boyer's OUR-MAN-ON-THE-SCENE deep voice (he speaks in a much higher register when he's not being paid to open his mouth), was exactly as dumb as it sounded.

"Are you sure?" he boomed.

Were they sure? The chief medical examiner of the City of New York doesn't call a news conference to make statements about visions that come to him in dreams. If he wasn't absolutely sure of his facts, he'd still be back in the morgue, scratching his head, not standing in front of seventeen microphones talking to the global village.

From behind me in the control room, I heard Ike speak into her link with the telex in Arden's ear.

"Arden, your fly's unzipped," she said.

I saw Arden dip his head to check his pants.

If Church had been a better sound tech, I'm certain we would have picked up audio of some grief from other representatives of the Fourth Estate, stuff like "No, Arden, the M.E.'s taking a wild-ass guess." Or "Hey, Arden, did your parents have I.Q.s?" Or "Way to go, Arden, ask him again! Only, this time, can you do it in Sam Donaldson's voice?"

But Dr. Richmond, not wise to how incompetent Arden is, answered the question as though it hadn't come from an idiot who had no idea how to do a Sam Donaldson. (Arden had once confided to me that his own idol was Connie Chung.)

"Yes, we're sure," Richmond said, but his brow was creased in a frown. "I mean, we're sure if you mean, are we sure Archie Thorpe died from a knife through the heart. Or did you mean are we sure he's dead?"

"The first thing," Arden managed. "We all know he's dead."

I could see Fillingeri, where he stood at Dr. Richmond's shoulder, shake his head slightly, like maybe a flea had landed in his ear.

Dr. Richmond, sad to say, evidently didn't think there was anything unusual about mindlessness in the media. "We know, from careful study of the dead man's heart, from the shape and size of the wound in the right ventricle, that a blade—about five inches in length and approximately half an inch in width—penetrated the myocardium, the middle layer of the heart's wall, and was the murder weapon a knife, in fact."

A *Times* reporter, thank God, fired off the next question, and his made sense. "This knife wound must have come as a surprise to you, Dr. Richmond, and to the NYPD, given the shotgun blast."

"Yes, I think it's fair to say we were all shocked."

The *Times* reporter followed up. "Were the men on the court searched for weapons?"

Fillingeri looked uncomfortable. Richmond stepped aside so Fillingeri could move up to the microphones.

"Every man on the court was injured by the discharge of the shotgun, which you have all reported. They received medical attention either at Madison Square Garden or, in the case of those men with the more serious wounds, at St. Vincent's Hospital. While no knife was uncovered during any treatment, we feel sure that one would have been found if any of the injured men had been carrying one."

"But you didn't specifically search those men for a knife?" That was from the CNN reporter.

"No. We had no reason to. Our assumption was that Thorpe had received the fatal wound from a shotgun fired from the stands."

From then on, it was up for grabs and difficult to tell who was asking which question. But the highlights went like this:

Reporter: "Have you traced the shotgun?"

Fillingeri: "No. The serial numbers had been deliberately destroyed."

Reporter: "Were you able to obtain fingerprints from the shotgun?"

Fillingeri: "None. The weapon was clean."

Reporter: "Are you now proceeding on the theory that says this murder was a conspiracy between at least two parties, the shooter and Archie Thorpe's killer?"

Fillingeri: "Yes. We don't think it's a coincidence that the two events were more or less simultaneous. There were two murderers. Or a murderer and an accessory. The particular charges will be for the D.A. to decide. But we know it took at least two people to commit this crime, and we're looking for two perpetrators."

Reporter: "Do you have a suspect for either role?"

Fillingeri, after a slight pause: "No."

Reporter: "In the course of your investigation, did any of the men on the court tell you they had seen any personal attack on the Big Chill?"

Fillingeri: "No."

Reporter: "Don't you think that's odd? Dr. Richmond said that the knife entered Thorpe's heart with great force. That must have been some attack."

Richmond traded places with Fillingeri at the microphones.

Richmond: "The attack must have been very swift. You don't make a deep hole like that by taking your time."

Reporter: "We've all seen the NTB television pictures of the warm-up during which the murder occurred. Have you examined that tape?"

Fillingeri's turn again.

Fillingeri: "We have. Nothing on that videotape shows an attack on the Big Chill by any man on the court."

Reporter: "We're all curious about that tape."

Uh-oh.

Same reporter: "How did NTB air those pictures if you had

them? Who has possession of that tape and when did the New York Police obtain it?''

Fillingeri (after clearing his throat politely): "The NYPD has had the full cooperation of NTB News. If you are suggesting that the NYPD has relied on edited material, you are making a bad assumption.''

Different reporter: "Then why don't the pictures show the murder? What was the *Morning Watch* crew taping? Each other's eyes shut?''

General laughter.

Fillingeri: "You will recall that when the shotgun went off, the television crew was in danger. They, uh, took shelter. That's where the tape shows what is essentially garbage. They've got a space on that videotape where they were down on the floor.''

Smart reporter: "So the stabbing must have occurred *after* the shooting, if NTB missed it?''

Fillingeri. "That is our assumption.''

Back in the control room, Ike hissed at me as I watched the live feed from 54th Street: "Abby, I want that infernal videotape cued up to show the warm-up. Be ready to cut out just *after* the gunshot, when you lose the focus and start shooting floor. We don't need to show what we *did* not get of the story.''

I nodded to Ginger Peloshian, the technical director, who sits to my right, and she got busy. I kept my eyes and ears on the conference.

Even Smarter Reporter: "How did the man with the knife know when to act? When he heard the shotgun go off? And how could the killer know he himself wouldn't be among the badly injured? If he was on the court, he got shot and could have been hurt too badly himself to attack the Big Chill. And how'd the killer on the court know when to get into position close enough to stab the Big Chill?''

Fillingeri: "That's what we're working on. All of that.''

Reporter: "How?''

Fillingeri: "We're starting over in our questioning of those present on the court."

Reporter: "Are you starting over especially on those known to have a record of personal animosity toward the Big Chill?"

Nobody murmured the names of Fedex Parker or Coach "Caucasian" Hall, but those names hung silently in the air in that small room.

Fillingeri (gruffly): "We're starting over on everyone."

Reporter: "Including the coaches?"

Fillingeri: "Everyone."

Reporter: "How many men were on the court at the time of the shooting?"

Fillingeri: "Twenty-one."

Reporter: "We heard Fedex Parker left the court before the shooting. Does that mean he's out of the picture? If he wasn't on the court, he couldn't have killed the Big Chill."

Fillingeri: "We have an eyewitness who says Parker was not on the court when the gun was fired."

Behind me, I heard Ike talking to Arden's telex.

Arden Boyer: "You said you haven't been able to trace the gun. Have you discovered anything about the gun that's un- usual or that leads you to conclude anything about the person who used it?"

The *Times* reporter gaped at Arden.

Fillingeri almost gaped at Arden, but he controlled his face in time and his expression came out looking more like he might have swallowed his chewing gum.

Fillingeri: "That's an interesting question. The gun was sawed off at both ends. The reason to saw off the barrels is to spread the shot in as wide a pattern as possible. That's what makes it so dangerous. The only reason I know of to saw off the butt is to make the gun small enough to carry and hide. The gun was new and in perfect condition."

Reporter: "Is the gun's newness significant?"

Fillingeri: "Maybe. It either means nothing or it means the shooter knew that a gun in that condition leaves very little residue or evidence of any kind behind. And a twenty-gauge is a shooter's gun. I'd say this shooter knows shotguns cold.''

Arden Boyer (with Ike's voice in his ear): "What do you mean by a shooter's gun?''

Fillingeri: "A twenty-gauge is for somebody who knows how to shoot. A marksman.''

Reporter: "Then you should be looking for an expert shot.''

Fillingeri: "We are. Believe me. And the man who stabbed the Big Chill. Remember: we're looking now for two perps.''

Once again Ike spoke into Arden's ear via the miracle of modern remote audio technology, and he asked a whopper.

Arden Boyer: "But, Captain Fillingeri, isn't it true that the gunshot last night in Madison Square Garden was the opposite of marksmanship? I mean, wasn't it more like anybody could have picked up that gun and fired it the way it was fired and hit as many men as were hit?''

Fillingeri blinked. "Yeah. That's a problem.''

Ike didn't take her eyes off the line monitor, but she pulled her mike down over her mouth and spoke to Hannah in the studio.

"Hannah. When we come out of the news conference, we're going to replay the tape of the warm-up, before the shooting. Do the same voice-over you did last night, but point out where the Big Chill is and how close any individual gets to him. Are you okay on the names of the players and coaches?''

I checked out the monitor that showed Hannah and J.D. at the newsdesk.

"I'm all set, Ike,'' Hannah said. "Can you ask J.D. to take a hike? His breath really smells.''

"*My* breath?'' J.D. said, exploding in the BBC accent of his Oxford education. "*My* breath? How can you smell anything over your own breath? You're worse than a Calcutta podiatry clinic in high summer, with all the windows closed.''

"Yeah, well, at least I didn't spend the night chewing garlic.''

Ike intervened. "Be quiet in there. I can hardly think.''

"I can still smell J.D.'s breath even when he's quiet," Hannah said, her tone sharp, her face turned so she could give J.D. the full benefit of her smoky delivery.

Ike flipped the key that closed her line to the anchors.

"I need this?" she said. "Their breath?"

That little anchor exchange cost us in the control room a couple of rapid questions and answers from 54th Street about the missing knife, but we had the whole thing on tape and could listen later at our leisure if it turned out that we'd missed anything good. Which Sally, on the scene with Arden, would clue us in on.

When we focused our attention back on the news conference after tuning out our own anchors, there were some technical questions about the myocardium and the angle of the knife's entry (straight in from the front of the chest), some questions about what procedures the paramedics had followed on the way to St. Vincent's with the Big Chill, some follow-up questions about the timing of the shooting and the stabbing, as well as more questions about where the investigation would go from what looked like a stalled position, but the three real nuggets from the conference had already been mined: The Big Chill had died of a knife wound. The person who had let off that shotgun blast wasn't some disgruntled neophyte playing around with a cute gun he or she had found in a trash barrel. And the shooter and the knifer had to have cooperated. There was no other logical way to account for the close timing of the gunshot and the stabbing.

Ike told me to cue Hannah and roll the tape, and then Ike opened the mike on her own headset.

Once again NTB's viewers got a chance to play detective as they watched the pictures of the Knicks and the Bulls shooting baskets. I also got a chance to see yet again what I'd already seen with my own eyes the night before, and there was nothing on that tape that made me suddenly jump up and shout, "Eureka! Will you look at that murderer?"

The Big Chill was under the basket just before the gunshot,

and nobody was closer than six feet to him. It would have taken a javelin, in my opinion, to put a hole through his heart in the time given. But where would you hide the javelin? During that warm-up, nobody looked or walked like he had a javelin stuck down his thin nylon pants leg.

Hannah didn't put it quite like that, but she gave a satisfactory commentary that ran over the video, even remembering the names of all the players I'd given her on the previous evening when we ran the exclusive footage the first time. She's nasty as hell and she reeks of Slims, but there's nothing wrong with her memory.

After the Garden video, we went to a commercial set, and Kathy Sills, our meteorologist, followed with a look at satellite photos of Hurricane Ricardo and a live chat with the director of the National Hurricane Center at FIU in Miami. The storm was still a category-three hurricane, but they were confident that Ricardo's winds were picking up speed as it made its way west. And *west* was what the computer models were projecting as the storm's course. Nobody seemed to think it would hit a bump and swerve north into a harmless path up the open waters of the Atlantic.

Ike apparently made the decision then and there to pull our crew out of Costa Rica. While we ran a taped feature on visiting the Louvre via the Web (this week's theme being *The Reach of the Internet),* she got on the phone and grabbed an associate producer, giving precise instructions about setting up reservations on the next flight from San José to Miami. Ike would contact the Costa Rica crew herself about the change in plans.

"Ike, you're shooting us in the foot for next week," I said. "We're not going to have enough material to run five days of programming on the rain forest."

Ike shrugged. "We may have a different story to cover, closer to home."

"Yeah. And what if we don't?"

She grinned at me. "Hannah can spend the weekend hauling

her fat ass over golf courses, interviewing the players in funny pants. We'll do a week on *really mindless games that pretend to be sports.*"

"I heard that, Ike," Hannah said, from her post at the news-desk. "You should close your mike when you want to talk about my ass."

Ike gulped. She spoke into her mouthpiece. "That was just an expression, Hannah. I'm sorry. A little joke."

"No, it wasn't a little joke. It was a *fat* joke."

"I said I was sorry, Hannah."

"Well, you can say it to Othello Armitage. I'm telling as soon as we get off the air."

Ike snapped her key closed. "She's going to tell Othello that she has a fat ass?"

"Hannah probably has a tattling clause in her contract," I said. "I wouldn't worry about it. I'll bet NTB's owner already knows Her Highness has a fat ass."

"Great," Ike said. "And now he'll know I've got a big mouth."

"You don't have a big mouth. You have a perfect mouth. Like a rosebud. May I kiss you?"

The other ten people who work in the control room were now looking at us.

"Stop that, Abby," Ike said, lowering her voice, a mean look in her weird eyes. "It's unprofessional. And we are divorced."

"Oh. Really? It's unprofessional for me to say you've got a nice mouth? What is it when *you* say our highest-paid anchor has a fat ass?"

Ike stuck her tongue out at me and with slow, dramatic flair flipped her line to the studio open. "Poetic license, Abby. I've actually always admired Hannah's figure. It's just jealousy that makes me say things like that. If Othello fires me, at least I'll have had the privilege of working with the best anchor in the business. Othello won't fire you, because directors never get fired, so it doesn't matter about what you called Hannah.''

Ike sat back, crossed her arms, and smirked at me.

Hannah's voice came into the control room loud and clear.

"Abby, what did you call me?"

I guess my eyes bugged out. They certainly felt sort of stretched as I stared at Ike.

"You little witch," I said—to Ike.

So much for control-room reality. Hannah thought I was answering *her* question.

"Abby, this is the first time I've ever had one hint that you're a man of discernment," our portly anchorwoman said. "I take your remark as a high compliment. And you may take me to lunch."

I swiveled back to gawk at the studio monitors.

I saw J.D. rip his telex out of his ear and stand up.

"If you need me for any broadcasting chores," he said, the disgust thick in his British accent, "I'll be in the Station Break Deli downstairs, ordering the breakfast special—the garlic omelet."

But Hannah was never one to let an opponent get in the last word.

She turned to J.D. and said, "Ordering the garlic omelet? Surely you'll work your way up to a raw onion? Why stop at merely making people feel sick? Gas 'em until they pass out."

Morning Watch was still on the air, and J.D. up and walked off the set. Just like that. He split. He vamoosed. He freaking *left.*

"Wow," the technical director said. "Hannah's finally got her own show."

"That's not all she's got," Ike said, her eyes mysterious, her smile smug. "She's got a hot lunch date."

I was horrified. We could spare J.D. for a few moments, but could I spare *me* for lunch with the Dragon Lady?

Ike pushed her lips into a mock kiss and winked at me. She leaned forward and smiled around the control room. "Hey, kids, it's show biz. Let's finish making this program!"

NINE

THERE WAS NO WAY I wanted to have lunch with Hannah, so I finally did fake a limp after all. And I went so far as to hike up my pants leg and show our anchorwoman the ugly chewed-up spot on my shin, received in the line of duty from a New York taxi.

"You weren't limping last night, Abby," Hannah said, a dryness in her voice that owed nothing to Virginia Slims.

"No. I think the cold weather kept the swelling down or something."

"We'll do lunch tomorrow, then."

"Tomorrow?"

"Yes. The day after today. You've heard of tomorrow."

"Tomorrow."

"I'll have my assistant make reservations." She walked off down the curving hall of the twenty-seventh floor. Ike was certainly correct about Hannah's hindquarters.

"Tomorrow," I mumbled to myself. "She'll make reservations. I already *have* reservations about this."

I stood there in the corridor for a few moments, trying to come up with a dandy lie, but I was blank. Tomorrow. Maybe my monthly quota really had run out. I couldn't think of a single lie. The only thing that occurred to me was that I should go out and make sure I actually did get hurt bad enough to cancel lunch.

Maybe I could throw myself under a crosstown bus. Or off the Brooklyn Bridge. Or down an elevator shaft. Or at Hannah's mercy. Any of those, and I was a dead man. Maybe instead I could rob Tiffany's and get myself thrown in jail.

My mind was so gassed out by the double disaster—a lunch date with Hannah and the sudden shutdown of my lying gland—that I almost forgot the 9:30 meeting. I practiced my limp on my way down to conference room 2718 and slumped into a chair next to Ike.

What the hell. A man's got to live. I reached under the table and put my hand on the soft green wool of her dress, just above her knees.

"Ouch," I said, when she retaliated by scraping the spiral end of her notepad across my knuckles, hard.

"I hope that hurts for real, Abby. And that limp better be a fake. Are you forgetting the waltz competition in two days?"

I looked across the table at Hannah, who was glaring at me.

"Abby probably won't be able to dance, Ike," Hannah said, in a deadly tone. "He's injured."

Ike put her notebook on the table. "Of course he'll dance. Abby'd only miss a contest if he broke both legs and lost his hearing."

Swell. Now I'd *have* to go to lunch with Hannah.

When Ike and I got divorced, which was not my bright idea, and divvied up the spoils of marriage, I got the stereo system and she got all the other stuff, but we awarded ourselves joint custody of our ballroom dancing. You can get a new husband anywhere, anytime, if you look like Ike. But a well-designed, custom-engineered, beautifully appointed, and perfectly matched dance partner is a man in a million. The Fred Astaire part of me, she kept. The last of the Abagnarros, she ditched.

The morning meeting consisted, in addition to strange looks from Hannah at me and ugly looks from Hannah at J.D., mostly of logistics for rearranging the upcoming week, changing things around so we were set either to cover a hurricane or to salvage our theme week on the rain forests.

J.D.'s brief walk from the set was carefully avoided as a topic, but his turn would come, probably with Othello Armitage, upstairs in the fabled green marble penthouse suite of the Emerald City. I liked J.D., but walking out in the middle of a show is considered a no-no, and he had something coming to him. I hoped what he was going to get would not be a longer walk, all the way out of the Emerald City, partly because we'd just broken him in as anchor, partly because if he got the boot, Hannah's next coanchor might not be as patient as J.D., partly because you don't change anchors when your show has just risen in the ratings, and partly because he hadn't really left *Morning Watch* in the lurch. I mean, it's not like we went to black or anything.

The network's legal arm was represented at the meeting, but not because of J.D.'s walk. George Fahrends, one of NTB's swarm of attorneys, showed up, and he took about ten minutes grilling us on what, precisely, had been the story on my removing evidence from the scene of a crime. He nodded and made notes while I told my story (it was all my idea to hide the tape), and Sally told hers (she advised me on where to hide it), and Ronnie told his (he pulled the actual switch), and Church—the biggest villain of us all because he was the videotape courier—smiled and acted like he didn't know what Fahrends was talking about.

Beyond those three topics—one journalistic in nature; one ethical and having to do with J.D.'s aerobic exercise during a broadcast, a topic left hanging silently in the air; and one legal, meaning was the show open to criminal charges—we had nothing but minor details of production to discuss. The joke about Hurricane Ricardo and the Knicks got retold, but that was just about as close as we came to discussing anything like coverage of the murder. From here on in, we'd follow the police investigation, Ike said, because we had no resources or insights to lead us into any active participation in the solution of the crime. Sally Goldberg-Petit was given the story: she'd be in charge of dogging the police for developments, covering the funeral and the memorial service, and keeping a file of the jokes about the Big Chill that would circulate among the media, especially on the Internet. Disaster humor is part of a producer's job description.

When Ike broke up the meeting around 10:15, she headed for her office, with Church at her side. Neither one of them looked especially tired, and I didn't like that. I happened to be going in that direction, and since Hannah had bolted for her office where she could embalm her bronchial tubes in tar and nicotine, it was safe for me to walk normally. Like Fred Astaire, instead of Hopalong Abagnarro.

I stopped at Ike's door and got a surprise. At least, it seemed at first like a nice surprise until I got the details.

"Abby, I was going to call your office," she said brightly.

"Why?"

"We're going to the Garden, and I want you along as our guide."

"Why?"

"Because you now know that place inside and out."

"I meant, why are you going to the Garden?"

"Because I want to see if we can sneak in."

"Why?"

"To see if it can be done."

"In broad daylight, Ike?"

"Yes."

"Why?"

She was standing in the middle of her cluttered office, on the one spot not crowded with newsjunk. Perfect position for stomping her foot, which she did.

"Because," she said, "somebody shot that gun. It didn't have to be someone with legitimate business in the Garden. Maybe it was someone who got in without having to account for himself. Somebody not on the teams, not on the coaching staff, not an employee."

"You mean, maybe, somebody in the United States?"

"You're making this sound stupid, Abby. It's not. I'm just checking the possibilities. In the news business we call that being thorough."

"At the meeting you turned this story over to Sally."

"This is a special assignment. With special personnel."

I gave Church the once-over. He was sitting on Ike's couch, the UN beret on his head. *My* beret. Well, maybe it wasn't my beret. But I'd worn it first, like a lot of other things I'd done first in Ike's office.

"Why is he going?" I asked, jerking my thumb at the guy wearing my blue Frisbee on his dark hair.

"Because he's an expert on sound. If nobody saw an attack on the Big Chill, maybe somebody *heard* something. Church will be able to tell me about acoustics."

"Oh, for God's sake, Ike," I said. "If you really want to sneak into the Garden, your chances of succeeding increase exponentially as you decrease the number of the troops you bring with you. You need me more than you need him, nothing personal intended. Even better, you should go alone."

She stood there in the center of her office, obviously considering my unchallengeable logic. A rare moment for the former Mrs. Abagnarro.

"Ike," I said gently, "you can't just commandeer a UFO and sail into the Garden like ET.... Wait a minute. I can't remember how he came to earth. Did we ever see his spacecraft? It seems to me there's a big hole in that film. If I was Spielberg—"

"Hello, Abby. What are you talking about?"

From the couch, Church Finnegan opened his mouth and out came his musical Irish brogue, no doubt enhanced by the UN beret.

"Ike's right, Abagnarro. We should all go. I know I'm not a real New Yorker, a navel like you, but I know how a few things work. A good-looking single woman, by definition, gets looked at. A guy on his own looks suspicious."

"That's for sure," Ike interrupted him, yet glaring at me.

"What'd I do?" I demanded.

But Church continued his musical interlude. "Two guys together look like they've been in a bar and are settling a bet. Two men and a woman look like a business meeting. Nobody'd notice that in this city."

Ike beamed at him.

I threw in the towel.

But not all the way.

"I'm not paying for the cab," I said.

At that hour of the morning, getting a cab was a cinch. We just walked out through the stingy revolving door of the Emerald City and three cabs pulled over immediately into the slush-filled gutter at our feet. It looked like slush, anyway. In New York, it could have been a half ton of raw oysters that fell off a truck. It was *something* gray and cold and slippery.

We stood there outside the towering, two-story sea green glass doors of the Emerald City, which no one ever uses and which have etched into them the faces of all NTB anchors, past and present. The Door-and-Etching Department hadn't gotten around to adding J.D.'s face yet, and I hoped they still would at some point. It sort of depended on whether J.D. had a clause in his contract that said he could take a snack break during the show if he reached the point where he couldn't tolerate his coanchor's breath. I doubted he had such a clause, but I've heard of anchor clauses more peculiar than that. The legends have it that one of the pioneers of morning news had a clause that said he couldn't consume more than a fifth of vodka before he went on the air. True story.

"Which cab do we choose?" Church asked. "I mean, how do you know? Is there some outer sign that indicates which one is safe?"

"Easy," I said. "Look for the least cluttered dashboard."

Cab number one had a pair of big stereo speakers, a compass, and a Mets cap on the dash. Strike one.

Cab number two's dash sported three Frederick's of Hollywood catalogs and the remains of an Egg McMuffin. Strike two.

Cab number three was imaginatively decorated with fake beige fur on the dashboard and six different styles of sunglasses laid out on the fur. Strike three.

Ike led the way and stepped across the slush into cab #1. Her reasoning, I suppose, was that the Mets cap was evidence that the driver at least knew what city he was in.

We squeezed into the backseat together, Ike in the middle.

"Abagnarro," Church said, "this driver isn't as pretty as the one we had last night."

I had to agree. Our present rented chauffeur was about seventy years old, had three separate bald spots that looked mildly green, and wore a navy pea coat that smelled like sauerkraut.

Ike idly smoothed the right sleeve of her green wool coat and said, "Your cab driver was a woman? A pretty woman?"

If Church hadn't been in the car, I might have shown some relish over the details, but he was in the car, so I gave Ike the plain facts.

"Oh," Ike said. "What a pretty name. Angel Rosenbloom. I like that."

"I've got her certificate number if you want it," I said. "You know, for beauty tips and stuff."

"You took her certificate number? Why?"

"I don't know. It just seemed like the thing to do."

Ike snorted.

"I took her certificate number," I said evenly, "because she made an encore appearance last night at the Garden. She was parked outside the employees' entrance when we left. I think she's interested in me."

"I'll bet. How come she really came back to the Garden, I wonder? You say she was parked? Didn't have a fare? Was she waiting for a fare?"

"No. She just took off after I, uh, joked around with her."

"If she's so interested in you, why did she take off?"

"That is a mystery, all right. I can't figure it out myself. Probably intimidated by my good looks."

Church leaned over Ike's lap and looked me in the eye. "Stop screwing around, Abagnarro. She came back out of a ghoulish instinct to be where the Big Chill got it. She hated his guts."

"How do you know that?" Ike said.

"She told us. She never said anything about being interested in Mr. Good Looks Abagnarro.'' Church sat back and crossed his arms over his chest.

Our driver got us to Madison Square Garden without getting lost and, miracle of miracles, without talking to us. Ike paid the fare and we got out near the entrance. The day was sunny and bright and a little warmer than it had been sixteen hours earlier when Archie ''Big Chill'' Thorpe was being killed.

''So what's your plan, baby?'' I said to Ike. ''Wanna try the front door?''

''Sure. That looks less sneaky than renting a jackhammer and going through the walls. And don't call me 'baby.' ''

I conducted a quick surveillance of the street. ''I don't see any cop cars. I wonder why not.''

''Maybe the basketball players slept late. It's them that Fillingeri wants to talk to.''

''They had a rough night. Even million-dollar tall guys wearing buckshot need a little R & R,'' I said. Nobody was paying any attention to me, so I shook my head and followed Ike and Church up the steps and into the Garden.

''Are we going to do this brazenly?'' I said, catching up with Ike and whispering in her ear. ''Or on the Q.T.?''

''Let's try brazen. Same theory as the jackhammer.''

And that's exactly what we did and it worked.

We walked past the lines already forming at the box offices, past the curiosity hounds pouncing on the chance to photograph the latest, greatest murder site (if only from the arena's exterior), past the black velvet rope that partially blocked the way to the upper floors, and we were inside.

There was no sign of a security guard, except one who had stationed himself near the box offices and wasn't looking at us. It's amazing the faith people have in velvet ropes.

It was easy. We strolled up into the quiet, quiet halls. The escalator was running, and we took that up to the fifth floor. With me in the lead, we entered the same tunnel gate our crew had used the night before and made our way down to the barrier between the seats and the arena floor.

The basketball court was gone. What we saw was the brilliant white ice that the Rangers would skate on that night. Two men with long metal poles—carried parallel to the floor the way tightrope artists do it—were walking back and forth on the ice, spreading thin mists of water from the tiny holes in the metal rods. The rods were connected to slim hoses that snaked over the ice after the men as they laid down a new veneer of ice. Very peaceful scene, very pretty to watch, very hard to imagine as the scene of a murder. Ike and I both love to skate, and there was a special tug of longing from the artificial winter wonderland we were watching.

However, hockey is one of those sports that Ike considers a major contributor to the S.G.Q., so the magic wore off for her quickly.

"What about the acoustics in here, Church?" she said.

"Pretty good with the shotgun mike. I got more talk from the court than I'd have expected."

Ike craned her neck and stared up, 192 feet up, at the ceiling. "Even in this much space, you say the acoustics are good?"

"Surprisingly so for a sports arena." He pointed up at the top tier, a long, uninterrupted line of private boxes above the seats. "There's some sound baffles up there that'll bounce the sound right back at you. The roof looks like acoustic tile of some sort. It was pretty quiet in here last night without fans and without the announcer. Just men talking, shoes squeaking, basketballs bouncing."

"Generally okay acoustics then?"

"Very good acoustics. Better even than the United Center in Chicago, which is a little bigger than the Garden, I think, but lots newer. I seem to remember reading that Streisand had her people okay the acoustics before her concerts here."

"If the acoustics are fairly tight, shouldn't your equipment have picked up some noise, some sound when the Big Chill was attacked with the knife? Like a shoe squeaking on the floor? Something? Anything?"

Church pursed his lips and seemed lost in thought. When he came out of his trance, he said, "It could be. We'd have to go back and run the videotape, this time with an eye on the sound levels. See how the needle's moving. We might see something. But, Ike, that shotgun produced a lot of echoes. The only way really to crank up the volume on what we've got is to use our eyes on the sound equipment. If the needle jumps or something, we can isolate an anomalous sound, but we may not be able to tell what it is."

I had a vague memory of watching the needle jerk around on the level display of the sound mixer when the crew was down on the concrete after the shot.

Ike stood thoughtfully and looked around.

Even though Ike had studied the videotape, I pointed out to her which end of the court the Big Chill had been on when he was stabbed, where I had found the gun, and the exit Fedex Parker had used when he left the warm-up session. I showed her the door the paramedics had used. I told her we were practically standing on the spot where the crew had taken its dive.

We left the arena, and I took Church and Ike down to the locker rooms. The doors were locked, so I couldn't show Ike where Fedex had stashed the money. We looked around the basement hall at the extra hockey goals, freshly painted and ready for each new game, because once a goal is used, it's so marked up from the sticks that it has to be put in the shop for some body work.

As we headed out for the box office, we were finally stopped by a security guard. This was after we'd been inside the Garden some forty minutes.

What the guard should have done was blow the whistle on us, or at least ask us to leave. Instead, he said something dumb.

"How'd you get in here?" he asked. Like I said, dumb.

So Ike smiled brightly, said, "Guess!" and we kept walking.

That's all there was to it. Easy.

When we were back out on the street, I was getting into position to hail a cab when Ike grabbed my arm.

"Wait, Abby."

"What for?"

"I want to see if we can get in the hard way."

"With a jackhammer?"

"Nope. It takes a relatively long time to get to the Garden's arena floor the way we did it. There must be a faster way."

"Last night we left by the employees' entrance."

"Then let's see if we can blow our way in there as easily as we handled the main entrance."

"You're kidding, right? We had a police escort last night."

"I don't care. I still want to try. Where's the employees' entrance?"

"On Thirty-third Street. You got plenty of money on you?"

"For what? Bribes?"

"Bail money."

"Pooh. It won't come to that."

"You're probably right. We can't be arrested for trespassing since we won't get beyond the door."

We trekked through the salt and cinders and slush on the sidewalk on 33rd and stopped at the door that was our target. There was a simple but extremely unambiguous sign painted over the door: EMPLOYEES ONLY.

"We're employees," Ike said, like she'd just solved an interesting math problem. "Just not of Madison Square Garden. I see no reason why this sign should bar us entry." She looked at Church and me.

Church shrugged and looked doubtful. Chicken.

With a manly grab, I pulled the door open and told Ike, "After you."

We acted like three people on legitimate business and explored the nether regions of the Garden, ending up back at the hockey goals.

"You've proven your point, Ike," I said.

"I certainly have. Let's all go home and get some sleep."

I raised an eyebrow. "All of us? Since when are you kinky?"

I thought she was going to kick me, so I backed up a step. My shin had already had its share of abuse. Too late I remembered that I should have been looking for an injury to get me out of lunch with Hannah.

We exited the Garden the way we had come in, three employed people merely using the employees' entrance. We stepped out into the sunlight onto the sidewalk.

Across 33rd Street, I caught a flash of bright metal reflecting the morning sun. Without thinking, I flattened Ike to the wet, filthy pavement while I hauled Church down by his vest.

And the shotgun blast sprayed about ten cars and the Garden door.

TEN

OUTSIDE, we didn't get the tremendous echoes I'd heard in the arena when the shooter had let loose at the basketball court. This time, after the explosion, the buckshot sounded like heavy rain, or hail. From my position on top of Ike, I checked the sidewalk. We were the only pedestrians, if you can call three people lying on the sidewalk "pedestrians."

Ike wasn't moving.

I pushed her curls aside and whispered in her ear.

"You okay?"

"Fine. Sleepy and contented. I could do this all day. What a lark."

"I get the picture, Ike."

"How many more shots can that person fire?"

"As far as I know, one more—then he has to reload. I think there's just two barrels."

"Great. Did you get a good look at him?"

"No way."

"Then why'd you jump me and plow me into the slush?"

"I thought I saw the gun."

She put her head down on the sleeve of her ruined coat. "Thank God for your eyes, Abby. And your quick reflexes."

I ruffled her curls softly and took a look at Church. He was flat on his belly on the pavement, his hands over his head.

"Church, are you awake?"

"Bloody hell. Of course I'm awake. Do you have to joke about everything, Abagnarro?"

I gave that a little thought. "Not everything."

"I think I'm hit."

"Where?"

"My right shoulder."

"There's worse places." I patted his left shoulder. "Hang on."

I eased my weight off Ike and rose to my knees so I could look through the cracked and crazily pocked glass of the blue Lincoln that was our impromptu fortress. "Stay down," I said. "I'll be back."

"Where are you going?" Ike said, rising to her knees.

"I said to stay down!"

"Well, who named you General of all the Armies?"

"The Directors' Guild."

Ike plopped onto her rear on the cold sidewalk and snatched her cell phone from her purse. She only punched in three numbers, so I figured she was going to chat with 911 before she called in to the NTB Radio Desk. Church, after all, was wounded, and besides, she probably wanted to know what I found out before calling the desk.

I crawled around to the front of the Lincoln and looked across the street. And I mean looked. I knew exactly where I'd seen that flash of metal, so I knew where to begin my search.

Unless our shooter was also crab-walking behind parked cars—and there were only three on his side of the street, in the no-parking zone—he was gone. On a thing like that, though, you don't want to take a chance on your assumptions being right. It's not like crossing on a green light, which lowers your risk of getting killed. My only experience—the previous night at the basketball court—told me that buckshot from a distance probably wouldn't kill me, but I didn't want even a tiny flesh wound. I'd rather have lunch with Hannah, I decided.

If this shooting was a return engagement of the other shooting, what was worrying me was that maybe somebody with a knife was around, waiting to complete the pattern of violence on us. I happened to be using my heart at the moment—I certainly didn't want to expose it to somebody who apparently knew a lot about heart carving.

The door to the employees' entrance to the Garden was open, and a little crowd had gathered there, pushing each other so they could see the street without getting shoved out into the danger zone. Larger crowds had gathered at both ends of the block, but nobody was rushing down 33rd to be a hero. Which was good. We didn't need any urban clutter.

What we needed was some cops and an M.D. And unless the shooter was David Copperfield, he must have been somewhere nearby, and I wanted to get an unobstructed glimpse of him. I took a deep breath and bolted across the street, taking refuge beside a UPS truck.

When I was a boy in Queens, trucks were always my friends when we played our brand of guerrilla hide-and-seek.

I made my way around the truck to the sidewalk, wishing I were wearing a Kevlar vest. I did not come face-to-face with anyone holding a smoking shotgun. There was nobody in sight.

How long had we been down on the sidewalk? I asked myself. I thought about it. Probably twenty seconds. Enough time for a shooter with good legs to sprint to Seventh Avenue. Or, even better, scoot across the street and down into Penn Station. Maybe get a train to Miami. Maybe hide in a bathroom. Maybe saunter out of the station and get a cab. Maybe go inside the Garden and get back to work on his regular job.

Without wasting time looking for a phantom, I returned to the blue Lincoln. Police cars and an ambulance were rounding 33rd from Seventh Avenue.

"See anything?" Ike said, her phone open in her hand.

"Not even my own shadow."

Church had rolled over onto his back and was lying there, studying the sky.

I squatted beside him. "Hurt much?"

He smiled. "Just a sting." There was a little blood on his shirtsleeve.

Police cars screeched to a halt a couple of car lengths beyond the Lincoln, leaving room for the ambulance. Ike must have given the dispatcher such exact directions that the cops and the ambulance driver knew to an inch where she thought they ought to park. She was used to being in charge.

Two paramedics jumped out of the ambulance and headed for the man studying the sky from the sidewalk. Fillingeri emerged from the passenger side of the lead police car and headed for me. All the cops had their weapons drawn, including Fillingeri.

"I'm beginning to think you're a quail, Abagnarro," he said grimly. "You seem to attract buckshot."

His uniformed cohorts spread out around and across 33rd Street. The paramedics helped Church to his feet and walked him across to the ambulance. Ike offered to go with them, but Church shook his head.

A van with a siren blaring roared toward us. The crime scene unit had arrived to dust, photograph, and fill plastic evidence bags with buckshot. I couldn't imagine what a ballistics expert could determine from a shotgun pellet, especially one that had not been fired from the same gun as the one that had been used to spray the Knicks and the Bulls, which was now in police custody, but maybe the CSU has a monthly evidence quota, like my lying quota.

"Captain," I said, "if I'm a quail, or any other predator's delight, I'd like to know why. I don't have any enemies." I stared into the middle distance for a second before returning my gaze to Fillingeri's face. "Except maybe you."

"I don't carry a shotgun, you ape. If I was going to ambush you, I'd use a nine-millimeter."

"So it was definitely a shotgun again?" I felt a little stupid. I mean, there were all those shotgun pellets.

He looked at the Lincoln and nodded. "Wasn't a howitzer."

"Was it just like the other gun, the one from last night? I mean, sawed off, same brand, that sort of thing?"

"From the wide dispersion of the shot, I'd say it was sawed off. As for the other stuff, I'll know that only when I see the gun. Nobody's handed me the weapon yet for this second shooting. You don't happen to have the gun in your pocket, do you?"

"Shame on you, Captain. I haven't even got a slingshot in my pocket. Wanna have me frisked?"

"No, thanks. You'd probably like it."

"Depends who does it."

He helped Ike to her feet, even as she was narrating current events to someone on the phone, probably the Radio Desk in the Emerald City.

Fillingeri signaled her to get off the phone. She rushed to the end of her sentence and snapped the phone shut.

"Let's go inside," Fillingeri said. "It's cold out here, and we need to have a talk."

And what are we going to tell him? I wondered. That we were minding our own business while finishing up our trespassing when somebody opened fire on us?

The crowd at the employees' entrance parted to let us in, and Fillingeri escorted us to a little office just around the corner from the locker rooms. We found chairs, sat, and Ike started paying attention to her slopped-up coat and dress. She hung the coat on the back of the chair to let some of the slush drip off and used her scarf to wipe the hem of her green dress. She crossed her legs to make the operation more efficient, and even with ripped nylons, her legs were simply outstanding as visual aids to what we'd been through.

"Tell me what happened," Fillingeri said, shrugging himself out of his perfectly clean camel's-hair overcoat. He looked like he'd just come from a session at Barney's. And, as usual, not a hair was out of place. And before he went to Barney's, it looked like he'd done a heavy workout at the police gym. I swear he buys his shirts a half size too small just so his muscles will make the cloth stretch.

I glanced at Ike, who was looking at me.

"I see," Fillingeri said, watching us. "A little nonverbal communication? There something about your story you need to get straight before you tell it?"

"Why are you treating us like the bad guys?" Ike said, rubbing her hem vigorously with her scarf. "We're the ones who just got attacked. And our sound tech is on the way to the hospital."

Fillingeri rubbed his jaw. "Habit, I guess. Let me start over. Why don't you just take your time and tell me what happened? I have a certain interest in shootings in this neighborhood, but lately I've positively got a *thing* about shotgun statistics."

"Well," Ike began, "we were taking a tour of Madison Square Garden—"

"One of those guided tours?"

"Self-guided."

"Self-guided? What's that? You mean you sneaked in?"

"We walked in proudly, with our heads held high, and nobody said for us to stop. I don't call that sneaking."

"Whatever you call it, I want to know your route, every place you, uh, self-guided yourself to."

I stepped in and gave Fillingeri the nickel synopsis of our stroll through the Garden. I knew the place better than Ike, and I figured my tale would have fewer "you knows" in it. Basically, I told him, we'd been pretty much everywhere in the Garden except in the ticket booths and the executive offices. And the bar.

He nodded, like he expected as much.

When I got to the part about us going back in through the employees' entrance, he didn't even let a muscle twitch. I finished with a detailed description of playing cowboys and Indians as we exited back onto 33rd Street.

He sat there for a minute, unmoving. Thinking. Deducting. Police mind at work.

Then he asked *the* question. I have to admit that Fillingeri has a way of cutting through a lot of unnecessary clutter.

"Did anyone come near you with a knife?" he asked, finally breaking the silence.

"No. No sign of *anyone,* much less anyone with a knife," I said. "In fact, no sign of the shooter."

"Except that flash of sunlight on the gun barrel that alerted you to get down?"

"That was it. The sum total. Oh. There's all that damage to the cars outside, not to mention whatever they take out of Church Finnegan's shoulder at the hospital."

"Yeah, I saw the cars. And Finnegan."

I sat back in my chair. "So who's after us, Captain, and why?"

"That's what I want to know. The easy answer is that someone has lost his mind and is taking it out on Madison Square Garden. I don't like that answer, because what happened last night to the Big Chill required two people. I get suspicious when two people go crazy at the same time. That bucks the odds. Lunatics, in my experience, are loners."

"I suppose that makes sense."

Fillingeri nodded, as if to say, *Good boy. You haven't yet flunked out of my School for Morons.*

"So," Fillingeri said, "I start thinking that you and Ike and that sound tech are not random targets. And why would that be? Why would anyone go after you? And the only answer I can come up with is that you represent a danger to the shooter. From there I start asking myself what could be dangerous about this television crew that's trespassing in Madison Square Garden. The answer that pops into my mind is that you know something, something the shooter doesn't want you to know or tell. Now, what could that be? Let me show you how the rational mind works. I conclude that you either saw something last night or you recorded something last night about the shooter. I can't read your mind, but I watched that videotape a thousand times. The place where the picture goes dark—did you edit that in after you got back to the studio?"

"Shit. We edited nothing before sending you that tape."

"Excuse me. *Copy* of the tape."

"Copy, schmoppy. You got what we got. No editing."

"We don't like copies of any evidence. We like the real thing. You know what? Something smells bad about *Morning*

Watch being here last night at all. What was the deal on that interview you were supposed to get? I find it hard to believe the Big Chill finally decided to talk to the media again and then chose you guys.''

"Yeah? Well, I find it tough to turn down Ike Tygart when she asks for something. Maybe the Big Chill felt the same way. Lots of guys do. Know what I mean?''

Fillingeri shifted in his chair and looked mighty uncomfortable. Good.

"Let me ask you something, Abagnarro. Why do *you* think you were shot at just now?''

"No idea. I'm without a clue.''

"Where did the gunman go?''

"No clue.''

"How'd you just happen to see the gun without seeing the gunman?''

"Well, this is only a guess, but maybe the gunman wasn't shiny. Didn't reflect the sun.''

"That's not very cute.''

"It wasn't meant to be.''

Fillingeri looked at his watch. He squeezed his hand into a fist.

"Ike," he said, without taking his eyes off his fist, "do you have anything to add?''

"Yes. Abby saved us from serious harm, maybe even saved our lives. You could give him some credit for that.''

"I could. I sure could. I could do that.''

Silence filled the room. I thought I could hear Fillingeri's watch ticking. Or maybe it was his mind, thinking about giving me some credit.

He broke the silence with a surprise. Apparently I wasn't going to be offered the Key to the City.

"If I was the Garden, I'd press charges against you three.''

"What!" Ike exploded out of her chair, dropping her scarf.

"You heard me.''

"Of all the hoo-ha I ever heard," she said, "that's the worst."

"Sit down, Ike," Fillingeri said. "The media has no special privileges when it comes to private property. The media has no civil mandate to investigate a murder. The media is not above the law. The media has no right to help itself to evidence and tamper with that evidence."

Ike did not sit down. The media has no civil mandate to play "Simon Says" with the cops.

"We tampered with nothing," Ike said, with as much dignity as I could imagine in a woman who looked like she'd been crawling around Manhattan on her hands and knees.

"Ike," Fillingeri said softly, "let's assume you didn't tamper with that videotape. Just assume. Now, what if your crew had gotten into an accident on the way back to the Emerald City? What if your truck had gone up in smoke? Where would that videotape be now?"

"Are you going to charge NTB News with obstruction of justice?" she demanded. "You're on the record publicly as having said we cooperated fully with the NYPD."

Fillingeri stood. "What I say for the record is the record. That's it. Final." He sighed. "For now. Until I know different."

I bent down to pick up Ike's damp scarf from the floor.

"Captain," I said, raising my head and looking him in the eyes, "are you a betting man?"

"What? Where did that come from? Betting?"

"Yeah. I'd like to offer you a wager."

"I'm listening."

"I'll bet you a year's salary—mine, not yours—against your badge, that nobody at the NTB Television Network sees the inside of jail on this shotgun or videotape mess. We're now officially victims. The public will eat its heart out over us."

"The public will eat whatever you choose to feed them." Fillingeri squeezed his fingers into a fist again.

"I'll tell you something else, Captain. No. I'll make it another bet instead of a statement. I'll bet you my wristwatch against yours that other basketball teams and hockey teams are giving some thought to games they're scheduled to play in this arena. The public will maybe eat its heart out over that, too.''

''What's that got to do with me?''

''It's going to come home to roost with the NYPD. It's your ball game.''

Fillingeri made a noise and turned abruptly to Ike, who was still standing and still seething. ''Tell me something, Ike. What were you looking for when you trespassed in the Garden?''

If she hadn't been so hot under the collar, she probably wouldn't have told him.

''A possibility,'' she hissed at him. ''If the three of us could get in without setting off some kind of security hoo-ha, then anyone could get in. Last night's shooter could be anybody. This is a big city, Captain Fillingeri. You've got a lot more work to do than we do. All we have to do is report *whether* you find the Big Chill's killers.''

Fillingeri reached for his coat and pulled it on with care, shooting his cuffs and smoothing his lapels.

''See that you remember your own words, Ike. Stay out from under my feet.''

ELEVEN

By THE TIME we reached the corner of 33rd Street and Seventh Avenue, the crime-gawkers had moved on, replaced by the normal thousand or so pedestrians who use that busy slab of pavement at any given moment, and Ike, who'd been yapping into her cellular, slapped the phone shut hard enough, I thought, to break the thing. Or at least hurt its feelings.

"Bad news?"

"Zero news," she said. She spat out her words so viciously that I was glad I was in New York where spitting can get you fined but doesn't show. "St. Vincent's won't tell me anything about Church."

"He's all right, Ike. All he's got is a nicked shoulder."

"Oh. And where did you get your physician's license, Dr. Abagnarro?"

After coping with two shotgun attacks in less than twenty-four hours, I was exasperated. So I said, not chummily, "The Medical Academy of Shit Happening—hereafter known as M*A*S*H. The classes were held in Panama, Saudi Arabia, Los Angeles, Bosnia, and Madison Square Garden. Some of the same places you studied for your diploma."

"Well, kiss my Major Hoolihan."

"Name the time and the place."

She made a noise, not an elegant one. "Hell. When it freezes over."

I glanced around pointedly at our surroundings, at the slush and the crowds. "Looks like we're there already. Bend over."

"Serve you right if I did, Abby. Just look at my clothes! I'm a wet, green, woolen, stinky icicle."

"All right, all right. You want to walk or take a taxi?"

"Golly, Abby, let's just take a gentle stroll. My coat and

dress are soaking wet, and I'd just love an opportunity to air-dry them on the street. It must be at least thirty degrees. Positively balmy for Hell."

It took me a few minutes to get a cab, with the lunch crowds added to the Penn Station crowds. We got a driver whose B.O. was so bad, he should have provided gas masks for his fares. My eyes were probably running a little when I told him to take us uptown. He had to go two blocks south before he could make a right turn and get us headed in the right direction.

Ike made it her business to sniff as loud as she could and mumbled at the cabbie something about "does your union prohibit bathing?"

"You want to be dropped at your apartment?" I asked her, merely requesting information. I did not request to have my head snapped off.

"If you hadn't already told the driver to go up Eighth Avenue, you bully, I was going to tell him St. Vincent's."

"What is it with Church and you? Is this serious?"

"I just like to take care of my people, is all."

"You're not answering my question."

"Why do you want to know? So you can have better gossip than everyone else?"

"You know why. The way I feel—"

The driver spoke over his shoulder. "Where to?"

"That's what I'm trying to find out," I snapped at him, resenting the untimely interruption.

"Keep going up Eighth," Ike told him. "I'll tell you where to drop us. Or he will. Just don't *nag* us about it."

It was the wrong time of day to make progress in a cab going up that avenue. Progress of any kind.

Lunchtime in Manhattan was designed by The Cosmic Mad Behavioral Scientist to produce the most chaos possible in the rat maze known as New York, New York. As the song should have said, *If you can make it here, it's not lunch hour.*

No matter what reward awaited us at the end of our successfully completed tasks, we couldn't get through the maze any faster or more intelligently than algae. In fact, I've seen algae on a stagnant pond move faster than traffic in Midtown during the lunch hour. And with better social planning.

One hundred thousand cabs were bumper to bumper; their drivers were all horn-happy; and the sea of pedestrians (who always think they have the right of way, no matter what color the light is) flowed around us so thick, we couldn't even see where we were. All I could tell when Ike told the driver that we'd let him know was that we were located at the elderly lady with the black fur hat, just south of the Korean kid carrying a package of pink carnations.

"This is crazy," Ike said, lifting the dank hem of her dress and fanning it up and down. "Let's make a pit stop until the traffic thins out."

"Like where?"

"Anywhere. I know! How far are we from Columbus Circle? We can go get dry clothes and our Rollerblades." She turned to stare out the window—longingly, I thought—at a man wearing a clean and dry orange sweatshirt that said I'LL WORK FOR MARLA TRUMP'S HIGH HEELS.

Since we weren't moving anyway, I opened the door of the cab and stepped into the street. I stretched to my full height and saw a street sign. I leaned into the cab.

"We're at Forty-eighth."

"About ten blocks from work." She heaved a sigh.

"You up to it?"

"I'll probably get pneumonia."

"Big deal. Your muscles will probably atrophy in the cab, at this rate."

"I wish we were near civilization," she said. She opened her purse, put some money in the dish on the plastic partition, got a receipt, and scooted out of the cab on my side.

We dived into the sea of pedestrians and made pretty good headway going north. Seemed like we were swimming with the current.

Ike's teeth were chattering by the time we reached the Emerald City and shoved our way in through the midget revolving doors. In the lobby, where the expanse of marble floor was dappled with distorted shadows of the anchor faces etched into the glass of the giant sea green doors, Ike yanked off her green coat and gave it a shake.

"Ick," she said, studying the gray and wet crud on the coat. "I bought this at Saks because it's an exact match for this dress. Does this coat look like it cost me five hundred dollars?"

I gave her green dress and her curves a thorough inspection—eyes only. "I'd say your dress is still an exact match for that coat. They both look like you bought 'em on the street from a hag lady."

She shot me a fiery glance.

"But," I said, in an attempt to thaw her out, "I happen to believe that you could glue raw salmon to your body and still compete in the Miss America swimsuit competition."

"Well, *that* certainly makes me feel better. You've got such a romantic mind, Abby."

"I think what I said *was* romantic."

"Salmons are not romantic."

"Okay, forget the salmon. Glue candles to your body. You can't say candles aren't romantic."

"Gluing anything to my skin is just plain cold-blooded, you simpleton."

She took off for the security desk, rummaging in her purse for her network I.D.

I took out my credentials and showed them to the guard. Like Ike, he was wearing green—though not from Saks. But his uniform was clean and pressed and as stiff as drywall from all the starch.

"Do you like candles?" I asked him, showing him my laminated card.

"Sure, Mr. Abagnarro. I guess so."

"You think they're romantic?"

He looked puzzled. "Romantic?"

"Yeah. *Romantic.* Like a candlelit dinner."

"I ain't never had one."

"You're a big help. Thanks a lot."

"So, uh, is that a problem?" he said.

I heard the *bing* that announced the elevator had arrived at the lobby. I hurried away from the guard.

"Is that a problem, Mr. Abagnarro?" The guard's voice trailed after me.

I boarded the elevator with Ike. She pushed the button for the twenty-seventh floor. We rode up in silence.

When we reached our floor and the elevator doors opened, I let her go first. The staff of *Evening Watch* was bustling in the curving hall we call the "tube" because it circles the twenty-seventh floor, and all the offices and studios open from it. Nobody gave Ike's slimy dress a second glance. They'd all seen worse.

I followed her to her office and waited while she unlocked the door.

She pushed it open and then almost closed it on my nose.

"Hey," I objected. "I've already been attacked once today."

She pulled the door open far enough to peer out at me. "I'm going to change my clothes."

"I'll help you with your zipper."

"No, you won't. I've got a special solvent to unglue all the crap on my body."

"I can spread the solvent around for you."

"Why don't you make yourself useful and call St. Vincent's instead? Use the phone in your own office."

"That sounds lonely."

"It will be—until somebody answers the phone at the hospital. Go away." She shut the door, not with a bang, but not with a whimper either. Just decisively.

I didn't get very far around the tube before I ran into Tom Hitt, boy broadcasting bigwig—approximately five feet of bigwigness, executive producer of NTB's flagship evening news program, and not likely to get any taller, even in his own mind.

"Abagnarro, the very crime victim I'm looking for. We want you live on *Evening Watch*. Is Ike here in the building, too?"

"I'm not hanging around until six-thirty this evening, Tom. Busy night, busy day, been doing the Lord's work."

"You've been doing *bupkes*. You didn't even manage to get one measly glance at a shooter firing over your heads inside the Garden last night. And then today. Are you a total weenie or did you see the guy who shot at you this very morning?"

"Tom, this time I saw him like he was painted on a billboard and surrounded by neon lights. I'll never forget him. Big guy, wearing a clown suit and carrying a sample case of Barbie dolls. I almost bought the Barbie and Clyde set. And the guy spoke with a marked Lithuanian accent. He didn't have any outstanding physical traits except for the rubber nose and the sawed-off shotgun."

"Great. Then that's *twice* now you've missed seeing him. You doing the Lord's work." Tom made a noise, not an affectionate one. "Which Lord are you working for?"

"If I'm so worthless, how come you want me on your show?"

"Not just you. You and Ike. And Church Finnegan. Because, as should be obvious to even your mean intelligence, the Garden Shooter is still at large and still taking potshots at people. You are one of those people. Therefore, you are part of the story. And, unlike last night, this network doesn't have any exclusive pictures of the second Garden shooting. We don't have any pictures at all. Three TV journalists attacked on the street, and we don't have any fucking pictures. You want me to spell this out further? I've got all afternoon."

"So far I'm with you, Tom. But I've got a question. If I stay for your show, who's going to do my sleeping for me?"

He stuck his hands in his pockets (either bought in the boys' department at Bloomingdale's or custom-tailored) and rattled his change. "You can do without sleep, Abby. I, however, cannot do without this breaking development in the sports story of the decade."

I shifted my weight and couldn't stifle a yawn.

"Tom, I am not a sports figure. I should be, the way I skate, but alas, I'm not."

"Nobody gives a crap about you, Abby. You're diddly in the sports world. But you're a sidebar to the Big Chill's story, whether you like it or not."

I yawned again, this time on purpose. "By your own words, my boy, you've just lost a sidebar. I am, as you so aptly put it, 'diddly.' I'm squat. I'm nothing. I'm leaving."

He planted his feet and crossed his little arms over his little chest and thought he'd bar my way.

That wasn't even worth a comment, but I was suddenly too tired to exercise any judgment. "Move, or I'll simply step over you."

"I'd like to see you try."

"No, you wouldn't, Tom. Compared to you, I'm practically all inseam."

"I'm calling our mutual boss and owner of your place of employment—Othello Armitage himself."

"Give him my regards."

I escaped by the easy and basic maneuver of stepping around him, but of course, I'd had recent military experience invading Madison Square Garden. Both were child's play, when I thought about it, but the encounter with Tiny Tom fit the description better.

When I inserted the key into the lock of my office door, I could hear the phone inside ringing.

I took my time, but the phone didn't give up. I'd forgotten to switch it to my voice-mail system.

I walked around my desk, got comfortable in my chair, and picked up the receiver.

"This is Abagnarro."

"Abby," my former wife said, and I wondered if she was standing stark naked in her office, "security just called up and Marie Celeste Thorpe—Mrs. Chill—is downstairs, wanting to see you. Holy cow!"

"Why'd he call you instead of me?"

"He tried. No answer in your office. What took you so long to get there? Oh, never mind. The big question is why she's here at all."

"Did she show I.D.? I mean, is the guard sure this woman isn't some television nut? I heard we got a lot of callers last night claiming to be Mrs. Big Chill, some of them from men."

"Of course he made her show I.D. I told him to send the widow up with an escort to your office. I called *Evening Watch.* This could be a monumental 'get' on the Big Chill story. I'll be right there."

"Are you decent?"

She hung up. Not so that it hurt my ear. Much.

At least my clothes were essentially dry, unlike those belonging to the crabby woman down the hall, because I'd been down on her when she'd been down on the sidewalk. Luck— my favorite surface *and* one of my favorite positions.

Ike came running up to my door, dressed in a pink sweater and black jeans, dragging a black parka and her Rollerblades. She was clutching a large white plastic bag, which I assumed contained a sloppy coat and dress destined for her dry cleaner. She ditched her wardrobe annex on the floor at the far end of my couch.

"I wonder what Mrs. Thorpe wants," she said, a little out of breath. "Tom's got a crew on its way, in case we can't lure her into a studio."

"What could Mrs. Big Chill Thorpe want with us? Probably not our money. She's got plenty of her own—now. She certainly doesn't want publicity."

Marie Celeste Thorpe, bereaved wife of the Big Chill, had stayed in her husband's shadow during their marriage, shunning photographers and saying almost nothing publicly. And she kept her mouth resolutely shut tight even when the paparazzi captured more than a few shots of Mr. Big Chill with other women around town—hell, around the globe.

For all I knew, these other women were all consultants in the cattle business, but other people had other guesses. What Mrs. Chill had guessed or had known was, apparently, her own business. The media knew very little about this tall, regal black woman except that she had a great profile, with a classic Nefertiti nose, and that she wore better clothes than Lee Radziwill. The only other dope generally available on Marie Celeste Thorpe, beyond vital statistics on public records, was that she never missed a home game. Maybe the Big Chill didn't deserve it, but she was loyal. Or, at a minimum, one hell of a New York Knicks fan.

Between his basketball salary and his unpopular but profitable beef ranches hacked out of Brazil's dwindling rain forest, the Big Chill had presumably left his wife enough millions to purchase the Knicks' franchise, if she wanted it, or more acres of rain forest to destroy, if she didn't mind having people hate her. She could buy NTB News, for that matter, if she couldn't get from us whatever she'd come for, which I suspected we didn't have anyway. We didn't *have* anything. The only thing I could figure was that she was here for revenge against me because I was somehow responsible for all the gunplay lately.

Ike studied herself quickly in the mirror behind my door, fluffing her blond hair. I figured she wouldn't let me share the mirror, so I should kill the time productively while Mrs. Thorpe got herself escorted up twenty-seven floors. I was too tired to stand up and dislodge the Manhattan phone book from under a pile of videotapes on my bookshelf, so I dialed information and got the number for St. Vincent's. After some twaddle with their computer menu, and some more twaddle from their information desk, and some twiddly poop from a goon in the E.R., I learned that Church Finnegan had been treated and released. Released both by hospital staff and, I could guess

from past experience, by police officers sent there to give
Church their own brand of examination, a close grilling about
this new shooting and why the gunman had rearranged the
pieces of the puzzle and there'd been no stabbing.

Like Church would know.

I relayed the hot news to Ike.

"Abby, is Fillingeri on to something?" she said. "What I
mean is, at least he had an idea about why we got shot at—
that someone is after us because of something we know. *Do*
we know something? Is there something on the tape? If there
is, the gunman will have to shoot a lot of people, because
there are now a lot of copies of that tape. I think the killer
must have been after *you* this morning. You must have seen
something and the gunman knows it."

"The gunman is not the killer," I reminded her. "The Big
Chill was stabbed on the court. The gunman had some other
purpose."

"That much is obvious, Sherlock."

"Dammit, Ike! I know that. His purpose had something to
do with giving his partner-in-crime a chance to stab the Big
Chill."

"The gunman had lousy timing. When he let off that shot
in the Garden, there was nobody within six feet of the victim."

"Maybe the shooter's trigger-happy, bad at planning."

She snorted. "You're a big help."

"Actually, I am. I've been thinking."

She raised her brows before promptly forgetting about me.
She stepped to the door and peered down the tube.

I wondered if her back was any more receptive than her
front. "I really have been thinking, Ike. Why did the shooter
leave the gun on the steps? It was sawed off to be carried as
a concealed weapon. Why not carry it out of the Garden with
him, concealed?"

She looked over her shoulder at me, grazing the soft pink
of her sweater with the graceful line of her chin. "Probably
afraid to get caught with it."

"Ike, I could have made it out of the Garden with a duck in a bad mood concealed under my jacket. There was a huge crowd downstairs, with a lot of distractions and a lot of noise."

"I guess he didn't leave the Garden, then, no? I wonder what's taking Mrs. Thorpe so long?"

I thought about what she'd said for a moment. "You know, Ike, I believe you just said a mouthful. Maybe he left the gun on the stairs because he couldn't leave the Garden with it—because he couldn't leave the Garden at all. Ike, that would be true if he worked there."

She curled her pretty lips at me. "Guess you just ruled out an independently wealthy shotgun nut and mayhem dilettante."

Tom, a cameraman, a lighting tech, and a sound tech showed up just outside my door.

"I'm talking specifically about a Garden employee, Ike, not just *anyone* who has a job."

"Tom," Ike said, ignoring me, "we don't know anything about what Mrs. Thorpe is doing here, or if she'll consent to cameras and questions and stuff."

I hate being ignored in front of Tom.

"Maybe she's brought a slide show," I said. "Or a confession."

Tom shook his head and gave Ike a sympathetic, comradely gaze. "Maybe Abby should just go home and get a short nap. We don't need him."

"Correction," I said. "You do need me. I'm the man Mrs. Thorpe wants to see." I leaned back in my chair, stretching out my legs. "And on the subject of snoozing, I specialize in *long* naps, Tom. *You* take short ones."

TWELVE

IT WAS A GOOD THING Ike had changed her clothes to something that didn't make a cruddy, slushy statement, because Mrs. Marie Celeste "Spine Chiller" Thorpe looked like she had stepped off the cover of *Fashion Tomorrow: The Guide to Dressing Without Fear*. She was wearing a spanking clean royal blue coat with diagonal chartreuse stripes and giant pearl buttons that looked like it had cost the Big Chill at least ten times what Ike had paid for her green rags, and unlike Ike's five-hundred-dollar garbage from Saks, this coat was so exotic, it sure hadn't come from any rack in America, or from the hands of a premier designer in New York. Not even the most determined designers in this city would risk making a garment so weird that only one woman in a million could carry it off.

If Mrs. Thorpe hadn't bought that coat on Jupiter, the next closest place I could think of with intergalactically strange but beautiful clothing was my home country of Italy—and I guessed she had probably acquired the garment on the same block in Florence where her matching blue and chartreuse leather boots had been purchased. I'm sure the boots hadn't cost more than a mere five thousand, American—although Mrs. Chill might have had to fork over an extra thousand for materials and labor, because her boots were in the size eleven range, or higher.

When they had been in bed together, lying on their backs, Mr. and Mrs. Big Chill must have made some serious bumps in the sheets with their feet—pup tents large enough for a few Chihuahuas to sleep in. But even with his size twenty-two tootsies, the Big Chill couldn't have sheltered more than two dogs in excess of his wife's capacity. I'd guess no more than two Chihuahuas and maybe a sedated canary.

Mrs. Thorpe dismissed her Emerald City security escort with a regal nod, but he wasn't taking that Interplanetary Czarina junk from her. He looked at Ike and got the sign from her that it was okay for him to vacate the premises. He left, slowly and with backward glances, but not before he indicated to Ike, with a security guard facial expression and a meaningful jerk of his left shoulder, that he'd hang around outside in the tube and be only too happy to wrestle Mrs. Thorpe to the ground if the rest of us couldn't handle her without a club. In fact, his fingers twitched around the butt of his nightstick like he was hoping she'd pull a fast one.

And, in a way, she did.

She took a seat across from my desk and casually slung one long, booted leg over the other, completely oblivious to Ike, Tom, the camera, the microphone, and the bright, hot glare from the hand-held frezzies out in the tube. I was waiting and prepared for her either to grab my head and shake out my memory banks or just massacre me with a blast of arctic air from her ray gun.

It turned out she had something different in mind.

And she didn't waste any breath on getting to know me, or Ike, or any of the crew in the tube. She didn't seem interested in any introductions, although I could almost hear introductions hovering unsaid in the air.

"You are Abagnarro?"

"Yes, Mrs. Thorpe. It's a pleas—"

"You were there in Madison Square Garden when my husband was killed, yes?"

"Yes, I was, and—"

"Did he talk to you?"

"There wasn't really time." I got that whole sentence out.

"Do you know why my husband consented to an interview with *Morning Watch?*" Her voice was deep and creamy, like she'd just woken up from a pleasant dream and was thinking about a cup of coffee.

Ike came forward and sat down on the couch.

"Mrs. Thorpe?"

The Big Chill's widow turned her head slightly in Ike's direction and looked down. "Who are you? I have come to see the man who saw my husband die."

Ah, I thought, an introduction is coming, at last.

Wrong. No time for that.

The widow turned her regal scrutiny back to me without waiting for an answer to her own question. Jesus, I thought, she even interrupts herself.

"So, you, Abagnarro, exchanged no words with my husband?"

"None."

"Not even before, when this interview was arranged?"

Oh, I thought, she thinks a television director is the boss.

"Mrs. Thorpe," Ike said, butting in on the royal conference, "didn't your husband discuss this interview with you ahead of time? I mean—"

Without looking at her, the widow said, "We discussed all matters pertaining to business. And it was clearly agreed that he would grant no interviews. His sudden change of mind with you people is why I am here. Please explain your understanding of the arrangement you made to talk with my husband."

"We'd like to tape *this* talk with you, Mrs. Thorpe," Ike said bluntly, gesturing at the crew and Tom in the doorway.

The widow nodded, as though granting an insignificant boon just to shut up the insignificant boon craver.

The crew immediately got into place, and Ike took over from her impromptu helm on the couch. I think she took over from Tom, but maybe she was taking over from the widow. The crew started taping, and the first line they got was from Ike:

"There was nothing very complicated about setting up that interview," Ike said, in a calm, soothing voice that was clearly wasted on the block of wood seated across from her in the blue and chartreuse coat. "*Morning Watch* will be doing a weeklong package of shows next week on the rain forests. I passed the idea by your husband's agent that it would be a good forum to air some of the negative assumptions about the cattle ranches in Brazil and get Mr. Thorpe's comments. Mr. Thorpe agreed. We decided to do the feature in the Garden, instead of in our studio, to emphasize his contributions to basketball. That was your husband's wish, and we agreed to it. I'd like to—"

"You are mistaken." Mrs. Big Chill spoke in the same rich, deep voice, but her eyes narrowed until they were almost shut. She never looked at the camera. I don't know *what* she was looking at. She abruptly opened her eyes as wide as they could go and gave Ike a bold stare, as if she'd never seen her before, and repeated her own first question. "Who are you?"

Ike rose and offered her hand. "Ike Tygart. I'm the broadcast producer of *Morning Wa*—"

Marie Celeste took Ike's hand tepidly and gave it a perfunctory jiggle. "You're very pretty, with such strange eyes: one blue and one green. Those are nice colors. I've never seen eyes like yours before. Were you sleeping with my husband?"

Ike gawked at her. Tom gawked. The crew probably gawked, but I couldn't take in all the details of all the gawking, and still get in my share of gawking.

When Ike got her mouth closed and swallowed hard enough to lubricate her vocal cords, she said, "Sleeping with the Big Chill? Of course not."

Marie Celeste nodded with dignified restraint, like she'd been practicing in front of Grace Kelly videos. She turned to me.

"You're the director, yes?"

"Yes, and I wasn't sleeping with your husband either."

She laughed softly. "No, I didn't think so." Then she nodded rhythmically, like she'd been watching *Gene* Kelly movies.

"Tell me, Mr. Abagnarro, did my husband tell you he would agree to that interview because of Fedex Parker and the criminal abuse on the basketball court that Parker was determined to continue?''

''Ask Ms. Tygart,'' I said, pointing at Ike, in case the czarina had forgotten again who the little blonde was. ''I had nothing to do with getting this interview set up. My only contribution was to supervise technical production.''

Even standing, Ike barely cleared a couple of inches over the seated Mrs. Big Chill, but Ike went into lofty mode anyway and took advantage of the only opportunity she was ever likely to get to look down on this Amazon. ''It was my understanding that your husband did indeed wish to discuss Fedex Parker. I was told that your husband was worried that Parker would get kicked out of the NBA for his behavior. The Big Chill apparently thought that would be a terrible loss to the game.''

I tried not to look surprised—just like, as the director of the show, I had a clue about all the devious dealings we had with guests. Editorial content is not my bailiwick, but this was great gossip, and you'd think *someone* would have let it slip. Ike and Hannah and Sally must all have been in on the conspiracy to keep me in the dark. In my experience, one person can keep a secret, but not three people, so the three women must have applied industrial-strength glue to each other's lips.

And, most peculiar, it was news to me that the Big Chill wasn't having really spicy fantasies about Fedex being shown the door by the NBA. The Big Chill wanted Parker to stay around?

Marie Celeste folded her hands in her lap, very proper and prim. ''Basketball gave my husband everything he had. He did not want to see the sport diminished by a public feud he did not start and did not want.''

''I know,'' Ike said. ''I mean, that's what I was told last week by—''

''So I think it is most odd that he was murdered the very night he was going to speak again to the media. Don't you?''

''I think it's odd that he was murdered at all,'' Ike said. ''And I frankly can't even understand how it was done. Do you have any ideas about how this murder was accomplished?''

"I have many ideas. And I have discussed them, of necessity, with the police. But the murder itself? That is an enigma of great darkness. It is like God. No one will ever solve it.'' She didn't say it like she was having a religious experience. She could have been having a harmless chat with her hairdresser. "But I did not come here to answer your questions about murder. I have told the police all my answers and they were all the same: I know nothing. I came to this building today to tell Mr. Abagnarro a thing, only now I see I have chosen the wrong person, even though he was present when my husband's life was taken from him.''

I felt like I'd misled this woman somehow, though I'd never in my life met her before. Was there some hyperreality where I could tell a lie without having finished a sentence?

The widow shifted position in her chair and faced Ike.

Tom's cameraman shifted his lens to follow her movement.

"Did *Morning Watch* offer to Fedex Parker the same opportunity you offered my husband—to bring this childish war out of the physical realm and into the relative civility of television conversation?''

"Yes,'' Ike said. "Fedex Parker had agreed to be a guest next week in our studio. But he indicated that he still intended to do his best talking on the court. In fact, he—''

"That man should not be allowed to talk at all. The wrong man was killed.'' Again Mrs. Big Chill could have been blowing a little meaningless gas with her hairdresser, the way she eased along without any emotion in her voice. Behind her, Tom started rocking on his little feet, his face tense, his fingers twitching.

The widow said, "I believe that knife was meant for Fedex Parker.''

Tom nudged his cameraman, clearly asking for a close-up on this extraordinary statement and its follow-up, if any.

I raised a hand and was rewarded by a killer glare from

Tom. "Hold on a minute," I said, defying Tom's nonverbal gag order. "Parker wasn't even on the court when the stabbing occurred."

"Yes," the widow said. "Clearly some mistake was made."

At that point Tom jerked himself into motion and came to stand beside Ike.

"You think your husband's murder was a mistake?" he demanded. "And that the knife was intended for Fedex Parker?"

"Of course."

I didn't gasp or turn pale or faint. She was just wrong. The Big Chill's murder seemed to me to have worked out just fine, as murders go. Even if Parker had been on the court—and he wasn't—it would be pretty difficult to confuse the heavily muscled, six-foot-four-inch Fedex with the seven-foot beanpole the Big Chill. He hadn't been the only man on the court at Madison Square Garden who looked more like a tree than a human, but he didn't look like Parker at all. The Big Chill's heart was easily eight inches higher off the floor than Fedex Parker's. If I'd been after Fedex, and the lights were on, and I wasn't committing murder in my sleep or on a quart of bourbon, I wouldn't have accidentally stabbed a man who was that much taller than my target. And in addition to the difference in height, the warm-up uniforms of the two men were unmistakably different colors, with Parker of Chicago in bright red with black trim, and the Big Chill of New York in pure white. Plus—and I didn't know if this was relevant—Fedex Parker probably could have dodged a knife better than the Iceman, having a lower center of gravity and a lot more speed.

"Why are you so certain your husband's murder was a mistake?" Tom said, his eyes glittering. "Is there something you know that has not been revealed to the general public, or to the police? It's common knowledge that Fedex Parker wasn't on the court when your husband was killed."

"And why in the world would anyone want to kill Fedex

Parker?'' Ike said, practically tumbling her question over Tom's, and then her hand flew to her mouth as she realized what she'd said—to the widow of the man someone *had* wanted to kill.

Mrs. Big Chill didn't even blink. ''Because Parker is a pig,'' she said, choosing to answer Ike's question and leave Tom's alone. ''I would have killed him myself quite gladly.''

Tom shifted his gaze to the camera. I could almost see his thoughts written on his forehead: *Shit, we've got it on tape that this woman thinks Parker was the murder target and that she would have been willing to kill him in a minute. What the hell?*

The widow inclined her head to Ike and to me. ''You are all laboring in the blackest of darkness. You don't know what you are dealing with. That is why I am here. To tell you. My husband agreed to your absurd little interview because he wanted to tell the world of his immediate retirement from basketball. Now you know the truth.''

She rose gracefully from the chair and swept out of my office. She cleared the doorframe without having to duck her head. I didn't hear any crash out in the tube, so she hadn't been tripped by the security guard.

Tom spread his little hands out in the air and then clutched his head.

Ike stuck her head out the door and watched for a moment.

''She's got that guard taking her to the elevator,'' Ike said, walking dazedly back toward my desk. ''I don't get it.''

''Pardon my barnyard French, but shit a brick!'' I said.

''Retire? The Big Chill? Why? That's crazy.''

Tom took a couple of steps toward my desk, too. ''You can't refuse to come on *Evening Watch*,'' he said. ''Especially now.''

''I can't?''

''Even before this bombshell in your office, Othello told me to cancel your refusal. You and Ike are both doing the show. And Church, if we can find him. Twelve million people want to know what happened to you three this morning outside the Garden. And now they'll want to know what just happened in your office.''

I hate it when Tom gets his way by tattling to Othello.

"You've got the merry widow's visit on tape, Tom. You saw and heard everything I saw and heard. We have nothing to say that can top what she just said.''

"I've also got you. Nice for a change to have you in a spot where you can't pull any sass on me.''

"Why do you have to bother with Church Finnegan?'' Ike said, and it came off as whining. "If he's going to be tortured on the air, too, won't it look bad with his arm resting heroically in a sling?''

"A sling would actually make better TV. You know that, Ike. But this is all if I can find him. Church is not at his apartment, or at least he's not answering his phone. I've sent a producer down there and sent a note to his E-mail address.''

E-mail? I wanted to swat Tom. "Betcha he was just sitting there at his computer, Tom, waiting to hear from you.''

"Smart people in this town really ought to get in that habit,'' Tom said, and I think he sort of meant it.

"Listen, Tom. Church is probably asleep, all tucked up in his warm little bed. Speaking of which, there goes my sleeping. There goes the waltz practice with Ike. There goes my dignity. I should have stepped on you out in the hall for the hell of it. I wish you'd minded your own business.''

"He's minding the nation's business, Abby.'' Ike ran her hand idly along the top of my desk.

"I don't want to think about Tom's mind. Let's get equipped.'' I yanked my Rollerblades out from under my desk, slipped off my shoes, tucked my jeans into the skates, and laced up. By the time I was finished, Ike was also ready.

Tom was twitching.

"What's the matter, Tom?'' I said. "Can't decide whether to keep this bomb exclusively for your show, and how? You do even one interview to confirm the widow, you've lost your exclusive. This story'll be all over town.''

I stood up, grabbed my jacket, and snatched my keys off the desk. ''Let's go get a couple hours of sleep.''

Tom was mad. That makes him especially nasty. ''Together?'' he said.

''Get out of my office, Tom. Or I'll tear your left arm out of its socket.''

''I'm right-handed, Abagnarro.''

''I know. I was being generous, Tom.''

He left my office, sort of marching, but I could still see the twitch.

Ike wiggled into her black parka and picked up her dry cleaning. I followed her out the door and locked up behind us. We skated to the elevator.

While we waited, I asked her how much time Tom was giving us on *Evening Watch*.

''He said two and a half minutes.''

''Are we the lead story?''

''We must be now. When I saw the lineup earlier, they were leading with the federal budget. With a sound bite like 'My husband was quitting the game,' who'll care about the country's budget?''

''What about the hurricane?''

''Just a graphic and a voice-over. Tom thinks everyone is overreacting to Hurricane Ricardo.'' Ike smiled. ''Tom actually said he wouldn't cover a hurricane this late in November because it would hurt his credibility. Like a hurricane could be a hoax or something.''

The elevator arrived and the brass doors slid open, disgorging a load of producers and techs. Ike and I skated inside, and I pushed the button for the lobby.

''That's good, Ike. A hoax. I guess he never heard of Hurricane Norma in November of 1953.''

''Have you been boning up?''

''Just a little Internet playtime. Did Tom happen to cite any natural disasters that turned out to be hoaxes? Phony earth-quakes? Bogus floods? Anything like that?''

''He did, sort of,'' she said, giggling. ''Well, not exactly.''

''What? What's so funny?''

''Tom mentioned Newt Gingrich's hairpiece.''

''That's a rug?''

''According to Tom.''

''I'll be damned.''

When we left the building, the sky was dark gray and a light snow was falling. Just enough to make it extra interesting to skate.

Ike was about to take off when I grabbed her elbow.

''Ike, what if that shooter doesn't confine his target practice to Madison Square Garden?''

She extracted her elbow from my grip. ''You mean we'll get shot at here?''

''Maybe.''

''Well, we don't have anything like an armored personnel carrier. What's the choice? Stay in the Emerald City the rest of our lives?''

We started skating up Broadway, and that's when I had the idea.

''Hey, Ike!''

She looked at me over her shoulder but kept skating.

I caught up with her and grabbed her dry cleaning.

''I have an idea,'' I said.

''About my dry cleaning?''

''About this shooter. About how to get a look at him.''

She circled into a speed stop, neatly completing a ring around a man pedaling a Chinese food delivery bicycle.

He may have sworn at her, or he may have simply been telling her that the moo shu pork was very good today.

I stopped.

''What's your idea, Abby?'' She brushed a few snowflakes off her nose. ''It can't possibly explain the impossible—the Big Chill quitting the game.''

"Nothing can explain that. I'm thinking about the other impossible thing—his murder. Let's lie on *Evening Watch* tonight."

She snorted. "You call this an idea? Millions of people get lied to every night on that show. What are we, politicians?"

"Just listen. You and I and the crew at the Garden last night know there's absolutely nothing on that videotape to incriminate anyone, right?"

"Right. Although Fillingeri thinks we may have doctored the tape to keep the information to ourselves, for our own use."

"Even better. So what happens if we hint, on the air, that there is something on the videotape—and only on the original tape—that will lead to the killer?"

"Easy. Fillingeri kills us."

"But before he kills us, what happens?"

The snow was picking up some volume, beginning to fall like a flimsy veil between us. But the glow kindling slowly in Ike's eerie eyes canceled out the effects of the white filter.

"I see what you're getting at, Abby. The killer will have to make another move on us." She put her hands on her hips and thought a moment. "No good—unless he also got his hands on the allegedly incriminating videotape. This won't work."

I gave that some thought, although I had her dry cleaning, so I couldn't put my hands on my hips like she did. "All right, then what if we hint that, instead of having something suspicious on tape, I saw something with my own eyes?"

"That would certainly paint a target specifically on your chest. The shooter will have to come after you again."

"Yep. And then we can get a look at his face."

"What if our own faces get blasted off first?"

A few people on the street had stopped to listen in. You have to do *something* while you're waiting for the light to change. And it was too windy to read a magazine.

I put my arm over Ike's shoulders and we started skating north again.

"I've got an idea about that, too," I said.

"I'll just bet you do. Is it as lousy as your first idea?"

"No, this one actually makes sense. The Big Chill was stabbed, right?"

"I'm not going to play any stupid guessing game. Of course he was stabbed. And now we know he was stabbed just minutes before he was going to tell the universe he was quitting basketball. What's your point?"

"My point is, since he was killed with a knife, why the shooting?"

"We've been over this. It was a diversion of some kind."

"From what? Who did it divert?"

Ike gazed at me as we skated across 69th Street. "Well, it sure diverted the crew. Is that what you're getting at?"

I dodged a cab that was dodging the light. "Yeah, the shot put us down on the floor. But what was the *major* accomplishment of that shot?"

"It hurt some people." I could see the exact moment when Ike plugged in. "Oh. You said the shot froze everyone on the court. Is that what you mean?"

"Turned them into statues. Maybe that was what the shot was designed to do. Freeze the action."

"Why?" she said, but I could tell she already knew the answer.

"It's easier to stab a big man who's standing still than a big man who's running around a basketball court."

The snow was thick now, and starting to accumulate under our skates. It was like having power steering all of a sudden.

"Even if you're right," Ike said, her wheels gliding through the powdery stuff on the street, "I don't see how that helps us."

"Think about it, Ike. Say we hint that we—"

"You."

"Of course. Me. Say we hint that I saw something, maybe

even saw the shooter—at the Garden last night or there in the street this morning. It doesn't matter which. I've set myself up. But I've got a secret weapon. Think about it. What do I do if someone opens up on me with buckshot?''

Ike clutched her hands together and squeezed them. I could tell she had it.

As we crossed 70th, she said it out loud.

''Don't freeze. Keep moving.''

THIRTEEN

I DON'T KNOW how well Ike slept that afternoon. I had made a left at 74th for my apartment building, and she kept going up Broadway to our former marital abode in the 80s. For all I know, she made a right at Central Park and went to the Children's Zoo. She didn't go to her dry cleaner, because I still had her bag of clothes. I dumped the bag on a chair and took off my clothes in what must have looked like the home version of Wrestlemania because I was trying not to touch any part of my skin with my frozen fingers. I crawled between the sheets.

I tried to shut out the clutter in my mind and get some rest, but I tossed and turned and wondered what it felt like to have buckshot under my skin. Hell, I couldn't even stand icy fingers.

I tried to think of comparisons, like bees and wasps and even chicken pox, but what I finally decided was that buckshot under my skin would feel like little balls of hot metal that were making me bleed.

I also saw what was wrong with my plan, conceived on the street but now gestating in my rumpled bed: If I let on to millions of viewers that I knew something interesting about the Madison Square Garden shooter, Fillingeri would be among those viewers and he'd arrest me as a material witness. When that happened, not only would I not get a chance to see the shooter's face, I probably wouldn't see many faces I wanted to see. Jail didn't seem a heck of a lot better than metal balls under my skin making me bleed.

I was still awake when my alarm went off at 5:30 p.m. I got up, showered, shaved, and put on some TV clothes, including the obligatory pale blue shirt and red necktie.

Patsy (short for Patrick) Heywood, the *Evening Watch* makeup artist, was already working on Ike when I got to the Emerald City. She was wearing a beige blazer over a dark blue turtleneck. Like me, she was wearing jeans. Unless you're planning to demonstrate cartwheels on a news show, you only have to be dressed appropriately from the waist up.

We had to talk in code, concocted on the spot, so the makeup man wouldn't rat on us. Patsy has a kind heart but a restless mouth.

"Have you spotted the catch in your plan yet, Abby?"

"Yep. The man with the perfect hair will offer me new lodgings and a quick-weight-loss diet of bread and water."

So maybe Ike, too, had lost some sleep—unless she had arrived peacefully in her dreams at the same conclusion about Fillingeri I'd reached by turning my bed into a nest suitable for turkey buzzards.

"I guess you'll just answer questions then, as best you can, for *Evening Watch* viewers and go back home?" she said.

"I'm thinking."

I got shoved gently back in my chair, and Patsy started working on my face. I closed my eyes.

"Abby?"

"Hmm?"

"Could you temporize?"

"Mmmph?"

"Sort of say maybe you saw that person we talked about, but maybe you didn't?"

"Uh, whhup."

"And say that sometimes things come back to you, especially when they're playing our song?"

She lost me there. I leaned forward in the chair and pushed the towel away from my chin, looking her straight in the eyes, not an easy task, although a pleasant one, for a man who can't decide if green is prettier than blue.

"What the hell are you talking about, Ike? We don't have a song. We never did."

She frowned at me fiercely and rolled her eyes at Patsy,

who was standing there waiting for me to put my face back in the work zone.

"I'm talking," Ike said, her voice dropping close to a whisper, which was silly because it only made Patsy lean over so he could hear better, "about keeping your present lodgings but admitting to some confusion."

"I *am* confused."

Apparently Patsy was not confused, though. He seemed to be hearing voices loud and clear.

"Oh, my God," he said, waving his highlighter brush around in the air, "are you two moving back in together? How sweet! Don't worry about the confusion. That's perfectly understandable at this point, after what you've been through." He sighed heavily. "This will make many people very happy."

"By golly," I said, offering my hand to Patsy, "you guessed it." We shook. "Congratulate me."

"Oh, I *do*, Mr. Abagnarro."

Ike nudged me with the toe of her boot. "You'll never change, Abby."

The makeup man was almost overcome. "That's very special." I thought he was going to weep. "Accepting your partner for what he is—that means so much."

"I know what he is, all right," Ike said, a nasty glint in her eyes.

I restored my face to the work zone and closed my eyes again. "Ike, could you please make it plainer to me what your big inspiration is?"

The highlighter brush tickled my cheeks and Patsy started whistling softly to himself, I think "I've Grown Accustomed to Your Face," from *My Fair Lady.* I couldn't be sure because Patsy's whistle needed some WD-40.

"Try to work it in on the air," Ike said, "that you think you saw something but you can't quite get the picture to come into focus in your mind. Say that dancing often helps you, sort of like meditation."

"You mean the waltz contest?"

"Exactly. That's tomorrow night. It's a safe environment. Anybody trying to, er, come between us would be bound to get caught."

Mr. Makeup clucked his tongue. "I just despise a person who would try to do that. They have no conception of true love. They use people."

"And," Ike went on, "they couldn't wait very long to attempt to get you, because they couldn't allow you the time for your memory to come into focus and for you to communicate with the man who'd like to change your lodgings."

"I have to think about this, Ike. Where's Church?"

"Last I heard, nobody knew."

"He's probably on his hands and knees in some pub."

"You're being just plain venomous and disgusting, Abby. Church isn't like that."

"I meant it to be venomous and disgusting."

"Now, now, Mr. Abagnarro," our makeup matchmaker said, soothingly, "don't spoil this moment with petty remembrance."

"Right. I forgot about not remembering."

Ike picked right up on that. "That's the spirit, Abby. You don't quite remember. It'll come to you."

I had this much figured out: The Emerald City would be abuzz with two nuggets after Ike and I finished our gig on *Evening Watch.* One, she and I, after half a year of breaking each other's hearts with our divorce, were reuniting. Two, I thought I knew something about the shooter, but I couldn't quite recall what it was. Something nagged at the edges of my mind. It might come to me in a day or so.

Sure. Ha, ha. Despite Ike's earnest suggestion that I indicate on the air that I often have bolts of lightning-like inspiration while on the dance floor, I wasn't going to say anything on *Evening Watch* about the dance contest. I knew I couldn't pull that off with a straight face.

Besides, the waltz is holy, and there are limits to what I will lie about. Not many, but they do exist.

By the time we were called from the Green Room for our live appearance on Tom Hitt's *Definitive News Statement to the American People,* I found myself wishing Church Finnegan would arrive to flesh out our thin story or give it some pathos. A sling or a bandage on a wounded man would have made better TV than two people who had been shot at but didn't have enough flair for drama to get even one tiny, decent injury between them.

After *Evening Watch* ran the tape of Mrs. Marie Celeste Thorpe talking in her spooky tenor about her husband quitting the game, Steve Holt, the show's anchor, interviewed Ike and me at the big newsdesk, knowledgeably, professionally, and as if we were total strangers to him, merely a couple of crime victims who might have information about the *important* crime victim everyone was really interested in: the New York Knicks' controversial center, the Big Chill.

We gave Steve our spiel on the morning's shotgun party outside the Garden straight, making nothing up and hiding nothing. The only tricky part, since we knew zippo about the Big Chill's surprise career plans, was where my lie came in.

This is what he asked me: "And, Mr. Abagnarro, you were present at both shootings. Is there nothing you can tell us about the person behind the gun?"

This was my lie: "That's kind of blurry, Steve. I mean, I saw a blur. Something about the blur seemed familiar to me. I think when the immediate shock wears off, I may be able to put together what it is that's bothering me about the blur I saw. I can still see that blurred figure quite vividly in my mind. I just can't quite put my finger on what was so distinctive about the shooter. You know? It's like a tune you can't get out of your head, only you can't remember the lyrics."

I was ready to leave then, after my lie, but Steve had been primed with another question.

"Mr. Abagnarro, do you think this was a personal attack

on you, or do you think the attack is connected with Madison Square Garden?"

"I hope it's the Garden."

"So you don't fear for your personal safety where this gunman is concerned?"

"It's not like I make regularly scheduled personal appearances in public places. I'm not a New York Knick. I just happened to be at the Garden this morning. The rest of the time, I'm anonymous, like any other New Yorker."

Steve smiled gently. "In some circles, it's fairly well known that you wear another hat when you're not directing television shows. You're a competitive dancer, aren't you?"

I could have kicked him under the desk. I glanced at Ike, wondering if she'd put this bee in his bonnet. Maybe she'd even given him the address and time of the waltz contest we were doing Thursday evening.

"Steve, I guess it's no secret that I dance."

And then Ike smiled brightly. "He dances very well. I think we have a good chance to place well in the waltz tomorrow night at Playtime-in-Brazil on West 72nd Street. Mr. Abagnarro could dance professionally."

I glared at her. Why didn't she just hang a sign on me that said "Go ahead and shoot! I'll show you some fancy dancing"?

Evening Watch got rid of us during a commercial.

Tom caught up with us outside the studio door.

"This is the first I heard you saw anything during the shooting, Abby. You're the Bupkes Kid. What was that all about?"

"I gave you an exclusive, Tom. That's more than you requested or deserved. Be grateful."

"I'm skeptical, not grateful. You're going to get it from Captain Fillingeri."

"Won't be the first time."

Tom put his hands in his pockets and looked up at me. Must have hurt his neck.

"When and *if* you actually recall details on the shooter,

Abby, I want it first. You broke the news on my program. It's now my story."

If I weren't so tired, I would have laughed. "No, Tom, it's *my* story, and I'm sticking to it. Like glue."

"We'll see about that."

"There's a lot of stuff we'll see about. Like the origin of the universe, the existence of God, what it was like for Lisa Marie Presley to be married to Michael Jackson..."

A muscle in Tom's jaw twitched. He pulled open the studio door, despite the red "on air" light, and stormed back toward the *Evening Watch* control room. One more pedestrian in New York ignoring the traffic lights.

The door opened again.

"Is it true?" Tom asked. "Are you two getting back together?"

Ike and I both laughed.

"Well? I'm standing here waiting for an answer."

"Make yourself comfortable, Tom," Ike said, and we strolled away, hand in hand.

When Tom was safely behind the heavy studio door again, I gave Ike's hand a squeeze, not gently.

"Thanks for introducing me to the nation as the next Isadora Duncan."

"Don't be such a baby, Abby. Nothing will come of it."

"Then why'd you say that stuff?"

"To increase public awareness of your whereabouts."

"Swell."

In Ike's office, she made another call to Church Finnegan's apartment. No answer, not even his machine. She pulled a sheet of paper out of her desk, ran her finger down a column of names, and picked up the phone again. This time she dialed Church's sky pager, dialing in the number of her cell phone at the prompt.

"You can mail him a postcard, too, Ike," I said. "If you haven't heard from Church in a week, we can have the cops put out an APB."

"This isn't funny, Abby. I'm worried about him."

"I didn't say it was funny. I don't think it's funny. I think it's sickening. Church Finnegan isn't worth all the pigeon shit in Bryant Park."

"You don't know anything about Church."

"I know enough."

"You think you know enough about everything. When was the last time you bothered to read a book?"

She had me there.

I broke down and confessed. "Four years ago, in a Dallas motel, I flipped through the Gideon Bible. I couldn't get the TV to work."

We used the elevator simultaneously, but I wouldn't say we were "together." Ike stayed on her side and I stayed on mine. We didn't speak. Not until the doors opened at the lobby and we saw what was outside the towering sea green glass doors of the Emerald City.

It was snowing like New York had been moved to the North Pole, or, more likely, like the North Pole had decided it was boring up there and had come to the Big Apple looking for a little action. And, worse, illegally parked at the curb, there was a blue and white car with a bar of lights on top and a uniformed officer getting out of the vehicle with a folded document in his hand. He was wearing sturdy black boots, and I didn't think there was any chance he'd slip on the slick sidewalk and knock himself unconscious before he delivered that document.

If that wasn't a warrant, I'd eat the transcript of *Evening Watch* and chase it with a shot of brake fluid.

"I don't like the look of this weather," Ike whispered.

We backstepped unobtrusively into the elevator and pushed the button marked LL, which stands for lower lobby. That lobby doesn't have neat etched-glass doors, but it has a handy back exit onto 9th Avenue in the rear of the building.

"I wonder how Fillingeri got a warrant so fast," Ike said.

"If that was a warrant."

"He probably keeps one on file for me in his desk drawer. I'll bet he just uses a rubber stamp to change the date."

We had to show I.D. to get out of the building, because that floor has the loading dock that trafficks in Othello Armitage's most expensive broadcasting equipment, and he isn't taking any chances on his employees going home with a Hitachi camera worth almost one hundred thousand dollars. We steal plenty of little stuff from our employer, but I think he budgets for that. The cameras are different. Even when NTB equipment leaves the building to cover heavy-duty events like the Tony Awards, it has to be signed out in triplicate, and the drivers not only show I.D., they probably have to swear an oath of loyalty. And leave their children as deposits.

I didn't think the cops were going to surround the Emerald City and flush us out with tear gas, but still, I opened the door carefully and scanned the street for anything that might have my name on it, with an accompanying message saying "Deliver addressee to the 54th Street Precinct House, C.O.D." It wasn't so much that I couldn't stand the sight of Fillingeri, or that I was reluctant to answer his questions, or even that a few hours in jail would have been unwelcome—I was ready to nap anyway.

What bothered me was that I didn't think *any* of those scenarios awaited me on 54th Street. What I suspected was that the NYPD and the Fates had a nice comfortable polygraph test scheduled for me. I'd never undergone a lie detector test, but I was fairly certain it would be beyond even my scope. I know that polygraph tests have pretty much been exploded as evidence, but Fillingeri wasn't going to put me on trial before a jury. He would use the polygraph machine as torture.

I waved my hand at a cab coming down 9th in front of a snowplow. He pulled over. Ike and I bolted from the Emerald City.

"Where to?" he asked, wearily, as we climbed in the cab, not an easy thing to do on Rollerblades. "If you say the airport, I'm gonna cry. All the bridges are a mess."

Ike patted his shoulder. "Thirty-five East Tenth Street. Is that okay?"

The driver shrugged. "If you don't mind, I'll let the plow get in front of me."

"No problem."

She sat back against the cushions. The plow passed us, and our driver pulled over into the space it had cleared and followed along in the Sanitation Department's contribution to our quality of life. Boy, was I glad I pay taxes.

"Ike, what's on Tenth Street? A safe house?"

"Church's apartment."

"Oh."

I thought about that.

"Ike?"

"What?"

"You got a key?"

She blushed. I wish she wouldn't do that. She used to do it when we fooled around, and my Pavlov's dog was responding.

"Of course I don't have a key. You know me better than that."

"Good."

FOURTEEN

THIRTY-FIVE East 10th Street is a clean, redbrick, four-story building in a quiet neighborhood near New York University. I could tell that nice people lived there. Nice, and also smart. They hadn't been dumb enough to plant any trees or bushes in their little two-by-three-foot rectangle of dirt beside the steps: New Yorkers steal and remarket shrubs, so the residents had put down white gravel over the dirt. Not too many people steal gravel.

The nice-people building had brass trim that was polished (who'd steal trim?), and their stoop was freshly swept, even with the snow still coming down. Lights were on in almost every apartment window we could see from the street, telling me that these people were not out gallivanting in Manhattan's fleshpots. Further evidence of niceness.

I was disappointed. I had wanted Church to live in either college-dormitory-type squalor (with black lights and Pink Floyd posters) or yuppie mediocrity, complete with the Eddie Bauer catalogue's charm—a railroad flat with silk plants and a faux loft. This address was just too, well, *nice*.

We gained entry to the well-lighted hallway by buzzing the building's superintendent. Even he appeared to be nice. He came down the hallway wearing an Icelandic wool sweater, blue corduroy trousers, and loafers that had a fresh shine. He looked like a history professor.

Ike explained that the tenant in apartment 2K was an employee of NTB News who had been injured earlier in the day by a gunman, that the tenant had been treated at St. Vincent's and released, and that since that release, no one at the network had heard from him. Could we please come in and knock on the tenant's door?

Ike offered her I.D. as a courtesy. The fact that he actually looked carefully at her picture cheered me up. Ike obviously was not a regular in this building. This nice guy had never seen her before. Good.

We showed nice manners and took off our skates in the hall.

The super accompanied us to the elevator and up to the second floor. Apartment 2K was at the end of the hall, meaning it was a *nice* place facing the street. Ike knocked on the door.

The super leaned past her shoulder and pushed the doorbell. Not only nice, but smart.

No answer.

"I guess he's not home," the super said.

"Or maybe his injury is preventing him from responding," Ike said, in a crisp, educational way. "Do you have a key?"

He scratched the back of his neck. "Well, I do. To the house lock. But not to those two dead bolts he installed himself. Would you remind me what your relationship is with Mr. Finnegan?"

"I'm his boss," Ike said. "And I'm worried about Mr. Finnegan. Will you try your key?"

The super pulled a large key ring from one of his deep pockets and sorted through about ten keys. When he found one he liked, he inserted it into the lock that had come with the apartment and started to turn the key.

"It's not locked," he said. "That's funny."

Ike reached out quickly and turned the knob on 2K. The door opened a couple of inches.

"Church?" she said, in a low voice, the kind you use in hospitals and libraries. No answer.

"Church?" she said, in a louder voice, the kind you use in train stations. Still no answer.

She pushed the door all the way open. In a building this nice, of course, there was no squeak from the hinges. Smooth and silent.

She took a step into the room. A small desk lamp with a fluorescent bulb was on, and I could see that 2K was a "junior one-bedroom"—meaning a large studio with a half wall creating a small space for a pretend bedroom.

The furnishings might have been nice, but it was hard to tell—someone had tossed them around and dumped out drawers and scooped the contents of the refrigerator onto the floor and messed up the kitchen cabinets. Anything bigger than about the size of a box of pasta was on the floor. The bottles in the spice rack, however, on the kitchen wall, were still neatly arranged, alphabetically by name of spice.

Across from the kitchen area, the one closet was open but blocked by a couple of suitcases that had been unzipped and dumped. On top of the suitcases were assorted shoe boxes and hats. The coats and clothing on hangers looked like they had been left alone.

The entertainment wall unit seemed undisturbed, except that a collection of videocassettes was in a jumble on the floor, including a real revelation about Church's character—he owned copies of *Aladdin, Beauty and the Beast,* and that Dalmations movie. I didn't know what his taste in movies said about him, but it certainly said something.

The power on the VCR itself had been left on, but there was no tape in the machine.

"You think we should call the cops?" the super asked.

"I most certainly do," Ike said. "In a minute." She stepped carefully around the mess and went to the divider wall. She looked behind it and took a deep breath.

"Abby."

A couple of strides and I was beside her.

Church Finnegan, his arm in a sling, his blue eyes open and staring at nothing, was lying on his back on a futon, sprawled diagonally across his New Age bed. There was a knife handle sticking out of his chest, and I had to assume the rest of the knife was inside. The bed was a mess. Church must have tried to fight, but with his arm in a sling and with some painkillers in his system, the fight hadn't been good enough.

"Call 555-4444," Ike said, urgently, over her shoulder to the super. "Ask for Captain Dennis Fillingeri. Tell him about this."

"Not 911?"

"No, 555-4444. And don't touch anything in here. You'd better call from your own apartment."

"Jesus, what's behind the divider?"

"Your tenant," she said. "I think he's dead. Do any doctors live in this building?" She was kneeling beside the futon, her hand on Church's neck, feeling for a pulse.

She got no answer on the doctor question because the super had skedaddled.

Ike put her hand on Church's chest, getting her ear as close to the knife handle as possible, and listened.

"Nothing," she said. "Abby, he feels cold."

I was feeling a little cold myself. The window above the futon was open about an inch, and a miniature snowdrift had formed on the ledge and looked like it was about to avalanche onto the futon.

I remembered the team doctor kneeling beside the Big Chill in Madison Square Garden, and how the doctor's ear was streaked with blood. I looked at Ike's ear. No blood. This heart isn't pumping at all, I thought, not one single beat.

I hoped Ike wasn't going to cry.

"Abby, I'd tell you to get out of here on the double, with Fillingeri on the way soon," she said, her voice unsteady though not tearful, "but that would only get you in more trouble. Dennis is going to believe the lie you told and shackle you in the dungeon until you cough up what you know."

"Which lie?"

"The one you told on *Evening Watch*."

"Oh. I'm having some trouble keeping my lies straight. That's not a good sign." I knelt beside her and put my arm around her shoulders. "Are you okay?"

She sniffed. "No."

"I think we should wait out in the hall."

"You think it's ghoulish to stay here?"

"It's cold in here, Ike. You're shivering. I'm shivering. Too bad Church isn't shivering. That really was the only bad fate I ever wished on him."

"That he'd shiver?"

"Last night. I just wished he was as miserably cold as I was."

"I'll bet you're sorry now."

"I'm sorry he's dead. I'm not sorry about hoping he was cold last night."

She stood. "Let's go. I don't want to hear any more about your wishful thinking."

I took her arm and we steered through the chaos toward the door. "I was jealous, Ike."

"Church and I had one date, Abby, not that what I do is any of your concern. For coffee, at the Barnes and Noble Superstore up on Broadway."

"I was hearing wedding bells on the grapevine."

"It's your own fault for listening to gossip."

"Most of the gossip was coming from Church."

"You're kidding."

"Cross my heart." I glanced back at the room divider. "Please pardon the unfortunate expression."

"Church was talking about us—I mean about him and me?"

"Like he'd entered a marathon sponsored by *The National Enquirer*."

"That's pretty stinky," she said, in her hospital/library voice. "Not to speak ill of the probably dead."

"He's dead, Ike."

"Yeah, I know."

We waited out in the nice hall, holding the fort until the murder officials showed up. The super did not return to the second floor. Perhaps he didn't approve of murder in his nice building. Or maybe he was out front, sweeping the steps for the arrival of New York City personnel.

"You're not going to mention that to Dennis, are you?" Ike said.

"That Church is dead? I expect I won't have to mention it."

"I mean the gossip, stupid."

"I plan to say as little as possible. That should keep me from slipping accidentally into a bunch of lies."

"Just how many lies have you told?"

I leaned my shoulder against the nice brocaded wallpaper in the hall and tried to sort it out. "I think two. One at the Garden last night, and what I said on *Evening Watch* tonight."

"Pooh. Two measly lies? Everyone lies about something to the police."

"Hell, Ike, most of them don't go on national television and lay on the B.S. as thick as I did. I might as well have used a trowel instead of my tongue."

"You're exaggerating, Abby. You didn't tell such a big lie."

"Well, maybe not big. But well spread. Have you ever lied to twelve million people?"

She giggled, but quickly checked the sound with a guilty glance at Church's door. "Not all at one time."

"I have." I tried to find the silver lining. "I don't think, however, that I've ever lied to twelve million people *one at a time*. I don't even know twelve million people."

The soft wail of sirens had been accompanying our little seminar on lying, but we had to end class right there because the sirens were suddenly too loud for us to speak without shouting in the nice hall.

The paramedics arrived first, with a folded stretcher. I pointed to the wall divider and they waded through the mess on the floor. They had other equipment with them, but I didn't think they'd be using anything but the stretcher. Unless they had a body bag in their gear.

Fillingeri wasn't far behind the paramedics, maybe three minutes. Not too shabby for a trip downtown on snowy streets.

He and his minions used the stairs. When he stepped onto the carpeted floor of the hall, he reached into his pocket and pulled out a document, which he handed to me without saying anything, not even "Hello, liar."

"What's this?" I said, holding the paper carefully between two fingers like it maybe had thorns.

"An invitation. RSVP, and get out of my way."

I wasn't in his way, so I didn't move. "Is this a warrant?"

"It ain't a collection of my favorite Calvin and Hobbes cartoons. Hang on to it. There will be a couple of uniforms here in a minute to show you how to use it."

He hurried into 2K.

What I need, I thought, is a *lawyer.*

I talked it over quietly with Ike, and we agreed that while NTB News probably didn't owe me an attorney from their stock, given that I'd abused their airtime even if they didn't know I'd done it, the network would probably supply me with one anyway because hotshot directors don't grow on every tree.

I flipped open my cell phone. The batteries were dead. "Damnation," I said. "Give me yours."

"I don't want you tying up my phone. I could need it at any second to phone in this story."

"What are you waiting for?"

"Official word that he's dead."

I loped down the stairs and found the super's apartment, which was easy because he was standing in the open doorway.

"Can I use your phone?" I asked.

"Is that legal?"

"If you let me use your phone, I'll ask my attorney."

"Be my guest." He showed me into a living room crammed with books. They were everywhere, even piled up on the window ledges. I glanced at some of the titles.

"Do you teach history?" I asked.

"Part time."

I couldn't help noticing, because the topic had played such an interesting role in *my* recent history, the guns he had in a glass display case on the wall beside his desk. Mostly they seemed to be the kind of thing you see in parades—muskets or something, those guns that look like sticks. I did not notice anything that looked like you could load it with shotgun shells and go have target practice in Madison Square Garden. These were old patriotic-type guns. I wonder if he had a fife collection in the other room.

"You like guns?" I said casually.

"I'm rather fond of these." He touched a finger gently to the glass front of the wooden case. "They belonged to my father—who also taught history—and they're worth a great deal of money. Are you a collector?"

"You could say so. But not guns. Lately I collect people who shoot them."

I sat at his desk and dialed the night operator at the Emerald City, explained that I needed legal advice immediately, repeated myself, answered some stupid questions a few times, and finally got patched through to George Fahrends, who'd attended the morning meeting and was already familiar with my rotten conduct.

"What's the problem, Abagnarro?"

I told him about what I'd said on the air and about Church and about the warrant for my arrest, which I was holding in my hand.

"Read it to me."

I obliged.

Fahrends was quiet for a moment. I thought he'd hung up on me or dozed off. But he must have been doing some attorney-type thinking, because he finally said, "Obstruction of justice is a junk charge in this case."

"Thanks. I don't much like it either."

"I don't want to know if what you said on the air was a lie, Abagnarro, so don't tell me."

How would you know if I was lying about lying? I thought, but I said, "Okay. What do I do now?"

"Stonewall. Act offended. Tell Fillingeri I'm preparing papers to sue him for false arrest. Stick to the story you told on the air. It's no crime not to remember something."

"Thanks. What will Fillingeri do?"

Fahrends laughed. "I doubt he'll do anything. You'll be home tonight. Fillingeri, by way of contrast, will be busy."

"I'd better not be home. I work nights, remember? I've got a highly rated two-hour morning news program to direct."

"Don't get cocky. Third place hardly qualifies as 'highly rated.' Just stick to your story. Change nothing. Don't get chatty and start embroidering this highly entertaining tale. You simply don't remember. Got it?"

"That should be easy, because I *don't* remember anything."

"Well, don't get carried away. You only don't remember that one thing—what the shooter might have looked like. You do remember everything else. Okay?"

"Thanks, George."

"Abby?"

"Yes?"

"You got a pen?"

I patted myself down and found a ballpoint in my shirt pocket. "Yeah. What?"

"Take my number. Call me here at home if you have to. I could be wrong about what Fillingeri's going to do. He may execute that warrant."

He gave me the number, said good night, and hung up.

I put the receiver where it belonged and almost knocked the super down when I stood.

He stumbled backward. "Was it legal?" he asked.

"Perfectly. My lawyer said you were just doing your duty, letting me use your phone. He said you were a fine American. Maybe you can use that in class, huh?"

"I don't teach patriotism. I teach history."

"I'd like to talk with you about your curriculum sometime, maybe when I'm not so busy being arrested."

He backed away from me again, this time deliberately. "For murder?"

"For lying."

I left him standing in his sanctuary and ran back up the stairs. Two uniforms were standing in the hallway outside Church's door, appreciating Ike.

"You can arrest me now," I said brightly, handing one of them the warrant. "I already talked to my lawyer and I've got this down cold."

The cop who was first able to take his eyes off Ike's eyes said, "The captain said you had a smart mouth."

"Indeed I do. But you didn't need Fillingeri to tell you that. It's all spelled out on the warrant. Don't you read your own threatening letters?"

"I just do what I'm told."

Fillingeri appeared at the door of 2K.

"Abagnarro, I want you in here for a minute. Ike, you too."

"Happy to oblige," I said. "Civic duty. I could teach patriotism."

"You could teach clown college. Get in here."

FIFTEEN

IKE DIDN'T look thrilled with leaving the accommodations out in the nice hallway and returning to apartment 2K.

"What do you want with us?" she whined. "Can't you interrogate us out in the hall? It's cold in this apartment. We're not crime scene specialists."

Fillingeri raised his right shoulder and gave it a couple of rolls, like he was stiff from a workout.

"Abagnarro is a different kind of specialist," he said.

Oh, oh, I thought. He needs a liar.

He opened his mouth to begin the inquisition on me but got interrupted by one of the paramedics, who had come around the divider wall with a bland expression on his face. "Captain, we've definitely got a DOA here."

DOA. Church Anthony Finnegan, a sound technician from Ireland, with a name of his own, had been transformed into a DOA.

Ike quickly got busy on her cell phone and started talking quietly into it. She wasn't teary-eyed, but she wasn't having a good time.

"Now, there's a news flash," Fillingeri said to the paramedic, sarcasm giving his voice an odd depth. "You're sure the body didn't get up, see the knife in his chest, and just keel over from the shock?"

"Yes, sir. I mean, I'm sure."

"Then what you've got is a DRT."

"DRT, sir?"

"Dead Right There. That way we don't have to worry about whether he arrived or we did."

The paramedic had enough brains not to comment.

"Stand by your DOA until our photographer can capture your diagnosis on the magic of film," Fillingeri said sharply.

The paramedic took a position beside the divider wall, ostentatiously not touching anything. A couple of plainclothes detectives were carefully sorting through the mess in 2K. They didn't pay any attention to the paramedic who had turned himself into a post.

"Ike," Fillingeri said, "what's going out on that phone?"

She covered the mouthpiece with the palm of her hand. "I'm phoning my gynecologist."

"At this hour?"

"You wouldn't understand. It's a girl thing."

"Not from a crime scene, it's not."

"Excuse me," she mumbled, "I feel faint."

She and her phone went out in the hall.

"Shit," Fillingeri said, more or less under his breath. He followed her out into the hall and brought her back, I think without touching her.

He made us tell him, and a uniformed cop who doubled as Fillingeri's stenographer, about finding the body. Fillingeri really seemed to be picking our brains with tweezers over the details—the door not being locked, the window being open an inch, anything we had done or not done to Church's body, anything in 2K we had touched, what time we'd arrived at the building, if we'd had any contact with Church since the morning's shotgun incident, the extent of the super's penetration into the scene of the crime, and who we had phoned besides him. I thought he was referring to us phoning NTB HQ, so I passed on mentioning my little conference with George Fahrends about a certain warrant for my arrest. I don't call *that* lying, exactly.

After Fillingeri got the story from us, he seemed to go off into a junior trance of some kind, gazing absently at Ike.

"Before the crime scene unit gets here," Fillingeri said, yanking his eyes off Ike's form and looking me in the eye, "I want you to tell me what they were searching for when they trashed this apartment.''

''Huh?''

''You heard me. Look around. This is a crazy way to toss a place. They bothered with some things; other things, they left alone.''

''Why are you asking me? You think I'm some kind of specialist in looting apartments?''

''Abagnarro, help me out, will you?''

''Okay.'' I shrugged my shoulders, puzzled but willing to play. ''I'll say the obvious: money? They were looking for money?''

''Don't be a sap. They were looking for something physically larger than money. They passed on the small stuff. They didn't touch the spice rack or the medicine cabinet in the bathroom or any of the small compartments in his desk drawer. On a bet, his clothing wasn't touched. His papers were not disturbed. They were not looking for money.''

''Maybe they found his wallet right away and didn't have to rummage around. Maybe he had it on him. Although, come to think of it, his wallet was on empty last I heard.''

''He had the wallet on him. He still does. He's got forty dollars in it.''

''Must have visited the ATM or mugged somebody.''

''What?''

''Nothing. Church didn't have any money last night, that's all.''

''Abagnarro, don't get me started on last night.''

''No problem. I'm all talked out about that.''

''Not yet, you're not.'' Fillingeri ran his hand through his gravity-conditioned hair. I don't think he knows he does that. At least, I hope not. I mean, not to the extent of practicing or anything. ''To me, this is something,'' he said, gesturing, waving his arm to indicate the apartment, ''you can figure out, if you'll use your brain for a minute. This is television-type crap.

Look at the video junk on the floor. The VCR is on. Whoever made this mess was looking at TV stuff."

I looked around.

But it was Ike who was using her brain.

"Captain," she said. "Dennis. Church should have his audio gear here. His mixer. I don't see it anywhere. Have your men seen it?"

"Audio gear." Fillingeri nodded slowly. "He usually takes it home with him?"

"Yes. Always. Our field techs do that routinely. Church could get called any time to go out on assignment. He always had it with him."

Fillingeri asked the detectives about the mixer, which Ike described for them. They hadn't seen it.

Fillingeri, who had seen mixers before, did not compliment Ike on her powers of description or critical-thinking skills. But he did thank her, which is more than he ever does when I answer a question or offer a suggestion.

"Thank you, Ike. Now, what's so special about his audio gear that someone would kill him for it and throw the apartment?"

"Nothing."

"That stuff has practically no street value," Fillingeri said. "You don't steal objects you can't peddle. Nobody knows how to use that mixer thing but the experts. So something must be special about it, that somebody would take it."

Ike opened her mismatched eyes, wide. "I can't imagine. You think they killed him for audio equipment?"

"I don't know. But they didn't kill him for his movie collection. In fact, I'll eat these Disney movies for breakfast if Finnegan's death doesn't have something to do with him being at the Garden last night. He was the sound man for your feature there. He witnessed a shooting and a stabbing last night. He was shot on the street this morning and then stabbed in his apartment. Same M.O. as the Big Chill, only the pieces of the M.O. occurred over a greater period of time. Finnegan's dead now and his audio gear is missing. If that's all coincidence, I've got one really bad meal ahead of me."

"I'll say," I said.

He ignored me.

"Ike, I know Othello Armitage takes very special care of his TV toys. Probably makes his people go through decontamination showers and tattoos his name on their arms before they use any of his equipment. Can you get me the serial numbers and any other identifying information on Finnegan's gear?"

"Of course. You want it now? I can phone for it." She waved her phone. "Thanks to you, I'm not using this instrument for calls to my gynecologist."

Now Ike is lying, I thought. *She caught it from me.*

"Yeah. Use your cellular. Don't touch Finnegan's phone."

"Be with you in a jiffy," she said. She flipped open the little gray phone and punched one of her speed-dial numbers.

While she was techno-busy, Fillingeri started on me again.

"Abagnarro, does that pile of videotapes mean anything to you, I mean anything pertaining to Finnegan's death, or the Big Chill's? I'm not looking for film criticism."

"Let me take a look. I haven't really studied them. We were only in here a few minutes, and like we told you, most of that time we were deciding how dead Finnegan was."

"He's plenty dead. Finnegan won't mind if you go through his stuff. Take a look at those movies. Look with your eyes, not with your fingers."

Ike stuck her free hand out at Fillingeri, and he reached into his jacket pocket to get her a notebook and pen. She tucked the phone against her shoulder and started writing something on the paper.

I got down on my haunches and ran my eyes over the videos. The only unusual item, as far as I was concerned, was a lack of certain items. Most sound techs keep copies of some of the pieces they've worked on, sort of like a portfolio. Church Finnegan didn't.

Or he did. If he did, his copies were gone. But I did a quick study of his video storage space and of the tapes on the floor, and it didn't seem to me like it added up right that Church's personal work collection was gone. I concluded he just didn't keep his pieces. Maybe he'd cleaned house before moving from Ireland to the United States. Or maybe he'd stored his audio portfolio somewhere else. In any case, who'd be interested in great SOTs—not even the thickest, rawest intern calls them "sound on tapes"—of Irish peat-cutting festivals and dog-breeding poetry recitals? I mean, who in New York would be interested in those things enough to steal Church's tapes?

"Captain, one thing. I don't think Church took a copy of the Big Chill's death video home with him. He could have, but frankly, he didn't seem all that interested. We've made a lot of copies of that tape, and Church could have had an editor make one for him. Most sound techs would want a copy of a tape they helped make and everyone's talking about. But there's no copy here. If I was the killer/shooter/stabber, I might have been looking for that tape. I might or might not have found it. I don't see anything else here that strikes me as peculiar, except that Church wasn't very keen on his own work."

"How do you mean?"

"He didn't keep copies of any of the pieces he'd worked on." I pointed at but did not touch the cardboard sleeve of the *Beauty and the Beast* video, which showed lots of wear and tear. "Just looking at this pile of movies and how the boxes aren't in mint condition, I'd say Church was more interested in a different kind of audio work than he was in news. Which could explain how lazy he was."

"Lazy? He practically took my tonsils out with that microphone last night."

"That was just to annoy you. The crew hit the deck right when that shotgun went off in the Garden, and Church just left the mike hanging on the barrier. He wasn't even trying to record any of the sound. Our cameraman, although he got bad shots, at least kept his gear running. He's a pro. Finnegan was playing in the wrong league."

"You were all under fire, Abagnarro." Fillingeri glanced behind him, found the arm of the couch, and sat down, looking at my face like he was seeing it for the first time. "You know what? I'm starting to think of you as the world's most dangerous man. Wherever you go, there's calamity, chaos, and pestilence."

SIXTEEN

WITH A COMRADE down and a long night ahead, I didn't want to lie down on Church Finnegan's couch and let Fillingeri analyze me.

"Can I go now? I have some calamity to spread around."

"You're forgetting the small matter of the warrant for your arrest."

"My lawyer said that was junk."

"You already phoned your lawyer?"

"I had to phone. He's not on the premises."

"Funny you didn't mention that when I asked about phone calls."

Fillingeri got up and took a quick walk around the little apartment, careful not to step on things, probably counting to ten. Or fifty. His lips were moving, at any event.

When he returned from his travels and got back to me, he said, "You're going uptown with us."

"My attorney is preparing the papers to sue you for false arrest."

"The hell he is."

I nodded. "The hell he is."

"He instructed you to clam?"

"He instructed me to tell the truth. Which, naturally, he didn't have to, since that's what I'd do anyway. But if you take me uptown, don't you have to read me that thing that says I have the right to remain silent?"

"I've got it memorized."

"What does your Miranda card say about polygraph tests?"

"Didn't you ask your lawyer?"

"Yep," I lied, feeling really stupid that I'd omitted that

important point when I'd talked to Fahrends from the super's apartment, "but I'm just checking to see if you know."

"I know, all right. Polygraph machines are going the way of the dinosaurs. Abagnarro, I imagine you could turn a lie detector into scrap metal just by reciting the alphabet."

"If you insist, I'll give it my best try. I can also recite the Gettysburg Address."

Fillingeri shot his cuffs and looked at his wristwatch. "I've got a full night, Abagnarro. I don't have time now to execute that warrant and diddle with you and your lawyer. But we've got the warrant, and I know where to find you, and you won't skip town unless you can fit your ex-wife in your duffel bag, so don't turn all warm and gooey from gratitude that I'm going to let you go. For now. I can get you any time I need you. And that time will be soon."

"I don't know what to say."

"The day you don't know what to say." I thought Fillingeri was going to smack his forehead, or mine, but he ended up raking his hair with his fingers. Probably sublimating. "For once, tell me what I need to hear. Stop dancing around. What you said tonight on *Evening Watch*. What's all this baloney about you *think* you might know something about the gunman?"

"I said I don't remember. I might remember later."

"Do I need to point out that what you *might remember* is vital information in a capital crime?"

"No."

"I don't believe you're going to have a sudden attack of memory. I think you know right now what you saw, and I think you're keeping it from the proper authorities, who will know how to use the information. That's obstruction of justice."

"I swear. I don't recall anything about that figure I saw after the shooting that could give you even the tiniest hint about who it was."

"Bullshit. You want to know why I don't believe you?"

I hoped he was not about to say because I'm a compulsive liar.

"I don't believe you because you don't miss things, Mr. TV Director. If you saw that shooter, you saw that shooter. You've got good eyes and you use them. You seeing a *blur* is like a Times Square hooker giving away free samples. It doesn't happen. Not in this space-time continuum. It just doesn't happen."

"It happened last night. The *me* thing, not the hooker thing."

"You're lying."

The odd thing was, *I wasn't lying.*

"Not this time, Captain. All I saw was a blur, a fragment of motion. All I can say for sure is, I think it was human."

"Human. But it could have been a giraffe?"

I shook my head. "Didn't move like a giraffe."

"Get out of here. Turn yourself into a blur, Abagnarro. I'd like to see that."

Ike handed over to Fillingeri his pen and notepad, with the information on Church's mixer she'd written down. It felt strange merely walking out. I'd expected to be dragged out.

Down in the hall we got our socks wet, getting at our skates in the puddle of gray water they'd manufactured in our absence.

We caught a cab going uptown, and several times we skidded and slid so wildly that I thought we'd end up as window displays in a couple of delis and a Thai restaurant. I wondered if we'd be better off getting out and skating up to the Emerald City. But we stuck with the cab, because at least it had a heater, and finished our joy ride with a sixteen-dollar fare because it took us so long. On a normal night that much money will get you within walking distance of La Guardia Airport way out in the New York boondocks—the Borough of Queens.

Ike had called from her cell phone for a crew to hustle down to Finnegan's apartment, but I don't think she had any real

expectations of getting pictures we could use on the air to tell
his story, and not just because of the weather slowdowns. The
NTB truck could probably compete with the plows for navigating the streets, but with Fillingeri on the scene, NTB personnel would not be welcomed or encouraged to go about their
jobs. But that's why we have writers—in television, a picture
is worth much more than a thousand words, but at least we've
got access to pretty good words when we need them.

The twenty-seventh floor of the Emerald City was quiet
when we skated out of the elevator. It was early for show
production to have generated much activity yet. I was dreading
having a long talk with Ike about the death of Church Finnegan.

But the quiet on the floor masked a story coming into our
computers. And no matter how we felt personally, it was a
much bigger story than the death of Church Finnegan, which
had itself already moved on the wires. And, like Church's
story, this one looked like it was also going to provide us with
problems getting pictures. Ike wasn't going to have any time
to grieve over any budding romance with Church, if that's
what she wanted to do.

She was either going to have to come up with some pictures
over the next few hours, against terrible odds, or we were
going to need more than our usual share of words. Hurricane
Ricardo, despite Tom Hitt's direct orders, had dared to approach the U.S. mainland. Ike had her computer screens up
almost before she took off her parka, and Ricardo, nearing
category four strength, was headed for Miami Beach.

The National Hurricane Center had posted warnings from
the Florida Keys up through the South Carolina coast, but
Ricardo was taking a steady aim so far at the historic Art Deco
District of Miami Beach. If it hit there, I didn't have much
hope for our satellite dishes or the phone lines in Miami. We
already had early pictures of the storm's approach—reporters
in slickers getting their hair whipped around their faces by
slashing rain and wind, people boarding up their homes and

businesses—but power would go almost as soon as the real force of Ricardo made landfall. You can't get pictures without power. I'd have to check with the Miami bureau on their emergency generators.

Even with generators, hard information of any kind would be in short supply, so our writers would be pressed to come up with enough words to report the storm. Unless they had a crystal ball to get full coverage of damage and deaths.

Landfall was predicted, if the storm stayed on its present track over the next several hours, for around 6:00 a.m. An hour before *Morning Watch* went on the air. Everybody on the show knew about Church's murder, but nobody had time to do more than know about it. The entire staff was in motion, trying to fill our video gap.

Nonexistent or outdated pictures of Ricardo, no pictures of the Church Finnegan murder, maybe used pictures from the *Evening Watch* coverage of Mrs. Big Chill's performance in my office—we had a big news hole to fill.

And a big sleep hole. I could tell Ike was exhausted only by how much she was blinking. I could tell how tired I was, as the hours passed, by how much my hands began to shake from all the coffee I was pouring down my gullet. We'd been through sleepless days and nights before, so our condition was not a new phenomenon, but it did occur to me that I wouldn't dance any better than a hanged man when the waltz contest rolled around, in less than twenty-four hours. Especially if I had to carry Ike around the ballroom.

Ike spent a lot of time overnight on the phone or on-line with the Miami Bureau. We took in their satellite feeds, but those were night shots, with no scope to show the storm's fury. We had photos and computer graphics from the National Hurricane Center at FIU, but we were in line overnight with the rest of the media for direct interviews with their meteorologists. Once the storm hit, though, the Hurricane Center would be no use to us. All they could do was tell us where the storm would hit—useful for us in trying to get our people in place, but after Ricardo hit, who would need the Hurricane Center? The predicting business would be for history buffs.

About three in the morning, Ike took a break. For her that means she stood up and paced around the control room for a few minutes. I'd been so busy with the Miami satellite and phone feeds that I'd almost forgotten about our other stories.

"Abby," she said, stretching her arms over her head, yawning like she was going to audition for the role of the Grand Canyon in *Thelma and Louise,* "can you take a few minutes and look at something with me?"

The control room was full of people being frantic about show production, but the frenetic pace of work didn't stop the outbreak of nearly simultaneous snickers—a chorus of in-the-know music whose basic message was that the word had gotten completely around the network that Ike and I had come to our senses, were reneging on the divorce, and romance was once again in bloom. When I heard the noise, I was hit by a sudden, happy inspiration: almost certainly Hannah would hear the gossip and might lose interest in having lunch with me—I'd be spared.

Ike commandeered an editor and a sound tech, and we all crowded into Editing Room 3, which, like all of our editing rooms, is about the size of a two-broom closet.

Ike had a copy of the video we had shot in Madison Square Garden. But she didn't want to watch it again. She wanted to listen to it this time.

Whoever had made off with Church's mixer, not to mention his life, was obviously no expert on sound. Maybe *concerned* about sound, but not in the know on the deep, dark secrets of recording it. We didn't need Church's mixer to examine the sound on that videotape. There was nothing special about Church's mixer, except that it was missing. Big deal. Mixers are so plentiful in the Emerald City, we could use them for doorstops.

The editor and the tech wired their setup, and instead of watching the pictures on the monitor screen showing the Bulls and the Knicks warming up, we watched the little window on the sound mixer, where the needle moves according to the sound it's picking up. Just like I had done right after the shooting, when we were down on the concrete and Church's mixer was in my face. I remembered the needle dancing around, trying to hit discrete noises among the echoes of the blast.

And just like in the Garden, that needle was jerking even as it swayed with the echoes. Ike had the editor slow the video, and we started matching the needle's twitches with specific sounds—like the squeak of a basketball shoe on the court. When we hit the exact moment of the shotgun blast, we watched that needle swing to the right at the speed of sound. Then it flickered left for a fraction of a second before it started that swaying motion indicating the echoes.

"What was that?" Ike said, putting the end of her pencil on the mixer's window. "Play back that last two seconds. Where the gun goes off."

The editor rewound, and we watched again that little flicker of the needle swinging to the left immediately after the gunshot.

"What is that?" Ike said. "Abby? What is it?"

"I don't have any idea. I've got good ears, but I heard nothing except that huge explosion. My ears hurt, I remember."

"Well, it's *something*," she said. She put her right hand on the editor's shoulder. "Slower."

He rolled it again, and again, and again. Still we heard and saw nothing on the videotape. All we saw was that needle's one interesting jerk.

"Slower."

The editor and sound tech, with agonizing adjustments, finally isolated the *something*. The editor played it.

"Okay," Ike said. "Abby, you were there. What is that sound?"

"This is the first time I'm hearing it, Ike. All I can say is the same thing you could say. It sounds like a librarian."

"What?!"

"You know. When they want you to be quiet."

"What the devil are you talking about?"

"It sounds like *shhh*."

"Like what?"

I put my finger on my lips. "I want to listen again. *Shhh*."

SEVENTEEN

WHILE we were puzzling over our shhh noise, a certain hurricane—scorned and practically ignored by NTB's flagship news program because Tom Hitt, executive producer of *Evening Watch,* thought the storm was a dumb idea—was pounding the east coast of Florida with screaming and howling winds that made our Madison Square Garden shotgun blast sound like a lullaby. Mother Nature wins again.

Ricardo hit Miami before it was scheduled. The eye crossed the mainland at 5:35 a.m.

The monstrous winds of the hurricane barely brushed Miami Beach, but they tore the hell out of Miami and unincorporated Dade County. Our bureau had to evacuate its offices on Biscayne Bay after the windows blew out of the building. The bureau moved inland to the facilities of our affiliate station in Miami, where part of the roof promptly collapsed. Their emergency generator kept their computers up—sporadically—so we could exchange E-mail, but there was no question of getting pictures out of Miami. The *Morning Watch* crew we had flown in from Costa Rica had plenty of pictures of the destruction, but no way of sending them to us in New York. No phones. No satellite dishes.

Around 6:20, Ike was sitting in the control room at her computer, her elbows on the desk, her head in her hands, her monitor screen dark.

I wanted to put my arms around her and tell her I had video of the hurricane's path in my pocket, but I try not to lie to Ike. It's like she's exempt from my quota.

Her cell phone, which was beside her on the sound engineer's board, made its distinctive *twir*ring sound. She reached one arm over to grab the phone and answered it without otherwise moving.

"Ike Tygart here."

She listened for a moment before suddenly sitting bolt upright like she'd gotten a nasty electric shock from the phone.

"I'll call 'em right away," she said, and snapped her cellular shut.

"What's up, Ike?" I asked.

She faced me, no longer blinking and exhausted. She looked, well, like the horse she'd bet a week's pay on was heading into the straightaway, a couple of lengths out in front.

"The bureau reached a cell in Tennessee and they patched the call here. The crew is headed up to the Broward County line. AT&T has a fiber-optic land line. They can send their pictures through that if we can reach AT&T to get access."

"Holy God."

"Holy Ma Bell," she said. Ike barely got the words out before she set herself into hypermotion, raking in producers to set up the *AT&T Fiber Optic Cable Salvation Show* and sending orders to the writers and printing out the mail from her computer that was now coming in from Miami and prepping Hannah and J.D. about the top of the show—because it now looked like we had a chance of having a television show instead of a radio program you could *see*.

Six minutes before we went on the air, the live coverage from Miami started coming in. A cheer went up in the control room when five of our sixty-six monitor screens came alive and we saw our people—wet, but ready to report the storm for us.

The one thing I'll never figure out about that morning is how, with suddenly and literally hundreds of things for me to do and do quickly, I managed to alert our Graphics Department to use their electronic bricks to build some Chyrons we would use at the end of the show, superimposed over our news set and anchors, acknowledging the help AT&T had given us. Part of my brain must have been on autopilot.

Hannah signed us on at seven o'clock and we cut immediately to the live feed from Miami. I could see from the monitors that the other networks were opening their morning news shows with pictures of their anchors' heads reading copy that had probably come straight off the AP wire. Since that's all they could do about Hurricane Ricardo, the competition soon went to what they *could* show, which was an overnight interview with Fillingeri on the snowy steps of 35 East 10th Street. I wondered why the super hadn't been keeping up with his sweeping.

The same Fillingeri statements concerning the murder of Church Finnegan were in our machines, having been sent from the microwave truck, but we had the luxury of waiting to use the Finnegan story. And we also had the luxury—rare for us—of a huge national audience. Even if Church's death was tied in with the Big Chill's, Fillingeri holding court on a stoop in New York was a local story, and he wasn't saying anything we didn't already know. Ricardo was the national story, and we *owned* it.

Tom Hitt showed up in the control room during the second hour of *Morning Watch*. He took a seat and kept his mouth shut, watching us scoop the world with the kind of story everyone hates but everyone wants to see. Tom was going to have a long day. The AT&T line and the Miami crew would be turned over to him and to our Special Events Unit when we got off the air—which was good, because NTB's exclusive coverage would be continuous. But from Tom's point of view, it was also bad, because he'd be eating *Morning Watch* dust again. Tom would prefer not to.

At 8:58:10 J.D. signed us off the air and our graphic went up, thanking AT&T for their quick action in helping us cover the disaster. Sixty-one of our monitors went dark. And we applauded *Morning Watch*. Even Tom put his little hands together and made a sort of flapping noise a couple of times.

The morning meeting was more crowded than usual, with Tom and Special Events personnel joining us. A case of champagne and a package of plastic glasses arrived by messenger at the conference room, addressed to Ike. She opened the card, laughed, waved it in the air, and then read it aloud:

"Will it be safe to assume that tomorrow morning you will be showing the nation an exclusive look at the CIA's War Room and their classified files? Good show. Othello Armitage."

The conference room got treated to a bubbly shower, but a lot of the champagne went down the throats of the senior staff of *Morning Watch*. Ike also sent bottles to be distributed around the twenty-seventh floor, so everyone who worked on the show could get a taste of what it was like to make Othello Armitage pry open the vault and spring for a party.

The party in the conference room, however, took a lurch before anyone could get a decent buzz.

Ike stood up and raised her plastic glass.

"He wasn't at NTB News very long," she said, and everyone in the room looked down at the table, knowing what was coming. "Last night we lost Church Finnegan, one of our comrades. Let's salute his memory and do our best to get the truth out about his killer."

We drank. Not with gusto.

Sobriety ruled the next hour as we planned Ricardo coverage and tried to pull together whatever threads we had on the Big Chill's murder, as well as Finnegan's.

We had that *shhh* sound on the Madison Square Garden tape. We handed over that little factoid to Tom and answered his questions, which weren't many: Tom may scoff at hurricanes, but he's got a healthy respect for TV technology. The M.E., on whom Sally Goldberg-Petit had been keeping a watchful eye, had not reported any flashes of inspiration. If he'd had any, he was keeping them to himself. None of our producers or Tom's, looking into the backgrounds of the men who had been on the court at the time of the shooting, had come up with a startling and powerful motive for killing the Big Chill or with eyewitness testimony from any of those men saying they'd seen the guy who plunged the knife into the Big Chill's heart. The slain center's personal physician had been interviewed (by every reporter in the city), and his only contribution was that the Big Chill was human and a knife through the heart could certainly be fatal. And we could quote him.

Nobody had confessed. Nobody had tattled. The gun had still not been traced. No gloves had been found in Madison Square Garden, unless you counted one fluffy pink mitten that might fit an eight-year-old and a grubby work glove so large that nobody wearing it could have fit his finger in against the shotgun's trigger to fire a shot.

Police ballistics experts had determined that the shot had been fired from somewhere near the spot where the gun had been found. I couldn't have figured that out from the entry angles of the buckshot in the men on the court, but I wouldn't have spent even five minutes trying, given the testimony of an experienced network television field unit. We had been present and jolly well knew where the shot had come from.

The NYPD thought that as many as three hundred MSG employees had been in the building at the time of the shooting, working in the restaurants, or in the ticket booths, or with brooms and mops, but the police hadn't wrung any clues out of them.

The Knicks' organization was considering the possibility of offering a reward for information leading to the killer, but no decision on that had been handed down. The widow had not come forward with any reward money.

Everyone was howling for any scrap of background they could find on the Big Chill's plan for imminent retirement from basketball, but nobody who might know the story or anything about the story was talking. Mrs. Big Chill Thorpe had turned into a stone, after giving us the one fact. Ike thought the best bet would be the dead man's personal physician, who seemed to like the media, but he suddenly got lost. She sent a crew to stake out his office, but so far they hadn't done anything more interesting than buy the doorman breakfast and look at pictures of his grandchildren.

Meanwhile, other NBA teams had expressed concern about security at the Knicks' home court and reluctance about playing their games in what was becoming known in the tabloids as "Madison Square Gundown."

Attendance at the previous night's New York Rangers hockey game against the Philadelphia Flyers, however, had been a solid, sold-out twenty thousand, showing either that a Rangers fan will go to any lengths to support his team, or that if you'd already paid for a ticket, a little buckshot scare wasn't going to keep you out of a seat around the ice. (The Flyers, adding insult to injury, had won the game, five to three.) Nobody in the National Hockey League had said a word publicly about the dangers of playing in Madison Square Garden. Apparently they thought the gunplay was strictly a basketball problem. Or maybe hockey players are just brave.

The ten-thousand-dollar wad of cash had been examined by the NYPD, photographed, and returned to Fedex Parker. Nobody seemed to know if the Big Chill's death had given Parker ideas (assuming he needed help getting murder ideas) and he'd gone out to spend some of the cash on a new shotgun or knife to go after Church Finnegan.

"Has anyone done any original thinking about covering this story?" Ike said. "Any angle we can try that hasn't already been tried?"

"I don't get his widow," Hannah said, brushing her dyed blond hair behind her ears. Since makeup had not done her ears, they looked too pale and too big for her head. There's nothing really wrong with her ears; it was just the contrast.

"What was her royal visit to the Emerald City all about?" Hannah continued. I couldn't help staring at her ears. "What I'm saying is, she could have phoned. Or had one of her slaves phone us." Hannah *would* think in terms of slaves. "Why show up in person? Marie Celeste Thorpe doesn't usually do her own dirty work. Doesn't anyone else here think that was peculiar?"

I guess Tom thought Mrs. Chill was his project—the one coup scored by *Evening Watch*, even if the coup had been donated by us—because he took the floor.

"I've thought about it, Hannah. She took us all by surprise. She meant to. She made herself memorable. I think she knew nobody'd believe her husband was retiring from basketball unless she herself said so, for the record, in front of cameras. I regret we didn't get any more out of her. But you know, I don't think she was going to give any more."

"Then what was that horseshit," Hannah said, "about Fedex Parker being the man who should have been killed?"

"Who knows? The widow won't talk to anyone now at all."

"You probably haven't asked right. Tell her I'll interview her. Bet she'll do it then."

Tom glared at her, but you don't really want to sass the anchors, not even when their egos balloon out and slap you in the face.

"Hannah," Tom said, with exaggerated patience, "you're welcome to try. I'll assign any producer you like. I'll go check the oil in your limousine. I'll do anything feasible to get that interview. While you're at it, find out from that woman whether the Big Chill, in what looked like an attempt to re-habilitate his image, planned to tell your show any facts and figures and bottom lines about getting out of the ranching business as well as the athlete business. I'll personally bend over and kiss your ass if you can do that, Hannah."

I was thinking Tom wouldn't have to bend over, not at his height.

"The Big Chill wouldn't give up the ranches, Tom. The man was adamant."

"He was also adamant about not talking to the media. He changed his mind about that. Nobody expected a young man like him to quit the game. Maybe *adamant* only went so far

with the Big Chill. His widow said that basketball had given
her husband everything he had, right?''

''Yes, Tom, I saw your little show last night.''

''Thanks for tuning in, Hannah, and swelling our audience.''

''Is that a crack about my weight?''

''No. It's a crack about your attitude.''

''Screw attitude. I get paid for presence, not attitude.''

''That's for sure. But I'm glad you brought up attitude, Hannah. Let's get back to the Big Chill and his attitude. His cattle
ranches were taking everything away from him that basketball
had given him. Nobody liked him. No all-star votes. No spot
on the Olympic team. No endorsements. No respect. No fans.
No worship. He could play, but he couldn't belong.''

''At least the Big Chill didn't date Madonna,'' Hannah said,
like she was delivering the best eulogy the Iceman deserved.
''I don't see why owning cattle ranches is worse than that in
the average public mind. Face it: who gives an authentic shit
about the rain forests? We've still got air left to breathe. Still,
if he was smart, he'd have dumped the ranches and stayed on
the court.''

''Dating Madonna doesn't destroy the rain forests,'' Tom
explained patiently. ''Not yet, anyway. But, Hannah, even
though I agree with your perception of the public mind, the
public mouth had spoken. The Big Chill was public crud. It
was like the latest fashion trend. Except for Fedex Parker and
some genuine Green Freaks. *Those guys* really hated the Big
Chill.''

''Thanks ever so much for explaining all that to me,'' Hannah said, sitting back in her chair and crossing her arms under
her ample bosom. ''Now I know who to ask about fashion
trends and all kinds of global thinking. Why don't you write
a book? Call it *How I Learned Everything.* In it you can explain why that ball player who owed everything to basketball
was giving up the game instead of his ranches.''

Ike was rubbing her eyes, opening her mouth from time to

time, looking for an opening to end the exchange so we could all go home.

"Tom," Ike said, through a yawn, "it stands out a mile that Mrs. Big Chill had a financial motive to kill her husband—I mean, beyond the obvious thing that she inherits his estate. Maybe she made that up about him quitting basketball, to throw everyone off. I can see her as the killer."

It would be fair to say that Tom laughed in Ike's face, except for the fact that he was fifteen feet across the room from her face.

"Marie Celeste Thorpe didn't kill her husband," Tom said scornfully and with a sort of withering certainty. "Not unless she disguised herself as a basketball player and was shooting hoops during the pregame warm-up. The Big Chill was killed by someone *on* that court."

Tom turned to me and caught me staring at Hannah's ears.

"What about it, Abagnarro? Hey! Snap out of it. Was anyone cross-dressing on that court?"

"Tom, you know, I didn't check."

Sally chuckled. "That's a good one, Abby."

"Thanks."

"Because the killer had to be on the court, at least we can eliminate some people," Sally said. "Fedex Parker. Our crew. The widow. The head coach, Max Hall, and Sam Rice, the team doctor. They, and we, were all away from the court at the moment the murder took place."

That made me think. A certain lovely taxi driver had been lurking around the Garden. She had hated the Big Chill but hadn't been on the court. Angel Rosenbloom was therefore eliminated as a suspect. Hell, who wasn't?

Tom made a face. "Thanks for the help, Sally. By that reasoning, we can eliminate most of the planet." I looked at Tom, wondering if he was reading my mind. He went on without noticing me, so I guess not. "In addition to the Big Chill, who did not stick a knife in his own chest and then hide the weapon, we've got twenty big strong men on that court. What have we learned about them? My producers have come up with two solid facts about those men on the court: fact one is, nobody but Knicks teammate Theo Hornacheck liked the Big Chill; fact two is, those ballplayers didn't like getting hit by buckshot any better. Very hard to believe that anyone would set himself up to get shot so he could go stick a knife in someone.''

"That's the conundrum in a nutshell, Tom," Ike said. "If I hadn't seen the videotape of the Big Chill on the floor, and the paramedics swarming all over him, and that doctor at St. Vincent's pronouncing him dead, I'd think the New York *Post* made up this whole story.''

"Well, they didn't. Make it up, I mean. And as far as I can tell, NTB news isn't thinking any more creatively than the *Post.* All we've had so far has been sheer dumb luck.''

"Bull," I said. "It wasn't luck that got that videotape out of the Garden and gave this network a major scoop. It was determination and basic guile and raw courage. I could devour a mastodon raw, I'm so proud of my primitive cunning.''

"I'll look for you in the *Post,* Abby," Tom said.

Black steam started pouring out of Ike's ears.

"Will you two stop it?" she said. "We've got a personal obligation now because of Church, on top of our professional obligation concerning this story. Do you mind if we stick to what we know and need to find out, and omit this macho posturing?''

Tom cleared his throat. "I wish I could figure out your romantic life, Ike. But you're right. The problem is like that old joke where this guy says, 'What do you know for sure?' and the other guy, an engineer, says, 'It takes a big woman to weigh a ton.' Where do you go from the obvious?''

I thought Ike would get Tom for sexism, but she ignored both the personal remark about her romantic life and the limp joke.

"Well, Tom," she said, "in your world view, just what do we know for sure?''

"Whoever stabbed the Big Chill had help from a confederate in the stands. That gun didn't go off by itself. So we need two people we can nail. Abagnarro, have you had any flashbacks yet? You opened your big mouth on national television that something seemed familiar about that blurry shape you saw after the shooting. In fact, you said it on my show. Cough it up."

I scratched my head. "Nothing's come to me yet, Tom. You know how it is."

"No, I don't know how it is. My memory doesn't fade in and out like an AM radio station out on the Plains."

Ike smacked the table with the palm of her hand. "What about motive? Has that angle gotten anyone anywhere?"

Hannah rolled her eyes. "The *New York Times*. Their op-ed page had a column about all the enemies the Big Chill had made in the ecology camps. Everyone see that piece of beef jerky?"

There was general head nodding. Everyone at NTB checks the *Times* to see if we're right about stuff.

"Well," Hannah said, "are we all agreed that's a crock? I mean, do we agree that nobody kills over the destruction of rain forests? I don't think we can productively explore any so-called motive connected to that cattle-ranching stuff, unless that motive is financial and personal, rather than idealistic. I must say, though, that op-ed piece was amusing, with its science fiction take on this murder. People gasping for breath in the year 2000 and begging for a tree. I think Kevin Costner ought to make a movie out of that."

Suddenly J.D., who had stayed out of the discussion, looked interested. "You're already gasping for breath, Hannah, with all those cigarettes. You probably won't make it alive to the next century."

"I'll beat you there, sonny." She tapped her cleavage, which showed above the tight red thing she was wearing under her blue blazer. "This model was built to last. And I'll still be on the air when you've got grandchildren supporting you."

J.D. shook his head. "What was I thinking? You'll be on the air until doomsday, as long as they don't run out of Preference, by L'Oréal."

"I don't dye my hair."

"Then how'd you get that nice two-tone effect with your dark roots?"

She gave him a mean look. "I don't get out in the sun enough."

I fixated again on Hannah's pale ears. She really *didn't* get out in the sun enough. I've never seen such pale ears.

"Abby," she said, yanking me out of my stupor, "despite all the sweet rumors going around about you and Ike, I assume that you and I are still on for lunch?"

"Lunch?" I'd almost forgotten. Repressed it.

"Lunch, Abby. The midday meal. I'm sure you've had lunch at some point in your life."

"Lunch."

"My girl made reservations at Gypsy's. I don't know why I've never been there. All the stars go there for lunch. I understand your mother is a big fan of mine."

Gypsy's. She had reservations at my mother's restaurant on 46th Street. Holy ground, and Hannah wanted to share lunch with me there. She was right, though, about my mother. Carole Abagnarro approves of Hannah. "That Hannah doesn't make mistakes like some of your parade of weird anchors," my mother says.

Everyone in the room was staring at me. The fact was sinking in: I actually had a date with Hannah Van Stone.

I played my last card. "Hannah, Gypsy's doesn't have a smoking section. Not even at the bar."

"I'm aware of New York City statutes, Abby. I don't worry about the ban on smoking."

"You don't? I mean, you can do without cigarettes?"

"Not at all. The restaurants pay the fines, not me."

She stood, smoothed her skirt over her central bulge, picked up her purse, and headed for the door.

"I'll be in my office," she said, smoothing her hair, perhaps for J.D.'s benefit. "Abby, pick me up a little before eleven-thirty." She put her hand on the doorknob and turned slowly back to face Tom. "Listen, sexist piglet. You got that joke wrong. My brother is a mechanical engineer, and they really talk like that. Here's how it's supposed to go: The first guy says, 'What do you know for sure?' and the second guy, the engineer, responds, 'A two-hundred-pound German shepherd is a big fucking dog.' Get it right, pork chop."

And she left.

Everyone looked at Tom and then everyone looked at me.

The silence in the conference room was not music to my ears. I could hear what everyone was thinking.

We'll never see Abby again. He'll disappear into that black hole with what's left of Hannah's dates after she devours the good parts.

I glanced at Ike's face, where I discovered an unmistakable smirk. This was all her fault.

She didn't let me get eye contact with her.

"Sally," she said, "I want to know how the Big Chill's insurance breaks down."

"You mean with the widow and how much, and all that?"

"No. I mean his team insurance. How much the Knicks carried on him. Who pays whom now. This won't be easy information to get."

Sally yawned and stretched. "Ike, if I wanted easy, I'd be working the circus, getting shot out of cannons. You'll have the information by this evening."

EIGHTEEN

WITH THE MANDATORY sentence of lunch with Hannah looming over my head, and given how long the morning meeting had run, and considering that I was half-asleep, and faced with the certainty that it wouldn't be long before Fillingeri arrived to pull Church Finnegan's personnel file and our collective pancreas inside out in the NYPD's investigation, I didn't have much time or inclination for playing with sound mixers again. But Ike hauled me, an editor, and a sound tech back into an editing room, and we went through the procedure of isolating that odd noise again. It didn't take us long this time, because we knew where the thing we were looking for was.

We just didn't know *what* it was.

We listened to *shhh* several times. We played it louder and softer. We sped it up and slowed it down. It still sounded like *shhh*, no matter how we played it.

"What can that be?" Ike said, mostly to herself, rubbing her tired eyes. "What an odd thing to hear in the Garden."

"Ike, it could be anything—from the swish of a mop to a librarian hiding under the seats telling us to be quiet. Maybe somebody didn't like the noise the gun made and that's why they said *shhh*."

"Abby, I wish you would take this seriously."

"I'm trying."

"Okay, was anybody using a mop?"

"The only Garden personnel I saw was that one security guard who escorted us in. Oh, and the people in the ticket booths."

"So let's assume that sound was not made by a mop."

"Okay."

"So what else could it be?"

"Maybe a pigeon got into the Garden."

"Did you see a pigeon?"

"No."

"Does a pigeon make a *shhh* noise?"

"No. They flap and coo. And shit."

"Then it wasn't a pigeon."

"Right." I yawned.

"And don't try to tell that idiotic story about the parrots."

"Now? I'm not that stupid."

"I'm so glad. Was the crew close enough to the shotgun mike to kick it or something? Could that noise be the mike sliding on the barrier?"

"No. I was the one closest to the mike and I did not touch it. I was hoping it was doing its job. Church might have kicked it if he'd been near it, but not me."

"Oh, because you're the consummate professional?"

"You can answer that question yourself, Ike. Would I screw with the equipment during a breaking story?"

"No. Not unless you couldn't help it."

"I hadn't lost my mind. I was just down on the floor."

Ike picked up a pencil that was lying on the console and started tapping the palm of her hand with it. "You think that noise is nothing?"

I'd been leaning against the wall of the tiny editing room. I slid down the wall until I was sitting on the floor, my hands on my knees. I thought hard.

"Maybe. It could be anything, Ike. But I'm going to vote that the noise is something. Something important."

"Why?"

"The timing. It doesn't sound like anything the crew did immediately following the gunshot. And the players froze after the gunshot. The noise, however, comes like a second, or a second and a half, after the gunshot. Something made that noise. And the noise was made when everyone else was quiet and not moving."

"Except, of course, the shooter," Ike said. "He had to have been moving, escaping."

"Then there should have been a *series* of noises from him, Ike, not one, not one single discrete noise that we can isolate on tape. We have no other sounds on here that indicate *any* movement on the part of the gunman. Hell, we don't even have the sound of the gun being dropped on the floor. It must have been put down very gently. The gunman was as quiet as we were."

"Then, with all those possibilities eliminated, it's time to ask the obvious. Could that noise have been made by a dart gun or something? Are you thinking what I'm thinking?"

"That was practically my first thought, but I ruled it out. I'm not making fun of you, Ike, but if the *shhh* sound came from some means of delivering that stab wound, where's the knife? Somebody not only stabbed the Big Chill but also *removed* the knife. I'm sure I would have known if the gunman was reeling in a knife after he got through shooting. That would take time. Therefore, someone had to be on the court to remove the knife. Therefore, someone on the court inserted the knife."

"Damn." She raked her hair with both hands, making a big mess out of her designer hairdo. "I can't even *think,* I'm so tired."

"Me, too. Think we can waltz tonight?"

"Oh, absolutely. We just can't win. Not unless all the other couples wear galoshes."

I pushed myself off the floor and got upright. "You want to pick me up at my place?"

"Yeah. I'll stop for you at seven-thirty. Be down in the lobby. And don't be wrinkled. And do be awake. You've got our music, don't you?"

"Yeah, I've got it."

Ike reached out to touch my cheek. "Enjoy lunch, honey."

"Maybe Hannah forgot. I can always hope."

"Despair, Abby. Despair. There is no hope. Hannah doesn't forget. Or forgive."

The word "hope" had treated me to a sudden pang of butterflies. I'd been forgetting for a few blessed moments that I had no hope. Before I could go home and get some sleep, I had to break bread with Hannah. Or whatever she broke. Raw crocodiles. Live rats.

Ike walked me to my office, leaving me there with a sweet, sad, parting smile lingering on her lovely face. Completely phony.

I collected my jacket from my office and took a deep breath. I locked my door behind me and walked—what was left of my spine curling—toward Hannah's suite of offices. I scarcely noticed the long line of portraits gracing the wall of the tube, portraits of NTB anchors, including Hannah. Hers, I did notice.

That painting is at least twenty-five years old, probably more. I stopped for a moment to look at what she had been like before she got like she is now. Her hair had been blond then (although I couldn't swear it was ever naturally that color), and her face had been wrinkle-free, but she had, even then, an authoritative glint in the blue eyes captured forever with oil paint. I didn't think that was license on the part of the artist. Hannah had been born to present the news on television. There was no doubt she had "it": poise, self-assurance, a no-nonsense hardness, shamelessly cold directness. Authority. She had steel, and it showed.

I hoped she wasn't going to use any on me.

Ordinarily when Hannah issues the command for a male to have lunch with her—or so the legend goes, confirmed by several hapless males at NTB—she's checking him out as a suitable sexual partner. I knew I'd be under scrutiny as a *toy* while we ate.

Maybe it was fortunate that Hannah had chosen to hold my viewing at Gypsy's, the Abagnarro family restaurant. If she got out of line, I could always holler for my mother.

I could smell the cigarette smoke twenty paces before I reached Hannah's lair. The Emerald City has a firm no-smoking policy, but Hannah has some clause in her contract that allows her to bake lung cookies from her *Virginia Slims Cookbook* in her suite of offices, even if there is no way to confine the stench to those offices.

One of the *Evening Watch* producers passed me in the tube as I hesitated at Hannah's door. He was holding his nose. He smiled knowingly, it seemed to me, either out of compassion or because he, too, had been there, or maybe out of pure meanness. I smiled back, like whatever his smile was all about, mine said, *I'm just here to deliver a script.*

Too late I realized I wasn't carrying anything but my jacket. My smile must have come off like somebody on death row seeing the tray arriving with his last meal—and it wasn't what he ordered.

I knocked on the door. Maybe she had forgotten.

There was no answer.

I waited at least two seconds and started to make my retreat.

The door opened. Hannah's secretary had her hand on the doorknob and no expression at all on her face. This was probably routine for her.

A couple of personal assistants were scurrying around inside the suite of offices, but I couldn't make out what they were doing, not with all the smoke cloaking their activities.

I wondered where the superintendent of this gas chamber was hiding. Hannah, however, soon emerged from her inner sanctum, following closely on the trail of a blast of smoke shooting out from her mouth.

She'd changed her clothes.

She wasn't exactly all in black. Her velvet slacks were black. Her boots with three-inch spike heels were black. Her velvet knee-length jacket was black. The thing she was wearing under the jacket was black, but there wasn't much of it. What there was *a lot of* was cleavage, and it certainly wasn't black. It was wearing powder that barely disguised the liver spots on her overflowing breasts. I tried to think back to the portrait I'd just seen, trying to remember if she'd always possessed this much acreage in the Grand Tetons, but the woman in the portrait had been wearing a shirt buttoned to the throat. All I could say for sure was that twenty-five years ago she'd had a throat, all right.

I attempted self-hypnosis, reminding myself that I'm a leg man, looked Hannah in the eye and studiously avoided the rest of the scenery. But I couldn't keep the thought out of my mind: was she wearing a bra or a forklift?

"You're right on time, Abby," she said, blowing a circle of smoke that landed on my nose and made me imagine she'd hooked me like a trout. "That's always a good sign. I like punctuality."

"One of the reasons Ike divorced me is that I'm often late."

"That was Ike. This is me."

"That's for sure," I said, but I thought, *A hell of a lot of you.*

"Why don't you come in while I do my lips and get my coat?"

"Oh. You've got a coat?"

She laughed. Sort of. Maybe it wasn't a laugh. It was more in the humming family. I started yanking my jacket on to cover up the shiver.

Leaving the main office door open, she disappeared back through the clouds of smoke obscuring her sitting room, on her way to her inner office/boudoir/laboratory. I stood there at the door, unwilling to plunge after her into the depths of her cancer factory. But I heard some people approaching from the east side of the tube, so I hurriedly stepped inside Hannah's suite, closing the door softly behind me. I didn't want to be put on the spot again, forced to plaster an indecipherable smile on my face.

I took a seat on the barber's chair Hannah keeps in the middle of that sitting room. I sat back and crossed my legs. It

was really comfortable. I closed my eyes. That suddenly ter-
rified me. What if she had a razor?

I almost leapt out of the chair—into her arms. She was
standing right there, looking at me.

"Ready, Abby?"

Ready? Were the Salem witches ready for a dip in the pond?
Was Joan of Arc ready for the stake? Was the Light Brigade
ready to ride into the valley of death?

"Ready," I said. What a man.

She tossed her half-smoked Virginia Slim into an already
full ashtray, a yellow ceramic object about the size of a bucket.
I think I saw something like it once in the Guggenheim Mu-
seum.

We left her office and marched together to the elevator—
marched because she was setting the pace. My legs are much
longer than hers, but mine seemed to have acquired some lead,
or maybe petrified wood.

When the brass doors closed on us and we were alone in
the elevator, she pulled something on me that changed the
whole picture and made me feel ashamed of myself.

"I've been very pleased," she said, "by the latest from the
rumor mill. I hope it's true, unlike most of the half-baked
bullshit that passes for internal news around here, that you and
Ike have finally come to your senses."

She bent her most penetrating stare on me, the kind she's
used on Bob Dole and Michael Jackson and every coanchor
she's driven off the set of *Morning Watch*. "Is it true, Abby?
You and Ike were once very happy."

*Now, here, I thought, is where a lie will really come in
handy. If I say the rumor's true, I can step out from between
the lion's jaws.*

I don't know why I told her the truth. It could have been
her authority working on me, and that penetrating stare.

"Hannah," I said, "I wish the rumor was true. The divorce
almost killed me. But I'm afraid what you've heard is half-
baked bullshit."

"That's a shame. Ike should have forgiven you by now. After all, what's a little infidelity?"

The doors opened at the lobby, and she marched out onto the green marble floor, her boots sounding loud enough for a troop of at least five women to be inside all that black velvet. Which was kind of also my mathematical reaction to the Grand Tetons that were *not* quite inside the black tank-thingie she was wearing.

Hannah knows, I thought. A little infidelity.

I caught up with her and we pushed through the revolving doors.

The sidewalks were clean, but the streets were sloppy, snow was piled in mounds at the curb, and the mounds—this always happens in New York when it snows—were covered with dog shit. Pet owners, for some reason, think they don't have to obey the pooper-scooper laws when they know the plows will be coming by.

"I'll get us a cab," I said.

She put her fingers in her mouth and emitted an earsplitting whistle that the financial grabbers probably heard all the way down at Wall Street.

Her white limo pulled up at the corner. The—I couldn't help noticing—*good-looking and young* driver leapt out and opened the door for her. When we were inside, she said, "Forty-sixth Street, honey. Gypsy's."

Carole Abagnarro, who's been running Gypsy's by herself since my dad died, still keeps the place qualified as a Theater District shrine by letting up-and-comers run tabs while the stars, who once survived on credit, now pay enormous prices to eat my mother's healthful, low-cholesterol, complex-carbohydrate-rich, fat-resistant creations. Her pasta is freshly made each day in the kitchen she remodeled after Dad's death, and she doesn't use eggs.

My mother, who, at fifty years old, looks forty—yet covers her bosom decently—was sitting at the bar with Liza Minnelli when I held the door for Hannah and we walked into the

restaurant. Here's a measure of how much Broadway's lumi-
naries treat Gypsy's like their second home: Liza wasn't wearing any mascara.

Ma excused herself from Liza and hurried to greet us.

"Hannah, it's so good to see you!" she said.

"I've always wanted to come here, Carole, so this is a
happy occasion. You've been well, I hope?"

"Great." Ma swept her hand toward the full dining room.
"You can see for yourself."

"You must be eating your own cooking," Hannah said,
frankly assessing Carole's figure. It was like Hannah had tape
measures rolled up under her eyelids. "You look like a teen-
ager."

My mother is too savvy to blush when somebody hands her
a load of Broadway baloney, but she smiled gently. "I've
saved you my favorite table. Let me take your coat."

Hannah divested herself of her black mink street-length
Czarina-of-all-the-Russias coat. She laid it over my mother's
waiting arms. My mother then got her first look at Hannah's
expanse of the Continental Divide. Carole Abagnarro is no
prude—okay, so she's a prude; what do you expect from a
fifty-year-old Italian mother?—but something in her posture,
or her bearing, changed. Stiffened. It was a slight change, but
I know Carole Abagnarro's disciplinary stances from experience, and she was *not* pleased to welcome Hannah's two
friends into Gypsy's.

But Carole is also too savvy to make a scene over somebody's topography making a scene, so carrying Hannah's coat,
she led us to the booth right under the clock given to her by
the original cast of *Cats*. It's a black and white cat whose belly
is the clock's face, and the tail ticks and tocks back and forth.

Carole looked Hannah in the eye and said she'd be right
back to tell Hannah the specials.

I was beginning to wonder if I existed.

"Nice place," Hannah said. "Do you have a wrench?"

"Excuse me?"

"Somebody ought to dismantle that clock. Tick tock, tick tock—it sounds like a game show."

In spite of myself, I laughed. "Better that than *American Gladiators.*"

"Abby, that is a game show."

I thought about it. "Maybe you're right."

"I'm right about a lot of things. I'm right about the Big Chill's murder. This conspiracy theory is stupid. Two perpetrators? The cops and the media can kiss my ass."

My eyes probably bugged out. I was amazed they didn't swing back and forth from their sockets and make tick-tock noises. I'd thought Hannah was here to fondle my thigh, and instead she was pulling my leg.

When I could think, I wondered if Hannah had been paying attention when we told Tom about that *shhh* noise. I said, "How in the world can one person fire a gun, put the gun down, race out of the arena, make it all the way down to the court, stab the victim, get off the court with the knife—all in a matter of some four or five seconds—without me seeing any of it?"

"It can't be done."

I sank back against the red leather of the cushioned booth. "Then what are you talking about?"

"I don't know how the thing was done. I just know human nature. The Big Chill was heartily disliked. That much is a given. But only a lunatic kills from simple dislike. The scenario as we now have it requires two lunatics. Try and tell me the last time you saw two lunatics cooperating with such precision. They'd get their straitjackets tangled."

"Where are you going with this, Hannah?"

"Motive. All the people who had real motives to kill that man were *off* the court. And you can't tell me that any of those players or coaches who were on the court when the Big Chill died is a hired assassin. Nobody on the court stabbed him. Somebody would have seen it. So the conspiracy theory falls apart right there. And think motive. It's not enough to dislike the guy—somebody who hated him was responsible for that fatal wound to the heart.''

"Who's on your list of the people who hated the Big Chill enough to kill him?''

"The wife, of course. She may have merely hated the fact that he had all that money to himself. She inherits and is therefore suspect number one. Plus, she can't have missed the fact that he was unfaithful to her, rather publicly.''

"Go on.''

"The coach. There's a history of racial hatred between him and the Big Chill.''

"Who else?''

"Fedex Parker.''

"He's an environmentalist, not a hater.''

"Grow up, Abby. He was physically attacking the Big Chill and willing to pay cash for the privilege. That's not idealism. That's hatred.''

"You remember that cab outside the Garden when we left?''

"The one with the woman? Of course. You were flirting with her.''

"I was not.''

"Whatever.''

"I wasn't. Anyway, she hated the Big Chill enough to sell her season ticket to the Knicks' games.''

"That's interesting. Make a good profit?''

"Sold it at cost.''

"That's pretty implausible. You think she dated him? She was pretty enough.''

"Never occurred to me.''

"You should get a copy of her Taxi and Limousine certificate and have an intern run her photo against all the pictures we have of the Big Chill's postmarital flings.''

"I don't know, Hannah. That's pretty wild.''

"Well, perhaps. But it's against human nature for her to drive her cab over to the Garden after the shooting just to look at reporters coming out the door. By that hour, she must have known the Big Chill was dead.''

"She did. She said she heard it on the radio."

"Then she wasn't parked outside the Garden in the hope of hating him in person. She was doing something else."

"Like what?"

"Like what anyone would do. Satisfy curiosity about the aftermath. Everyone else with a motive had the opportunity to satisfy that itch."

"Hannah, tell me. I'm into human nature as much as the next man, but there's a problem of simple logistics. If nobody who hated the Big Chill was on the court, how'd he get stabbed?"

She shrugged, which caused an interesting cascading ripple effect down the mountainside of her upper anatomy. "My guess is he wasn't stabbed."

NINETEEN

MY MOTHER, who has radar where most people have ears, zoomed in on Hannah and me with the specials menus. Pointedly maintaining eye contact with the cat clock instead of gazing at Mount St. Hannah about to erupt out of that black outfit, Carole said, "That ballplayer wasn't stabbed? You think somebody threw that knife?"

"What knife?" Hannah said, opening her menu. "Nobody ever found a knife."

"Well, *something* stabbed that man, and—"

I was taught not to interrupt my mother, but there comes a time when the lessons we learn at our parents' knees start to look a little knobby.

"Ma, the M.E. said he was stabbed. The M.E. is supposed to know about that sort of thing. And nobody could have thrown a knife without being seen—by someone. And if it wasn't thrown by someone on the court, but by the gunman up in the stands, it wouldn't ever have had the force to kill the Big Chill."

"You interrupted me, Abby," she said. "I was about to say what you said."

Hannah looked up from her menu. "What's this 'TBA' under the salads?"

Women can do that. Carry on two conversations at once without getting them mixed up.

"To Be Announced."

"I know *that*. So announce it, will you?"

"Belgian endive with capers and lemon-pepper dressing."

These two women (each old enough to be my mother, one of whom might want to fondle my thigh, the other more likely to grab me by the scruff of my neck) might as well have been stirring cups full of capers into my brain with wooden spoons.

"Let me get this straight," I said, fanning my menu across my brow. "You both think nobody on the court could have stabbed the Big Chill. You both think nobody off the court could have stabbed the guy. Hannah, at least, thinks he wasn't stabbed at all. The M.E. says absolutely that the Big Chill was stabbed. *What the hell do you think made that hole in his heart?*"

"Are you swearing at me, Abby?"

"No, Ma. I'm just swearing."

"Well, you better not be."

"I'm not; I'm not."

"Good."

"Ma, what in the *world* made that hole in the Big Chill's heart?"

"He was gunned down in cold blood, Abby," my mother said, just like they say it in Westerns. "Have the pasta primavera."

I was expecting her to say "on the streets of Laredo" instead of "have the pasta primavera."

Hannah snapped her menu closed and ordered fettucine Alfredo. I wasn't going to tempt fate, so I ordered the pasta primavera.

Hannah opened her purse, pulled out a fresh pack of Virginia Slims, peeled the wrapper off, tapped out a cigarette, flicked her Bic, and lit the damn thing.

"You can't smoke in here," my mother told Hannah, in the same tones I'd heard when she had said something like "No, Abby, you can't have a horse in a Queens apartment."

"Could you find me an ashtray?" Hannah asked sweetly. "So I can put it out? I'd hate to grind it on your nice clean floor. I don't know how you keep it so shiny in this weather."

My mother gave Hannah that horse-in-the-apartment look and whisked herself off to the kitchen. Hannah dragged deeply on the cigarette dangling from her lips.

"Abby," she said, "let's forget for a moment about the Big Chill. We have another murder to talk about. How many people do you think it took to kill Church Finnegan?" The smoke curled around her nose as she used her nostrils for exhaust pipes.

"One, I guess. I mean the one who stabbed him."

"And how many people did it take to shoot Church on the street when you were all together, sneaking out of Madison Square Garden?"

"One."

"Do you think they were the same person?"

How odd, I thought, *of course they were.*

"Yes," I said.

"Then, by analogy, or by hindsight, whichever you prefer, can't you apply that retroactively to the Big Chill's death?"

"No. Because the circumstances were not the same. Plus, I was there when he got it. I saw what happened."

"No, you didn't."

"But, I—"

She was smoking as fast as she could, but she can smoke and interrupt at the same time. "You saw nothing useful in the Garden."

The people at tables near us were muttering and glaring at Hannah.

After some nudging and whispering from the little brunette at his side, a guy in a blue suit pushed his chair back with some unnecessary noise and came over to our booth. He looked vaguely familiar.

"Aren't you Hannah Van Stone?" he said—meaning Hannah, not me—in a crisp British accent. "People like you should be thrown in jail."

"People like you ought to mind your own business."

"I'm sorry, but this is my business."

"Sod off, limey. There's some of the Queen's English for you. Are you getting my drift yet?"

"Madam, you are polluting my air."

"Well, how perfectly ghastly. Pollution. What a thing to happen in New York City! Why don't you go outside and stick your nose up the tailpipe of a bus?"

"I say! There's a law about smoking indoors."

"We have many laws in this city. Do you own a dog?"

"Yes, I do. What difference does that make?"

"I'm wondering," she said, blowing smoke right at him, "if you cleaned up after him on your most recent walk."

"That's none of your business." He was getting red in the face.

"Of course it is. I use these streets. I pay taxes for these streets. You pollute my streets, I pollute your air. It's self-righteous British creeps like you that turned Boston Harbor into the world's largest cup of tea."

"That's not awfully funny."

I had him placed now. I should have recognized him sooner.

"Oh, get a stiff upper lip," Hannah said, smoking at him.

He stood there, his arms doing a miniature Muhammad Ali at his sides. I knew what he was thinking: *Can I hit a woman?* And that thought was probably followed by *Especially this famous TV newswoman?*

My mother pushed her way through the swinging doors and hurried to our table with a saucer. She handed the saucer to Hannah. The cigarette was nothing but filter by then, but Hannah ground it into the saucer.

My mother took charge. "Go eat your lunch, L.W. I'll handle this."

The guy didn't even mutter. Like a good little boy, the richest composer of musicals on the planet slunk away. He just did as he was told.

Carole picked up the saucer, took our menus, told us she'd bring us the special salad with our entrées, and a nice glass of Chianti, and took off for the kitchen. Reminded me of a lot of meals at the Abagnarro Ranch back in Queens, where I'd learned early that you can only have one glass of wine.

"Did you know who that was, Hannah?"

"Certainly," she said. "So what? He's overrated. Forget him. Abby, let's talk instead all about that fib you disseminated on *Evening Watch*."

"Which one?"

"How many times have you been on *Evening Watch*?"

"I meant which *fib*."

"The one about your remembering something about the shooter."

"How'd you know I was lying, Hannah?"

"Years of experience at the anchor desk. I can usually tell."

It frightened me to think I was that transparent to Hannah, of all people. "What do you want to know about it?"

"Why you did it."

"Isn't it obvious? It's probably obvious to the shooter, assuming he had the bad taste to tune in to *Evening Watch*. I had an idea—at least, I think it was my idea—that I could draw the creep out to come after me. Then I could get a look at him."

"You're likely to get more than a look. I'd say you might get yourself blasted down to 14th Street, if not across the Hudson to East Orange."

"Nobody really got hurt with buckshot, Hannah. And I know what to do if this loony shoots at me."

"I'm thrilled to hear it. Fry him with your heat vision?"

Carole appeared with our meals, and the next ten minutes or so were rather quiet. I'd often thought the only reason my mother fed us at home was to get us to shut up for ten minutes. You don't waste mouth-energy on words when Carole's cooking is in front of you.

The only substantial talking came when my mother returned to collect our plates.

"I've decided the team doctor killed that Chill man," she said, reaching over the table to gather our dishes.

"Why, Ma?"

"Because he'd know where to find the heart."

"Sam Rice wasn't on the basketball court. He was summoned after the shooting and after the Big Chill was down on the floor.''

''Aha! I've solved it.'' Carole was beaming and rocking back and forth on her heels, balancing the dishes in her hands.

''Come on, Ma. Not even the NYPD has seen their way around this one.''

''Just listen. The gunshot scares the Chill man, the man falls down, somebody yells for the doctor, and the doctor stabs the man while he's down on the floor.''

I was stunned. Hannah looked stunned. It made perfect sense.

It was brilliant.

Except for one thing.

''Ma, how would the doctor know the gunshot would scare the Big Chill so bad he'd fall down in a faint?''

''He's a doctor. They know these things.''

''Or,'' Hannah said, ''he simply took advantage of an opportunity.''

''That's some opportunity,'' I said. ''I guess the doctor just happened to have the knife on him—maybe a scalpel?—and saw his chance. That still doesn't explain the gunman.''

Hannah sneered at me. ''Abby, you're supposed to have a good visual memory. There's something else wrong with this picture.''

I sat back and closed my eyes and saw it. ''The red stain on the Big Chill's pure white warm-up jacket. It was there before anyone yelled for the doctor.''

''Good boy.''

I opened my eyes.

My mother had already left the scene, no doubt gleeful about having solved the crime of the century.

''That was a nice meal,'' Hannah said, lighting a cigarette. ''I'll have to come here more often. Shall we go to my place now?''

I swallowed hard and thought fast.

"Hannah, I've got to get some sleep. There's that dance contest tonight."

"You can sleep at my place."

"My tuxedo is at my place."

"So we'll go to your place."

I swallowed hard again and thought. Nothing slick came to me.

"Uh, Hannah. Ike's going to pick me up at my apartment." She looked at her watch.

"It's not even one o'clock. We've got hours. Let's go."

"Would you excuse me just a minute?"

"Don't be long."

I slid out of the booth, stepped around the crowded tables, and headed for the front door. I needed some fresh air. Not that I was likely to get any out on 46th Street. City fumes would have to do, in the absence of anything like oxygen.

Of course, I could always flag a cab and ask the driver to take me to the Poconos. If I had any money on me.

I pulled open the shiny chrome and brass door of the restaurant and took a step out onto the sidewalk, half expecting Hannah's black boots to scrape my heels.

Two men in matching red plaid woolen coats passed in front of me, holding hands and obviously very much in love. I watched them as they neared the corner and began the tricky negotiation of the mounds of snow and garbage. It helps to have a partner when you go rappelling in New York City.

Inspiration on how to avoid Hannah's ambush without turning her into *Godzilla Scorned* still eluded me. I looked around. No cavalry.

I'd just have to suck it up, I decided, and tell her the truth. I didn't *want* to play. Not with her, anyway.

Then the one I wanted to play with suddenly hove into view, gliding around the corner on Rollerblades. I was never so glad to see anyone in my life.

It would take a lot worse than a few inches of snow and slop to keep Ike off her skates. She was wearing a shiny pastel blue down vest over her dark blue turtleneck. Her blue jeans were tucked into her skates, the pink laces tied in giant bows. Her cheeks were blushed by the cold. Her hair was windblown and beautiful.

I grinned, took a step, and raised my right arm to wave at her.

Too bad I'm right-handed.

The blast came from across 46th, from a silver-gray van doubled-parked a few doors down from where I stood in front of Gypsy's. I never saw it coming.

My right arm stopped waving and started burning as it came down—without me telling it to—to my side. I was so surprised by the gunshot, I didn't even think to get down. I just stood there and watched the expression on Ike's face as she slid and cruised into a speed stop about eight feet from me.

Other people were quicker than I was. The men in red plaid coats had dived into 9th Avenue, using the mound of filthy snow as a fortress. A few other pedestrians were down on the sidewalk.

My own words echoed in my mind: *I know what to do if this loony shoots at me.*

I had done precisely what the men on the basketball court in Madison Square Garden had done when the loony shot at them. I'd frozen in place, a statue of a television director waving at his former wife. Only there was a touch of the Venus de Milo about my right arm. I still had the arm, but I almost wished I didn't because it hurt like the fires of hell.

I was vaguely aware that the van had muscled its way into the eastbound traffic on 46th. I was vaguely aware that suddenly I could smell Italian food. I turned my head slowly to the right and saw that the window of Gypsy's was shattered. Even that had a vague, cartoonish feeling for me.

But I was hyperaware a second or two later when I caught a delicate whiff of Chanel No. 5. Ike was at my side, her phone open in her hand.

"Hi," I said.

"Oh, *fine*," she said, putting the phone up to her ear. "Stand there and tell me 'Hi' like we'd just run into each other in the cafeteria. Stand there and drip blood on the street. Stand there and gaze at the windows. Stand there— Dennis, this is Ike. I'm at Gypsy's. Send an ambulance. Abby's been shot."

"Well, *excuse* me," I said.

"You and your bright ideas."

I still couldn't remember if telling that lie on *Evening Watch* had been my idea or hers.

"Ike, did you get the license number of the van?" I said, somewhat bemused at how slow I seemed to be talking. And how fast she was talking.

"What do you take me for? Of course I got it."

"Good. Now I don't have to go home with Hannah."

"What?"

My knees buckled and I floated down to the pavement. I don't recall whether it was hard.

TWENTY

HE CERTAINLY won't be much use for a while." I heard what seemed to be Hannah's voice buzzing around in the cold air. "And just what was Abby doing with his arm? Some sort of macho City League basketball semaphore that said 'Hey, I'm open. Pass the ammo to me'?"

"He was waving." That was Ike. "To me. And how can you be so cold-blooded? Abby's hurt."

"Not any worse than he asked for. What are you doing here?"

"His mother phoned me and said Abby was in trouble."

"How long ago was that?"

"About twenty minutes."

"I wonder why she did that. He was safe and sound in her restaurant."

"How should I know? Carole just said to get down here."

"That woman must be working with a Ouija board. The shooting happened only in the last three minutes."

I was tuning in to other sounds, other New York voices. Mostly sirens. I tried to push myself up off the sidewalk onto my elbows. Ouch. Wrong idea.

I put my head back, slowly, on the pavement. If I turned slightly, I could see black boots with three-inch spike heels and a pair of Rollerblades with huge pink bows. And, it seemed, a bunch of wet knees and dirty pants legs and sloppy Timberland boots. The scene looked like an L.L. Bean catalog that had been lying in an alley for a few days. People were squatting and kneeling and standing around me.

As the ambulance came crawling around 46th, the bullhorn freely ordering lunchtime New York to get the hell out of the way, I heard my mother's voice, louder than the bullhorn:

"Move it! Clear the way. He's my son!"

I tried again to sit up, and this time I made it, with Ike's help. My butt sure was cold.

"Abby, don't try to stand," Ike said. "Your arm doesn't look too bad to me, but you'd better let the medics do their thing."

I studied my arm as though it belonged to someone else. My jacket would never go to lunch at a three-star restaurant again. The right sleeve was way beyond any tailor's skill. Maître d's would shun it....

"I was wrong, Ike," I said. "I was supposed to keep moving. This is my own fault."

"What is he talking about?" my mother demanded. "He's lost his mind."

Ike put her arm around my shoulders. "He's okay. He just wasn't expecting this to happen here."

"So who does? Is there something wrong with my restaurant?"

"No. It's a long story. Abby and I had this all worked out—we thought."

I was glad when I saw the uniforms of the paramedics. I don't like doctors and I don't like hospitals, not since my dad died, but my head hurt about as much as my arm, and I didn't feel like explaining to my mother, under the circumstances, anything about the way my mind works when Ike winds it up.

I sat there on the sidewalk while the paramedics quickly and efficiently moved the crowd back and started doing things to me. They took my blood pressure, my pulse, and checked my respiration. They got my ruined and sticky jacket off without killing me and draped a blanket over my shoulders. One of them wrapped my right arm several times around with gauze, and the other rolled up my left sleeve and got ready with a needle.

"I don't need that," I objected. "What are you doing?"

"Starting an I.V., TKO."

I searched the paramedic's face for signs of comedy.

"TKO?" I said. "Technical knockout? It was a gunshot."

"TKO means 'to keep open,' meaning your vein."

"I like my veins *closed*, thank you."

"This is just a precaution. Simply so we have immediate access to your system."

"Oh, God, my system's open," I said, probably whining.

My ex-wife, thank God, is not like my mother, who probably would have been happier if the medics had shot me full of morphine and operated right there on the street. Ike didn't stop them, but she also didn't encourage them.

"Don't whine, Abby," Ike said softly. "This will go more quickly if you keep your sass to yourself."

I leaned against her hip. "Good. Quick is good. I can probably only spare about fifteen minutes from my overloaded schedule. I've got to get some sleep."

I didn't rate a stretcher, which made my mother furious.

"You're making him walk?" she yelled. "What kind of monsters are you?"

They didn't bother to answer her. Ike was giving them my name and other vital statistics, like about my health insurance, I think. They bundled me into the back of the ambulance, which, I am happy to report, was nice and warm. I'd been thinking my can would never thaw out.

They gave Ike a lift up into the ambulance because she couldn't make it herself on Rollerblades. Before they could shut the back of the ambulance, a hand attached to a man with gravity-groomed hair grabbed one of the doors. He flipped open his card case and showed his badge to one of the medics.

"I'm riding along," he said. "Roosevelt Hospital?"

"That's right."

Fillingeri and one of the paramedics hopped in with us. The doors clanged shut. The ambulance started moving, and the bullhorn was a lot less bothersome from inside the vehicle. I guess that was the point. It was supposed to bother people *outside*.

"Abagnarro, this proves it," the captain said. "You're nuts."

"Me? Me? I'm nuts? What does that make the guy who *shot* me? King George the Third?"

"I doubt the gunman is a member of the royal family. Okay, who did shoot you?"

"I don't know."

"What do you mean, you don't know? This is the third time some bad hombre has fired a gun practically in your face and you don't know? What's the matter with your eyes?"

One of the paramedics added some tape to the I.V. and said, "Captain, he may be in shock. Not from loss of blood. There wasn't that much. It looks like he got the fight-or-flight adrenaline response, couldn't do either one, and that confused the body."

"He's confused, all right."

"You're not being fair, Dennis," Ike said sharply. "Give Abby some space. Besides, I was there this time. Why don't you badger me?"

"You saw this happen?"

"The entire thing. Somebody—all I saw was a gun sticking out of a van—shot Abby when he came out of Gypsy's. I've got the license number and I can describe the van."

She briskly dictated what she had, and this time Fillingeri did his own stenography.

I looked out the window. The ambulance was trying to back out onto 9th Avenue. The driver was really using his bullhorn now. A Pepsi delivery truck had pulled out behind us, having squeezed through an alley.

Fillingeri looked up from his notepad and raised his eyebrows at Ike. "Can you describe the gun?"

"All I know is that it had long barrels. It wasn't a sawed-off."

"Very good, Ike," he grunted. "You know how to keep your wits about you."

I couldn't let that pass. "Oh, and I don't?"

"The record speaks for itself."

"Well, so do I. And I say—"

"Shut up. We all know you speak. Christ! That's all you ever do."

"Not true. Sometimes I sleep. Sometimes I dance. Sometimes I even go to work. Oh, and I eat."

Fillingeri pretended he was in an ambulance with a blow-up doll attached to an I.V. and turned back to Ike, a living human being with some brains.

"Lend me your phone, Ike," he said, holding out his hand.

She had to wriggle around on the vinyl bench to pry the phone out of the back pocket of her jeans. I looked around for a scalpel to help her, but—wouldn't you know it—they don't keep scalpels within eyesight of their passengers in ambulances.

Ike punched in her security code and handed the open phone to the captain.

I tuned out a little at that point. I was vaguely aware he was telling someone the license number Ike had supplied him with and talking to crime scene people outside Gypsy's, but I didn't want to think about that. He was yapping about long barrels and how this shooting was meant to kill me outright, not just scare the hell out of me by flicking my hide randomly with buckshot. From the van's distance, as Ike had described it, and from the appearance of the gun, it looked like someone was taking aim this time at a small target—my head, for example— not the broad side of a barn.

I wanted to sleep.

"Where's Hannah?" I said, suddenly enough to surprise even myself.

"Boy, can that woman produce a wicked whistle," Ike said. "I mean, without any mechanical aids. She just puts her fingers in her mouth and out comes this piercing noise from the ninth circle of Hell. The minute she does that, her cicisbeo comes running with the limo."

"Her *what?*"

"Cicisbeo. Passionate wooer. Lover-on-call. Escort. Get it?"

"You mean Hannah and her driver are doing the wild thing?"

"Everyone knows that."

"I didn't."

She gave me a look, fairly sour, I thought, since it was directed at a man who was responsible for giving her a free joy ride in an ambulance through the streets of New York.

The ambulance had prevailed over the Pepsi truck, and we headed down 9th, making a right turn on 45th Street.

When Fillingeri handed Ike her phone, she kept it open and started using it. She does all that one-handed—holds the phone in her left hand and dials with her left thumb. *Come to think of it*, I thought, unconsciously flexing the muscles under the gauze covering my right arm and clenching my teeth against the agony, *maybe I should watch her technique closely*. Learn quickly how southpaws manage to get around in a right-handed world. I wondered, for the first time, how badly damaged I was, or, rather, how permanently.

"I'm in an ambulance with Abby," Ike said. And then she cussed. A little steam poured out of her ears. "No, Tom, and I resent such suggestions about kinky behavior. That remark tells me a lot about how your mind works."

Fillingeri leaned across toward Ike, his face showing he might be interested in hearing both sides of this conversation.

Ike tried to turn sideways to get some privacy. There's something I picked up on right away, however. Ambulances are not built to provide the wounded or their escorts with privacy. Ike was stuck with either telling her story with Fillingeri in her face, or journalistic abstinence.

"We're in this ambulance," she said, having made a quick executive decision, "because Abby's been… Oh, you heard about it on the scanners. Anyway, in the event you are planning to get on Abby's case because once again he's not bringing in pictures of a crime committed in his vicinity, I want you to know this was an unpremeditated crime on Abby's part. You know what I mean. I'll call you from Roosevelt Hospital and let you know his condition. If you want to send an *Evening Watch* crew to meet us there, that's up to you. It's your budget. Now, patch me through to the dayside editor for *Morning Watch*—I think Frank Savaglio's on today.''

She held the phone against her ear and gazed at my arm.

"Does it hurt much?" she asked, with real concern in her blue and green eyes.

"Depends on how you define 'much,'" I said. "More than a few bee stings, less than if a jaguar gnawed on it for lunch."

"Thanks for the zoo diagnosis, Abby."

"You're welcome."

We had reached 10th Avenue and the ambulance started making the kind of time an ambulance ought to make.

Ike started up with her cellular again. "Frank? Ike. Listen. Oh, wait a second." She covered the mouthpiece with her hand and drilled Fillingeri with her eyes. "Must you listen in? Don't you have some police work to do? You don't need to hear my every syllable. This is network business."

He shrugged and held out his hands, palms up. "What else I can do is maybe something you've got ideas about. You carry a set of earplugs on you?"

She made a face at him and resumed with the phone.

"Frank? Abby's been shot. He's okay, but now I'm really mad. First Church and now Abby. This killer has taken the fight to us. Are you ready?" She paused a few seconds. "Okay. Round up the right people and start digging—with earthmoving equipment if necessary—into the Big Chill's business dealings, paying special attention to recent sales or pending sales. Especially real estate. Right. And despite the fact that he wasn't on the basketball court at the time of the stabbing, Fedex Parker needs a closer look. I don't know what the NYPD has done"—a pregnant glance at Fillingeri—"but I want his entire biography, from kindergarten. And tell Sally to call me on the cell. She's working a different angle."

I waved my left fingers at her.

"Just a second, Frank," she said. "Abby wants something."

I didn't really want to say what I had to say in front of Fillingeri, but I didn't think I'd get a private moment with Ike any time soon.

"Hannah had a suggestion," I said.

"Go."

"Well, a couple of suggestions."

"Hurry up."

"Look into the head coach and the team doctor."

Fillingeri butted in. "Those two were not on the court when the player was stabbed. We've got witnesses. You're one of 'em."

I didn't feel like explaining human nature to the captain. I hadn't minded the topic over lunch, but that was before somebody's human nature shot me.

Ike must have seen the look on my face and read it right, because she showed she had some humanity in her nature.

"I'm not going to ask why about those men, Abby," she said. "You can explain later. Anything else?"

This was the part I'd rather have discussed privately with Ike. "Get a copy of Angel Rosenbloom's Taxi and Limousine photo and compare it with our archived tapes of the women the Big Chill hung out with. I mean other than his wife."

"Angel Rosenbloom?"

"You know, that taxi driver who took me and Church to the Garden Tuesday night when the Big Chill got it. Remember? We told you about her. She was back at the Garden after the shooting, parked out on Thirty-third when we left."

Ike nodded. "Oh, yeah. The pretty one." She started relaying Hannah's suggestions to Frank Savaglio.

Fillingeri's face was turning red under his year-round tan. "What the hell is this? Othello Armitage is now running his own private little police department over at the Emerald City? You keep your own secret suspects? Next thing you'll tell me is that you have a jail of your very own up on the twenty-seventh floor, and maybe even an electric chair. I'll bet you've got a whopper of a pension plan. And real fancy badges.''

"You don't understand," I said. "Hannah didn't make this connection until a few minutes ago."

"Between you and Hannah Van Stone, I'd rather believe Pinocchio. I don't care if you pass out from those wounds, Abagnarro. I want chapter and verse, and I want it now."

"You just said—"

"Never mind about the Pinocchio stuff," he growled, turning his notebook to a new page. "What's the taxi's certificate number? What was that name? Where did the driver pick you up? When did you see her again? Have you spoken with her lately? She gonna have your children?"

"Not unless she knows something about reproduction they didn't teach us in school or in X-rated movies."

The ambulance had dashed up 10th, and we were crossing 57th Street against the light. That should have been fun, but it didn't seem to matter to me. It would have been more fun if I'd been in a motorcade and they were holding the lights for me because I'd just returned from the moon or won the Super Bowl.

"Stop messing with me, Abagnarro." Fillingeri held up his right thumb and forefinger, slowly narrowing them almost completely together and shoving the whole picture in my face. "You see this? I'm this close to arresting you on about six charges."

"In an ambulance?"

"Wouldn't be a first for me. How about you?"

My right arm was actually talking to me much louder than Fillingeri was, so I decided to save energy by giving him what he wanted. I told him everything I could think of about Angel Rosenbloom. Which wasn't much.

I guess I did a good job, though, because when I'd finished my little story, Fillingeri didn't have any questions. Not about Angel Rosenbloom, anyway. He switched directions on me.

"I want to know about this lunch at Gypsy's. You were there with Hannah?"

"Yeah."

"Anyone else?"

"There were other people in the restaurant."

"I mean with you."

"Just me and the anchorwoman."

"You plan this lunch?"

"She did."

"Who else knew you and Hannah were having lunch at Gypsy's?"

My head really hurt. It was hard to think. "I don't know. I think everyone in the building probably knew I'd been summoned to lunch. But at Gypsy's? Probably just her personal assistant, the one who made the reservation. Oh. Ike knew, because I told her." I looked at my ex-wife, who was still on the phone. "Ike, did anyone else know Hannah and I were going to lunch at my mom's?"

"Well, kind of."

I knew what that meant. "I guess the gossip got around."

Fillingeri nodded and put his hands together, a self-righteous look on his handsome face, like gossip was the foe of decent law enforcement personnel all over the world, but he could accept that.

"Did you notice anyone following you?" he said.

"We came in Hannah's limo. I was busy noticing the limo. Besides, you know how it is. With traffic the way it's done in New York, *everyone* could be following me. How'm I supposed to know which cars are going about their business and which ones are going about mine?"

"Ike," Fillingeri said, as she shut her phone. "I want a deal."

"What kind of deal?"

"I can get that taxi certificate faster than you can. You've got the videotape archives and the gofers. You can get the pictures of the Big Chill's women faster than I can. This Angel

Rosenbloom is a brand-new shiny suspect for me, one of your NTB state secrets. You owe me a deal.''

"Why are you being so cooperative all of a sudden?" Ike said, suspicion clear from the frown on her face and the way she was swinging her leg. Impatiently.

"Because I'm smart, Ike. I can tell from past history that you guys are not about to cooperate with me. So I cooperate with you."

"Okay." She nodded. "But I want to say I think it's lousy that it takes three shootings to make you treat us like humans instead of low-down dirty rotten snakes. Just as soon as we get Abby squared away, you've got a deal. We'll do this together. But only if you give as much as you get. This better not be a trick.''

The ambulance screeched to a halt under the canopy of St. Luke's-Roosevelt Hospital. Tom had managed to get an *Evening Watch* cameraman in place, so I was immortalized as I winced getting out of the ambulance. The paramedics escorted me into the waiting room of New York's biggest casualty ward, which was SRO. When I saw the crowd, I was grateful, at last, for Fillingeri's company.

If anyone could cut through the red tape here, it was New York City's finest, represented by Captain Dennis Fillingeri.

Pulling every string he could and flashing his badge and throwing his weight around, NYPD Homicide Captain Dennis Fillingeri made sure Ike and I got out of Roosevelt Hospital's emergency room in a few minutes under three hours.

TWENTY-ONE

THEY TOOK six pieces of buckshot out of my right arm. With a local anesthetic, that wasn't so bad. But the tetanus shot (not in my arm) felt like Ben Hur had galloped up behind me at full speed in his second-best chariot and poked me with the decorative bronze figurehead of Athena.

The really weird part, however, wasn't the surgery. I'd never had Demerol before, but now that I have, I don't want it again. They told me it would make me feel drowsy. *Au contraire.*

That injection turned me into Superhero *FLASH* Abagnarro, Speed Freak. If someone had asked me to conduct a delicate bit of brain surgery, I would have grabbed the nearest pair of pliers and taken a shot at it. If Ike and I had not been divorced—or if we were and she didn't care—I'd have given her the afternoon of her life and either won her heart or broken her into smithereens in the process.

Those reactions lasted about an hour.

Then it got worse.

My eyeballs almost popped out of my head and I couldn't sit still. The sling they had given me in the E.R. stayed on for the first hour after we left Roosevelt Hospital. After that, I was tying the sling in knots and swatting imaginary tennis balls with it. Among other things.

I had wanted, even demanded, another ambulance ride, but nobody would take me seriously. So Ike, Fillingeri, and I had found a cab willing and able to take us the two blocks to the Emerald City. We made Fillingeri pay the $2.75 fare. He screwed the driver on the tip.

I had trouble getting my I.D. out to show the security guard, so I wanted to swat him with my sling, but Ike pulled her I.D.

and said the rest of us were her guests. We rode up in the elevator, and I found myself mesmerized by the distorted images we cast on the brass plates of the elevator's walls. Fillingeri looked short and dumpy. I, however, looked tall and mighty. Ike just looked cute.

I don't remember walking to the control room, because I was still busy, I guess, wondering if Fillingeri was permanently short and dumpy after that elevator ride. I was having a little problem with cause and effect.

Ike thought I should phone the hospital and report the odd reactions I was experiencing on the Demerol.

I shouted at her loud enough to make her cover her ears: "WHY PHONE 'EM? I LIKE HAVING SEIZURES! YOU LET ME ANYWHERE NEAR THAT PHONE AND I'LL RIP ITS ARMS AND LEGS OFF. I'LL SHOVE IT DOWN MY THROAT IN ONE GULP. I'LL FLING IT OUT THE WINDOW AND TEN BUCKS SAYS I KNOCK THE TORCH OFF THE STATUE OF LIBERTY."

My shouting, although it seemed perfectly normal to me at the time, must have been fairly audible, what with the good acoustics at NTB News World Headquarters, judging from the number of curiosity seekers who stopped by to see what was going on in the control room. We'd left the heavy door propped open with a big carton of beta tapes, because I had an idea that our control room was an alien ship trying to abduct me and I needed an escape hatch. Demerol Man might have been crazy, but he knew a UFO when he saw one.

"UFO!" I shouted. "How come nobody ever talks about FO? That's what they took out of my arm—FO!"

"Do you think we ought to get him some coffee or something?" Fillingeri asked.

Ike almost barbecued him with the flames shooting out of her eyes. "Coffee's a great idea. Let's really rev him up." She rolled her eyes and smacked her hand on the sound engineer's console. "What Abby needs is a two-by-four against the side of his head."

Fillingeri smiled. "I wouldn't mind trying."

"You touch one hair on my head," I hollered at him, "and I'll snap you in two. I'll toss the bottom half into the incinerator and the top half off the roof of this building. We'll see which part of you is really tough!"

"If you weren't on drugs…"

By this point I was beginning to come out of it some, but it was fun to have a free turn at Fillingeri. Sweet revenge for all the times he's accused me of having a smart mouth. I'd show him a smart mouth.

Besides, I owed him. He'd left me all alone in the E.R. at Roosevelt Hospital, a victim of all the Dr. Frankensteins.

Fillingeri had abandoned us to go back to Gypsy's while I was being turned into a maniac. Ike had burned out the battery on her cell phone about halfway through my transformation; she, too, abandoned me, having finagled a phone from Roosevelt Hospital, and started working on *The Case of the Buckshot Bad Guy*. Fillingeri's defection, however, had not been total. He'd left instructions not to release me without his say-so and his personal presence to sign me out. Apparently he was my new guardian. My pal. Perhaps even my dog.

The result of all that furious communicating Ike had done from the hospital, and Fillingeri had had his minions do, was that certain items arrived at the Emerald City's biggest control room around four o'clock that afternoon, before any life-forms had time to make off with me and drag me back to their sector of the galaxy.

A uniformed police officer, escorted by an Emerald City security guard dressed in green and a sweet smirk, brought us a perfectly clear Xerox of Angel Rosenbloom's photo—from the files of the Taxi and Limousine Commission. She was photogenic.

Tom Hitt had detailed a production assistant from the staff of *Evening Watch* to help us out (not from altruism—Tom wanted in on this rare deal between us and my police attendant, or valet, or whatever Fillingeri thought he was), and

Tom's slave had looted the NTB tape archives for all the footage Ike had requested: tapes of the Big Chill with his women and tapes of the Knicks' head coach, Max Hall, making remarks about skin color and subsequent remarks from him attempting to pry the size-fourteen Nike out of his mouth with a crowbar.

We had only a few sideline pictures of Sam Rice, the Knicks' team doctor, from game footage. But why would we have more of him? I mean, who pays any attention to team doctors?

We also had no tapes of Mrs. Big Chill, because nobody did, not because they didn't care. They did care. She just wouldn't let cameras near her.

Fillingeri had gotten attacked from out of nowhere by a bright idea, and had sent a platoon down to Madison Square Garden's press office, where they requested and were given a promotional videotape that included almost twenty seconds of the Queen of Photo Reticence in her private box overlooking the basketball court. Those private boxes cost normal people (meaning corporations) two hundred thousand dollars per year and they seat twelve people (meaning people). Mrs. Big Chill had one box to herself (meaning an Amazon in eye-catching designer clothing), and since she was big enough to require a little extra elbow room, nobody could possibly accuse the Garden or New York's Big Chill of having wasted money on her accommodations, *unless you were just a lowlife Knicks fan who struggled to make ends meet and had paid for your lousy season ticket in the upper tiers with a loan from your credit card, your friendly local bank, or your uncle Eddie, assuming you were lucky enough to have an uncle with thousand-dollar bills lining his pockets.*

Fillingeri didn't need a bright idea to get some of the other stuff we needed. All he needed was an NYPD flunky who faxed to us the typed summary of the Big Chill's recent financial background, which had already been prepared in detail as part of Fillingeri's investigation of the murder of Archibald Tyrone Thorpe, basketball marvel and cattle rancher.

"Now, Abagnarro," Fillingeri said, once we had all the materials gathered, "I want you to explain to me, please, just why we're so hot all of a sudden on these people who could not possibly have stabbed the Big Chill on the basketball court of Madison Square Garden—for the pure and simple reason that they were not *on* the court at the time of the stabbing. Do you mind helping me out here? Hello. Can you hear me? Abagnarro, are you receiving?"

"Of course I can hear you," I shouted. "I'm not deaf. I'm in an altered state."

"I'd like to alter your state. Maybe Kansas will take you."

"You want an answer or do you want to talk about geography? I can tell you the state capital of Kansas. And while I'm at it, did you trace the license plate on that van? You may recall there was a van with a shotgun in it. See my arm?" I held the offending limb out to him, which was the sort of thing my sling was supposed to prevent me from doing, but then Roosevelt Hospital shouldn't have given me one that was just made for swatting imaginary tennis balls. "I got this in front of my mother's restaurant!"

"Your arm?"

"No. I got that at birth. I'm talking about THE WOUNDS! Did you trace the license plate on the van or have you just been writing parking tickets all afternoon?"

"We traced it hours ago."

"Are you saving the information for my Christmas present?"

"I got other ideas about giving you something for Christmas. That van belongs to Madison Square Garden."

"Well, well. Was it hot-wired?"

"We haven't located the van. Yet."

"Your men on lunch break?"

"Abagnarro, in this business we have a saying about information: 'You can have it good, fast, or cheap—pick two.'"

The Demerol wired in my head didn't make that an easy thing for me to fathom, but I finally got the gist.

"Are you releasing this information about the van being the property of Madison Square Garden?" I said.

"No."

"Because you can't find the van? Makes you look bad?"

"Abagnarro, I wish that shooter had aimed a little better."

"Just for that I'm telling Tom Hitt about the Garden van."

"Just for that I'll tell him you're lying."

I thought about that, sort of. The Demerol, however, made thinking a little like pole-vaulting while strapped in a canoe. "Tom will probably believe you, Sergeant Fillingeri. If I hadn't been telling so many lies lately, he'd believe *me*. These are the wages of my sins."

"I'm not a priest, Abagnarro. I'm a police *captain*. Just talk to me. About this stabbing baloney."

I was only too happy to talk. It gave my tongue something to do, which was excellent, since I'd been biting it accidentally and it was starting to protest, even over the Demerol. I speed-talked my way through Hannah's lunch philosophy about human nature. I quoted my mother's theory on why the doctor was her favorite suspect. I went over the cab trip that had been brought to Church Finnegan and me courtesy of Angel Rosenbloom, and I gave a competent if loud report on her return to the Garden a couple hours later in her cab.

"This is exactly why I'm up here on the twenty-seventh floor of Ike and Abby's Secret World," Fillingeri said, giving me an ugly look. "This is the same kind of crap you guys pull all the time. You should have told me right away about the cab driver."

Just when I thought I'd have to threaten Fillingeri again with a little Demerol violence on his person, Ike took me by the hand, slam-dunked me into my chair, and patted my head. She picked up the phone to summon an editor and, while he was trotting over to the control room, diverted Fillingeri by explaining about the noise we had isolated on the tape we had so flagrantly smuggled out of the Garden Tuesday night, if you believed Fillingeri on the practice of smuggling. Personally, I thought *smuggling* was a misnomer. You can't smuggle something that

a. you own
b. isn't contraband
c. the cops could have asked you for directly if they'd had the brains to think of it and you would have turned it over gladly but they didn't.

Fillingeri was surprisingly mild when Ike told him about that *shhh* noise on the tape, which I thought was a better secret we'd kept from the police than Angel Rosenbloom.

"I can't insist that you hand over to me the product of your own independent thinking," he said, in a level voice, "but I can *wish* you'd shared this discovery with the NYPD, Ike."

"Even if I knew what that noise was, Dennis, which I don't, I haven't a clue to its meaning. We naturally thought of the noise representing a second weapon, like a dart gun, but we ruled that out because nobody ever found the knife that killed the man. No knife, no weapon to throw it, no relation to the *shhh* noise. And I don't believe you can just use your hand and throw a knife with enough force from where the gunman was standing and kill someone under the basket at the Garden. Not and penetrate the heart by—what was it?—five inches?"

Fillingeri nodded. "I agree, Ike, nobody just threw that knife. But there are delivery systems, all of them outlawed by Congress a few years ago, that can hurl knives great distances."

"Yeah, I know about those. You can shop by catalog."

Fillingeri shook his head. "Catalogs. Simple as ordering a bra from Victoria's Secret. Just pick up your phone and have your credit card ready."

"Then the killer could have had such a system, no problem."

"Anyone can have one. The FBI will be on to him like a crow on roadkill, though, but you can't make an arrest until the buyer uses the thing. But, Ike, in the Big Chill's case, we've got a big problem. The problem is just what you said a few seconds ago. Where's the freaking knife? Somebody had to be down there on the court to remove it and take it away, or we would have found it sticking out of the Big Chill's heart. I want to hear that *shhh* noise, but even so, you see, I'm having trouble with this human-nature theory that says we've got only one killer. Somebody had to fire the shotgun; somebody had to stab the Big Chill and remove the knife. That's two people. At least. And one of them was on the court. Church Finnegan's murder, I can figure out, at least how it was done. But it has to fit in with the Big Chill's murder, which, from where I'm standing, is not a likely fit."

Fillingeri waved his hand over the pile of print and electronic information that had accumulated on the consoles in the control room, brought from many directions by several flunkies, all at our request.

"What all this is going to tell us about the murders of Archie 'Big Chill' Thorpe and Church Finnegan is your part of the deal, Ike. Start showing me yours, and I'll show you mine. I'm not spending my time up here because I'm a TV groupie."

Thorpe. And Finnegan. Not "Abagnarro." I felt sort of bad that Fillingeri didn't include me in his list of victims, but I consoled myself with the fact that the victims he did mention were dead. I was merely nuts.

Ross Greenberg, our editor *du jour,* came in through the open door of the control room, and I leapt to the Demerol conclusion that he was after me. I nearly tried to escape from him through one of the monitor screens, on the theory that I could make it into Studio 57. Ross gave me a funny look, but that's exactly what an alien being *would* do.

Ross is pretty laid-back, and he doesn't mess with higher-ups any more than he has to, so he just did what Ike said and played the archive tape showing a free-form collection of images of the Big Chill out in public places with women who did not happen to be his giant spouse. It looked to me, although the Demerol still had me bug-eyed, like the Big Chill preferred his extracurricular females on the small size, at least compared with Marie Celeste Thorpe, the Colossus of Couture.

Case in point, Big Chill-preferencewise: Angel Rosenbloom.

There she was on the tape, at a party held by the Brazilian Embassy on Park Avenue, drinking champagne with the Big Chill and behaving as if he'd already autographed her stomach with a laundry marker but would help her scrub it off later.

Ike told Ross to freeze the shot, and she held up the photo of Angel beside the monitor screen. Same Angel. Same Big Chill. No cab. No basketball. Just two people at a party, apparently oblivious to the camera. From the graininess of the pictures, I could tell, even in my Demerol haze, that it was a hand-held camera used without proper lighting. But it was good enough to show that the basketball star and Angel Rosenbloom were having fun. And good enough to show the nuances that said it wasn't the first time they'd had fun together.

I read the label on the sleeve of the box the videotape had come from. Some NTB employee had taped this off of *Hard Copy.* I wondered how much *Hard Copy* had paid the amateur who shot the video.

I thought back to that cab ride with Angel and Church.

"My God!" I shouted. "That's the link!"

Fillingeri goggled at me like he was the one on Demerol. "What?"

"Their names," I shouted. "Angel and Church. They're both holy, you know?"

I thought Fillingeri was going to hit me.

"Abagnarro, I was born at night—but it wasn't *last* night!"

Ike cut in. "Listen, boys," she said, "we just nailed a really tight connection between the Big Chill and someone who was definitely hanging around the scene of his murder. Maybe the tightest connection.''

Even I got that one. ''The woman scorned,'' I said, surprised to hear my normal voice. I nodded to myself. ''Scorned. Had to have been scorned. She hated him.'' I looked at Ike. ''Wanna know something?''

She looked wary. ''Depends.''

''No, this is a good one.''

''All right. What?''

''That season ticket she said she sold?''

''Yeah?''

''Bet she made a nice profit.''

''She said she didn't, Abby.''

''And you believe *her?*'' I yelled. ''It's so obvious. Her ticket was a gift from the Big Chill. The whole thing was profit. I figured there was something fishy about that ticket from the start. Nobody in this town sells at cost. Use your brains, Ike!''

Fillingeri, who had been swiveling back and forth in the technical director's chair and might have been the navigator on this UFO, was probably hooked up to a universal cosmic translator, I thought in my Demerol haze, because he started talking again, not in an alien language. He was suspiciously familiar with English.

''So, we've got one cab driver with a motive that looks like one I can believe in. Old-fashioned jealousy, or whatever it is that a woman scorned feels. She made a point of her hatred of the guy. And she was on the scene. And she must have been very familiar with the arena, given her relationship with Thorpe. And you guys proved anyone can get into the Garden without one of those Star Trek things that beam you down.''

I jumped up from my chair. ''Holy Moses!'' I shouted. ''You are an alien.''

He smacked the flat of his hand on the console. ''I wish you'd knock it off with the foghorn routine, Abagnarro!'' Now he was yelling. ''I can hear you.''

I sat back down and looked at his head. "I finally understand your hair."

He shoved his chair back to get some distance from me. "You ought to go back to the hospital."

"No, this makes sense. It's like, you know how your hair never gets messed up? I mean, even when you do this?" I imitated that characteristic hand-raking thing he does with his hair. "I figured out you have your hair cut by a gravity expert. Well, we don't have those yet on *this* planet."

"That does it, you stooge." He stood up, rather too suddenly for a Terran life-form. "Ike, you've got to get him some medical help. Jesus. Look at *his* hair. He's beginning to look like an alien to me."

Ike had her head down on the sound engineer's board, her shoulders shaking. When she looked up, I could see tears on her face. She was laughing so hard, she couldn't make any noise, at least not anything louder than some death-rattle gasping.

"Straighten yourself out, Ike. This man ought to be locked up or hanged."

I resented that. "If they hang me," I yelled, "I'll sue the executioner for whiplash."

Fillingeri stood there gaping at me for a couple of Earthseconds and then he started laughing.

"What have you done with the real Fillingeri?" I demanded. "He doesn't laugh."

That was when Ross started laughing, which was fine with me because he wasn't doing any editing and I'd ruled him out as an alien because I'd forgotten he was in the room.

Ike and Fillingeri carried on like a couple of drunks who'd been sipping from the hysteria fountain. He fell into the chair beside her. And I began to feel paranoid. What did they know that I didn't know?

It was while they were going at it that Tom Hitt walked into the control room.

"This is just great," he said. "Are you holding a bachelor party in here?"

"Don't be such a poop, little green man," I yelled. "Have some champagne on me." I waved vaguely around the control room, forgetting we didn't have any champagne.

"It looks like you guys already drank a truckload."

Ike had found some Kleenex and was wiping her eyes. She handed a wad of tissues to Fillingeri.

"Tom," she said, hiccuping, "Abby's been mainlining Demerol and he thinks we're aliens."

Tom arched his eyebrows so high, it must have hurt, but doing so didn't make him any taller.

"That's the first sensible thing I've ever heard from Mr. Abagnarro," he said. "Does anyone else have something sensible to say? I need some hard news. Like, what's the word on that van?"

"That van," I told him, "shot the bejesus out of my arm." I held out my wounded limb to show Tom. "Want me to take the bandages off on national television? I am living proof of the existence of UFOs. Only, unlike some publicity hounds, I ain't baring my arm or anything on your show for free. I'll trade you an interview with me for your ray gun." I nearly tripped myself on my own feet when I turned back to face Ike and Fillingeri. "You know," I confided to them, "I've always wanted a ray gun. I can probably bargain Tom up to a set of three if you guys want one also."

Ike wailed and collapsed again on the board. Fillingeri had his head down practically in his own lap, shaking with laughter.

Or maybe it was his native planetary language.

TWENTY-TWO

TOM DIDN'T stay long in the control room. His audience of twelve million viewers was waiting breathlessly in America's living rooms to learn what *Evening Watch* thought they should know.

He was pretty disgusted when he didn't get anything useful and exclusive from Demerol Man and the Aliens that would have made him look like both Woodward and Bernstein, except shorter.

We had only two things that nobody else had—proof that one of the Big Chill's former and bitter girl-toys had been present at Madison Square Garden around the time of his murder (pretty hot stuff, if only we had a photo of her with a shotgun in her hands), and a fascinating noise we had pulled out of the echoing chaos of sound on tape during the murder itself. But Tom couldn't put any of that on TV.

He also couldn't put me on TV. Here I was, the latest victim of a shotgun attack in Manhattan, an attack probably related to the murders of New York's Big Chill and Church Finnegan, and I was so wired and spazzed out on Demerol that Tom didn't dare let me loose on the air. He was, as a result of having his expectations dashed, enjoying a bad attitude.

Tom crossed Ike and Fillingeri off his list of guest speakers for the show on account of the fact that they were secondhand news. I have no doubt that Tom had been counting on slapping Fillingeri into a chair at the newsdesk of *Evening Watch* for an interview—only now it was clear the NYPD had gotten nowhere with its investigation. Bummer.

"I don't know why I bothered with you twits," Tom said. "I should have known you were just yanking my chain."

Ingrate.

Thanks to *Morning Watch*, Tom would be leading his show with almost thirteen minutes of Hurricane Ricardo coverage. The other networks by this time were up and running with their own pictures of the billions of dollars of destruction that had turned Miami from paradise into a third-world country, but NTB had more personnel on the scene because of Ike's forethought in pulling our crew out of Costa Rica. We also owned the advantage of our Special Reports throughout the day, made possible by the AT&T fiber link. Those reports made us the network to watch on this story, and Othello had licensed some of our pictures to CNN just to prove it. CNN had to run NTB credit with the pictures, so we were drawing some of their highly dedicated audience into our programming.

My arm, which hadn't been bothering me as much as my delusions, started calling attention to itself around five o'clock. They had supplied me with Demerol tablets at the hospital, but I wasn't going to take any of those. Dr. Ike prescribed Tylenol, and I swallowed it without much hope but also without fear for my sanity.

I sat slumped in my chair at the director's console, which had turned into the helm of the U.S.S. *NTB Starship Demerol*, while Ike and Fillingeri read and reread the typed summaries of the Big Chill's recent financial history. The Knicks' star had died intestate, so it looked like the widow, as next of kin, would get everything, which was a lot. Intestate, I guessed, because he still wasn't certain he was as mortal as other people.

"Outstanding motive for murder," Fillingeri said, tapping the sheets of paper in his hand. "The only problem is, it looks like she was spending as much as she wanted anyway. Why go to all the trouble of murdering her husband for his money when she already had it?"

"Here's a better motive," Ike said. "She can't have been pleased about his public dalliance. Dalliances."

I knew this was my cue. "The widow is another woman scorned," I said, without much enthusiasm. I was paying at-

tention to my arm, thinking if I just concentrated hard enough,
I could extinguish the flames by shooting water at them from
my tear ducts.

"Yeah," Fillingeri said. He was reading the typed sheets
again. "But what about this? It says here that his business
manager was about to close a sale on that gonzo ranch in
Brazil. I'm not good at numbers, never having made any
money myself, but this looks like a get-out-of-here sale. The
Big Chill was going to lose money."

"Maybe there was some tax advantage?" Ike said. "A big
loss could be a substantial help with the kind of taxes he
paid."

"Probably not a foreign loss. Our experts are looking at
that. We're not exactly sleeping down on Fifty-fourth Street,
waiting for NTB News to break the case. Jesus, Ike. I'm only
up here because I thought you had something for me. And to
keep an eye on that walking bull's-eye you call your former
husband."

"I'm giving you everything we have, Dennis."

"That'll be the day."

"It's true, Dennis. I know we've had our differences in the
past—"

"Differences? Give me a break, Ike. You've walked all over
the NYPD."

"We have not!"

"I've got the boot marks to prove it."

"Well, if you're going to be oversensitive, why don't you
just leave? We don't need you."

"I think you'll learn you need me plenty. Abagnarro's not
going out on the street alone." He gave me a look, not
chummy. "Ike, the NYPD has turned over every stone we can
find in these murders. And I've given you what we found. It's
your turn. What the NYPD needs is my concern now. For
instance: What else did the widow say when she was here?
Everyone knows that part about her husband quitting the
game, although we have only her word for that. I saw the

show, but was there something you guys didn't put on the air?''

Ike pursed her lips and gazed into the middle distance. I was past the point where I could suspect she was seeing alien beings floating in the air. She was just thinking.

"*Evening Watch* has all of that on tape. The widow said nothing except that the wrong man had been killed and that the Big Chill was stepping out of professional basketball. She left so fast, we couldn't follow up. And now she's not talking."

"Well, Ike, did you have any hint of this before, when you were setting up the interview?''

"Negative. Positively negative. The way I understood it, from his agent, was that he wanted to rehabilitate his image. He didn't want to be the Rain Forest Bandit anymore.''

"I don't see anything there, Ike. She wouldn't kill him merely for talking to NTB about a different, surprise agenda, and neither would anyone else.''

"I agree." Ike heaved a deep sigh and frowned. "Dennis, she's an unusual woman. I don't know much about her. What about her? Where's she from? Where did she go to school? How did they meet? Why is she so reclusive? You give a little.''

"I'm giving you a lot. And I'm beginning to think you've got nothing to trade. You're bluffing.''

Ike sighed again. "Okay, don't tell me. I'll get it from public records, just not at this time of day.''

He sighed and rubbed the side of his neck. "It's not that big a deal, anyway. She's from Rio. The Big Chill met her down there when he became a land baron. Her maiden name is Rocha: R-O-C-H-A. Pronounced like 'Hosha.' The family is wealthy and claims some really creative royal background. They don't think it's proper for a woman to be in the limelight. Especially not a royal princess or whatever she is.''

My cue: "She's a royal pain. She interrupts all the time and thinks the rest of us are dirt. And she's not my idea of a princess, which is maybe why the family taught her to keep herself under wraps. She looks like a man in drag.''

"That's not really fair, Abby," Ike said. "Some people consider her quite handsome."

"Ha! Handsome is right. A princess should be *pretty*. Like you, Ike."

Ike didn't even bother to blush. She yawned in my face.

I couldn't be bothered to feel insulted. "Well, you and your policeman friend—or enemy or whatever he thinks he is—can stand there all day and look at typing," I said. "Marie Celeste Princess Rio de Janeiro's motive stands out a mile. A royal princess is obligated to kill a philandering commoner like the Big Chill. It's like a law in phony South American aristocracies. I read that somewhere."

Fillingeri made a noise. He tossed the sheets of paper onto the console.

"Let's put your editor to work, lunatic. I want to see those tapes of the head coach talking about his daughter and the Big Chill."

"Anything you say, boss," I said. "Wait a minute. You know those tests your crime-scene technician did on Fedex Parker's hands?"

"Yeah?"

"Did you get the results back?"

"Not yet."

"That one he had to send to the nuclear facility in Missouri—is it too late to run the same test on other people who might have handled a shotgun?"

"No."

"Then I have a suggestion."

"You don't have to spell it out, Abagnarro."

"Good."

"But we can't do that test randomly on as many people as we can find. One test alone costs a fortune. We thought we had a sure thing with Fedex Parker. He'd been off the court at the time of the murder and could have shot the gun, and he had plenty of motive. He stood out then as our best possibility."

"Too bad you didn't know then about the knife, Mr. Sure Thing." I turned to Ross and nearly howled when I scraped my arm across the keys and switches on my board. Tears sprang to my eyes. "You got that tape loaded, Ross?"

He nodded, punched a key, and we all watched and listened as New York Knicks Head Coach Max Hall told the world, back when the Big Chill was dating Didi Hall, "I'd rather see her marry Bobby Knight and have him kick her ass across the court every time Indiana loses. Knight's mean as hell, but he's Caucasian."

The subsequent attempt by Hall, under duress by Knicks management, to take back the comment didn't come across as really good screenwriting. He said, "Bobby Knight and I are old friends. I'm sorry my remark about him caused this whole ruckus. I was just kidding an old friend. In no way was I making a racist statement about any player in the NBA."

Sure.

"What's wrong with that," I said, "besides the obvious, is that Hall's words gave *the Big Chill* a motive for murder. What was in it for Hall to kill his star player, especially when the star player was safely married to royalty: *spooky,* but royalty nonetheless? Plus, the Knicks are—excuse me, *were*—favored to win their division."

Ike put a hand on Fillingeri's sleeve. That was the only time I was grateful she had touched his arm instead of mine.

"Where's Didi Hall now?" she said.

"You gonna put this on the air?"

"It must be good or you wouldn't ask. I'll put it on the air if there's a reason to. I won't air it just to say, 'Hey, look what we know.' We don't do that, Dennis."

He really gave Ike the evil eye. "When it comes to putting news on the air, that's when I trust you the least."

"Do I have to get this information from, like, her driver's

license? I can do that with a couple of phone calls to perfectly legal computer dweeb-detectives.''

Fillingeri shrugged and rubbed the side of his neck again. I wondered what was wrong with his neck to make him keep doing that.

"It's hardly that much of a secret," he said. "She's in a nice little township in New Jersey. With her daughter."

A faint memory stirred in my mind. I'd heard something about Didi Hall having a kid, but it must have been in the New York *Post* or some rag, because I never paid much attention. Besides, I didn't care if she had started a family.

"Wait a minute," I said, struck by my own keen intelligence, fostered, I thought, by the Demerol. "What color is Grandpa Hall's little granddaughter?"

"I haven't seen her myself," Fillingeri said, a wry note in his voice. "But I'm told she's not the same exact color as her lily white mother."

"Been out in the sun, has she?"

"Either that or the African-American man who's paying nine thousand dollars a month in child support is the kid's father. I don't know why else he'd pay that kind of money."

"The Big Chill?"

"It ain't Amos or Andy."

"Does—I mean *did*—he visit the kid?"

"The Big Chill?"

"Yes! I wish you'd pay attention. You're not even drugged. Or are you?" I gave him a keen glance, I think. "I was talking about the Big Chill."

"He did not visit the child. Just had his money people send the check to New Jersey every month."

"Nice father," I said.

"Maybe it wasn't so easy to be a nice father when Grandpa Head Coach liked the color of your skin just fine on his basketball court but not on his family tree."

I mulled that over. "You know. Here's a thought. Sometimes I prefer aliens to humans."

"Well, you'd be the expert on that, Abagnarro."

"Damn straight!"

I took a look at the line clock. Almost six o'clock.

"I'm hungry," I announced.

Ike said she'd call down to the Station Break Deli and have them send up something light because we didn't want "to puddle heavy cement in our stomachs, tonight of all nights."

Fillingeri looked like he was trying to pop his ears. He opened his mouth, moved his jaw around, closed his mouth, and repeated the operation, cocking his head a little to the side while he did all that. At least he didn't rub the side of his neck again.

When he was done, he said, "Excuse me if I'm butting in on something personal between you two, but when Abagnarro leaves this building, he's going to have a police escort. In fact, I may not let him leave this building. What's so special about tonight?"

"The waltz contest," Ike said, blinking at him like she wondered where he'd been to have missed this item of news.

"At Playtime-in-Brazil," I said.

"We've been practicing like demons," Ike said.

"We've got the coolest music," I said.

"And my dress is a dream," Ike said.

"You're under arrest, Abagnarro," Fillingeri said. "You're not going anywhere. Especially a public place like that. I never heard anything so stupid in my life. When was the last time you got any sleep? How's that Demerol gonna play in front of the dance judges? Want to get shot again? You *feel* like waltzing, do you? Well, you can do a little two-step in a jail cell before I let you loose on the streets of New York. Why don't you both screw your heads back on?"

"What's the charge, Captain? My lawyer says that obstruction of justice thing won't hold up."

"You jaywalked today getting into the ambulance."

Now, what Fillingeri said wasn't so tough. But the look on his face finally clued me in that he wasn't playing around. His jaw was set, and a muscle was working on its own under the skin.

"You're serious, aren't you?" I said.

"Dead serious. I'm tired of picking you up off of sidewalks."

"Blow me down! I didn't know you cared."

"I don't care. I never said I cared. I said I was tired."

"You look tired," I said, studying the tiny crow's-feet and the dark circles under his deep brown eyes.

"Thanks. You should see what you look like. Forget the waltz. You're being escorted home or you're going to jail. Your choice."

Ike plopped down on the floor and put her face in her hands.

"You can't do this," she mumbled. "Months and months of practice. Dennis, you just don't understand what this means to us."

In a gentler voice than he'd used with me, Fillingeri said, "What I understand is that you're too tired to think straight."

"We're used to being tired. We're always tired."

Fillingeri nodded at her. "Ike, do you understand that this baboon playing with his pretend UFO is in shock and on a drug that doesn't like him? And someone is trying to kill him." He squatted beside Ike. "You can't do it, Ike. It's just not reasonable. You can think straighter than this."

"I don't want to think straight. We have a lot invested in this dance contest. We've got a real chance to win. We *never* win, except for one lousy tango thing."

"Well, you'd better think straight. Do you want Abby to die?"

She burst into tears. "NO!"

Beside me, Ross cleared his throat and excused himself to the men's room. "I'll be back in a bit," he said, and scooted.

"So let's just forget all this talk about waltzing and get back to what we can do," Fillingeri said, apparently unaware he'd scared off our editor.

"I can't forget it," she said, sniffing.

"You have no choice. It's wrong, Ike."

She sat there, breathing deeply and pulling her hair. It looked like she was pulling it hard enough to hurt.

"Okay, Dennis. You win." Ike snuffled and grabbed some more Kleenex. "What's left to do here?"

"Good girl." He helped her to her feet. "The team doctor. I can't help thinking Abagnarro's mother wasn't so stupid—"

"My mother is not stupid!"

"Sorry. I can't help thinking your mother may have had an idea about the doctor's role in the Big Chill's murder. He did have access to the heart right after the shooting, like no one else did, at least for a few minutes. Let's see that part of the tape again."

Since Ross had bolted, it was up to Captain Jean-Luc Abagnarro to violate union rules and change the tapes in our playback, cue up the next tape, and flip the key that made the pictures appear on the screen. I used to be an editor before I became a big shot, so cheating the unions on any equipment is fairly standard practice for me. I'm sure Ross couldn't have pressed the buttons any better than I did, only he probably wouldn't have half killed himself from the activity since his arm hadn't been mined for ore at Roosevelt Hospital.

We watched in silence as, up on the monitor, Sam Rice came racing onto the court, felt around on the Big Chill, put his ear to the chest, and grabbed gauze from a small green canvas bag to pack the wound. Rice did not remove a knife.

"Dennis," Ike said, "the full report was never released by the M.E., was it?"

"It's being typed."

"That's what you always say when you're not ready to release something."

Fillingeri shook his head quickly. "There's nothing in that report but a stab wound and a couple of pieces of buckshot."

"Just thought I'd ask."

We kept watching the monitor as Sally Goldberg-Petit, our producer, and Coach Hall stood talking together beside the dying player and the doctor. And we listened, because that's where Sally's interview picked up. She asked the coach if there had been any preexisting medical condition that could account for the Big Chill being on the floor when the other players were just full of buckshot and hopping around mad. We heard the coach hotly deny Sally's suggestion that he would let a sick man play basketball.

Nowhere in all that did we see the doctor do anything that could remotely be construed as removing a knife or inserting a knife or doing anything with a knife. So much for my mother's theory.

Fillingeri rubbed his forehead. And rubbed and rubbed. He gave it quite a massage. Nice change from his neck.

"I just can't see it," he said. "I just can't believe it. There's absolutely nothing on that tape and nothing from living witnesses and nothing on God's earth to explain this murder."

"I have an idea," I said.

"I'll just bet you do." He didn't look at me. The massage had his full attention.

"Let us do the contest tonight."

He kept up the massage, steadfastly ignoring me.

I don't mind being ignored by Fillingeri. I believe he hears everything no matter what he's pretending to do.

"You can put a hundred cops in plainclothes—well, they'll have to be *nice* plainclothes—in the audience," I said. "One of two things will happen. We'll dance and nobody but us and the judges will care. Or the shooter will come after us and you'll get him."

"The NYPD doesn't play games like that, Abagnarro."

"Perhaps that's because you don't get such good volunteer bait every day."

The massage continued but slowed down. "I have to think about this."

"Think fast. The food will be here any second. Ike and I have to get our music and get changed."

"I hate this idea. We don't need to go to such extremes. Let me see what you have on Fedex Parker."

"It's not much," I said, forming words as clearly as possible, "if incriminating is what you're after. We've got that famous foul on the Big Chill. And all the usual hero stuff. Fedex's tape file is big because everyone loves him, even photographers."

We watched NTB's own *Fedex Parker, American Hero* movie. I never got tired of seeing Parker in action, and the man could read defense and pass and handle the ball probably better than anyone in the game.

But the spectacular foul was great, even better than watching Parker make pretty plays. The Big Chill was up in the air, reaching for a pass, and Fedex snatched his ankle with both hands and sent the big center sprawling facedown on the court. I'd never seen anything like it. The sound was great, too. There was a collective gasp from the fans.

Say what you will, basketball fans know that the game is a contact sport, and they're just as clued in as hockey fans on the fine points of hurting your opponent. There was no question about this flagrant foul, and no question about the satisfied smile on Fedex Parker's sweating face.

It was great TV. Great basketball. Probably assault, too.

While the delivery boy from the deli was putting our food on Ike's big console, we kept our eyes glued to the monitor. You just couldn't help watching Parker move. He was smooth, error-free, and just plain beautiful when he went for the basket.

The phone rang and Ike picked it up. She listened. And she talked. When she hung up, Fillingeri and I both looked at her.

"That was Sally. The Knicks insured the Big Chill against injury on the court for twenty million dollars. If he couldn't play, they'd get paid. Coverage is up at the end of this season."

"Yeah?" Fillingeri said. "Why? Why would they stop his insurance?"

"According to what Sally said, the insurance runs out on

all the players. They have to get it annually. They're all up for renewal.''

''What if he dies?''

''The Knicks get the money. But it's not as financially rewarding as play-off money and winning the championship.''

''Great,'' Fillingeri said. ''That helps a lot. Jesus.''

We went back to the monitors.

We had pictures from a game against the Celtics, where Parker sent it into overtime with a shot nobody believed then and nobody has topped since. Even though I'd seen his move a dozen times on tape, I watched Parker like it was my first time as he tossed the ball from midcourt, and you couldn't hear a thing as the ball passed through the hoop because that toss was all net. But maybe we could imagine a faint silken swish as the ball passed through for an impossible three points at the buzzer.

''I'll tell you one thing,'' Fillingeri said, reaching for a turkey sandwich. ''We may be looking at the game's greatest player. Fedex Parker sure can shoot.''

TWENTY-THREE

THE DANCE CLUB on West 72nd Street was in for a thrill that night.

So was I, in more ways than one.

My senses were tingling, on full alert. Everything was heightened for me—Ike's perfume, subtle touches from the soft clouds of her ice blue chiffon floor-length dress, the music, the extraordinary polish of the dance floor at Playtime-in-Brazil, the exquisite twinges in my right arm, the starch in my shirt, my peripheral vision. Colors, shapes, the rush of dancing with the only woman I've ever loved.

I don't know how much was due to the last traces of Demerol in my system, how much was adrenaline in anticipation of a shotgun attack, how much was the piercing pleasure of the waltz—the only dance that allows a couple to fly together, to flirt with the laws of physics, to defy the grasp of gravity.

But I knew that Ike must have felt it, too, whatever it was. I could see the electricity in those lovely mismatched eyes, and I felt her wildness when I finally touched her waist with my right hand. With the first measure—as I stepped forward on my left foot and she floated backward simultaneously on her right, her dress swirling out so the pale blue chiffon lifted gracefully around us and opened to reveal the deep blue underskirt—I knew that this was the dance of my life.

We had chosen "The Man on the Flying Trapeze" as our theme, and the small orchestra—obviously delighted that they didn't have to produce yet another predictable "Blue Danube," which had been danced by seven out of twelve dance pairs so far—played our song with enthusiasm and, it seemed, *with* us.

I know I wasn't tired, as I should have been, but Ike looked at first like she was sparkling with false energy, some elixir she'd found in a medicine cabinet, a thing she would never do.

I convinced myself I knew just exactly what was in Ike's thoughts, and her heart, during our performance of the Trapeze Waltz (as it was later dubbed in the media) because, in the dark hours of that night, when it was all over and Ike was home in her apartment, getting a few hours of sleep, I couldn't close my eyes. I paced in my little apartment. There was no end to the dance for me yet. I couldn't stop the music in my head. I couldn't put the tuxedo away in the closet, exchanged for a pair of jeans and a shirt. I needed to stay in costume because I was still that Man on the Flying Trapeze.

I went in to the Emerald City around midnight, restless and unable to shake off the exhilaration of the waltz. I also couldn't shake the two NYPD detectives constituting my police escort until I was in the lobby of the building.

I went upstairs and, on the way to my office, noticed the steady blue light flowing softly through the two inches between Ike's door and the burgundy paint of the jamb. She never leaves her door open unless she's in the building, so I tapped on the wood and went in, with every intention of taking her in my arms again and dancing her out into the hall. No Ike.

Her swivel chair was tucked neatly into the kneehole of the desk. Her computer screen was on, the blue light moving out at me from behind the white text she'd left. I looked around. No purse. No Rollerblades. Spooky.

I decided to wait for her, the phantom strains of the melody of ''The Man on the Flying Trapeze'' clinging to every molecule of the air in her office. I took off my black tuxedo jacket and loosened my tie, and the pain that flicked my wounded arm from those simple actions seemed to belong to someone else outside of me. I threw my stuff on her couch and pulled out her desk chair.

I sat, stretched out my legs, and got comfortable. I glanced at her blue screen. My heart skidded when my peripheral vision caught the words "The Daring Young Man." That could only be me, or the waltz, or the whole evening—anything but coincidence. That document on the screen sure wasn't the lineup for the morning's show. I was afraid to look at it. I was afraid not to look at it. I was afraid to invade her territory at all. I was afraid that if I didn't read it, I'd never know something I desperately wanted to know. Something had touched Ike enough to drag her in to the Emerald City (like me) and, apparently, write down the experiences of the evening before they had faded for her. Or maybe it was just a cold recounting of the facts, a record she'd have for some later appointment with official justice.

With butterflies in my stomach, I swiveled the chair and confronted the screen and "The Daring Young Man." For better or worse, with temptation gnawing at me like a rat with a dead taco, I shut down her computer.

The melody and the lyrics flowed through my mind as I stared at Ike's dark screen. What had she written? What had she been thinking about our waltz and "The Daring Young Man"?

I think I know Ike. Maybe she would have been sensible at first, and be certain we never should have entered into such a mad compact with the devil. But she would have fallen under the spell of the dance.

I did not want my euphoria ripped from me through learning that the woman I had waltzed with so intensely was a consummate actress. I wanted that woman to have been real. If any unhappy memories had intruded between us on the dance floor—what was for me a dangerous perfection—there was something wrong with my heart and my hands and everything I know about intimacy.

When I had touched her slim waist—me, the daring young man on the flying trapeze—and we flew through the air with the greatest of ease, she wasn't thinking that we were putting

ourselves at grave risk for nothing more than a stubborn desire
to win a fancy silver cup for dancing in three-quarter time.

I felt in her body and saw in her eyes the sparkling arro-
gance I knew was in mine: two people convinced they could
go round the ballroom more stylishly, more gracefully, with
greater originality, than any other couple—and by so doing,
outmaneuver, outperform, and escape a killer.

The new waltz figure, which I had invented and we had
practiced until I had only to press my fingers on hers to elicit
the steps, had that night entered the language of ballroom
dancing as the "Abagnarro Twinkle," or "Fallaway Reverse
Pivot." And flying over the floor in this new waltz step, I only
vaguely remembered, somewhere in the background of my
mind, the other purpose of our dancing at Playtime-in-Brazil,
vague, flitting memory residue of the NTB sound tech with
the high-range mike, and the police in the audience who, almost certainly, had no idea that we were making dance history
before their eyes.

But the judges knew, and most of that well-versed audience
knew, for even over the music and the hypnotic, smiling gaze
of the woman who was once my wife, I could hear and feel
the deep concentration of our peers and certainly I caught their
sharp inhalation and applause as I took Ike quickly through
the reverse chorus where I had incorporated the new waltz
figure I'd designed for the blonde with the misty, mismatched
eyes.

> *She floats through the air with the greatest of ease*
> *You'd think her a man on the flying trapeze*
> *She does all the hard work while he takes his ease*
> *That is what has become of my love.*

My love. It seemed I'd loved her all my life, even before I
met her. Despite my stupid conduct in Moscow, the mistake
that cost us both the marriage, I never wavered in my feelings

for Ike. Never. That sparkle in her eyes, that smile on her face, the oneness of the dance—I felt like a husband again.

When Ike and I dance well together, we're not two people anymore. And we'd never danced better than that night. We had such superb control over each other's bodies, such union—it was almost like making love in a very private place.

There, in Ike's office, still in my tuxedo, I heard the strains of our waltz come alive again in my mind:

> Packed her bags and eloped after midnight
> And with him with the greatest of ease
> Up from two stories high he had lowered her down
> To the ground on his flying trapeze.

I had been that man on the flying trapeze.

We were the second-to-last couple to dance. By then, any nervousness had disappeared. When I touched her to begin the dance, it was almost like I had her to myself, like there was no audience, no cops, no orchestra, and certainly no killer. I could barely tolerate my own feelings—a sexual high, a heightened erotic response so powerful, I thought I could hear my own heartbeat in the music. Or hers. It was not getting off on danger, but rather a purely emotional intoxication. I knew it wasn't the shreds of Demerol. I wanted to dance her to consummation, and if adrenaline produces an altered state, then my own body was drugging me.

I think of that moment, the beginning of any dance, when the nervousness vanishes and the music becomes the commitment, as *curtain time.* I like my job in news, with its highs of curtain time, and I guess that's why I'm in news, no matter how many offers I get to go direct shows for bigger or easier money. I live for the highs, just like when I dance with Ike: I feel like a wolf, consuming the savage pleasure in our ballroom performances for the sheer *ride* of curtain time.

Wolves. That made me remember. Fillingeri never saw our curtain time that night.

His face was way too well known for him to have taken a prominent place in guarding us at Playtime-in-Brazil. If the shooter had seen him, there would have been no action taken against Ike and me on the dance floor. So the city's top murder cop got shut out, left behind, outside in an unmarked car parked around the block from Playtime. I know that his position galled him, but even I know that Fillingeri's a good cop before he's anything. He was there to grab a killer, however he could.

The most important part of the plan we had worked out with Fillingeri—and this came from my experiences with the killer, was that if there should be shooting—Ike and I must on no account stop dancing. The fatal error made by the Big Chill had been to freeze. That same error had almost gotten me killed on the street in front of Gypsy's. Only the sudden sight of Ike rounding the corner on her Rollerblades—and then waving at her—had caused me to move just enough to escape the trueness of the killer's aim. And I didn't have any doubt I had saved Church's life once, by acting quickly to get us down on the sidewalk outside Madison Square Garden—to knock over the setup for that target practice.

No matter what happened in the ballroom this night, Ike and I had known we must not allow ourselves to interrupt the fast revolutions of the dance, or change any of my innovations, the dance movements no one could predict but Ike and me. Our only safety was in movement.

While the first contestants went through their routines, so beautiful and traditional that I was positive the judges would give them high marks, whereas they would be skeptical of our strange and new "Trapeze Waltz," Ike and I had searched the stands for faces that had pertinence in the life of the Big Chill, and perhaps in his death or Church Finnegan's. We remained hidden near the entrance to the dance floor, staring out at the audience in their seats.

The problem, which we should have anticipated, was that the lights were set up to illuminate the dance and the dancers, especially the feet of the contestants. The audience was in deep shadow. We could see the blaze of white shirtfronts on the males, the occasional sparkle of sequins or rhinestones on the females, but the faces were scarcely distinguishable from each other.

Ike recognized no one in the audience. As for me, with that sharper eye that turns mere technicians into the best TV directors, I was pretty sure I could tell who was a cop in fancy clothing and who was a dance fan. But that was all.

When our number was shown on the light board, I glanced at Ike's face, wondering what she was thinking. She was staring at me, a faraway look in her eyes. I remembered suddenly, in that moment, a story Ike had once told me in bed. It was that thing Audrey Hepburn had once said about Fred Astaire. "Was he good-looking? I think so, because charm is the best-looking thing in the world, isn't it?"

I smiled at her, hoping I'd read her right.

We did not enter the dance floor until the first notes of our waltz were struck by the orchestra, and we entered dancing, a whirl of thirty to forty measures per minute.

> *He floats through the air with the greatest of ease*
> *The daring young man on the flying trapeze*
> *His movements are graceful, all girls he does please*
> *And my love he has purloined away.*

What the judges were looking for was a progressive dance of smooth and continuous motion. I think they must never look at our faces or we'd always win waltzes, for to me, the essence of the waltz is in what happens between the partners as a result of the motion of the dance. I may be kidding myself, but it always feels like we're falling in love again when we waltz. If you're talented, you get to a point where you can sort stuff like that out. When we tango, I think she wants to kill me.

At any rate, I could tell Ike was turned on.

"The Man on the Flying Trapeze" was a risky choice for

us. It's an old song that brings to mind circuses, not stately grandeur and high romance. But the new figures I had choreographed demanded a different sort of music from the traditional ballroom Strausses. I sure as hell wasn't going to twirl Ike out and let our new dance figures get drowned while the orchestra was pouring Strauss out onto the floor in huge floods from "The Blue Danube."

About three minutes into our dance, which was flawless—even the sizzling pain in my wounded right arm, my *leading* arm, made me concentrate on Ike like a starving wolf—and which had stunned the audience into silence and immobility, the shot rang out. Only one shot. My grip on Ike's waist tightened immediately. I said, "Dance. Just dance. Remember. Faster and faster. No stopping."

There were some few murmurs from the audience, but to my surprise, most of the people did not move or panic. I believe that they thought the gunshot was part of our surprising waltz, a sort of punctuation mark to the rise and fall of the dance. The orchestra, which had been alerted to keep playing unless they themselves were in danger, did play, though as we whirled past them, I saw that their faces were grim.

I saw a piece of buckshot sparkling on the floor, the mirrored globe suspended over the dance floor continuing its smooth rotation and casting changing lights on the shiny pellet. It was only a brief glimpse, a flicker of sight, as we twirled past that spot.

I quickened our pace until specific images of the ballroom were almost impossible for me to select or isolate. But I did see one dazzling white shirtfront on the move, twisting and jumping toward us from the stands. The movement of the dance was taking us away from him. That anonymous figure in a black tuxedo vaulted onto the dance floor near the doorway where Ike and I had begun our dance, hesitated, then disappeared.

The crowd shifted impatiently as policemen and policewomen in formal attire pushed their way down through the audience and followed the gunman through the doorway.

The progress of the dance had taken us back to the orchestra, where the band leader waved frantically at us and shouted, "Hey, we can stop now, right?"

I'm not stupid.

I pulled Ike even closer to me with my wounded arm and said, "The hell! I ain't done with her yet. Play on."

Ike laughed. The beginning, the middle, and the end of appreciation.

I grinned at her, and she raised an eyebrow, smiling back. And we finished our waltz. For a long moment there was no reaction at all. Then the audience, which seemed to have been holding its breath, stood and applauded us, as if, all through the evening's contest, there had never been any other couple on the dance floor until we whirled out before the judges and the audience in a spiral of blue chiffon and a new variation on the waltz.

Only after the applause did all hell break loose. But for me, all the rushing figures were shades of memory or wisps of the original chaos that had formed the world.

The hell with that world. Ike and I were in a separate world. I gazed down at her, moving my hand to clutch her waist more fiercely, and started singing the lyrics softly to her. I tried to make every syllable clean and clear over the clouds of random noises surrounding us. I think the band, near the end of our waltz, might have stopped playing, but I can't be certain.

Now once I was happy but now I'm forlorn
Like an old coat that is tattered and torn
And left in this wide world to fret and to mourn
Betrayed by a maid in her teens.

And the dance was over. Gone. And so was what Ike and I had just shared.

Shit. Just gone. I'd been replaying somebody else's videotape in my mind. The occasional waltz is the most painful, powerful, and pleasurable reminder of the continuous progress that had been total union with this beautiful woman.

That's over for now—until the next waltz.

Fillingeri then had custody of another sawed-off shotgun, a twin of the one I'd found in Madison Square Garden. And when the crowd had cleared, our sound tech, knowing exactly what to look for, had quickly located the blip of the needle on his mixer and another *shhh* sound. But this time there was no knife. No one was hurt.

Three officers had been assigned the task of keeping an eye on the dance floor—I mean the floor itself—and all three swore that they saw no knife there and that none of the crowd spilling onto the floor stooped to pick anything up.

I thought we had to conclude with certainty now that the *shhh* noise was somehow linked to the firing of the gun. But in the absence, again, of a knife. I didn't think we had done anything to establish that there was only one killer, someone who not only blasted the basketball court with a shotgun but also managed to deliver a fatal stab wound to the man known as the Big Chill—from that one position in the stands at the Garden. The *shhh* noise, as far as I was concerned, could not imply a weapons system that delivers a knife. There was no knife. And apparently there never was.

The music had faded from my mind completely. It was late, and time for facts. The chief fact was that Fillingeri and the other cops had not caught up with our shooter in the tuxedo.

I felt hollow. The euphoria was gone.

I rose slowly from the chair, putting too much pressure on my right arm and not caring much about the resulting shower of fire that ran down the arm.

"Screw the pain," I said. "Screw the goddam pain."

I left, closing Ike's door all the way, and went on to my office. I lay down on my couch, knowing I should try to sleep. We had a two-hour television show to get on the air in a little more than six hours.

What I had seen in Ike's eyes kept running through my mind, and the song's lyrics blurred together:

> She floats through the air with the greatest of ease
> You'd think her a man on the flying trapeze
> Her movements are graceful, all men she does please
> But her love she has purloined away.

I got up and took some Tylenol.

TWENTY-FOUR

THE PHONE woke me up at five o'clock that morning.

I was cold, headachy, but as far as I could tell, my right arm was still an arm. It was a little difficult to move and felt heavy, with an eerie sensation that things were rolling around and rubbing against each other under the skin when I shifted position, but I didn't scream in agony.

In fact, the worst part about that arm was the wrinkled sleeve of my dress shirt. It looked like I'd used the sleeve to wrap fish.

I reached for the phone with my left arm.

"This is Abagnarro."

"They found the van in the East River."

"What van?"

"Wild Bill's Traveling Target Range and Snake Oil Wagon. What van do you think I mean? The van that was used so somebody could ambush you with a shotgun outside of Gypsy's."

"Ike?"

"Abby, did you take more Demerol?"

"No. I'm hallucinating on Tylenol."

"You should really see a doctor."

"You know I don't have a doctor. That's a woman thing, having a doctor. Guys just rub soil in their wounds."

"Where'd you find enough soil in Manhattan to treat your whole arm?"

"Easy. I dusted my apartment."

"Don't you want to know about the van?"

I yawned, not on purpose. I felt funny talking to her. I mean, after that waltz, and my replay of it, and what I wanted it to have been, and here she was talking business.

"Tell me about the van," I said courageously.

"It had the keys in it."

"Anybody in the driver's seat, holding on to the keys?"

"Not a soul. No soul, no gun, no nuthin' but what Chrysler put in there. Except I don't suppose Chrysler included the dirty water."

"How'd you find out? Fillingeri camping in your office?"

"I get around. It moved overnight on the AP wire. "Abby?"

"Hmmm?"

"The wire stories about Playtime-in-Brazil all mention your new dance figure. They've even been calling it 'The Trapeze Waltz.'"

"It was nice, Ike. I don't care what people call it. You liked it, didn't you?"

"Yes." There was a hesitation. "I've been liking it the whole time we practiced. It's very geometric and precise."

Geometric and precise.

Not "overpoweringly romantic" or "sizzling with sex appeal." Geometric and precise. That was BS if ever I heard it.

"Do we have any pictures of the van being hauled out of the river?"

"You won't like 'em much, Abby, but I'm happy to have them. It's amateur video, and we didn't have to compromise our budget or our reputations by putting out any money to buy the tape. The guy offered it to us *gratis.*"

"I wonder why the amateur guy didn't offer his video to ABC—or anybody with a bigger audience."

"You're forgetting we are now 'anybody.' But this Good Samaritan photographer said it had to do with NTB being the victims in this crime spree. Very nice man. He said it was just like the media to make a big deal out of the Big Chill's death and practically ignore the death of Church Finnegan. He said he thought we'd remember that this killer got Church, too."

"The media are sensationalist buggers, all right."

"That we are. Can you come to the control room right now and take a gander at the van stuff?"

I looked down at my tux. I wished I'd changed my clothes. The Man on the Flying Trapeze had come down in the world and looked more like the Man Who Isn't on Speaking Terms with His Dry Cleaner.

"Yeah. Ike, you're not going to lead with them recovering the van, are you?"

"No, we're still going with Miami, which the bureau down there is now spelling M-A-I-M-I. Get it?"

"I didn't smoke so much Tylenol that I'm incapable of understanding a dumb joke. I'll be right there."

"Abby?"

"I'm here."

"How's your arm?"

"Just splendid. Well, maybe 'splendid' is going too far. Let's just say it's still working, but I'd rather not work with it."

"Abby, are you sure you don't need to see a doctor?"

"Yes. I'm not going anywhere near a doctor. They're trying to mess with my mind. I'm on my way to the control room."

There was some booing and hissing from the folks in the control room when I strolled in wearing my wrinkled tux. Ike gave me a funny look.

That's not the way she looked last night, I thought. She'd changed back into Ike the News Boss. Ike, the newshound from Hell. Ike, the terror of network journalism. Which was all probably more than the workings of my groggy brain. She really can work from different compartments of her brain when she has to. That's part of the problem, part of why I can't get around her defenses. Some bigmouth—me, for example—ought to tell her.

But then she smiled. *There's the look again,* I thought.

She was dressed all in white: a fluffy white sweater, which made me want to pet her like my faithful poodle, and tight white jeans, which made me want to say, *What's the deal on this earning-a-living junk? Let's go to your apartment, which also used to be my apartment, and fool around.*

I took my seat at the director's console, vetted the amateur video, pronounced it usable, and got ready to look into the electronic mirror: We had sound and video—professional—of the shooting episode at Playtime-in-Brazil, including a murky shot of the white shirtfront and dark pants legs vaulting out of the audience and escaping through the dance floor doorway. Whoever it was, was tall.

"Who do we know that's tall?" I said, to the control room at large.

One of the technicians laughed. "Tom Hitt on stilts."

Except for that crack, nobody bothered to answer me right away. But after a long silence, Ike said, "How tall is Angel Rosenbloom?"

"By golly. I'm not sure. I've only seen her sitting down. Wait, on the video she didn't look so tall next to her date, the Big Chill. But then, who would?"

"I never thought to look at her vital statistics on that fax Dennis had in here. We should find out how tall she is."

"Great idea, Ike. The Taxi and Limousine Commission offices open at nine. If you can't wait until then, why don't you just phone her and ask?"

Ike gave me a nasty look. No more Ms. Trapeze Partner. "What's her number? I suppose she gave it to you."

"She didn't give me the time of day. Look it up in the phone book."

"Oh. Look up *Rosenbloom?* In New York City. Good thinking. Got any idea which borough to start with?"

"She sounded like she was from Brooklyn."

"That doesn't mean she lives there now. Besides, I'm not calling her up before the sun even rises and ask her how tall she is." Ike picked up the phone, dialed an in-house number, and gave instructions to an intern to hunt down one Angel Rosenbloom and find out how tall she was.

I'd had such bad luck with my Angel idea that I took it upon myself to stick my neck out with a harmless question.

"Do we have any statement from the cops?"

"Yeah," Ike said, starting to run her hands through her hair and stopping just in time when she realized she had braided it. "Too bad it's Dennis. He and his driver were the only cops not in evening clothes. The captain in a penguin suit would have been pretty neat television."

I screened the Fillingeri tape. The only bite from it we'd use, I assumed, was the dynamite insight that the Iceman's killer was still at large and probably gunning for me, his presumed motive the fact that it was pretty well known that I'd gotten a look at the shooter in Madison Square Garden and needed to be eliminated on account of the scrapbook I was supposedly carrying around in my head, which was a lie on my part.

I left the technical director and an A.D. with orders to requisition the art we needed from the Graphics Department, dictated by the editorial content of our news stories, and told them to spell Fillingeri's name right before we supered it across television screens in America's grumpy morning faces.

"Ike," I said, grabbing the tape of the waltz, "may I have a private word with you?"

She looked up from her computer screen, but her fingers kept typing.

"Why?"

"Humor me."

"Oh, all right." She finished what she was typing and pushed the "send" button. She exited her mail program but left the machine on.

As we walked together from the control room, I heard some remark—which I ignored—about "the Mr. and the Mrs." Ike ignored it, too.

As we walked around the tube, we didn't seem to have anything to say to each other more personal than Ike's "Where to?" Not chitchat of really amorous caliber.

"Your office," I said. *God, that's romantic,* I thought. "My beta player is being temperamental again."

"You're the director. Why don't you just get it fixed?"

"The director doesn't get his gadgets fixed. I've ordered a new one. It doesn't even come out of your budget."

"Boy, do you ever have the life."

"Yeah, it's great. I'm blessed. I get a new beta player. I think I'll write a TV movie-of-the-week about my life."

She laughed. I didn't.

She unlocked her office and we went in. That is to say, we threaded our way across her carpet, littered with all her news-junk, which now included a basketball, which I hadn't noticed earlier that night. I stooped and one-handed it off the floor, just one of my many talents. The ball was signed by all the New York Knicks—with one glaring omission.

"Where'd you get this?" I said.

"The Garden press office sent it over."

"Do you want it?"

"Not especially. Why?"

"Gimme."

"Take it. It doesn't mean anything to me."

I cradled the ball in my left arm, handed her the tape, and lowered myself tenderly to her couch without reinjuring my arm any more than could be handled by minor screaming and writhing, which I kept manfully to myself.

She inserted the tape in her player. "So what do you want to see? How the waltz looks from the outside?"

"I want to see if I can make any connection between last night's gunman and the blur I saw in the Garden the night the Big Chill got it." I thought hard. "Tuesday."

"Good luck." She pressed the play button and we watched. The waltz was different from the outside looking in. I thought it was beautiful.

"Ike, it never occurred to me until now. Did we win?"

She shook her head, apparently disgusted. "There was one

more couple, remember? After us. They didn't get to dance. They get a separate chance tonight before the same judges."

"Well, that just sucks."

"I sure hope *they* do."

I sat up. "Pause it right there."

"Here?" She paused the tape.

I bent forward, the basketball in my lap, my right arm resting on it, and squinted at the picture. "I wish the lights were better."

"We could hardly have used our frezzies or HMIs. Nobody could have danced while blinded by those things."

I squinted some more at the picture. "It's just a blur. Only this time it's a blur in a tux. Whoever that is in the tux came ready to play the right sport and wearing his game face."

"Game face?"

"Slang. Means 'intending to win,' or something like that. You've got your game face on if you're serious and concentrating and focused."

"Abby," she said, putting her face close to mine and gazing into my eyes, "you're wearing your game face right now."

"Maybe. But I'm on the injured list, Coach Mary Ellen Tygart. Anyone ever tell you that dancing with you is like holding an angel?"

Her voice was a whisper. "Not in those words. But you told me, Abby."

If it hadn't been for the basketball and my sore right arm, I'd have grabbed her right there.

By the time I deposited the basketball on the floor, she'd moved away. Proof that sports do contribute to bad relations between the sexes.

She was restarting the tape.

"Back it up," I said. "Right to the gunshot."

She fiddled with the remote and got the tape cued up. "Ready?"

"Go."

She pushed "play."

"Stop it."

The tape froze.

"What's that?"

"What?"

I stood without much grace and put my finger on the screen, on a silvery streak running across the picture, above the shoulders of that striking couple dancing the Trapeze Waltz.

"You're the technical expert," she said. "You tell me. It just looks like, you know, a flaw or camera shake."

"That's not camera shake."

"Then what is it?"

"I think it's a knife."

"They didn't find a knife."

"Okay. Then it's a magic knife. And the murderer is Houdini."

"You can't tell from that junk on the screen that you're seeing a knife. Can you?"

"Maybe you can't, but I can."

"I'll take your word for it, Maestro."

"That's why I get paid the big bucks, not to bring up an uncomfortable topic in front of a peon working the editorial side. We can enlarge that shot on an ADO. We ought to anyway, to show Fillingeri."

"To make up for stealing the Big Chill's Death-in-the-Garden tape right from under Dennis's nose?"

"It's a sort of penance for being a bad boy, yeah. For now, though, follow the trajectory of the silvery thing you see. Where would that knife land?"

"Assuming it's a knife, it looks like it was supposed to land in your forehead. We moved just in time."

"But where would it go, having missed my head?"

She cocked her head to one side and studied the frozen picture on the screen. She pressed "play" and watched. She paused the tape again. "It looks like it might have hit the floor—see? Right at the edge of the orchestra's platform. But the cops didn't find a knife, Abby."

"Then the knife somehow disappeared on its own."

"I suppose you think it sprouted legs?"

"Dammit. I think it did exactly what it did in the Big Chill's heart."

"What?"

"Went up in smoke. Vamoosed. Scrammed. Without anyone touching it. Took a powder. Left. Vanished. Melted into thin air."

"Melted."

"Melted. I said that?"

"Melted. Yes, Abby, you said *melted*. If it was made out of ice, it would melt and the police wouldn't find it on the dance floor."

"But the M.E. would find water in the Iceman's heart, right? I mean, melted ice. You know what I mean."

"Let's call Dennis."

"At this hour?" It was 5:37 a.m. "He won't be there."

"Home number," she said.

"Home number, home number. What's he got that's so great that you have his home number?"

"*Shhh.*"

She grabbed her phone and dialed. It apparently took about ten rings for her to get him on the line.

"Dennis? Finally. Where were you? Oh. Sorry I asked. Listen. Do you have the M.E.'s report handy?"

At home? I mouthed.

I maneuvered myself back onto the couch and picked up her other phone. Fillingeri was talking.

"...what I remember. And that's it. A stab wound in the heart, no stabbing implement found present in the wound, two pieces of buckshot in the right leg."

"Did the M.E. find any water in the heart?"

"Water? Water?"

I could hear Fillingeri rustling around in his sheets. I wished he hadn't.

"Ike," he said, with exaggerated patience, "why would he find water? You mean H-two-O, I assume?"

"Just tell me."

"Fuck. I'm gonna put you on hold."

We waited, close to four minutes. He came back on the line, but I could hear that the three of us had been joined by another party on another phone line.

"No water," a stranger's voice said. "Only the fluids you'd expect to find in a heart. I'm assuming you mean tap water, Captain. We took sections of the heart. We did not find any of the cellular disruption that would be present if water had been introduced into the tissue."

There was a silence. Ike broke it.

"Dennis, who's on the line with us? How come he's so sure about everything?"

"Ask him yourself. David Burns. He's an assistant M.E."

"Oh." Ike scratched her head.

"Listen, Ike," Fillingeri said, and I could hear more sheet noises, "is this one of those stupid riddles or something, where you're sitting around a campfire and you tell stories about a knife made from ice? Wouldn't that be neat? An ice knife killing the Big Chill?"

Ike held the phone away from her ear and gave the thing a dirty look. She put it back against her head.

"Yes, Dennis. I'm sorry I bothered you."

"Oh, it's no bother. I've been asleep at least two hours. Call me any time you have a kindergarten guess."

"It wasn't such a stupid guess," Ike said huffily.

There was a polite sound on the line, something like "er, uh, well, may I..."

Fillingeri growled into the phone. "Spit it out, David. You're the medical expert. What are you trying to say?"

The A.M.E. spoke. "It *was* actually quite a stupid guess, about a knife made from ice, I mean. I've heard that old story a million times. Sometimes it's an icicle, sometimes a knife. It could kill, but nobody'd get away with it. The autopsy would always show the icicle in a melted form. It wouldn't evaporate. There'd be a puddle in the heart that we'd see almost right away. Unless emergency resuscitation, uh, smooshed the stuff around. And then we'd still see cell disruption. Can't be done."

"Forget it, Ike," Fillingeri said. "You heard him. The cells didn't show water. I got woken up for this children's story hour? Ike, why don't you call me when you've got something for adults to chew on?"

"You bet I will," Ike said, not cordially. "Do you have anything better to suggest?"

"No. No. No. A thousand times, no. The NYPD's got a big load of nothing."

"Is the A.M.E. still on the line?"

"Right here."

"Can you tell me if the autopsy showed anything odd about the heart itself ? I mean, odd on its own, before the stabbing?"

Burns spoke up, bright and alert. "Irrelevant. The stabbing was and is the official cause of death. No contributing factors."

"You're evading my question."

Fillingeri snapped, "Burns? You have anything or not?"

Heavy sigh from the A.M.E.'s end of the line. "A real funny aorta, since I'm speaking with a layperson." When Ike heard that "layperson" stuff, she ground her teeth. "Stretched, you might say. It could have gone at any time. But it didn't. The stabbing killed the basketball player."

"What was wrong with the aorta?" Ike said.

I heard the A.M.E. flipping a piece of paper.

"It's called Marfan's syndrome. You see it in unusually tall people mostly. Long arms, long legs. It affects the skeleton, the eyes sometimes, the heart almost always. It's congenital, and gets progressively worse as the body ages."

"That's what killed Celtics captain Reggie Lewis, isn't it?" Ike said. "His heart just sort of ripped itself apart?"

"Yes, indeed. And Hank Gathers of Loyola. And women's

volleyball star Flo Hyman. You might be interested to know that medical detectives are now certain that Abe Lincoln had the disease. But Gathers and Hyman didn't get any help from a shotgun or a knife. They just keeled over as a direct result of Marfan's syndrome. We've studied this carefully. For your very definite information, the syndrome did not cause the death of Archibald Tyrone Thorpe."

"The syndrome didn't even contribute to his death?"

"I already said that."

"Somebody with Marfan's. They shouldn't be playing basketball, should they?"

"Absolutely not. They should be in a Barcalounger, watching PBS. Physical exertion can and will rip the aorta. Poof. You're dead in a hurry."

"That's really interesting. Dennis, are you still there? Isn't that interesting?"

"Fascinating, Ike. Listen: Marfan's had nothing to do with the death of Archie Thorpe. The funny aorta is in the official report being typed, but only because the M.E. lets nothing by."

"Don't hang up yet. I don't suppose you've made any progress finding the person who tried to interrupt our dance last night, have you?"

"No, but we found the goddamned van. You want a miracle?"

"God! You don't have to jump down my throat. I was just wondering if you had a theory yet about who shot that gun at Playtime."

"Just this—I think it was Harry Houdini. He didn't have an alibi for those hours last night, and neither did anyone else in the city. Yeah, yeah, we've talked to the widow, the coach, et cetera."

"Houdini. How odd. That's what Abby said."

"What Abagnarro says." Those rustling sheet noises were really bothering me now. "He have any other pearls?"

Ike's eyes twinkled. "As a matter of fact, yes. He wants to know how tall Angel Rosenbloom is."

"What for? Is he buying her a new door?"

"I don't know about that, but from what we can see on the tape NTB shot last night, and which you have a copy of, the gun person was tall."

I heard Fillingeri put his receiver down on something hard, and that was followed by the rustling of something that wasn't sheets. Maybe a crocodile was in his bed. When he came back on the line, he sounded like he was playing a game where nobody had told him the rules.

"Angel Rosenbloom, taxi driver and sometime escort to a certain seven-foot basketball player before he was dead, is five seven.

"Then, unless she was wearing elevator shoes, I don't think she was at Playtime-in-Brazil with a gun last night."

"So?" Fillingeri was getting just irritated enough to light the fuse that would explode the phones in our hands. "Who said she was?"

"Nobody. Hold on a minute." Ike covered the mouthpiece of her phone with her hand. "Abby, that blur you saw in Madison Square Garden, when the Big Chill died. How tall was it? Really tall?"

I closed my eyes and thought. And tried to picture that fragment of darkness I'd seen. I pictured it against the outlines of the tunnel leading out of the arena. I opened my eyes.

"Yes. A *really* tall blur."

Ike took her hand off the phone.

"Dennis? Abby remembers something about the Garden gunman."

Fillingeri snorted, or at least made a noise that sounded like an animal with a prominent nose. "Such as? Something really distinctive, like a tattoo of a Buddha drinking milk?"

"No. The person was tall."

"Dagnabit, Ike! You call me at this hour, I think you've got something for me. Shit. Eight million people in this town, some of 'em have to be tall. Thanks for the tip."

TWENTY-FIVE

NATURALLY, NTB News was the only broadcast outfit present at the Playtime-in-Brazil shooting. (It's like an unwritten law that we don't alert CBS and company when we're sneaking around.) *Morning Watch* broke the pictures, if not the story, of the Trapeze Waltz. Granted, our pictures didn't show much of any crime, but by jimminy, they were nice pictures to start any day with. Our dance—the little we showed of it—probably woke up more viewers than the shooting story itself or a couple million cups of coffee across America. I felt like applauding—they looked like such a *nice* couple—and that dance! Let me just say that Fred and Ginger would have been pleased with us.

Power was still out over much of Miami, so *that* market couldn't get the Trapeze Waltz mixed in with its salsa rhythms. The hurricane cleanup and the long lines for food and water in that city were the big stories of the morning, much more consequential but a lot less pretty than what Ike and I had personally done to provide news for the early audience. I thought it was a shame the people of Miami didn't have power because going without power makes life miserable, but it was also a shame to deny them the dance pictures. Miamians needed some entertainment in the midst of all those tears and all that rage and all that unfathomable despair.

And they should have seen Ike's dress.

After J.D. signed us off the air at 8:58:30, Hannah's voice came rumbling into the control room, and I looked up at the studio monitor.

"Abby," she said, and I cringed. "When your arm is feeling better, let's not forget that we had some plans."

Hannah couldn't hear the control room from the newsdesk

in the studio unless we were stupid enough to open our keys—
not that it would have made any difference because her ego
is so well padded that direct insults simply bounce off it like
hail on a tin roof—but the ribbing I took from the staff was
clearly directed at me only because everyone else was wary
of messing with Hannah. Look where messing around had
gotten me—*lunch*.

On the monitor I saw her snatch a crumpled pack of Virginia Slims from her jacket pocket and head for the hills.

I felt Ike's hand on my shoulder.

That was quickly followed by additional personal commentary from the staff as they bolted for their offices. What exactly
is hanging on the grapevine around here? I asked myself. Are
they saying I'm dumb enough to service the voracious anchor-
sow while I mend relations with my ex-wife? Or are they just
saying I'm plain stupid where women are concerned but with
the strength of ten?

"Abby," Ike said, and I was rather surprised to hear a voice
other than my own suddenly register in my ears. "Are you up
to another trip to the Garden?"

"Do we get to wear bulletproof vests?"

Ike sighed. "I sure wish we had a couple."

"With sleeves."

She smiled sympathetically but looked preoccupied. I rose
and grasped her elbow, mostly for something to hang on to
rather than from any gentlemanly impulses, and steered her
out of the control room.

"Why is someone trying to kill you, Abby?"

I blinked. "You're kidding. You know as well as I do that
the Big Chill's killer thinks I can identify him."

I closed the control room door behind us.

"Maybe you *can* identify him."

"Bull. All I saw was a blur. Period." We passed a couple
of big-eared *Evening Watch* producers in the tube. I smiled
wanly at them and leaned ostentatiously on Ike. When they
were twenty feet or so down the hall, I straightened up and

told Ike, "I wouldn't know the difference between the killer and the Eiffel Tower, except that one of them is in Paris."

"Describe what you saw."

"Blurry and dark. That's all. Now, wait—come to think of it, I guess now I have to add *tall.*"

"Dark? You said 'dark.' You mean dark-skinned?"

"No, just dark. Dark all over."

"Maybe wearing a dark covering of some sort?"

"Ike, all I saw was a blur."

"The Garden maintenance staff wears dark coveralls. Dark blue. I noticed that on our first foray. Remember that crowd at the employees' entrance when Church was shot on the street? Some of them were wearing the coveralls. With zippers. In and out quickly. That kind of garment."

"They probably don't have any choice about what they wear. Ike, what are you trying to prove?"

She flipped both hands over, palms up, and looked at me. "Don't you think the shooter has to be connected somehow to the Garden? Or do you think he or she is just some florist from Queens who's gone nuts from riding the subway with the rats—and the Big Chill's death is one of those murders that will never be solved?"

"Ike, I'll go with the only scenario that makes sense to me. We got into the Garden okay without a connection inside, but most people wouldn't think they could. I mean, most people wouldn't chance a murder as carefully timed as the Big Chill's if they weren't sure they could be in the right spot at the right time. Correct? So forget the florist. It was an insider."

She nodded. "That's what I think. And there's the van the shooter drove to come after you in front of your mom's restaurant. That van belonged to the Garden. Somebody with access had to have taken it. They had keys. That van was not hot-wired."

We stopped at her office, and she opened the door. I kept yapping and followed her in.

"But to continue with this florist idea," I said, "we also

know the killer can't be an anonymous nobody fan-type who'll never be seen again, or they wouldn't be so afraid of me suddenly putting two and two together. I can't possibly do any math with an unknown quantity. It has to be someone I'd recognize on sight.''

"Right. So we should be looking for a known quantity, a quantity with a motive.''

"Bottom line, Ike: the killer has to be someone I've seen at least once in my life, for a long enough period of time to log him or her in my memory and therefore identify later. I can spot a New York Knick and give you his height and the number on his shirt and what position he plays and his stats for the last year, but I don't see how the guys on that court could have killed their star center. Now that I've had a taste of buckshot under my skin, I know I wouldn't set myself up to be on the receiving end of it again. That's why Hannah's got to be right about human nature. She just had the reason wrong. There had to be only one killer simply because—answer this question—who could convince a confederate to stand down there on the court and take some buckshot before stabbing the Big Chill? The pattern of spread on the shot was so wide, there was no way to predict who would get hit and in what part of the anatomy. It hurts to think about it. And anyway, we know what happened: every man on that court did get shot. Therefore, none of those men was in any conspiracy with the shooter. Athletes like that take plenty good care of their million-dollar bodies. So I rule out a conspiracy. The Big Chill was stabbed—the M.E. says so. But the man was not stabbed by anyone on that basketball court.''

"Then the knife had to have been a projectile, thrown by someone *you* could conceivably identify.''

"Not thrown. You'd have to be Superman to throw a knife that hard and that accurate to penetrate the chest. That thing went in all of five inches, according to the M.E.''

"After seeing what you pointed out on the tape of the Trapeze Waltz, I've been thinking about that. And I might have an idea, which I'll explain. But first, how many people fit those criteria? You know—you have seen them before or since the shooting, they have good access to the Garden, they had a reason to murder the Big Chill. Oh, and don't forget it's some-one tall. And somebody not on the basketball court, which rules out all of the New York Knicks and Chicago Bulls, doesn't it?''

''Yes, ma'am.'' I held up my left hand and raised a finger for the name of each person I thought fit our composite mur-derer: ''Mrs. Marie Celeste Iceman Thorpe, Amazon of the Amazon, maybe royalty way back when, but now, and much better, heiress *du jour*. Fedex Parker, protector of rain forests and public mauler of the dreaded Big Chill. Knicks head coach Max Hall, grandfather and racist. I'm going to put Sam Rice, the team doctor, in the pool just because my mother said he was the killer. That's four. I assume we do not include Angel Rosenbloom, former lover and current hater of the star center, because she's not tall enough.''

''That's about what we have to work with.''

''Unless, like Fillingeri, you think we should count each of eight million New Yorkers, skipping, of course, the florists.'' I picked up the horseshoe puzzle from her coffee table and started playing with it, trying to put the ring back on.

''That's baloney,'' Ike said, pulling out the rubber band that kept her braid in place. She rubbed her head with both hands, separating the braided strands. The result was a pretty sort of crimped look, like out of the forties. Or maybe I mean the thirties. ''Dennis doesn't believe this was a random killing. You just don't understand his sarcasm.''

I folded the horseshoes back against each other, jiggled the links in the puzzle, twisted them, and slid the ring onto one side. I grabbed both horseshoes and pulled them away from each other. The ring was back on.

''Hey! I did it,'' I said, holding it out to Ike. ''Look.''

She had a weird look in her green and blue eyes. ''You might just have done it. You put the hardware together.''

"That's sort of what I said."

"I'm not talking about that puzzle thing. Put it down and listen."

"I can listen and hold it."

"Oh, have it your way. We're a couple of brick-brains."

"I like to think so."

She glared at me. "The gunman deliberately left the gun on the stairs at Madison Square Garden, right?"

"So?"

"But there was no knife."

"So?"

"He shot Church Finnegan on the street, but the cops didn't find a gun there."

"So?"

"But they found a knife in Church's chest."

"So?"

"And whoever-it-was shot you on the street in front of Gypsy's, and I saw the gun."

"So?"

"And last night the cops found the gun at Playtime-in-Brazil. You think there was a knife. But nobody found a knife."

"So?"

"Abby, is this the parrot joke?"

"What?"

"You keep saying the same thing."

"Sorry."

"Where was I? Oh. The weapons are never found together. One or the other is always missing."

"So? Oops. I mean, what are you getting at?"

"We have to put the hardware together, like you just did with that puzzle. Abby, let's forget the killer and look for the hardware. As we say in Missouri, the best way to get fertilizer is to follow a horse with a shovel. Hardware, Abby, hardware."

"And so we go to the Garden. Is that why you asked me to go, because you figured this out about the hardware?"

"No, I only thought of the hardware when you put that puzzle back together. I wanted to go to the Garden because it was home ground for the first killing, and the shotgun attack on us and Church, and for the van. But now we have a really specific goal. We want some hardware. Look at it this way: If anyone, like the cops, found suspicious hardware in the Garden, it would either implicate no one in particular or one of several people with motives. It wouldn't point directly at one person. The Garden would be a safe storage place."

"Correction. A *big* storage place. Are you proposing we search the entire building? I'll start down in the subway and you can start at the top floor—we can meet in the middle, say at the basketball court, next May."

She got her hands in her hair and started pulling. "I'm not going to yell at you, Abby, because of the fact that you are a wounded person who cannot be held accountable for all of his faculties, but doesn't it make sense to concentrate on the offices and locker rooms and all that smelly stuff on the ground floor? All the other areas of the Garden are somehow public and they'd be cleaned on a regular basis."

"You know, you're right about my faculties. What's wrong with the NYPD's faculties? Why doesn't Fillingeri get a warrant and do this? He didn't get shot in the arm. I did and I resent it. Fillingeri should search the Garden."

She narrowed her eyes at me. "He probably already has."

"What makes you think we'll have any better luck than he did?"

"Because he was looking for a knife or ammunition or a gun."

"What are we looking for?"

"Houdini's magic trunk. Let me just make one phone call."

"Who to?"

She raised her eyebrows. "My gynecologist, if you must know."

"Not again? Do you call her on a daily basis? Are you preggers?"

"Not likely, Dumbo. I've got a question about body fluids."

"Yucky stuff?"

"Scientific stuff. God! Men are such weenies."

I left her to her yucky stuff and retreated to my office to get my skates. I didn't need Ike to tell me that my police escort, waiting for me down in the lobby of the Emerald City, was not going to be invited along on our raid. They were on foot. Therefore, we would be on wheels.

I managed to mangle myself into my old maroon parka, which contrasted unpleasantly with my tuxedo trousers. The skates were no problem for me to handle with an injured arm. I've got the new Velcro fasteners—skates designed for injured and maimed folks who, because they belong in psycho wards, want to cruise around the streets of New York City on Rollerblades.

Ike was outfitted by the time I returned to her office, the yucky stuff apparently all taken care of between her and her body-fluids pal.

Ike looked really cute, with her black parka over her white jeans and sweater. Her skates, which used to be white before all the weather she'd slopped through, were sort of pearly gray, but her pink laces looked bright and clean. Since I was now in the detective business, I deduced she'd put new laces in her skates. V. I. Abagnarro.

We took the elevator directly to the lowest level this time, without stopping at the front lobby, to repeat our previous escape from the cops. How things change. Then they had a warrant for my arrest. Now they were my nursemaids.

Never let it be said that Captain Dennis Fillingeri is stupid. Damned if we didn't skate out onto the loading dock and almost knock over two uniformed cops waiting there, like two pins at the end of a bowling alley. If we hadn't applied the brakes in time, we'd have scored a spare.

"Excuse me," one of the cops said. Excuse him? We were the ones with the bad manners. "You're Abagnarro."

"That's what some people call me, sonny."

"Oh yeah?" He looked confused. And freckled.

"Yeah. But some people call me the daring young man on the flying trapeze." I grabbed Ike's hand and we turned together in a smooth circle, picked up speed, and went flying down and over the short flight of rusty green stairs to the sidewalk.

The cop started down the stairs and yelled after us. "Where are you going?"

"To the other side of the Big Top. We'll be back. We always come back."

We slipped into the river of traffic flowing down 9th Avenue and had great luck with the lights. The street, while damp, was fairly clean if you looked out for the pothole wells dotted around—'Bladers call them "skater craters."

The sun was shining, the air had warmed up to forty-two degrees, which I knew because the MONY clock's version of the temperature is always correct when it's working at all, and if I tucked my right arm across my lower back, I felt pretty good.

Ike was laughing. "Just imagine. If anyone didn't know you were the King of Rollerblades, they might think you were crazy. Those cops are probably really worried about you. And their captain's wrath."

"More likely they're hoping I'll get shot."

"They'll have to tell Dennis, or whoever is in charge of Operation Abagnarro."

"Oh, I hope so," I said, a big grin on my face.

Those two cops from the loading dock hadn't even tried, after a couple of automatic steps, to follow us. We were flying.

The great thing about Rollerblading in Manhattan is that you really are in the driver's seat. If you've got well-developed thigh muscles, good peripheral vision, and the kind of nerve it takes to live in New York in the first place, you can name the game when you skate the streets. That's why everyone else on wheels of any other kind hates us. Traffic is meaningless to us, we don't give a damn about double-parked cars and blocked lanes, and we can pretty much thumb our noses at all the new laws that are supposed to be cracking down on 'Bladers in the Big Apple. We are tough dudes to enforce.

Even though city hall is after us lately, they'll never catch up. We own the streets, and I don't think even a cop on a horse could pull me over if I didn't want him to. Plus, there's this advantage: We don't have license plates, so once we're gone, we're gone. You can't track a 'Blader through the DMV.

DMV? BFD. That's my attitude.

We cut over to 7th on 36th Street and cruised down to the Garden. The pedestrian traffic wasn't bad yet since it was a couple hours before the lunch marauders would come out, and we controlled the sidewalks, too.

"What do you think?" I said. "The back door?"

We stood looking up at the massive building. It takes up an entire block of Manhattan real estate. Up the stairs and past the plaza, I could see people inside already, lined up to get tickets at the box-office windows.

"I like the idea of joining that herd," Ike said, pointing a finger at the ticket lines. "Safety in numbers. The Garden just might have a better grasp of security at the employees' entrance after the prank we pulled."

"Not to mention the fact that we almost got gunned down just to dramatize our prank. Probably called a certain amount of attention to that door."

"That, too."

Skating up to the main entrance of Madison Square Garden is a cinch. The stairs are wide, and the raised plaza is smooth, and it's neat to look down on all the pedestrians on the sidewalk. It's kind of a nice metaphor for how low-life pedestrians rate compared to wizards on Rollerblades.

There aren't any signs posted about skating in the Garden (I mean, if you're a civilian; I'm not talking about Wayne

Gretzky). But I don't think you're really supposed to engage in the sport in the halls. Ike and I stood on one of the ticket lines for a few moments, waiting. What kept us waiting was our need for the security guard who was standing by the velvet rope to go find somewhere else to stand. He was standing there, stroking that rope clumsily like it was his first date. I thought he'd never leave, and the line was moving rather quickly. *What'll we buy tickets for?* I thought.

The guard finally let go of the velvet and departed, away from us and around the curving hall, toward some unknown danger that only security guards can face. Or maybe he was just going to the john.

Ike and I cruised out of the line, slid around the rope, and followed the guard. It didn't seem likely that he had taken off only to follow his own tracks back in a hurry, so our course looked like the right and safe one.

We coasted to the elevator, summoned it, used it to take us down to the secret heart of the Garden, where the athletes get to be human before they go upstairs and turn into superbeings.

We skated out onto the gray-painted concrete floor of the locker room level.

"Well, Ike," I whispered, "what are we looking for?"

"Salt, I think."

TWENTY-SIX

As a pair of secret operatives, Ike and I immediately flunked the James Bond Superspy Clandestine-Agent Creeping-Around Urban Field Test.

We lost points right off the bat on the all-important *don't get caught* portion of the test.

Just as we skated quietly around the corner from the elevator, Ike plowed right into Fedex Parker, who smelled of ivory soap and was very natty in a conservative gray sport coat that was obviously custom-tailored. If there'd been a referee handy, I expect Ike would have been called for a personal foul. Maybe also a technical, because she was so surprised, she cussed. One little word, but it happened to be one of those words that sensitive referees frown on.

Parker caught Ike gently by her arms (better her than me) to keep her from falling and hurting herself, or maybe to prevent her from skating between his long legs and tickling him.

He gave her his boyish and very genuine *Sports Illustrated* smile and said, "You might want to watch how you trip over an NBA player, Ike."

"You know my name?" she said, bewilderment on her face, but no minxish blushes. She saves those, I think, for when somebody makes a pass at her, me included, and I don't mean a basketball pass.

"Of course I know your name. My publicist briefed me because I'm doing your show on Monday. Then I saw the television news of that waltz." He smiled again in his ferociously happy way. "I hope you won't take offense if I say you've sure got the smooth moves."

"So do you."

She's such a fibber, I thought. *She thinks basketball is for dummies who can't count higher than two.* She'd told me recently that a basket was worth only two points because that's as high as a player could make it with numbers. When I pointed out to her the three-point shot, she just said, "Big deal. Three. Two. It's the same thing." And when I further pointed out to her that the difference between three and two is one, she said, "Congratulations. Why don't you try out for the Houston Hornets?" So I felt obligated to correct her, telling her she meant the world-champion Houston *Rockets,* and she said, "Whatever. You'll notice it's not the Houston *Rocket Scientists.*"

I wondered, in that awkward moment, there in the basement of the Garden, if Ike thought Parker was so dumb that she could just come right out and say, "Did you assassinate the Big Chill?" and expect him to answer her with a full confession.

But evidently her scorn for NBA intelligence only extended to men *caught in the act* of playing the game.

He let go of her, she got her balance, and she stuck out her right hand. "It's a pleasure to meet you, Mr. Parker. I'm looking forward to having you on *Morning Watch.* Your work for charities has impressed me—as it has moved many people worldwide—especially the rain-forest project you conduct for elementary schools."

Parker's smile dimmed and his huge brown eyes took on a melancholy look. He grasped Ike's hand, and they shook.

He said, "I hope we can talk about that on Monday, on the air, but I suppose now you'll want the interview to rehash the trash. Me and the Chill."

Ike nodded at him. Up at him. "You couldn't blame me for that, could you? I haven't seen anything in the media from you on what happened Tuesday night."

"I haven't spoken with the media. I have nothing to say." The words he used are the basic mortar of the stonewall, but he said them so gently, in such a soft voice, that it was difficult for me to call up my usual reaction to that kind of attitude, which is to hope the subject swallows the lock on his tongue and forgets the first rule of No Comment, which is not to comment at all.

No Comment goes against human nature. Try it at home. At parties. Among friends.

Ike, who is practically deaf in the presence of No comment, was not going to let such an opportunity slip by. I almost expected her to yank her cell phone from her pocket and send for a camera crew while she grabbed Parker's lapel and hung on.

"Mr. Parker," she began.

"You can call me Lasalle."

"Thank you. Lasalle, everybody knows about that ten thousand dollars in cash you had with you. Will you tell me what you were planning to do that would cost that much in NBA fines?"

Parker had not had good coaching on No Comment, although he'd obviously had some. "I don't know," he said. "What I did would have depended on what the Chill himself did. But I would have got to him somehow. I think laying him out on the wood worked pretty good the last time. I guess something like that would have been about right."

That was pretty good No Comment for a comment, since it played the story his legal team would like best. He had intended to hurt the Big Chill, not kill him.

"You didn't care if you hurt him?" Ike said.

"Of course I cared! I meant to hurt him."

Ike didn't gulp or back away. "Lasalle, I'm also interested in why you left the basketball court during the warm-up on Tuesday night. You were lucky, you know, to escape buckshot wounds."

"Not like this man standing next to you, huh?"

Ike's hand flew to her mouth. "Oh, I'm sorry." She nipped at my arm with her other hand—my wounded *right* arm, for God's sake. "This is our show's director."

Parker faced me like he was sizing me up, or, in this case, *down*. "You're Abagnarro. I heard about you getting shot— bet that hurts like hell."

"It's not too bad," I lied. I might have wanted some sympathy, but not from a surefire future Hall of Famer and maybe the best guard ever to play the game. "I have to ask, or I can ask you on Monday—what's the secret, the real lowdown, on your three-point miracle shots? I mean, you can really give that ball a two-dollar cab ride."

Ike tried to scorch me with her eyes for asking an S.G.Q. question when she was after murder secrets.

Parker laughed out loud. "Miracle shots. That's about right. You know what it is? Zen."

"Zen?"

"I meditate before every game. Plus four times a day. The body's not smooth if the mind is wrinkled."

I don't know much about Zen, but what he said sounded like the real thing to me. I mean, that's the way they *talk*.

Ike poked her nose into my education. "Lasalle, is that why you left the court during the warm-up? To meditate?"

He nodded.

The next question, he must have answered a thousand times.

Ike said, as if she just couldn't help herself, "How tall are you?"

There was that famous grin, back on his face. "I'm an official six feet six inches tall, Ike."

"Official? What does that mean?"

"I'm six four," he said. "In life. But not in the game program." He grinned. "It's okay. I *play* tall."

I kept waiting for him to ask us what we were doing there in the Garden, and then it struck me that I could ask him what *he* was doing there.

So I did. "What are you doing here today, Lasalle?"

"I'm allowed. I like being around the court. And I can't go home."

"You can't?"

It happens this way a lot. You get somebody talking, and "No Comment" might as well be "No Problem."

"I was going to leave New York last night," he said, reaching into the inside pocket of his expensive jacket and extracting a piece of paper. I'd seen paper just like that not all that long ago. "This is a restraining order or something. The cops say I'm needed for questioning." He flapped the document against his hand. Big hand. "It's like a request for my cooperation."

Ike sputtered. "How come I don't know about this? I haven't even heard a rumor. I'm intimate with this story. I'll kill Dennis Fillingeri. I'll mow him down. I'll grind his bones. Abby, did you hear about this piece of news?"

I shook my head. "Negative."

"That's because my lawyer said I wouldn't want to brag about it," Parker said, smiling. "Guess I just did, though, huh? You can't quote me, however, because all I did was show you a piece of paper. I didn't say any words."

"Well, you said a *few* words," Ike corrected him.

"I expect you can get all the words you need out of the cops. Their lawyer probably didn't tell them to keep their mouths shut. That okay with you, Ike?"

I felt sorry for Parker. His lawyer would probably gun him down in cold blood for this exchange of pleasantries with network crud.

And it didn't matter if Ike said it was okay with her if we all forgot this encounter. That Ike Tygart had missed this morsel of the Big Chill/Fedex story meant nothing, except maybe that she was tired. And that she'd be pissed off for about three days because she didn't know everything. I'd have put a hundred dollars down on the spot that forty reporters, from all sorts of news outlets, covering the police beat had already dug this injunction out of public records. It had to be all over the wires and all over the tube and all over the radio and just plain all over. That Fedex Parker was being held in New York, even if on his own recognizance, was headed for some front pages and had probably already made a few. Ike and me getting it from the horse's mouth—that was just weirdo *kismet* or something.

Ike merely stood there, rooted to the spot on her Rollerblades. She wasn't going to agree to keep quiet about Parker talking to us—walking dead square into a hole he dug himself—but I was guessing she didn't want to hurt this man's feelings. He seemed, well, sweet.

Parker rested his hand lightly on her shoulder. "Nice meeting you folks. I'll see you on Monday."

He walked away. Athletes of Parker's caliber aren't like the rest of us. He even walked cool.

We watched him go. In a low voice Ike said, "I'm not going to phone in. NTB doesn't need us to hand them this chance meeting. The Emerald City has better sources than us right now on this. Well, maybe not better. But sources nonetheless."

I knew how she felt. "Of course they do. Parker's living in a fantasy world right now. Coming down here to shoot baskets or whatever. He's homesick."

"I like him, Abby."

"Me, too." I patted her tush with my left hand, in a friendly way. "Maybe I'll try Zen."

"You'll try anything. Keep your hands off me."

"One lousy little pat on the—"

"Lousy is right. You don't have any *right* to pat me."

I held up my hands in surrender. "Calm down. I won't do it again."

She gave me the screw-eye. "You'd better not."

"Unless you ask me to."

"Ha!"

"Ha, yourself."

It looked like we were going to have a staring contest in Madison Square Garden, probably a first for that sports palace.

"Oh, never mind, Abby. Let's get busy."

"What's this salt mystery all about?"

We started skating toward the locker rooms and the coaches' offices.

"The knife nobody can find. I think it was a melting knife."

"Fillingeri—no, I think it was the assistant M.E.—said there was no water in the heart. He could tell because the cells weren't disrupted or something. There'd have to be water if the knife was made out of ice."

"I don't think it was made out of water. That's why I called my gynecologist."

"I don't get it, Ike."

"Saline. That's normal, regular, ordinary liquid you'd find in the body. And it's real easy to make. Just add salt to water. My doctor said you can use table salt. And there'd be no telltale cellular disruption.

"Can you freeze saline?"

"Of course. You think I'd forget to ask about that? It's only zero point eight five percent salt. It'd freeze like water. Just about. But it would melt a little faster."

We had reached Coach Hall's office.

"Ike, they'll have salt tablets down here for the players."

"But it would be hard to measure a salt tablet accurately. You'd have to smoosh it up. It would be hard to measure that right. And you'd have to get it right. That's a precise figure, you know, not a ballpark figure from my doctor—saline in the body is zero point eight five percent in solution in human body fluids. It's called isotonic saline and is very specific in its ratio of salt to water. If you didn't get it right, the medical examiner would pick it up. If you did get it right, the M.E. would never, *ever* suspect a thing."

"Zero point eight five percent? Give me a better idea. That sounds really tricky. You'd need a lab to measure something that accurately."

She looked smug, like she'd designed this feature of the human body herself. "Check this out: one tablespoon in one cup of water. A Styrofoam coffee cup is ideal. Simple. It may sound like a lot of salt, but that's because there's so much space between the crystals of table salt. It's really not all that much actual salt. You'd be measuring out some empty space. And you'd end up with zero point eight five percent saline solution."

"Your gynecologist is *good*, Ike. I wonder how her apple pie tastes."

Ike tried the handle of the coach's door. Locked.

"Damn," she said. "You'll have to break the window."

There was indeed a big window in the wall, near the door. "Me? Break it? You'll have security here in no time. Besides, how am I supposed to break it? Bang it with my head?"

"You're such a crybaby. Stay here."

She skated off in a huff, but she returned quickly in triumph. She had a hockey stick in her hands.

She took off her parka and handed it to me.

"Hold that over the window, as near as you can to the door," she said.

"Oh, Jesus," I said. "You're gonna kill me. First my arm gets shot and now you're going to bludgeon me with a hockey stick."

"Abby."

I folded her coat in two, placed it over the bottom left corner of the window with my left hand, flattened myself against the door, and closed my eyes. I heard a terrific *whoosh* and then a thud. I opened my eyes.

Ike was smiling like she'd won a gold medal. And she was wielding the hockey stick like she'd just knocked off five pigeons with a club in one blow.

I pulled her coat gently away from the window in the wall. Former window. I handed her the coat. Very carefully, I pulled out a large fragment of glass from the corner of the window. And then another fragment. She'd hit a home run on her first shot.

I dropped the pieces of glass inside the room, onto the carpet.

"You'll have to open the door," I said. "It'll take a right hand."

"No problem." She placed the hockey stick down quietly on the concrete floor, stuck her hand in through the hole she'd made in the window, reached for the door, and twisted the handle.

The door opened inward about a quarter of an inch.

"After you, Mr. Abagnarro," she said. I don't think I imagined the smug triumph in her tone.

TWENTY-SEVEN

WE SPENT fifteen minutes in Coach Hall's office. If there was any table salt in there, he'd hidden it grain by grain in his carpet.

"What now?" I said.

"The doctor's office."

"Coach Hall isn't going to be pleased with what we've done to his window. I'd put some tape over that hole if I were him. I'd do it myself, but I'm sort of busy now, trying not to get caught in here."

"A known racist doesn't need any favors from us. Let him call maintenance."

Sometimes I think Ike's got a real problem with megalomania. *She* broke the window, but it was the coach's problem.

We locked and closed Hall's door behind us, which was just silly. Anyone could break in through the hole we'd created in the window on that wall beside the coach's door.

Ike stooped and picked up the hockey stick. We skated down the hall and around the corner.

The wall of the doctor's office, thank God, didn't have a window. All he had was wall and a door. I didn't want to play goalie again with Ike and the hockey stick. I didn't even have a face mask on.

"You got any ideas on this, Ike?"

She looked stumped and leaned on the hockey stick like it was a crutch. "We have to get in there, Abby. I think Sam Rice is the best bet. He'd have the medical knowledge. And he'd always have ice on hand to freeze the saline into a solid knife. Team doctors are always smacking ice packs on players. I think they do it even for chicken pox. Plus, we have it on tape: Sam Rice held gauze over the Big Chill's heart as he lay dying on the court, and that would help to keep the heat in the man's heart. The knife would be sure to melt quicker that way. And it melted totally inside the wound. Nothing was left of it.''

"Rats. I wanted the killer to be the widow."

Ike ignored me and stood in thought. I decided to try thinking, too. The door just stayed put.

"Stand back," she said suddenly.

"What are you going to do? Beat down the door?"

She turned the doorknob and walked into the doctor's office.

"Well. He must be around nearby, Abby. He'd never leave his office unlocked and go away for long. There must be drugs and shit in here."

"Oh, cool. If he comes back, we can ask him how he treats chicken pox. I hope he doesn't prescribe a shotgun blast."

"Hurry up. I'll take the desk. You do those shelves."

I found what we were *not* looking for almost immediately. It was a plastic graduated cylinder, about four inches long, marked off in teaspoons and quarter tablespoons, with a plastic scoop on the end. I showed it to Ike. "This, Ike, does not belong here."

She looked up, her hands in one of the desk drawers.

"Abby, that's a medicine doser for children."

"I know what it is. And children do not play basketball in the NBA."

"Let me see that."

I handed it over. She looked at the lines marking off tablespoons by quarters.

"This gadget," she said, "is perfect."

"That part, I figured out. But what about the water?"

She raised her eyebrows at me. "I told you. A Styrofoam cup, dummy. You wouldn't want some mondo-bizarro mug from Las Vegas in the shape of a chorus girl or something. Don't be so slow."

"Great. Good. Fine. But you still haven't got a knife or a means to deliver the knife. The doctor did not stick that knife in the Big Chill after running onto the court to treat him. I saw the stain on the player's jacket before Rice showed up. No knife of any kind came from Rice's hand."

"The answer is here somewhere, Abby. Try those cabinets." She stuck her hands all the way into the back of the drawer. She pulled out a large box of Morton's salt and held it up.

I opened cabinets. "These doors won't need the hockey stick. They're wide open to anyone who needs a Band-Aid." I looked back over my shoulder. "Ike, the doctor probably uses that salt in his soup."

"He must really like it salty. This is a big box."

"Maybe he gargles with it."

"Oh, sure. And maybe he uses it as baby powder after he showers, too." She gave the box of salt a shake. "What a harmless, homey, familiar thing this is. Good old Morton's salt. I think this is a murder device, Abby. Or part of one. No doctor in a modern, powerhouse sports facility like the Garden would be making his own saline solution by the gallon. This box of salt may not prove anything, but it's out of place here."

We searched Sam Rice's office thoroughly, but we didn't find any means of making a knife. I did find some interesting drugs in a locked glass case, but I'd already had my drug-induced frenzy for the week, so I didn't get excited. There was a little freezer full of ice and ice packs. That was nice. That was handy for Ike's theory. That was convenient. That was exactly what you'd *expect* to find in a team doctor's office.

Plus, this particular recipe Ike was cooking still lacked a crucial ingredient: a Jell-O mold in the shape of a knife.

We put everything back where we'd found it and left the office, closing the door softly behind us. Sam Rice did not leap out of any corners at us. The hallway was empty.

"Something's bothering me," Ike said.

"Me, too. My arm hurts."

"Be quiet and let me think."

"Okay. I'll just stand here and do some Zen on my arm."

"Fine." She stood staring at the wall. I didn't see any answers written there.

"Abby, let's go back to the coach's office."

"What's bothering you?"

"Marfan's syndrome. God bless our terrific producer. Sally Goldberg-Petit is the best in the business, by golly, and she had the correct direction from the get-go. We all heard her on that videotape you sneaked out. Tuesday night, practically the first question Sally asked the coach was if the Big Chill had any preexisting medical condition that he knew of. Remember?"

"Like it was just Tuesday."

"Don't be funny. Remember how Hall reacted?"

"Furiously. I thought he was going to strangle Sally."

"Abby, what do you suppose would happen to a coach who knowingly played a man with Marfan's syndrome?"

"He'd be fired. Immediately. That's the minimum. I expect he'd also be prosecuted, if not by the D.A., then certainly in some civil court. Doing something that irresponsible and downright life-threatening, to my way of thinking, would be attempted murder. He'd be trying to kill his own player."

"Do you think Coach Hall knew the Big Chill had Marfan's syndrome?"

"He could hardly not know it. These players have regular and thorough physicals, which are not kept secret from the coaches. It's the coaches who want to see the results of the physicals. I'm guessing, but I'm guessing good. No. I'm not guessing. I'm stating the obvious. Trust me."

"The Big Chill probably would have died on the court, sooner or later, yes?"

"From what the A.M.E. said on the phone, yes. Only a matter of when. Putting the Big Chill on the court was setting a time bomb."

"And when he did die, and it came out about Marfan's syndrome, everyone would say the coach had been trying to kill Archie 'The Big Chill' Thorpe."

"Well, Ike, Hall obviously was trying to kill him."

"And," Ike said, making a mighty sour face like she'd been sucking on a lemon, "so Hall killed his star player to hide the fact that he'd been attempting to murder the Big Chill for a few years.''

''Why'd he wait so long?''

''I don't know. Maybe it took Hall that long to figure out how to do it. Or maybe he waited until those support payments for the grandchild had piled up some. Or maybe the Big Chill's symptoms had gotten worse suddenly.''

''That must be it, Ike! That's why the Big Chill was quitting the game. The players would know the results of their own physicals. You know that eavesdropping assistant M.E., that guy who told us about Marfan's? He said the disease was progressive, getting worse as the guy ages. *If* it was diagnosed right, and the Chill knew about it, can you imagine how much he loved the game to keep playing as long as he did? Every game he'd get worse and worse. I wonder if Mrs. Chill knew?'' Ike just shrugged at me. ''Bet he didn't tell her. She'd have put him in a half-nelson until he gave up the women, if not basketball—all that physical exertion. I don't see her letting her golden goose go around the town with his floozies, risking his heart when he should have been tending his hamburger ranches, which is really too bad, because, Ike, she *looks* like a killer. Besides, if she wanted him dead, she didn't have to kill him—he was dying anyway just by continuing to live as he'd been living. So, she's out. Well. We can't have everything. In fact, we *don't* have everything. You have to explain why the hell the coach fired a shotgun at all of his own players and how he made a knife out of saline and how he got that knife into the Big Chill's heart.''

''We already know why he fired the shotgun.''

It took me a second. ''Oh. To freeze the action on the court,'' I said. ''To stop the Big Chill dead in his tracks. To create a stationary target. The coach needed a nice, clean, open shot at the heart. But with what?''

''Dennis said there were delivery systems for knives, and I've seen pictures of some myself. But they all have metal blades. Ejectible metal blades. I don't see any reason why you couldn't put a frozen saline blade into one of those gadgets. That's what Hall must have done."

"Then how come it's the doctor who has the Morton's salt in his office?"

"Somebody instructed Hall on the medical facts," she said. "I doubt the coach phoned a gynecologist like I did. Rice had to have been part of the deal to cover up the Marfan's syndrome. It may have gotten worse, but the condition was there all along."

"So which one fired this mythical salty knife?"

"The coach. The doctor made it to the court too quickly for him to have been in the stands firing a knife. Now we at least know the coach had easy access to everything needed."

"You still can't make a knife with just a cup of water and a tablespoon of salt."

I heard the sound of footsteps coming down the front hall. I grabbed Ike's hand, put my finger to my lips, and we skated quietly around the warren of offices, back to the coach's office. We stood and listened. The footsteps had stopped. We heard a door close. "Sounds like it must have been Sam Rice's door," I whispered in Ike's ear. "The right distance, the right noise."

She took a deep breath.

"Noise. Abby. That *shhh* sound we located on the tape. That was the knife being shot or hurled or whatever. And that's why Church was killed. He was the sound man on that assignment. Hall must have at least practiced with the knife to know that it made a little noise. And he thought Church had recorded and heard the sound."

"The sound's on the videotape."

"I know that. You know that. But *Hall* probably didn't know that. The average Joe sees a sound technician, average Joe thinks the tech has the sound. Right?"

"Maybe. But so what if our sound picked up a knife? I'll grant you it's easy to make a zero point eight five percent saline solution. How do you get a saline knife out of saline?"

Ike looked mad, maybe not at me. She reached through the

broken glass and opened the door to Coach Hall's office. I
followed her in and pulled the door shut.

Ike stood in the center of his office, turning a slow circle
on her skates, letting the images in the room whirl past her at
languid speed. She made two complete revolutions before she
stopped short.

She skated over to a metal filing cabinet against the wall.
Over the cabinet hung two framed pictures—Knicks team photos, the only two New York teams ever to win the NBA championship.

The frames—containing portraits of the 1970 and 1973
World Champion Knicks, each signed by Willis Reed, the
MVP for both series—were unusual, a little too thick for photos. Ike reached up and across the filing cabinet and lifted the
framed photo of the 1973 Knicks off the wall. She turned it
over to look at the back. I skated over to her side.

The frame's backing was Styrofoam, about half an inch
thick, perhaps a little thicker. Ike moved the metals clasps on
the back of the frame, removed the Styrofoam, and turned it
over. It was just a slab of Styrofoam.

"It probably gets moist down here," I said. "You know—
a basement, athletes, sweat, showers. That Styrofoam is a good
idea. If I had Willis Reed's signature, I'd take good care of
it, too."

"Willis Reed?" Ike shrugged. "Name sounds familiar."

She hung the frame back up on the wall. She looked at the
other frame, the one holding the immortal 1970 World Champion Knicks' portrait. The first world basketball championship
ever brought to New York City. It gave me a chill to look at
the men in that photo. And to see Reed's signature flowing
across the top left quarter of the picture. His name sounded
familiar?

Ike lifted the picture off the wall and turned it over.

This one had Styrofoam in its frame, too. Ike removed the
backing and turned it over. Carved into the Styrofoam was a
perfect mold, in the shape of a five-inch knife blade.

Ike sat back against the desk.

"This is ugly," she said.

I was looking at the junk on the coach's desk. I was seeing things differently from our first break-in. Among the junk and papers on the desk was a plastic bottle. I picked it up and read the label. "Ike, look at this."

She turned. "What?"

"Contact lens wetting solution. Hall wears contact lenses."

"So what? You got something against contacts?"

"Ike, read this bottle. The contents are written right here. It's isotonic saline." I shook the bottle. "He wouldn't have had to *make* any home brew."

TWENTY-EIGHT

HEAD COACH MAX HALL never took the stand at his own trial, and so he himself never had a chance to implicate the team doctor. The jury took only seven hours to convict Hall of the murder of Archibald Tyrone Thorpe, the Big Chill of New York. Hall was sentenced to life in prison.

That conviction and the sentence couldn't possibly satisfy Knicks fans completely, who, bereft of the Big Chill, never got a smell of the play-offs. In death, the former popularity of the Big Chill had been partially restored to him. New York's loss implied what had once been a huge presence in our town.

That was the fan reaction. In the media, we had a different grievance. Coach Hall was never tried for killing Church Finnegan. There wasn't, according to the D.A.'s office, enough evidence against Hall to mount a trial. So the file on Finnegan is still open.

And so is the file on Hall, in a way. His case is in appeal while he shoots baskets up in the gym at the state penitentiary in Ossining, New York. He may not be there for the rest of his life, but Hall, in my opinion, will be doing some significant time during the appeals process alone. The defense team is basing its appeal on how well and with what exactitude it was documented in the Knicks' organization that Thorpe suffered from Marfan's syndrome. The case will probably be in appeal for fifteen years while all the doctors have their say.

Ike and I did some time ourselves, on benches outside the courtroom downtown during Hall's trial. We were, you might say, the star witnesses for the prosecution.

Star witnesses do a lot of hanging around. And that gives you too much time to think, which is especially bad in Ike's case. When she's not busy, she comes up with some really gloomy ideas, like the gem she'd had about divorcing me. She had some morose moments while we waited outside the courtroom, with nothing to do but try to stay awake after working all night.

While the prosecution was inside establishing motive, Ike had her worst attack of the blues.

"Abby," she said, "Hall's motive is sickening."

"You mean killing a guy to cover up the fact that you were killing him?"

"I really meant that it would have been more noble, sort of, if the Big Chill had been killed because he was screwing us out of our rain forests." She touched my knee. "Not that I mean it would be okay to kill him for any reason. But it makes me sad to realize that nobody would commit murder to save the planet. We'll kill for almost anything else."

"That would be a new one."

"What do you mean?"

"Killing for the earth. I guess we'll just go on blithely committing mass suicide. Does that make you feel any better?"

"Oh, yeah. Lots. I feel great."

It was during a dreary afternoon, I think about the second week into the trial, when Ike and I were parked on a bench that was getting harder by the hour, that she brought up the subject of the parrot joke. I'd forgotten all about it.

"You must be really bored," I said, "if you're asking me about one of my jokes. You always hate my jokes."

"I'm so bored I could hang myself by my tongue. Tell me the joke."

"Lemme think a minute. It's been a while, Ike. I'm not even sure it's a joke. It's maybe more like a tale, or a fable or something."

A seedy little man in a bowler hat who was hauling a bulging briefcase sat down beside us. He dumped the briefcase on the worn, scratched linoleum floor and tipped his hat to Ike. He slipped a couple of business cards from his suit jacket and gave us each one. They read:

Coren St. James Birnbaum, Esq.
Personal Injury and Estate Planning
They do; I sue.

I nodded to thank him for the card and stuffed it in my pocket.

"Okay," I said. "There's these three parrots who fly to the seashore with a big net to go fishing."

"Abby, that doesn't make any sense. Parrots don't fish."

"Assume they do. Anyway, the parrots are there all day and they don't catch anything. They're about ready to give up when they feel something really heavy yanking the net."

"They caught a flying fish?"

"Very funny. No. They pull in their net and they've captured a beautiful mermaid."

"I suppose she has big breasts, the whole mermaid deal?"

"The parrots don't care about her breasts. They're *parrots*, for crying out loud!"

"Go on."

"So the mermaid cries and cries and begs for the parrots to release her back into the ocean. The parrots refuse. They think they've got a pretty good deal. Maybe they can sell her to the circus."

"Monsters."

"Just listen. The mermaid says that if they'll let her go, she'll grant them each a wish."

"Oh, boy. They each ask for a cracker?"

"Do you want to hear this story or not, Ike?"

She sighed heavily. "Go ahead."

St. James Birnbaum, to my left, chimed in. "I think I've heard this joke."

I considered one-handing him off the bench. "I don't care what you've heard. Let me tell it, or I'll give *you* a personal injury."

St. James Birnbaum looked around at the crowd in the corridor, which happened to include some uniformed police officers. "I wouldn't try it, buddy. I've never seen a better bunch of witnesses in my life. I'll sue your pants off."

"Forget I said anything, okay?"

He sized me up. "For now."

I cleared my throat and turned my back to St. James Birnbaum. "Let me go on. The parrots agree, yielding to the mermaid's request. The first parrot tells the mermaid he wants her to double his I.Q. She nods her head and—poof!—he starts quoting Shakespeare and explicating all the really difficult passages."

Ike leaned her head back against the dirty wall.

"The second parrot says he wants twice the I.Q. the first parrot got. Poof! The second bird starts rattling off chemical formulas while speculating on the problem that sections of the universe are older than the universe itself."

St. James Birnbaum opened his mouth. I put up my hand.

"Please, Birnbaum. This is my story. I can tell you're about to object. We're not in court." I turned back to Ike. "The third parrot likes what he's seen so far, but he takes a moment to think."

Ike smirked. "Using parrot I.Q."

"Right. And he tells the mermaid he wants ten times the I.Q. of the second parrot. The mermaid looks thoughtful and tells the bird he'd better think again, because he doesn't understand what he's asking for. For one thing, if she grants his wish, he'll start playing golf. But worse, if she grants his wish, he'll always regret letting her go. Of course, the parrot, being a parrot, doesn't understand her. He insists on ten times the I.Q. of the second parrot. The mermaid nods regretfully and—poof!—the parrot turns into a man and she swims away, leaving him lonely and lovesick, with only golf to take his mind off his loss."

Ike sat up straight. "Is that supposed to be hilarious or something?"

"It's got a moral. Be careful what you wish for or you might end up worse off than when you started."

"Hmmph." She relaxed again against the wall. "What time is it?"

"Excuse me," St. James Birnbaum said. "You really loused that story up. You totally missed the punch line. Let me tell her the way I heard the joke."

Ike rolled her eyes. "Does it stink, too?"

"No," he said, "I think this will appeal to you. Well, as the mermaid is swimming away, the man yells after her, begging her to come back. She stops and turns. She tells him that she'll take pity on him if he'll ask for something different. The man stands there, a slow smile creeping over his face. He figures he's gotta be smart to catch this beautiful mermaid again, so he says he wants one hundred times his current I.Q."

"And what happens?" Ike said.

"The mermaid shakes her head. She says he doesn't know what he's asking for, that if she grants his wish, his whole view of the universe will change, that he's asking for more than he can handle, that no man can handle that much I.Q."

"But the guy refuses to back down, right?" Ike said.

"Right. He says she promised and he wants one hundred times the I.Q. he's already got. The mermaid shakes her head and then nods gently—poof !"

"Well?"

"Well, he's a woman."

Ike laughed out loud and smacked her palms on her knees.

St. James Birnbaum settled back against the wall. "Don't forget you've got my card, anything happens to you."

"Thanks a whole lot," I said.

"Personal injury. Any time, pal."

Pal. He was company that loved misery.

I, too, leaned back against the wall, and sort of wished a mermaid would swim by.

That didn't do any good, so I thought about my coming testimony and the prosecution's case against Coach Hall.

That Friday back in November when Ike and I had discovered the Styrofoam blade mold behind the picture frame, the NYPD had obtained a hurry-up search warrant, and what they'd found in Hall's luxury apartment in the East 80s was being presented in court, along with that photo of the 1970 World Championship team.

In Hall's bedroom, Fillingeri and his minions had found what they called a "ballistic knife," an ugly thing with a thick handle containing a simple spring mechanism, and a collection of metal blades that fit the handle. The handle had a trigger button.

Fillingeri had directed one of his experts to do some test shooting with the knife, and I invited myself to the range to watch. Those blades came shooting out of the handle when the trigger was pushed, at about the speed of a bullet.

The ballistic knife, we all learned from the trial, was not illegal. You can have as many of them as you want. The part you have to be careful about is the spring inside the handle. Congress outlawed *the spring only*.

But you can buy springs at a hardware store, if you need one for, say, repairing your child's toys.

The cops also found a catalog in Hall's bedroom from Arisen Systems, Inc., that offered a lot of "G.I. Joe's-a-Maniac" toys and accessories, for surprisingly reasonable prices: night vision glasses, pepper gas dispensers, U.S. military infrared transmitter beacons, and—I swear I'm not making this up—an electric-powered pick gun, I suppose for burglars who didn't mind the noise when they were letting themselves surreptitiously into people's homes.

The NYPD traced the ballistic knife back to Arisen Systems, which had made the sale to Hall. Arisen claimed they had not sold him the spring, since that's illegal.

Hall had served in Vietnam, and his service records were introduced at his trial for the murder of the Big Chill. Hall had qualified as a marksman in boot camp, and had gone on to kill a depressing number of Vietnamese people, whom—if his remarks about his star center were a trend—Hall had probably called "gooks."

The prosecution never tried to make a case against Sam Rice, over strong protests from Dennis Fillingeri, if you believe Fillingeri. If the team doctor had helped Hall, we'll probably never know. The way it stands in the court record, from the prosecution's closing arguments, is that Hall acted alone.

Rice was "retired" by the Knicks organization, and there's no way he'll ever get a new job hanging around with basketball players.

That Friday we found the salt in Rice's little infirmary and the blade mold behind that championship photo in Hall's office, and the contact lens solution on Hall's desk, we phoned Fillingeri from Ike's cellular. We didn't reach him because he was already on his way, having learned from the uniformed bodyguards we had left behind on the loading dock at the Emerald City that Ike and I had bolted. Fillingeri doesn't need much time to put two and two together and get Madison Square Garden as his answer.

By four o'clock that afternoon, Coach Hall was in custody. Ike and I were out on the pavement at the corner of 8th Avenue and 33rd Street.

There was no question of skating up to our separate homes on the upper west side. It had been a long week, and we hailed a cab.

The driver was weird. He spoke English and his radio was tuned to a classical music station that was doing an hour on Strauss. No reggae, no all-news, no Christian broadcasting. Strauss, of all things. I thought back to the Trapeze Waltz.

When the cab stopped for the light at 74th, which is my block, I blurted it out: "Ike, will you marry me? I mean, remarry me?"

She turned to face me, and I got the full impact of her eerie eyes. "Are you talking to me?"

"I'm serious. We belong together. Take another chance with me."

"Abby, sometimes I think your brain is dead. This is Friday after one of the most exhausting weeks of my life. We've been through hell these past few days, we're both nuts with fatigue, your arm must hurt like the dickens, we've lost a comrade, and you ask me to marry you?"

"That's right."

"Well, God! What I need is two days of sleep before I can even think about my laundry, much less the rest of my life."

"Two days?"

"Yeah. At least two days. What are you doing? Keeping my social calendar?"

The light changed.

"Hold it!" I told the cabbie.

He obeyed. Cars behind us on Broadway started honking.

"Two days, Ike? You mean like a weekend?"

"Something like that. That'd be two days. What are you getting at?"

I kissed her quickly, opened the door, exited the cab, and before I closed the door, I said, "Thank God it's Friday."

Ike blinked. I shut the door reverently.

The cab started to pull away and she yanked open the door and yelled at me.

"Hey! You stuck me with the fare again!"

FOWL PLAY

A MOLLY WEST MYSTERY

Birds of a Feather

After fifteen years in rural Ohio, Chicago native Molly West is still considered an outsider, but as director of the local meals-on-wheels program, she's becoming more at home. The murder of a local woman and the abduction of a prize rooster are on everybody's minds.

Intrigued, Molly starts digging into the mystery. The trail leads to illegal doings and into the sport of cockfighting. However, the fowl deeds of the ring are minor compared to the blood sport of murder....

Patricia Tichenor Westfall

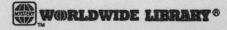

WORLDWIDE LIBRARY®

WPTW273

DEADLY PARTNERS
A KATE KINSELLA MYSTERY

SEASON OF DISCONTENT

A working holiday to the Isle of Wight is just what nurse-medical investigator Kate Kinsella needs to revive her lagging funds and sagging spirits. It's a missing-person case: hotel owner Nigel Carter has disappeared.

Posing as an heiress interested in buying a hotel on the island, Kate steps off the ferry and into a bizarre murder, then into a jail cell as the chief suspect. With the help of her friend Hubert Humberstone, Kate draws closer to the shocking truth that lies at the heart of a very elaborate deception.

CHRISTINE GREEN

MYSTERY WORLDWIDE LIBRARY®

WCG274